WOLVER CRAFT MANOR

CASE CROWE

TANGLED TREE PUBLISHING

WOLVERCRAFT MANOR

CAS E CROWE

For information, contact the publisher, Tangled Tree Publishing.

WWW.TANGLEDTREEPUBLISHING.COM

EDITING: HOT TREE EDITING

COVER DESIGNER: BOOKSMITH DESIGNS

E-BOOK ISBN: 978-1-922679-90-1

PAPERBACK ISBN: 978-1-922679-91-8

PROLOGUE

Wolvercraft Manor.

Nestled among steep hillsides and thick forests, Wolvercraft was a French-styled stone chateau of unrivalled beauty. Tourists from France, England, Normandy —all over the world—arrived on the island of Ashvall to explore the Wolvercraft estate. They'd marvel at the Romanesque gardens, the water fountains, and the terraces, but it was the house that captured their imagination. Charming, gothic, monstrous, Wolvercraft Manor was blanketed in white fog and veiled in constant gloom. Century-old trees lined the impressive driveway. The manor's cathedral-like architecture reached up to the sky in tall peaks, coiled with the intricate sculptures of gargoyles.

Furniture was tidy. Books were neatly stacked. Every room, hall, and stairway rivalled the great manors of Europe. Tourists laughed in delight. Envisioned themselves living the grand life. But at night, something lonesome wandered Wolvercraft's empty rooms. It lurked in the shadows.

Waiting.

Watching.

Hunting.

ONE

Saige Wolvercraft was a mess. She woke in the bathtub, her head lolled to the side at an uncomfortable angle, her cheek pressed into the ceramic. Last night's bottle of red floated on the surface, the water diluted to a cherry pink. It gave the impression that Saige had bled during the evening. The tips of her fingers and toes were wrinkled, her skin white.

"No! No, no. no." She scrambled out of the tub, her head swimming. The small clock face on her wristband, which she'd discarded on the tile floor, read 9:20 a.m. Panic clutched her chest.

They'll be waiting for me.

She normally didn't drink, but what she was about to face today had forced her to self-medicate. Her therapist wouldn't approve. She could imagine Dr Grigori's frown of disappointment. *"Stay on your medication. Get lots of rest. Eat healthy."* That was the doctor's advice. Drinking wasn't included, unless it was water. For the most part, Saige had managed to follow the recommendation and curb her anxiety, but today... was different.

Today was her worst nightmare brought to life.

Saige grabbed a towel and ran into the lounge. Muted light leaked in through the partly closed curtains, last night's Chinese takeout cold on the table. The hotel had been a last-minute decision and the only place she could afford on her measly wage. It smelt of mould and cheap detergent, but it had a bed and bathroom, and that was all Saige required for her one-night stay.

At least, I required one of the necessities.

She made a poor attempt at drying off her sodden skin, the spontaneous half of her brain laughing at what an idiot she'd been.

Stupid, stupid fool.

She rummaged through her suitcase. Undies, bra, jeans, flannel shirt, hoodie. Not flash by any stretch of the imagination, but it would do. Dressed, her fingers and toes still pruned, she returned to the bathroom and risked a glance in the mirror. Her strawberry-red hair created a damp curtain around her face, her freckles more pronounced against her fair skin. Her eyes were red, and her lips needed moisture. She probably would have looked just as good in a potato sack.

She grabbed her watch and attempted a bit of make-up, and then she was out the door, her suitcase in tow. There was no time for conversation in the lobby. She tossed her hotel key card on the desk, much to the annoyance of the clerk, and barrelled outside.

Which direction is the cab rank? Left or right?

She chose right because that was the direction of the

sea, which she could just make out on the horizon. She hurried through the tight seaside streets. The port town of Southammon consisted of crammed, unappealing buildings that looked like brick boxes with windows. The entire town seemed to have been beaten down by wind and weather, the locals unfriendly and aloof. It was June, but the nights and mornings were cold. Saige had spent one day here, and she regarded herself lucky that she'd seen the sun once.

A smile tugged her lips.

Zoe must be freaking out.

No sunshine will ruin her perfect day.

Saige hailed a cab. Five minutes later, Southammon's scenery had changed from derelict slums to a super-hip, modern marina village, complete with waterside homes, shops, restaurants, bars, and boutique hotels.

The cabbie slammed his foot on the brake. The car squealed to a stop. "Berth 56. You sure you're in the right place?" He gave her shabby clothes a once-over.

Saige handed him a small amount of cash and fought the urge to give him the finger.

Unfortunately, Southammon's Marina Village was exactly where she was meant to be. Half an hour ago. She actually hoped they'd given up on her and left, but her heart gave a small twist of disappointment when her eyes caught the magnificent superyacht, *Sunsurfer*, berthed at the moor. The media was there, of course—journalists, photographers, and nosy fans who'd probably travelled miles just to get a glimpse of the Wolvercraft family.

Saige stepped out of the cab. She wished she could jump back in and demand the driver take her all the way home to London, but he'd already left as soon as she was clear. Gulping deep, damp breaths, she pushed her way through the crowd. Her stomach was queasy from last night's wine indulgence, and the floating dock did nothing to appease the nausea in her throat. The flash photography didn't help.

Why are they even bothering with that? It's not that dark or cloudy out here.

Sunsurfer was an enormous white vessel that looked like something out of a James Bond film. Its sundecks, balconies, and outside café bar were already packed with the lucky guests invited to the wedding.

You'd think we were frigging royalty.

Saige swallowed.

The wedding. This is such a bad idea.

Tears glistened in her eyes as she bubbled up with panic.

I can't do this. I can't go there.

It was too much. The crowd. The noise. The entire scene made her ill.

Saige turned away, but someone latched on to her shoulder with a firm hand. "Saige, where have you been?"

She flinched.

Great. Just what I need. A pep talk from Dad.

Derrick Wolvercraft was six feet tall, broad-shouldered, with red-blond hair bordering toward grey, and just a few wrinkles around his mouth and eyes to indicate his age. At sixty-five, the papers described him as one of the sexiest *old guys* alive, which just made Saige cringe. This was her father they'd been talking about, but then again, he did own most of the British papers. It would be career suicide not to write about him in a favourable light, right?

There was nothing favourable about the way he was looking at her now, though. He took her elbow and steered her up the gangplank. His voice was a sharp whisper in her ear, but he still managed a smile for the cameras. "What happened? Did you get held up? Zoe is beside herself."

Saige rolled her eyes. Zoe beside herself? More likely she had fretted over what Saige's absence meant for her wedding plans. "Why did you wait, Dad? You should have just gone."

Derrick exhaled a tense sigh. "You're part of this family, and your brother wants you at his wedding. I want you there too. Are you taking your medication, Saige? You look tired. Are you still seeing Dr Grigori?"

"Yes, Dad." Saige hated hearing the concern in his voice.

They stepped onto the deck.

Now she had the entire frigging Wolvercraft clan to contend with. The only times she dealt with these people were at Christmas and at funerals. Great-aunts and uncles and distant cousins. She barely remembered their faces. The extended family was worse.

"There's my sweet girl." Aunt Violet sashayed up to Saige in her Louis Vuitton pastel dress, a phone in one hand and a champagne flute in the other. She air-kissed the sides of Saige's cheeks. "Have you been taking your medication, dear? You look tired."

What the hell is wrong with my family? They dish out insults like they're expensive caviar.

Before Saige could answer, Violet linked their arms and sauntered her niece around the deck. Her father walked close behind them. "Now," Aunt Violet purred, "you remember Chris, Clarissa, Beatrice, Tom, Danny, Phillip, Sam, Patrick, and Isabelle, don't you?"

"Um." Blood pounded through Saige's legs to spiral back into her head. She desperately needed to use the bathroom—to be sick.

It didn't matter if anyone recollected her or not. They were too engrossed in their conversations to offer her anything but a brief smile.

Aunt Violet's girlie laugh tinkled in Saige's ear. "Something to drink, dear? Some juice?"

They meandered over to the outdoor bar. Saige pleaded with her eyes at her father for help. Aunt Violet was a kind woman and had taken on a motherly role with Saige, but God, she was annoying.

Derrick watched her. Deep inside, Saige knew he was assessing her for damage. The lines in his brow creased. She hated disappointing him. She hated making him worry. Worst, she hated that she couldn't be the daughter he wanted—the socialite who attended newsworthy events and extravagant gala parties. She wasn't anything like Zoe, her soon-to-be sister-in-law. No, Saige was the outcast daughter. *"The one with problems."* It hadn't helped that Saige had been chased by paparazzi as a young girl, her photograph snapped when she'd been forced into hospital, her picture displayed in the tabloids with an insinuating headline and a false story. At least now in her late twenties, they'd learned to leave her alone. Saige had made herself as boring as humanly possible. She worked for a local London magazine writing trivial social stories. She loved it, but the pay could have been better.

Aunt Violet babbled on about something. Saige tuned

out. She spotted a tall, red-headed young man walking in her direction. For the first time all morning, a genuine smile sprang to her lips.

"Sis." The young man hugged her, crushing her in his arms in the way only older brothers could do.

Saige breathed in the familiar scent of cedarwood and geranium that was in his cologne. It reminded her of Christmas. Xavier Wolvercraft—or Xav, as she remembered he preferred to be called—was as tall as his father, had water-blue eyes that most girls found dreamy, and the chiselled arms and chest of a swimmer. Seeing girls swoon over her older brother in high school and later at university had made Saige retch, but now she could understand how he'd managed to catch the attention of supermodel Zoe Ruiz. He was good-looking. And he was rich.

He's happy. That's the important thing.

Zoe might be a snooty-nosed bitch to me, but at least she makes Xav happy.

Saige felt her breathing relax with her brother at her side. Big brothers had a moral responsibility to protect little sisters, and Xav had always done his best to protect her, even from the tabloids. It saddened her that since Xav had met Zoe, their sibling relationship had become distant.

Saige took a glass of orange juice from the barman and gulped greedily. She was so thirsty.

Her brother tilted his head to the side. "Careful. I think that has vodka in it."

Crap.

He laughed, but the smile didn't reach his eyes. "How have you been, Saige? It's been a while. I didn't think you were going to come." He scrutinised her face slowly. "You look tired."

Dear God. How many people are going to say that?

"Have you been sleeping?"

Saige looked down at her feet.

An alcohol-induced sleep doesn't count, right?

She divided glances between Xav and her father. "I'm sleeping fine. Just a bit nervous, that's all."

Derrick made a deep sound she couldn't decipher. "You need to learn to put that day behind you, Saige. Your brother's wedding is a joyous occasion. I understand that this is hard for you. It is for all of us. But this wedding is a new chapter. A new chapter of happiness for all of us. No more grief. No more guilt."

Saige couldn't look at her father as he spoke.

That's all very well for you to say. You didn't have to witness it. You didn't have to be plagued by nightmares for years later.

A coppery taste filled her mouth. She couldn't do this. Not here. Not now. "Excuse me."

She ducked to the bathroom. Even the *Sunsurfer's* ladies' room was exquisite. Her dad had spared no expense when he'd built this yacht. It was all jade marble tiles on one side, with gold handrails and faucets, black sinks, and vanity mirrors on the other. And, of course, there was a floor-to-ceiling window, just in case you wanted to admire the view.

Saige locked herself in the last stall and emptied her stomach in the toilet.

That is the last time I am ever drinking red wine. And vodka with orange juice.

She shut the lid and sat on the seat until the urge to cry faded from her eyes. Her skin was damp, and the small of her back was wet. Beneath her hoodie, her flannel shirt was stuck to her. She was just about to leave the stall to wipe water on her face when voices carried into the bathroom. Chatty. Happy. Catty.

"Oh my God, Zoe. I saw your whacky soon-to-be sister-in-law. What is she wearing this time? She looks like she just crawled out of bed."

"Did she even use make-up?" another voice piped up in an equally vindictive tone.

Saige crept back from the door.

Zoe's here.

Probably with two of her bridesmaids. Saige mentally counted off the list. At least she didn't have all seven of them in the bathroom. She peeked through the crack in the door. The women fluffed up their hair and applied lip gloss.

Great. Luisa and Kya, two blonde jumped-up Barbie dolls with heads as empty as the toy. Saige had met them once before, a long time ago, and had found them so full of their own self-importance that she was surprised they hadn't ruptured.

Saige recognised Zoe's voice, which escalated with high, vicious laughter. "Calm down, girls. Saige is a lost cause. I doubt Xav and I will have much to do with her once we're married. She keeps to herself most of the time."

"She has problems, right? Is she, like, dangerous?" Kya turned on the faucet and dampened some of the stray hairs from her curls.

"Dangerous?" Zoe stepped in front of the mirror,

brushing her fingers down her jet-black ponytail, which had been pinned to the side with a diamond brooch. "She's harmless."

"What happened to her?"

"Her mother died."

"That's it?" Kya sounded disappointed.

Zoe beamed in the mirror. Saige recognised the enjoyment that lit in her eyes. Zoe had always loved attention. "Not exactly. Her mother suicided, right in front of her."

"Jesus. That's rough."

"Yep. It happened on the cliffs just outside the grounds of Wolvercraft Manor."

There was silence for a moment.

Zoe's gossipy voice went up another octave. "That's not even the best part. So you can't tell another soul about this. I promised Xav I wouldn't speak a word, but you girls are my besties. So." She paused for dramatic effect. "Saige sees and experiences things that aren't really there."

Luisa's head snapped around. "What do you mean?" Curious excitement seeped out of her voice.

"Five years ago, Saige arrives home in London announcing to her father, brother, and aunt that she's engaged. She's been seeing a guy for a year, and he proposed. Naturally, the family are excited for her. They set another place at the dinner table. This mysterious man of Saige's is meant to arrive at 8:00 p.m. sharp."

"And?"

"Did he arrive?" Kya piped up.

Saige recognised the eager nastiness in their tones.

Zoe's lips shifted into a wicked smile. "Of course not. Eight o'clock came and went with no sign of him."

"What happened? Did he die? Is that why she's really... you know, depressed?"

"Jesus, Luisa. You are dumb. He never existed. Saige imagined for a year that she was in a relationship. Her father had her shipped off to a mental hospital, or some-place where they send crazies. She's been on medication ever since."

"Shit, Zoe. She sounds eternally screwed up. You should keep your distance from her."

"Like I said, Xav and I will have nothing to do with her when we're married. She's a loner anyway. Prefers to be by herself."

Saige flattened a hand to the wall for support. She felt sick now for an entirely different reason. How could her brother have betrayed her like this? Zoe was a spiteful, vindictive little bitch. He had to know she'd blab.

Saige waited long after the women had filed out of the bathroom before she left the safety of her stall. She wandered onto the outdoor deck and ordered a glass of water at the bar. She was getting off this ship. No way was she going back to Ashvall Island or that creepy house. She was going home. Back to London.

Saige was halfway across the yacht when she stopped. The glass in her hand trembled. They were already out at sea. The coast was on the horizon. Her father's yacht was so frigging big that she hadn't even been able to tell that they'd left the marina.

Shit. Shit. Triple shit.

She'd just decided to go and hide in the bathroom again when a cold, wet substance pooled at her feet. Saige had been so shocked by the scene before her that it took her a second to realise she'd dropped her water. Glass shards surrounded her in a broken mosaic around her boots. Everyone stared, but for the first time, she didn't care. Her eyes were firmly pinned on the man her brother was talking to.

Jasper Young.

Her ex.

TWO

What the hell is Jasper Young doing here?

And talking to her brother, of all things. Saige didn't think the pair were friends anymore. She grasped desperately for understanding. For an escape.

Abort. Abort. Abort.

But where could she go? It wasn't like she could jump overboard and swim to shore. Or could she?

Shit.

"Saige."

Her brother had spotted her. He waved her over.

She felt as if someone had forced acid down her throat. Trying to keep her cool, Saige strode casually toward her brother, who she wanted to strangle, hoping she didn't appear too stupefied. She sensed Jasper's eyes on her. Her cheeks flared in response.

Xav's smile stretched. "You remember Jasper, right? My friend from school."

Yep. She certainly remembered him. She remembered the taste of his mouth on hers when they'd hooked up underneath the bleachers... in the science lab... in her bedroom after school. He was two years older than Saige, and, at the time, that seemed like a huge, exciting risk. She'd caught the attention of an older boy. Her brother's best friend. But now whenever she looked back on the memory, all she experienced was a sense of shame with her younger self. They'd kept their relationship a secret because that was what Jasper had insisted, right up until the moment he'd left for Juilliard's Conservatory Program in New York City without so much as a goodbye. She'd been heartbroken, but she'd gotten over it.

And then six years ago, they'd run into each other unexpectedly in London at the Night of Hope Charity Dinner. Jasper was a big-time musician with a band and was performing at the event. Saige was a last-minute backup for her brother's absence. Xav was meant to be the Wolvercraft representative that night, but he'd taken ill. Saige and Jasper had met, and she'd fallen in love all over again.

Stupid. Stupid. Stupid.

For the longest moment, Saige couldn't find her voice. She looked at Jasper's handsome face, determined to give him the bored once-over. "Yes. I remember him." She attempted cold indifference, but her voice shook.

If Jasper was uncomfortable, he didn't show it, his face composed and good-humoured. She wanted to punch his perfect teeth from his perfect smile. His eyes were a dark shade of brown, his natural curls styled messy down to his shoulders. Wearing black trousers, boots, and a leather motorcycle jacket—yes, real leather—with a casual white T-shirt, Jasper effortlessly pulled off the rock star bad boy with preppy aesthetic. Saige hated him. The stubble beard was new. It annoyed her how much it suited him.

Xav was talking, but Saige didn't have it in her to listen. She was too focused on how all the women in the vicinity turned to check Jasper out. They giggled and whispered.

It's like high school all over again.

"Saige?"

She jumped. "What?"

Xav's eyebrows drew in a line. "I asked if you could introduce Jasper to the family. Zoe's asking for me. I have to go. Thanks, sis."

Before she could answer, he zipped away into the crowd.

Her heartbeat turned erratic. He'd left her... here... with Jasper.

The musician's grin was erased, his shoulders now taut. The pair of them stared at everything but each other.

Saige scrambled for something to say, but Jasper beat her to it. "How have you been? And I mean, really been?"

It was a casual enquiry, but hearing the subtext in his voice made something inside Saige ache. He knew about her breakdown. Who was she kidding? Everyone knew about her frigging breakdown.

Introduce him to the family? Sure, Xav. He's five years too late.

She tossed Jasper an indignant look. "What are you doing here?"

She had hoped her voice would sound confident and strong, but it had come out petty, mean, and jealous— exactly what an ex-girlfriend sounded like, or rather, a *meaningless* ex-girlfriend, because that was all she'd been in the end to Jasper. Meaningless.

A muscle in his jaw twitched, but otherwise, Jasper remained annoyingly calm. "The happy couple asked me to perform at their wedding. I'm playing the piano at the ceremony and singing at the reception. Any requests?"

"Yeah. I request that you leave."

His lips tipped at the corners. "Can't do. I've already received my pay cheque."

"Then I request that you stay away from me."

"Yeah, I figured that." He raked his fingers through his hair. "Saige, listen. You look—"

She pointed a nasty finger at him. "If you dare say I look tired, I will throw you overboard."

He raised his hands in surrender. "I was going to say you're looking...."

Saige was grateful that he shut his mouth for once. She'd loved fashion, make-up, and jewellery. She'd taken pride in her appearance once, but that had all changed five years ago. Saige had always had problems with anxiety, but heartache had sealed the deal, throwing her into a deep, spiralling depression she neither could, nor was motivated to crawl out from. Now, she was thin and tired and didn't care. Had she even brushed her hair today? She couldn't remember.

Jasper's eyes crinkled at the edges, the way they always did when he offered an apologetic smile. "I'm assuming you never told your brother about us? Or your dad?"

Saige crossed her arms. "Xav certainly wouldn't have invited you to his wedding if I had. And my father would have ruined you if he knew how you broke things off between us. You hurt me, Jasper. You promised me everything. You said you'd be there for Christmas dinner, that we'd announce it together, and then you just... left."

He squeezed his eyes shut, the first sign of weariness etched in his expression. "Saige, listen, I'm sorry. I just couldn't... at the time—"

Her cheeks grew hotter. "Save it. I have nothing to say to you."

She marched away, her legs trembling from anger and resentment. How dare Jasper Young turn up to her brother's wedding. Even if he was invited, their history should have made him reject the invitation immediately, or at least make up an excuse for why he couldn't attend. Why was he here? He certainly didn't need the money. Jasper was a rock star, his band famous all across the globe. He spent most of his time touring and hooking up with women, or so Saige had read. Every time she'd seen his picture in the papers, she'd drawn a big fat *X* over his face and given him devil horns and a forked tongue. It had become Saige's therapeutic obsession. Eventually, the administration officer at her work had been forced to take all the magazines away from the staff lunchroom.

Saige shoved her way through the wedding guests into the dining stateroom. Her father's mega yacht was a supreme water beast on the outside and full of luxury and comfort on the inside. Honestly, the décor looked like something that should have been in a great manor house or a trendy hotel. Crystal chandeliers hung from the ceiling, and every wooden surface polished and gleaming. The parquet floors were clean enough to eat off. The red upholstered chairs and burgundy couches matched the gold-plated fixtures.

Dad must have thought he was rebuilding the Titanic.

Waiters in black-and-white served canapés and drinks. She ignored the young man who offered her a glass of champagne and made a beeline for the elevator. It was far too early for drinking anyway, but when you were as rich as these guests, rules didn't apply.

Saige stepped out of the elevator onto the upper deck where the swimming pool was located and looked down over the helipad. The deck was empty. She flopped onto a sun chair and gazed out at the sea, grateful to be alone.

Why had she let herself be convinced into going to her brother's wedding? Why had Zoe insisted the wedding take place on Ashvall Island?

At the *house*?

Didn't Zoe want to go somewhere where there was sunshine? A tropical getaway? A beach? Definitely not a church. Zoe was no saint.

Saige smiled.

A church would fall over if Zoe crossed the threshold.

A dark feeling stirred inside her. She remembered the cruel story Zoe had shared with her bridesmaids in the bathroom. It had been half true. Everyone believed Saige's fiancé wasn't real. In the end, heartbroken and empty, Saige had decided to just go with it and let her family think she needed help. It was far easier to believe Jasper Young really *had* been a figment of her imagination.

SAIGE WOKE UP WITH COLD AIR BLOWING ON HER cheek. She cringed at the soreness that spiked down her back into her hip. The wooden sun chair hadn't been designed for sleeping, not without a cushion at least. She hadn't intended to doze off. All she wanted was to close her eyes for a second or two, but blissful unconsciousness had tempted her into its black depths. She didn't feel refreshed. Sleep never did clear her groggy head. Saige had been a zombie for years, just going through the motions. Work. Dinner. Bed. Repeat. She didn't eat breakfast. She barely ate lunch. Instead, Saige threw herself into her work, the one thing that distracted her from what a mess her life was.

She checked her wristwatch. Her eyes widened in dismay. It was early noon. She'd missed lunch, not that she'd intended to join the dining hall, but her father would be disappointed. Aunt Violet would be frantic. They probably thought she'd jumped overboard.

She staggered onto her feet, her sea legs doing little to help her stand. She grabbed the handrail at the same time her eyes caught the landscape ahead. Her stomach cartwheeled. Ashvall Island hadn't changed since she was a little girl. Wild, rugged, and unspoilt coastline stretched to the west, the east dotted with sea towns and villages. Seagulls squawked overhead. She remembered going down to the rocky cliffs with her father when she was little to see the turtles. She wondered if the creatures still visited.

The *Sunsurfer* drifted to the east, giving her a clearer view of beautiful St Albert Port, the major town and capital of Ashvall. Small yet charming, it had a French style but English flair. Yachts, fishing trawlers, catamarans, and deck boats dipped and bobbed in the marina, the hills beyond speckled with stylish restaurants, hotels, and churches. Saige could already make out the walking trails and cobblestone streets. Tourists meandered among the museums, galleries, and cafés. They sat outside the bars and pubs, feasting on the local seafood and beer.

She really had been too hard on Zoe. Ashvall Island

was a beautiful place and a fairy-tale location for a wedding—if you liked rain. Unlike its sister island Guernsey, which saw frequent sunlight in the summer, Ashvall Island was battered by ocean winds and severe storms. It was either grey, rainy, or shrouded in mist. Saige recalled as a child never seeing the sun for more than ten minutes before another rain cloud swept over the island and drowned it in a deluge.

The *Sunsurfer* gently manoeuvred toward the marina. Some of the crew on the deck below put the fenders out and prepared the lines.

This is it.

After all these years, Saige had returned to Ashvall. She stared at the first town she had ever known. People didn't visit Ashvall for the beaches, the weather, or the climate. They came for the history. St Albert Port ended at the base of forested hills. Steeped in folklore and tales of witches and ghosts, the forest was home to eerie tombs, Napoleonic towers, and World War Two bunkers. She'd even heard rumours of tunnels that led to a Nazi hospital ward, but no one had ever found them. And, of course, people came to the island for Wolvercraft Manor.

Saige shivered. She didn't want to look, but her head turned in that direction regardless. Beyond the coastal dunes, Ashvall's famous Cliffs of Eden jutted from the deep water. The rocky headland spanned miles, but it was this craggy arch that made fear leap in Saige's chest. She blinked, hoping the image she saw wasn't real, but when she opened her eyes, the scene hadn't changed. A woman stood on the tip of the cliff face. Her white nightdress and long blonde hair flapped like sails in the wind. Was she... staring at Saige? No. It couldn't be possible. Not at this distance. But the longer Saige stood frozen to the deck, the more she believed this woman had her fixed in her gaze.

Saige swallowed the metallic taste in her mouth.

It's not real. It's not real. It's an impression. A memory.

The woman turned, looked down at the water, and just... dropped.

Saige screamed. She watched the woman plummet to the craggy inlet below. The way she had fallen—not stepped off, not jumped off, but toppled into gravity's embrace—well... there'd been nothing natural about that movement at all.

"Saige?"

She spun around. She hadn't realised how tight she'd been holding on to the handrail. Her clammy fingers stuck to the polished timber.

Her father and Aunt Violet stood by the yacht's luxurious pool. Aunt Violet was pale in the face. A strangled sound worked up from her throat.

Her father moved toward her with cautious steps. He brought his hand forward. "Saige, come away from the edge."

What?

She looked down at her feet. Shock spasmed through her. She had climbed onto the rail.

How? Surely I'd remember doing that?

"Saige."

Her father's tense voice cut through her senses. She jumped down and staggered backward, knocking over a deck chair in the process. "I don't know what happened. I didn't mean to...."

Mean to what?

What had I been about to do?

Jump?

Drown myself in the water?

No. I'm not that crazy.

She peered back at the cliffs, but she knew there would be no sign of the woman. What Saige had seen was an event that occurred years ago, a memory that had embedded itself into the rocky terrain. For her only to witness, it seemed.

Aunt Violet stepped forward and wrapped Saige in her arms. "Come on, dear. Let's go inside and get you something to eat. I think you should rest when we get to the manor. That sounds good, doesn't it?" She threw a worried glance at Saige's father. It was a look that said *"This wasn't a good idea."*

Well, serves you both right.

Saige hadn't wanted to come to the island in the first place.

Derrick Wolvercraft stared at his daughter like he didn't know her.

That's because he doesn't know me. None of them want to know the real me.

She allowed Aunt Violet to lead her across the deck. Just as she was about to step inside, Saige stole a final look at the cliffs.

Yes.

The Cliffs of Eden were famous.

Made famous when her mother had plunged off the edge.

THREE

She wasn't staying on the island. Not now. Not ever.

Her father's guests had disembarked the *Sunsurfer* and made their way up the dock. She watched them from the deck, sickened by their snobbery and thoughtlessness. They snapped their fingers at the porters hired to help with their luggage and waved at their society friends—the same people they probably ridiculed and gossiped about.

An Ashvall tourist coach had been arranged to take the guests to Wolvercraft Manor. Saige mentally assessed the line. It would take the coach at least three trips. She remembered the roads being narrow and winding, the trees often overgrown and obstructing part of the lane. She recalled how often she stared out the car window as a kid, hoping to spy fairies or witches. Back then, Ashvall's local folklore and dark history had fascinated her. Now, it caused a cold prickle to shimmy across her scalp.

"Saige." Her father approached. He passed her a look that made her stomach clench. "I think I should have Dr

Grigori flown in. If these episodes are starting again, I want to make sure you're safe—"

"I'm not staying." Saige stared at her father with icy determination. "This yacht has many rooms. I'll stay here tonight. Tomorrow, I'll catch a ferry and return home."

Derrick gave an annoyed shake of his head.

Saige wasn't finished with him. "I told you I didn't want to come here. Why couldn't you have just left me alone?"

Why did Zoe have to have her stupid wedding at Wolver-craft Manor?

Derrick pulled on a patient smile, but Saige recognised how strained it was. "You'll be coming to the house with me and Aunt Violet. A room has been arranged for you. My associates are staying on the yacht. There's no room for you here, Saige."

"Then I'll find a hotel."

Or I'll sleep on the frigging deck.

She stormed off.

"Saige," her father called. "Your suitcase is already on the coach."

She turned around and raised her brows at him. "Then I'll have you send it to my hotel. I'll be in touch."

She darted down the stairs, ignored Aunt Violet—who slunk away beside the outdoor bar, pretending she hadn't been eavesdropping—and didn't look back.

***

"What?" Saige couldn't believe her luck, or rather, lack of it.

The bar attendant, a scruffy woman with greying hair

and arms the size of thighs, shot a disparaging smile at her. "It's high season, and an eccentric billionaire's son is marrying an eccentric supermodel. We're fully booked. We haven't a room to spare. Not that I'm complaining. The wedding has been good for business." She took up a tattered old tea towel and dried a glass tankard. "What? Why you staring at me like that? You want something?"

Saige shut her mouth, realising too late that her jaw had dropped. The Grubby Handmaid—a questionable pub and hostel—had been her last choice of preference along St Albert Port's charming seafront. The Peninsula Hotel, the Queen's Inn Bed and Breakfast, and the St Albert Self-Catering Cottage were entirely booked out. Even the Sandy Beach Bungalows and Ocean View Camping Park had turned her away.

I may actually have to sleep on the Sunsurfer's *deck, after all.*

That was fine. She'd slept in a lot rougher places.

"Thank you," she said, determined to make her voice sound anything but thankful, and returned outside with a scowl.

Saige didn't fare any better at the Ashvall Ferry Port.

"Sorry, love." The attendant's shaggy blond hair fell over his forehead. He took a sip of his coffee and bit greedily into his iced donut. "All the ferries departing Ashvall back to the mainland are booked out for the next week. It's high season, and some hoity-toity billionaire's son is marrying a singer, or supermodel... or some good-looking bird. Your best bet is to book a ferry to Guernsey. From there, you may be able to get a flight to London, but like I said, its high season. All the islands are busy."

Saige had thanked him and then found a bench seat to settle on.

Now she stared at the ocean, calculating her options. St Albert Port was the central town, but there were other smaller villages in Ashvall. It meant an expensive cab fare around the island in search of accommodation, and the chances that every hotel, pub, inn, cottage, and caravan park was booked out was high.

Damn it, damn it, damn it.

Someone sat down next to her.

Saige cut a curious glance at him. Anger fizzed her blood. "What the hell do you want?"

Jasper offered her a polite smile. "Chip?"

He must have discovered Ashvall's famous Sea Fuel, a fish and chip café she had loved as a little girl. The smell was intoxicating.

A spark of emotion danced behind her eyes. She remembered their first date. Fish and chips at the beach during the sunset.

Absolute arsehole.

Was he deliberately taunting her with that memory right now?

She stared back at the sea. "No, thank you."

Jasper popped another chip in his mouth. "Your loss."

She glared at him. "What do you want?"

He shrugged. "I saw you arguing with your dad. I wanted to make sure you were all right."

"Like you care."

"Things might have ended between us, Saige, but that doesn't mean I don't care. I know how much this island... the house... freaks you out." Concern lit in his brown eyes. It was a familiar stare—that serious, smouldering look that had made teenage girls all around the world lose their senses. She hadn't grown immune to it, and she hated herself for it.

She tilted her chin up. "I'm surprised you remember."

"I remember everything about you."

"A pity you didn't remember to break our engagement off."

Instead of taking offence, he watched her closely. His voice was infuriatingly calm. "I'll organise an Uber to the house. There's no accommodation left, Saige. It's time to go home."

So now he'd been watching her too. He'd ghosted her for years. No phone call. No email. No text. But now it was okay for him to follow her around like an overly protective guard dog.

She stood, distressed that Jasper was right. Her father would never let her sleep on the deck on the *Sunsurfer*. There were photographers, journalists, and paparazzi everywhere on the island, and it wouldn't be a good look for the family if Derrick Wolvercraft's daughter was caught asleep on a deck chair like a penniless tramp.

She squeezed her eyes shut, wishing she could dissolve into water and sink away into the ocean. "Fine. Let's go to the house. And there are no Ubers on the island. Most residents don't own a car. We'll be lucky if we can even find a cab. We'll have to walk."

"Walk?" Jasper looked like he'd choked on lemon peel.

"Yes, Jasper. It's called putting one foot in front of the other."

She started down the road, satisfied for the first time all day.

"HOW MUCH FARTHER? MY FEET HURT."

Jasper's complaints made Saige's heart accelerate. She'd been looking at her phone, searching maps for the most direct route, but the signal was patchy. She massaged a small circle into her temple. "Seriously, Jasper, we haven't even left the central town yet."

"I thought this island was small."

She turned around to face him, a hand on her hip. "How is it that you can look like a male underwear model and not be fit?"

It's so unfair.

"I'm fit." Jasper's out-of-breath voice hinted otherwise. "I'm just used to training in an air-conditioned gym. Plus, I'm not wearing the right shoes."

Join the club.

Her boots were rubbing on her toes. She sensed blisters sprouting.

My feet are going to look great with high heels later. Zoe will likely have a brain aneurysm seeing them. Everything has to be a hundred percent perfect for the big wedding.

Jasper wiped sweat from his brow. "And these hills... Saige, they're insane. You actually used to play on these things?"

Saige's mouth twitched. "The hills around the manor, yes. But not here. My father would never let Xav and me venture to town alone. We couldn't be trusted to stay on the hiking trails."

There were far too many lurking dangers in the woods between St Albert Port and Wolvercraft Manor. Rain caused frequent mudslides, and often many of the walking trails were closed. She hated to admit it, but she felt strangely reassured by Jasper's company. Yes, he was still a superficial jerk and an arsehole for what he'd done, but she was glad she wasn't alone. Saige remembered the stories her grandmother had told her about the Hauteville Woods—of witches' huts and fairy mounds, and mystical magical beasts. Back then, the stories had been fascinating. Now, it made her entire body run cold. Her mother's suicide had been... *strange.* No one, not the doctors, not the councillors, or the police, had believed her story. They'd recorded Saige's account of the incident as child trauma, a trick her mind had conjured to protect her from the truth. In the end, Saige had believed it herself. Or at least she'd tried to.

Jasper caught up to her. His eyes gave her a critical once-over. "You're quiet. What are you thinking about?"

She knew he was worried. The last time she'd been in woods, she had followed her mother down to the Cliffs of Eden. Saige wished she'd never shared that with Jasper. He was going to treat her like a porcelain doll that could crack any minute. It was the way her father, brother, and aunt had treated her for years.

"Nothing," she lied.

Jasper frowned. "Why do all the buildings have ledges beneath their chimneys? It's a real eyesore."

She examined the tavern they walked past. "They're plinths. It's said that witches used to travel across the island on their brooms and were in need of a place to stop and rest. If there was no seat, then the witch could come into the building to seek refuge and curse the owner for not thinking about her comfort."

"That's cheerful."

Saige offered a brief smile. "Ashvall's full of legends."

"So long as it's not full of ghost stories. I hate ghost stories."

MILKY LIGHT STREAMED THROUGH THE TREE branches. The Hauteville Woods hadn't changed. It was like the forest had been stuck in a time capsule, resistant to age or decay. Saige admired its beauty, the way it could look both peaceful and sinister at the same time. Gnarled, twisted roots created an intricate network along the leaf-strewn ground, the canopy abuzz with birdsong and insects. The towering wall of trees, overgrown and bulbous, swayed in the wind. The air in the forest bit into her skin like teeth.

Saige stared reluctantly at the rocky path ahead. They had left the road half an hour ago, taking a more direct route through some of the various hiking trails. Neither Saige nor Jasper had spoken much, but she sensed he had a million questions on his mind. They'd encountered a few retired couples walking the tracks. Only once did Jasper get recognised. A young woman with her parents had turned into a hysterical, blubbering mess and insisted on getting a selfie with her celebrity crush. Saige had swept her eyes up to the heavens and continued walking. She didn't need to see Jasper idolised like a god by another, much younger woman.

The sun had come out for the first time all day when the pair left the woods and entered the grounds of Wolvercraft Manor. The house was exactly as Saige remembered. Sprawling and foreboding. Gargoyles with demonic faces were interspersed among the steeply pitched roofs, towers, and turrets, the façade symmetrically balanced with two projecting wings. Above the front door was an incredible staircase tower, its winding balustrade carved with statues of angels, their faces smoothed down by age. The tower traversed all four storeys of the house, its spire piercing the sky.

Saige shivered. The building stood on the hill, an enormous white monument that reminded her of an elaborate mausoleum. The dark forest surrounding it gave the impression that the manor was alive and haunted, the windows its eyes, which stared straight at Saige and beckoned her to come inside. At least, that was what she imagined. With every step closer to the house, she felt more afraid, not less. She was hollow and cold inside, as though Wolvercraft Manor had sucked everything warm and cheerful away from her.

Jasper's wide eyes betrayed his surprise. "This place is a frigging mansion. I was expecting a cottage. I can't decide whether royalty should live here or the Addams family."

Grey rain clouds swept over the sun again, shrouding the house in shadow.

Saige wrapped her arms around herself.

Home sweet home.

But she knew Wolvercraft Manor was anything but sweet.

FOUR

Stepping into the house where she'd been born took Saige's breath away. The interior was exactly as she'd remembered it. The foyer, also known as the Winter Hall, remained decorated in the richly ornamented style of the French Renaissance. Priceless collections of antiques and art were on display: marble busts, family portraits, floral wallpaper painted in gold leaf. Two winding staircases met at a mezzanine, the ceiling painted with angels from the Sistine Chapel. A crystal chandelier hung from its centre. Saige squeezed her eyes shut. Her ancestors had never spared any expense when it came to showing off.

Neither did their descendants.

Her father, Xav, Zoe, and the wedding guests had joined a large tourist group that was gathered around for the last guided tour. Wolvercraft Manor might have been privately owned, but Saige's father had allowed the National Trust of Ashvall to conduct public tours. Thanks to Xav and Zoe's exclusive wedding, the house would be closed for the next week. It seemed to Saige that many tourists were taking the opportunity to see the house while they could.

Jasper stood taller as he marvelled at the house's beauty. At six feet, he made her feel more slight than usual. "I'm glad we didn't miss this. I wanted to go on the guided tour."

Saige scrunched her nose. "The *what?*"

"The guided tour. Here." He took out a brochure from his back pocket and unfolded it. "See? This is the wedding programme. The events run over the course of the week. First up is a tour of the house. Tonight there's an introductory dinner." He winked at her.

Saige remembered how much Jasper loved his food. He'd often eaten half her meal as well as his own on their dates. She groaned inwardly, not wishing to recall any more of their awkward past.

Great. A week-long wedding programme. That had to be Zoe's idea.

"Good afternoon." The tour guide was a woman in her late sixties with greying red hair and high cheekbones that even the most cosmetically enhanced models would envy. Saige couldn't help but notice how vintage her clothing was. A long linen skirt and beige jacket, with black rounded glasses on top of her head. She looked like a librarian from the 1920s.

"My name is Prue, and I want to cordially welcome you to Wolvercraft Manor." She beamed at the group. "After six years of construction by more than a thousand workers, Wolvercraft Manor was officially opened in 1846 by Frederick George Wolvercraft. The house consists of two hundred and fifty rooms, which includes forty-five bedrooms, twenty-three bathrooms, and sixty-five fireplaces. This afternoon, we will explore several of these rooms and parts of the summer gardens. The eight-thousand-acre estate is open all year-round, and I highly recommend that you explore the forested trails and the gardens after the tour. This way, please."

Prue led the large group through the house. Distinct childhood memories surfaced in Saige's mind as the assembly swept through different rooms. She remembered playing with her dolls underneath the large dining room table, her nanny frantically searching for her throughout the house. She recalled leaping up and down the grand staircase, determined to skip as many steps as she possibly could. She was amazed she never rolled an ankle.

Saige shook off the memories. She'd been a sweet girl back then, naïve of the dangers that lurked around her. The house had swallowed up that innocence the day her mother died.

While the tourists, Jasper included, admired and gaped at every furniture piece, ornament, and artwork the house offered, Saige smelt centuries of accumulated odour—of hundreds of Christmas dinners, birthdays, and deaths, of the lingering scent of rotting wood and decaying parchment, replaced with new timbers and paint. The house was old, tired. Saige sensed it in the way the floors creaked and the walls groaned. Wolvercraft Manor was like an aged person waiting to die. The National Trust of Ashvall, even her father, wouldn't let it go to sleep.

Jasper leaned close to her ear. "This house is incredible."

She shot her eyebrows up. "Yeah, it's real amazing."

They were in the library, which was a bibliophile's dream. Centuries-old books lined the massive shelves that went right up to the ceiling, the woodwork carved with cherubs and flowers. On the other side of the library, large windows offered spectacular views of the gardens. On any normal occasion, the curtains would have been drawn to protect the books. As a child, Saige remembered how dark the room became, even during the day. She'd imagined monsters lurking in the shadows waiting to snare her. As a result, she'd never entered the library alone.

"Seriously?" Jasper's long stare made her uncomfortable. "You never wanted to come back here. You and your brother are set to inherit this place, right?"

She crossed her arms. "Yes. Eventually. But I'm giving my half to Xav. After the wedding, I want nothing to do with it."

She'd resigned herself to the fact that the only way she was getting off this island was her father's yacht in a week's time. She exhaled an exhausted sigh. Her family was going to get exactly what they wanted: Saige stuck in Wolvercraft Manor.

Jasper's eyes narrowed. Uncertainty hardened his face. "I think your dad's right. You need to move on from your mother's death... as tragic as it was. This house, it has such potential. You could do so much... become so much with this place."

She scrambled for a response.

He doesn't understand. How could he? You never told him the truth.

She was afraid if she'd confided in Jasper when they were engaged, he would have thought she was crazy and run for the hills.

Turned out he ran anyway.

Her heart beat faster, but she managed to keep her voice level. "Enjoy the tour, Jasper."

He held her gaze a moment longer, then, seeming to give up, shook his head and turned his attention back to the guide.

Saige withdrew to the window. In a room full of people, she'd never felt more alone.

Prue talked about the elaborate furnishings that Frederick George Wolvercraft had purposely travelled to France to purchase, but Saige zoned it all out.

No. That's not right.

She could no longer hear Prue.

Sound was playing tricks in her ears. Dizziness rushed at her.

Why is it hard for me to breathe? Am I having a panic attack?

She was overly hot, and her underarms were slick with perspiration. She stumbled to the open window.

Breathe, Saige. Breathe.

As she focused on her inhales and exhales the way Dr Grigori had told her, the pounding inside her chest started to calm.

Saige stared out at the gardens, relishing the cool air on her face. A few tourists had set blankets down on the lawn and picnicked. Others were exploring the fountains and duck ponds. Her eyes travelled to the Hauteville Woods that seemed to wrap around the estate like a constricting snake. She imagined birdsong and cooler temperatures among the maples, pines, and oaks.

Something white flashed among the trees.

She blinked.

Was that...?

Had she truly just seen what she thought?

A woman in the trees, staring right back at her. A woman in a white eighteenth-century gown with raven-black hair.

No. That isn't possible.

Saige examined the shadows between the trees. A wintry, white fog, the kind of cloud cover seen coasting over a lake in the early hours of the morning, shrouded the woodland. Shock jolted through her, as cold as ice cubes sliding down her back. The woman had returned, only this time she was in the tree. No. Not in the tree. Hanging from it. A rope hung from a branch, the noose tight around the woman's snapped neck. Her feet twitched, reminding Saige of a skink's skittering tail. Even from this distance, she had the distinct impression that the woman's bulging eyes stared straight into her own.

Saige leapt back from the window.

Not again. No! Not again!

She pushed her way through the tour group, not caring who she barrelled into in the process, and hurried through the maze of rooms back to the foyer. It was the farthest room from the woods, and its windows looked out at the long drive that... eventually led back to the woods, but at least Saige couldn't see the trees from there.

Oh my God. No. Please, no!

She had thought, hoped, that time of her life was over.

Her heart was a jittery mess again, pounding through her body right down to her toes. She sat in a chair and leaned forward, bracing her hands on her knees and sucking in mouthfuls of air.

I can't see them again.

I won't survive the week if I do.

Not even a day in this house... on this island, and it was all coming back.

Saige must have been there for a full twenty minutes hyperventilating when the tour group returned. She quickly hid behind a door between the foyer and a sitting room and watched through the gap. She couldn't see her father, Xav, or Zoe, thank God. They must have left the tour early. Jasper was there. He was like an overgrown child, the house a playground he desperately wanted to climb. He watched and listened with eager curiosity, one hand curled around his elbow, the other cupped around his jaw.

Prue clapped her hands. "That concludes the tour of Wolvercraft Manor, but before you leave, does anyone have any final questions?"

A teenage girl, surrounded by a cluster of boisterous friends, put her hand up. She giggled nervously. "Is the house haunted?"

A silent anticipation filled the foyer.

It was a common question Saige had heard as a little girl. It never ceased to amaze her how the most rational-minded people were intrigued by stories of the super-natural.

Yet so quick to dismiss someone who's experienced para-normal events first-hand.

Prue didn't lose her smile, but her eyes remained care-fully expressionless. "Of course, a building is so much more than just bricks and mortar. There have been many stories of strange phenomena surrounding Wolvercraft Manor. From 1940 to 1945, the Nazis occupied Ashvall Island. They built camps, bunkers, air raid shelters, and concrete fortifications—using prisoners, of course—

around various parts of Ashvall. This house became the headquarters. It is said that somewhere beneath the manor is a maze of prisons where people were detained, interrogated, and killed. Having said that, the basement has been searched, but no prison cell has ever been found." Prue dabbed her tongue against her lips. "There are stories of ghost sightings in the woods. People have said they have heard the screams of a woman at night. It's all hocus-pocus, of course."

A man somewhere in his forties raised his hand. "Can you tell us any stories about the Hauteville Woods? I'm interested about the witches who used to reside there. Some of them were hanged in the forest. Correct?"

Prue pulled on another patient smile. "There are ghost tours that leave from the Ashvall Library in the centre of town at nine o'clock every night. If anyone is interested in Ashvall's spookier history, I suggest you buy yourself a ticket. Thank you, and have an enjoyable afternoon."

Everyone meandered outside to the lawns except Prue, Jasper, and Saige.

Prue laughed coolly. "Is that my favourite niece hiding in the doorway?"

Saige straightened. She was feeling only a little better. "I'm your only niece."

"Which means you have to be my favourite. Come here and let me see you."

Saige did as she was told. Aunt Prue, her father's older sister, took up Saige's hands and gave them a firm squeeze. "It's good to see you, sweetheart. I'm sorry you had to hear that last question. It's asked often, I'm afraid." She took Saige's jaw in her hand and assessed her. "You're looking a little thin, dear. Have you been sleeping?"

From the corner of her eye, Saige saw Jasper laugh.

"Aunt Prue, this is Jasper Young. He'll be singing at the wedding."

Jasper shook Prue's hand. "Hi. I've heard so much about you."

"Really?" Her eyes widened in surprise. She passed a teasing look at her niece. "How long have you two known each other?"

Saige's face coloured. "Xav is friends with Jasper. *They've* known each other since school."

Her voice came out a little too fast to be believable.

It was evident by the way Aunt Prue examined her that she knew Saige was lying.

Jasper put a hand up like he was at school. "I have a question about the house. There's a blank spot up there by the stairs. I just want to know who's supposed to be there."

Saige and Aunt Prue glanced along the mezzanine's wall, where portraits of the Wolvercraft Family dating two hundred years back hung. Saige had the distinct impression that her ancestors were looking down on her and judging.

Jasper was right. Near the staircase was an empty space where a portrait had undoubtedly been. Saige remembered this spot always being vacant, but she'd never been interested enough as a child to know why.

Aunt Prue shrugged. "That is a mystery of the Wolvercraft household. I suppose at some stage the portrait was damaged and taken down for repairing. Perhaps it was lost."

Jasper stared back at the empty space. "You don't know who it was a portrait of?"

"I'm afraid not."

He rocked back on his heels and gazed outside to where the tourists waited. A group of young women was watching him. A smile stretched across his lips. He slapped a heavy hand on Saige's shoulder. "I have some fans to attend to. See you around."

He stepped out of the foyer into the cold afternoon outside. Saige watched with a jealous pain as Jasper was enveloped by the giggling swarm. Each of them seemed to go redder in the face, bursting in hysterics as they snapped selfies with their idol.

Saige linked her arm with her aunt's. "Makes you sick, doesn't it?"

Aunt Prue only smiled. "He's a very nice young man. Not too bright, but... handsome. Is he single?"

"Aunt Prue! He's young enough to be your son."

"I meant for you, dear."

Saige swallowed discreetly.

FIVE

"YOU LOOK TROUBLED, SAIGE."

Aunt Prue watched her niece, her brow furrowed.

Saige focused on the roses that surrounded them. The gardeners really had done an exquisite job this summer.

And they should. My father pays them a small fortune to maintain the grounds.

No matter how hard she focused on the flowers, though, Saige couldn't ignore her aunt. She felt Prue's gaze biting into her.

The temperature had dropped dramatically as the afternoon slipped closer to dusk. Saige hugged herself, wishing she could thaw the cold out of her chest. "I've been on this island for less than five hours, and its already started." She laughed, half in surprise, half in despair. "I'm seeing things."

Aunt Prue took up both of Saige's hands. "My dear girl. It'll be okay. Wolvercraft Manor is *just* a house. Ashvall is *just* an island. Yes, some terrible things have happened here. Tragic accidents." She wrapped her delicate fingers around Saige's cheek, gently wiping some of her niece's tears away. "What you see isn't real. Your brother's wedding is a happy occasion. Focus on that. It'll remove the negative energy."

Saige offered her a weak smile in return. "That's what Dr Grigori said. She told me to come to the house. See it for what it really is. Just bricks and wood and glass. But how am I supposed to ignore these... *things* when they seem so real to me?"

No one understands.

Worse. No one had answers.

Aunt Prue's breath seemed to catch in her throat. "Your father told me what happened on the yacht. He wants you to sleep in Aunt Violet's room tonight."

Saige shook her head. "Aunt Violet snores. Can't I stay with you?"

Aunt Prue lived in a small cottage on the outskirts of Wolvercraft's estate. Unlike the rest of her family, she hadn't followed her brother's success to the mainland but remained on the island, a curator, librarian, and historian. She loved Ashvall Island and worked hard to help the National Trust keep the tourist trade alive.

The knot of fear in Saige's chest tightened when Prue didn't answer. "I don't think it's a good idea that I stay in the house," she persevered.

Her aunt bit down on her lip. "I'm sorry, Saige. I invited Dr Reynolds, a fellow historian, to the wedding. She's staying with me. I have no room."

"I could sleep on the couch."

"I discussed that option with your father. He wants you to stay at the manor."

The revelation made Saige feel like she'd been shoved

off a high diving board without warning. Of course her father wouldn't want to inconvenience his sister. Saige was a handful. A diagnosed handful. As a teenager, she woke up screaming from nightmares. She'd had panic attacks and migraines throughout her twenties. The medication had helped, but the only time she had ever truly been free of her "problem" was when she'd been with Jasper. She'd felt safe with him, happy, comfortable… at home. She hadn't seen anything that wasn't real. Sure, Jasper had wanted to keep their relationship a secret, but so had Saige. If the media hounds had gotten even a whiff of it, rumours and gossip would have been plastered all around social media. Saige could have imagined the headlines: *"Rock Star Bad Boy Dates Deranged Schizophrenic. How Long Will It Last?"*

Yes, keeping their relationship a secret had been the right call. Saige had wanted to share the news with her family first, then let the world know. It turned out she needn't have worried. After Jasper left without any communication, her depression resumed. The nightmares, sleep paralysis, and panic attacks returned. The media had gotten word about her condition and splashed it online. Medication and psychotherapy could only do so much when the entire world thought you were crazy.

Yes, I'm a handful my aunt doesn't deserve.

Saige tipped her head back and looked at the sky. "It's been a really long day. I think I might go inside, find my room, and take a nap."

She would absolutely not do that. Saige had been asleep for most of the morning. What she planned to do was find her bedroom and cry. Her throat felt sore and swollen, her eyes barely holding back unshed tears. Today had been hard. Tonight's dinner promised to be harder. How could she pretend to be all right when she most definitely was not okay?

Aunt Prue squeezed her shoulder. "Do you want me to come with you?"

Saige turned to face her. "No. I'll be fine."

It's time to face the house.

She stood there for a moment, unsure whether she should ask. She trusted Aunt Prue, more than she did her father or Aunt Violet. Even Xav. They had all looked at her like she was a poor, disturbed little girl, but Aunt Prue was different. Her favourite saying was "There are always two sides to every story."

Perhaps she would listen to Saige's story now.

Prue brushed her fingers through her impeccable side parting, seeming determined that the wind wouldn't ruin her hair. "What is it, dear?"

Saige's voice was so small, she struggled to hear it herself. "Mum saw the same things as me. Maybe I'm not...."

Crazy.

Maybe I'm sane, and everything I've seen in the past is real.

Aunt Prue watched Saige with careful consideration. "Saige, no one can ever truly trust their eyes, ears, and brains. Your mother was ill. That illness took her life. You have the same condition, but you're not like her. You're stronger. Perhaps you're right. Go inside and get some rest. I'll come and get you before dinner."

Saige nodded. The hope in her stomach dropped to her feet.

She walked back to the house, remembering the story her mother had told her.

About the woman she'd seen hanging from the tree.

THE UPPER FLOORS OF WOLVERCRAFT MANOR HAD always been, in Saige's opinion, too dark. She remembered as a child that even on the warmest summer days, with the windows open and the curtains drawn back, the sun could never seem to reach the manor, as though the house preferred to remain in eternal darkness. Now with dusk settled in and night approaching, Saige wandered the halls and passages with the acute sensation that she was being watched. It was the same feeling she'd experienced as a child. Her mother had told her they were spirits—entities that remained in the house. Elaine Wolvercraft, with her stunning blonde hair and ocean-blue eyes, had been a dedicated mother, but there were some things she insisted her daughter never tell her father, or her brother for that matter. The ghosts who walked Wolvercraft Manor were to remain their little secret.

Saige shivered and rubbed her arms.

Ghosts? Or madness?

She turned down a passage where the shadows seemed to close around her like hungry, cavernous monsters and fought to ignore the queasy tap dance that bounded in her stomach. Wolvercraft Manor hadn't been accustomed to housing guests in decades, and each door had been marked with a number tag hung around the handle. Saige had been told in the foyer by her father's hired concierge that she was in room twenty-two. No way was she staying with Aunt Violet. She'd never be able to deal with her aunt's energised, bubbly personality, the way she verbalised all her thoughts and feelings, or her squealing, high-pitched laughter. Honestly, Saige had seen that woman's squawk terrify a flock of birds.

She found her room, stepped inside, and fumbled for the light switch. Soft light lit her surroundings. Saige gasped as the memories took a moment to settle. This had been her bedroom as a little girl. She'd had a pink princess bed in the corner with a white canopy, her doll's house sitting beside it on a small, rectangular table. On the opposite wall, her dolls had been arranged in order from favourite to least favourite. Saige wondered how she'd managed to sleep with them all staring at her.

The room had changed, of course. Thick draperies now shielded any light from the outside. A four-poster bed with a rich mahogany headboard was placed along the wall, the matching dressers on either side decorated with a glass vase of white flowers. The room was large and airy, with high ceilings and light fixtures in the shape of rosebuds. A fireplace that Saige recalled had never been used was stacked with timber.

Just for show.

She was positive no one would actually be allowed to light a fire.

Saige dropped onto the bed, feeling as though she'd been sucked into a memory where nothing made sense. Someone—probably one of the many staff her father had hired for the wedding—had brought her suitcase up and placed it near the wooden duchess. On the chaise lounge beside it was a wrapped package. She moved from the bed and picked it up. There was a note.

. . .

PLEASE PUT SOME EFFORT IN TONIGHT. FOR YOUR brother's sake. Zoe chose the dress. Also, I want you to sleep in Aunt Violet's room tonight. She is next to you in twenty-one.

Love, Dad.

INSIDE WAS A LIGHT PURPLE SILK GOWN, THE KIND of frock worn at cocktail events. Saige bristled, her entire body stiff.

Put some effort in?

I don't even want to frigging be here.

She dropped the dress, wishing she had scissors to cut it into large chunks. She flopped back onto the bed, but staring at the ceiling didn't relax her.

Put some effort in, indeed. I'll put effort into not showing up.

She closed her eyes, urging her brain to turn off, the way she did whenever she didn't want to face her emotions. They were too overwhelming. Too suffocating.

The wind picked up outside, casting an eerie howl around the house. She shut it out. She didn't need nature screwing with her mind too. The wind developed into a gale, which made Saige pause.

Why does that sound like it's coming from inside the house?

From above?

Why does that sound like…

Crying?

Horrible, mournful cries that iced her to the bone.

Saige sat up.

The lady in the attic!

Saige had followed the voice once as a child. It had led her to the attic, but she had never gone up there, too afraid of what she might have found. She'd often heard those painful, wailing sobs at night, as though her ear were pressed right to the attic door.

Saige scrambled off the bed, found her wireless earbuds in the front pocket of her suitcase, and connected them to her phone. She found a track to listen to and dropped back onto the bed, shoving the pillow over her head, determined to drown out those miserable cries. She knew no one else could hear them.

Block it out. Block it out. Block it out.

She closed her eyes.

* * *

THE DREAM STARTED IN WOLVERCRAFT'S ROSE garden. Saige was eight years old again, playing dolls with her mother. Elaine had her hair loose, and it shone golden in the warm sunlight. She was still dressed in her white nightgown. She'd been ill, and Saige was afraid that playing outdoors would be too much for her mother, but Elaine had insisted. She was still beautiful, her lips full and plump, her eyes alive and perceptive, her skin creamy and smooth. How could Saige's mother be sick when she looked so... healthy?

The pair pretended that Saige's dolls were fairies in a rose kingdom. Butterflies flew among the flowers. Insects buzzed. Birds chirped. It was a little girl's dream come true. But when clouds drifted over the sun, something changed in Elaine. She dropped the doll. It landed on a stone, a huge crack ripped through its porcelain head.

"Mum?"

Elaine didn't answer. She stared at the trees. The huge maples and oaks no longer looked tranquil or inviting but twisted and gnarly. The hanging branches and roots were a gigantic web, and Saige imagined the forest preying on people like a spider. Sunlight had filtered out of the forest, replaced with cold streams of dark as the clouds coasted across the sky.

"Mum?"

Elaine stood up. She moved toward the forest, her long gown trailing over the grass like a ghostly bridal dress.

"Mum? Where are you going?"

Elaine never answered.

Saige discarded her doll and followed her mother out of the rose garden. She tried to slide her hand into her mother's, but Elaine's fingers were stiff and cold.

Like dead hands.

Saige was afraid. She'd never seen her mother act this way.

It has to be a fever, right?

Saige had read in a book that people could behave strangely under the influence of a fever. She dashed after Elaine. They crossed the lawn and approached the Hauteville Woods. Saige stopped. Her parents had always told her never to enter the woods alone, and yet her mother was doing exactly that.

Mum, stop. What are you doing?

Her father would never forgive her if something happened to Elaine. Saige made the uncomfortable decision. She stepped into the forest after her mother.

Saige had always admired the deciduous trees, blanketed by white and blue wild flowers, ferns, and moss. The stories of fairies and witches had always excited her, but now she wasn't so sure. The forest didn't smell sharp and earthy but of rotting vegetation and decay. Saige could have sworn her mother wasn't walking but floating, her white nightgown twisting around her legs in the breeze. She continued to follow, struggling against the branches, using her small arms to slap away overhanging vines. She could no longer see birds or small animals skittering through the underbrush. The woods were empty, abandoned by all living things.

"Mum? Please come back."

Her call went unanswered.

Tears of panic ran down her cheeks. Misery and silence encompassed her as she stumbled through the remainder of the woods and came out to the Cliffs of Eden. Her mother was standing at the tip of the peak.

Saige froze all over, her feet cemented to the grass. "Mum?"

Elaine turned around. Her eyes, which had always been a dazzling blue, were milky white orbs. Her blonde hair flapped in the breeze like reeds. There was nothing kind in the way her lips pulled back into a grisly smile. "Don't let the wedding go ahead, Saige. Love is a curse."

She fell back like a snapped tree, silently spinning into the depths.

Saige screamed.

She sat upright, the remnants of the dream still staining her eyes. Her skin was drenched in cold sweat, her breath heavy in her chest. She'd had this nightmare—

memory—before, but it had never been so vivid. And her mother had never spoken to her.

"Don't let the wedding go ahead, Saige. Love is a curse."

She tore off the bed on shaky legs. Saige stilled as her eyes met the window, the blood suddenly icy in her veins.

No. That's not possible.

The curtains were pulled back, and the window was open. Saige had a clear view to the Hauteville Woods. For a moment, she caught something white hanging from a tree, but it vanished in an eyeblink.

Saige stepped away. She most definitely had not drawn the curtains or opened the window. She backed into the bedroom door at the same time something pounded against it from the other side. Saige shrieked. She looked around the room for something to use as a weapon.

The door opened.

Saige held her breath.

Her father's head popped in. "Saige, what's wrong? I heard screaming."

She collapsed onto the floor and sobbed, her heart giving in to violent shudders.

SIX

Under her father's watchful gaze, Saige swallowed three large pills and opened her mouth to prove she'd consumed them. She'd told Derrick she'd had a nightmare, but Saige hadn't revealed what it had been about. Her father didn't need to know. It would only worry him.

She decided the dream had been a result of stress.

The open window?

Well, she'd sleepwalked many times before. She must have opened the window herself. Still, the whole event had given her the heebie-jeebies, and Saige no longer wanted to be alone. The woman hanging in the tree. The lady in the attic. Her mother plunging off a cliff. These were all thoughts she didn't want to revisit. Dinner with the family and Wolvercraft guests started to feel appealing.

Saige showered quickly while her father waited in her room. She knew he was too afraid to leave her alone. He'd demand she sleep in Aunt Violet's room tonight. Saige no longer had a problem with that.

In the mirror, she ran her fingers through her hair before tossing it up into a loose bun, then shimmied into her purple dress. Guilt racked her chest at the thought of how terrified her father must have been at the sight of her in a collapsed heap on the floor. She had to make it up to him and decided she really would put some effort in tonight. She'd brought minimal make-up with her on this trip, but she had a trained hand from happier days and was able to create something that, while not stunning, was acceptable and pretty.

"I'm sorry," she apologised again when she stepped out of the bathroom. "I must be making you late for your guests."

Derrick patted her on the arm. "Just make sure you stay on that medication, Saige. I don't want to lose you like I lost your mother."

She looked down at her feet.

The memory danced in her mind. Her mother's wild, possessed eyes. Elaine's hands, thin and skeletal and cold.

It's just stress. The house. My condition.

What I dreamt was just a memory. A very warped version.

But she had trouble believing it.

Saige drummed her fingernails on the dining table. She'd sworn to Derrick that she'd make an effort, and she intended to keep that promise. But it was hard. She hardly knew any of the elderly couples who'd been seated at her table, which she guessed had been Zoe's doing. Eating a three-course meal while trying to engage with strangers who were hard of hearing had been tiring and tested her patience.

She couldn't drink, not after taking her medication, and sipped on water instead. She swallowed it with a grimace. The waiter had given her sparkling. She hated sparkling.

Damn you, Zoe.

She watched her future sister-in-law bop and frolic on the dance floor with Xav. Her dress was long, white, and backless, and she had no shame as she showed off her tanned leg through the slit. Saige blew out a huff of frustration and focused on the other couples. Wolvercraft's ballroom had been elaborately dressed like a scene from a picture two centuries ago. The round dining tables were covered in soft white tablecloths, embellished with peonies as the centrepiece, and finished with vanilla-scented tealights. Wineglasses. Champagne flutes. Silver utensils. It was all a little overboard for Saige's taste.

Have I missed the wedding? Because this feels an awful lot like a reception.

She realised Zoe had never just wanted a wedding. She'd wanted a week's worth of celebrations where she could shine and be the centre of attention. Saige knew it just from the amount of media personnel and photographers in the room. Their flashing cameras would give her a serious headache.

But it's better than going back to my room and being alone.

Saige still didn't know what to make of the dream, or the image of the woman hanging in the tree, or the cries of the lady in the attic. Were they just hallucinations her mind created like her doctors had said? Or were they something else? Something more... sinister?

She scanned the room. On a small stage in the corner sat the band, classical musicians in tuxes playing violin, cello, drums, and flute. In the centre on the piano was Jasper. Saige wanted to look away but couldn't. His fingers glided effortlessly over the keys. It made her heart ache, bringing back too many painful memories of when they'd been together, nights of him practising his music in his studio, Saige listening to the beautiful harmony. She looked down at her empty glass, wishing she could fill it with wine, or something stronger.

Someone dropped into the seat beside her. An older woman with greying hair tied back in a tight bun. She wore a floor-length painted floral dress. Her lipstick was blood red, which Saige didn't think suited her green eyes, her eyelids decorated in dark purple eyeshadow.

The woman extended her hand. "You must be Saige Wolvercraft. I saw you sitting here alone and looking sorry for yourself and thought I'd make an introduction."

Gee, thanks.

Saige shook the woman's hand. She caught a whiff of her perfume and struggled to hold in a sneeze.

The woman drew closer and took out a business card. "My name is Dr Harriette Reynolds. I'm a historian and curator and have worked closely with your aunt Prue."

Saige recognised the name. "You're staying with my aunt at the cottage?"

"Yes. It was very nice of her to invite me to her nephew's wedding. It was a huge surprise. You see, I have a very special interest in Wolvercraft Manor and its incredible history."

Saige faked a polite smile. "Most people do. It's why tourists come to Ashvall."

She gazed jealously over at the young couples on the dance floor.

Why do I get stuck with the oldies for the night? Why can't I just be normal and be like other women my age, dancing with young men and drinking until I'm giddy with joy?

Harriette patted Saige's arm in a grandmotherly gesture. "You're very brave to return here."

Saige froze. She started breathing a little too hard. "Excuse me?"

Harriette waggled her eyebrows, as though the pair were in on a juicy secret. "I must confess that I came to Wolvercraft Manor with an ulterior motive. Your affliction... what your mother suffered all those years in this house, it's fascinated me since—now, please don't leave, Miss Saige."

Saige had stood up, repulsed by the woman's boldness. She'd dealt with these acts of vulgarity from the press when she was a teenager—their prying questions, their prowling behaviour—and she didn't fancy a replay.

Harriette gripped her arm. "Please, just listen to me. I have information that may benefit you. Your mother wasn't crazy. And neither are you." Her eyes briefly roamed the ballroom before continuing. "The things you have seen in this house... on the island... they're real."

Saige sat down. Doubt, even disgust, still tugged at her insides, but Harriette had caught her attention.

The doctor smiled, but her lips were stretched too thin for it to be genuine. She drank from her water glass, her fingers leaving sweat marks on the crystal. "When your aunt told me about your mother's suicide, it got me thinking about all the other deaths that have occurred at Wolvercraft Manor."

"Other deaths?" Saige ignored the no elbows on the table rule. She leaned forward and watched the historian closely.

"Yes. Since Wolvercraft's existence, there have been five noted suicides, and I suspect a great many more. All the deaths were of young women who had married into the Wolvercraft family." Harriette went silent for a moment as a couple drifted past them and headed for the dance floor. "I have done my research on the house. Five women. Five deaths. Your mother's included."

Saige's heart did an unexpected flip. "Did one of the women hang herself?"

The doctor scooted her chair closer. "Yes. Josette Wolvercraft. She hanged herself in the Hauteville Woods not far from the house. And then there was poor Bridgitt Wolvercraft. She died on her wedding night. Flung herself off the highest tower of this house."

A chill tiptoed along Saige's skin. Was it possible that Harriette Reynolds was making this all up? "Why have I never heard any stories like this before?"

"Well, my dear, the last known suicide was your mother's. It's unlikely your father or aunts would tell you the story, isn't it? But there are accounts of the events in the history books. The Ashvall library has journals and newspaper articles that date the suicides."

"I'd like to see these articles." Saige forced a hint of challenge in her voice.

Was Harriette just another loony seeking attention? Did she think Saige was so far gone with her condition that she'd believe whatever came out of the doctor's mouth? Saige had to test her. She didn't trust strangers, even little old ladies who were acquainted with her aunt.

Saige sat up straighter. "So you believe the things my mother saw were, in fact, ghosts?"

"Yes, dear. And I believe you have seen one or two of these ghosts yourself."

Saige didn't deny it. "I want to meet you tomorrow. Will you take me to the library so I can see proof?"

A muscle twitched in Harriette's neck. Saige imagined the lady's pulse had edged up a degree.

Harriette reached for her water again. "If your aunt permits it, of course."

"My aunt will know nothing about it. This is a sealed deal between you and me." Saige's knees wobbled, but she kept her gaze steady on the doctor. "I'll meet you tomorrow at ten o'clock in the library. I want to understand more about these suicides." She dug her fingers into the table and stole an anxious glance around the room. "What would make five women suicide?"

Harriette shook with dismayed laughter. "Saige, my sweet thing. You don't honestly believe the deaths were suicides, do you?"

"But you just said—" Saige felt herself go pale in the face.

"Wolvercraft Manor is not kind to strangers. The house doesn't like outsiders." Harriette gazed around the room, as though the very walls, floor, and ceiling could hear her. "There is something inside Wolvercraft Manor. Something that brings death. Something that doesn't rest."

Saige jumped when the grandfather clock in the ballroom chimed, announcing 10:30 p.m.

Harriette gave Saige's hand another friendly tap. "I best find your aunt. It's getting late."

She hobbled out of her chair and disappeared in the crowd.

Saige remained sitting, too cold to move.

A DULL ACHE HAD TAKEN UP RESIDENCE BEHIND Saige's eyes. She was desperate for painkillers, but she wouldn't leave the ballroom. Not alone. Harriette's story had frightened her, and she was too afraid to venture through the house in case she saw... *ghosts.*

For so many years, she questioned whether she was crazy, and now that she had met someone who believed in Wolvercraft's ghosts, well... that just made the possibility more terrifying.

It was late, nearly eleven thirty, when guests started to meander upstairs.

Right. Get back to your room. Grab your things and get inside Aunt Violet's room. Take a sleeping pill. Listen to music. You'll be out cold. No dreams. No ghosts. You'll be safe for the night.

Saige slipped away from the table and dashed as quickly as humanly possible through the throng in her high heels. She hoped to avoid her father's stern eye. He'd be disappointed that she hadn't made the effort to talk to people her own age.

Blame Zoe. She's the one who organised the ridiculous seating plan.

Saige was nearly out of the ballroom when she saw something that made her pause.

Oh hell no!

She couldn't breathe. On the dance floor, Jasper was engaged in a slow dance with a blonde in a tiny black dress and stiletto high heels. Luisa. Saige hated her before, but now she wanted to snap the bridesmaid's legs in half.

Saige knew she should look away. It wasn't any of her business, but heartache and jealousy got the better of her. Jasper's and Luisa's bodies were linked just a little too snugly together, like two jigsaw pieces that fitted perfectly. If they hadn't already passed the friendship zone, Saige knew it wouldn't take much longer.

Probably tonight.

She balled her hands into fists and stormed away. Painful tremors racked her throat, as if someone had stuffed nails down her windpipe.

I don't care. I don't care. I don't care.

Her emotions didn't calm down when she finally reached her bedroom. She collected what she needed, returned to the hall, and knocked loudly on Aunt Violet's door.

Oh, come on. What's taking so long?

She knocked again, this time with more force.

Nothing.

"Aunt Violet? Are you there?"

Saige pressed her ear to the wood. She couldn't hear anything beyond the thick mahogany. Her sweaty fingers made it difficult to clutch the handle. The door didn't budge.

She's locked it.

Saige waited twenty minutes in the hall, leaning against her aunt's door. She fixed her eyes on the various guests who wandered back to their rooms, wishing them a pleasant evening. She tried not to let frustration bleed into her voice.

Where the hell is Aunt Violet?

She typed a quick text to her aunt, but the signal was patchy, and the message failed. Saige blinked furiously. She dialled her father, but the call didn't go through.

An ominous prickle rushed over her skin. She could no longer hear the music from downstairs. The party was over, and all the guests had returned to their rooms. Both ends of the hall were lost in darkness, like an abyss. The silence pulled onward, surrounding her. A sense of foreboding ran through her body. She itched to run. Fear spiralled through her legs, making her tremble. Something was present. She could hear it breathe. Wicked. Harsh. Fierce. Right in her ear.

A macabre scream tore through the house, magnified through the empty hall. The sound rang through her skull.

That came from the attic!

Saige couldn't take it anymore. She ran on unsteady legs back to her room and locked the door behind her.

HER PULSE STILL RACED. THE PAIN IN HER HEAD had climbed to a migraine. Saige listened to music, determined not to hear anything but Kate Bush. She brushed her teeth in the bathroom, downed two painkillers and a sleeping pill, and changed into pyjamas. She glanced at herself in the mirror. Her eyes were red and swollen from crying, and without her lipstick or moisturiser, her lips now appeared ashen and chapped. She looked like she'd been deprived years of sleep. But the truth was Saige spent more hours asleep than she did awake, and that took a toll on her physical appearance too.

Careful not to wet her earbuds, she washed off her ruined make-up in the basin, flicked off the bathroom light, and scrambled into bed. She must have been lying there for half an hour in the dark, letting the music soothe her, waiting for the pills to kick in, when she saw a reflection of movement in the window. For a moment, Saige had been convinced it was a face. A grey, puckered face surrounded by wild dark hair hanging in wet tangles.

It's the trees outside. The moon must be casting palls of shadow against the branches. It made me think there was a woman outside.

Saige slipped out of bed and tiptoed to the window. She pulled the curtains closed.

Funny, I could have sworn I shut these before I left for dinner.

Saige dived back into bed and tried hard not to think about ghosts, about Harriette's theory, about Jasper's arms circled around Luisa.

Jesus, why aren't the pills working? I should be unconscious by now.

She pulled the quilt cover tight, not because she was cold but because it was her only source of comfort. Sleep tugged at her eyes, pulling her into smooth black waters.

There it is. Sweet emptiness.

Even over the music, Saige had the vague impression that she heard the slow sweep of curtains drawn back and a tapping on the window, but then darkness fully submerged her, and she heard nothing.

SEVEN

SAIGE NEVER HAD TROUBLE SLEEPING AFTER A PILL, but tonight was different. She dreamt she was back on the cliff with her mother. Elaine stood at the edge, half in moonlight, half in shadow. Her white nightgown danced in the wind like a phantom presence, her skin so pale it was practically translucent. The side of her face that was on display was smiling, while the other half, which Saige had to strain her eyes to see through the shadows, was crushed. Saige knew if she stepped closer and let her eyes adjust, she'd see a face that resembled a pulped watermelon, sticky and mangled with blood. That was what had happened to her mother when she'd hit the rock pools far below. The side of her face had shattered on impact. At least, that was what Saige imagined.

Elaine raised her arms, beckoning her daughter to come forward and embrace her. Saige stood still. The only part of her that moved was the sharp rise and fall of her chest. She was immobile, panicked. This had never happened before in her dreams.

"Mum?" The wind snatched Saige's voice away. She wasn't sure if her mother had heard it.

Elaine's manic grin transformed. Black lips pulled back to reveal stubbed teeth, the skin around her eyes sunken to the bone. What Saige mistook for roses blooming across Elaine's chest became clearer. Blood. It pooled from deep cuts, soaking into her nightdress.

That must have been where the rocks skewered her.

"Saige." Elaine's voice was shrill, an echo that struck like lightning and the cawing of crows. "Don't let the wedding go ahead."

Saige watched, horrified, as her mother's body arched backward at an unnatural angle. Elaine's spine crunched, arms and legs bent outward as she plunged off the cliff.

Saige woke up gasping. She was drenched in sweat again, her heart hammering against her ribcage, her earbuds lost somewhere among the sheets.

No. This can't be happening.

She was on her medication, damn it.

It's meant to stop these nightmares.

She tossed her quilt cover aside, savouring the cool air against her skin.

Hang on. I put the heater on.

A shudder of fear rippled through her body. The window was open, the curtains drawn back.

I definitely shut those.

She took a bracing breath, climbed out of the bed, and walked to the window, her eyes alert for anything that might jump out. She half expected something with hooked fingers and crooked teeth to wrench her onto the tiled roof below, but the night outside was empty. Nothing dark or sinister lurked in the shadows. The glass seemed to shake in the wooden frame when Saige locked the brass latch. It had been cold outside, maybe even drizzling at some point, and condensation leaked down the glass. Her hand froze on the ledge.

Had that been...?

No. Surely not.

But Saige had the impression that she'd seen something tall and white hanging from a tree outside.

That's it. Aunt Violet must be in her room by now.

She wasn't going to remain a minute longer by herself.

Saige hurried out of her room, every nerve in her body twitchy with anxiety. She flinched as the bedroom door glided shut behind her. The hallway was dark except for a long shard of moonlight that leaked through a stained glass window. Saige looked around for movement that shouldn't be there, then tiptoed to her aunt's room. The floorboard beneath her groaned. The house wasn't as still or silent as she'd first perceived. Parts of the building seemed to grind and constrict, as though Wolvercraft Manor had been asleep and she'd interrupted its slumber.

A crack of light leaked from underneath Aunt Violet's door.

Thank God.

Saige tapped the door.

Come on. Please. I don't want to go back to my own room.

The door opened.

Saige swallowed a startled gasp. "Jasper!"

The handsome rock star's face scrunched into a frown. "Saige? What are you doing here?"

"Me doing here?" It took her a second for her brain to

catch up with the unexpected surprise. "What are you doing here? This is my aunt's room."

He looked at her as though she'd sprouted a second head. Understanding shone in his eyes. "Oh, right. Yeah, we switched. Something about the sunlight in the morning. It interferes with your aunt's sleep pattern. Anyway, she asked if we could swap. I said yes."

"Sun in the morning! There is no sun on this damn island."

"Okay. Someone's cranky."

Saige couldn't believe her bad luck. She became embarrassingly aware of what she was wearing. A black tank top with white seahorses and a matching pair of boyshorts with crabs. Jasper examined the boy shorts with a sarcastic twinkle in his eyes. "Nice pyjamas."

Why did I even buy the bottoms? No wonder the sales attendant had been laughing.

She wanted to slap a hand to her head. Once again, her naivety had brought her total humiliation.

Jasper leaned on the architrave. "I know it's summer, but don't you think it's a little cold for pyjamas like that?"

To be fair, Saige had been freezing when she'd returned from the ballroom and had cranked the central heating in her room to a temperature deliciously warm and toasty. Her father had organised the entire house to be fitted out just for this occasion. It was the first time in a long while that Wolvercraft Manor had been modernised.

Jasper's cheeky grin vanished. "Saige, what's wrong? You look frightened."

She let go of a conflicted sigh. "What room is my aunt in?"

"Thirty-six."

Saige's skin broke out in goose bumps.

Thirty-six!

The next level of the house.

It would require Saige to take the staircase and walk to the east wing. She hadn't done that since she was a little girl. Since the night she'd seen....

She felt as though her heart were being squeezed. She couldn't get enough air into her lungs.

Maybe I should stay in my room, after all.

But what if she was troubled with more nightmares?

And the window. She couldn't explain how it had opened... on its own.

No, I definitely can't be alone tonight.

Jasper's eyes swept down the hallway. "So, do you want me to walk you to your aunt's room?"

"No."

Yes.

A floorboard creaked under Saige's foot, which made her jump. "Thanks, I'll be leaving now."

She couldn't help herself. She tipped her head to spy a quick glance over Jasper's shoulder. His bed was empty.

Good. Luisa isn't in there.

Jasper's teeth gleamed white in a heart-gripping smile. "Is there anything else in my room that you would like to examine?"

Saige felt her cheeks flare. "Goodnight, Jasper."

She tore away. A moment later, she heard him chuckle and shut his door.

Arrogant, egotistical jerk.

But he did have a point. Saige couldn't run around the house in nothing but her tank top and boyshorts.

She poked her head into her bedroom, scanning all the

shadows and dark nooks. After the dream and window incident, she'd rushed out so fast that she hadn't bothered to turn on a light. Shadows stretched across all the furniture, walls, and ceiling, making Saige imagine monstrous, crooked fingers bending down to snatch her. She hurried inside, all the time feeling a cold whisper of air around her, and grabbed her dressing gown from the chaise lounge.

Out in the hallway, her steps were slow and cautious. Saige had the impression that she was walking down a passage in a dream that stretched out forever. Gold-framed oil paintings of her ancestors seemed to watch her as she passed. All the gothic arches, columns, and tapestries could have come straight from a cathedral in Europe.

She took an adjoining passage to her left, then followed another to her right. As a child, she had run down these halls and passages pretending to be a princess fleeing a hungry dragon. She hadn't forgotten the layout of the house. Some intrinsic part inside her knew which way to go.

She came out to the grand staircase. It was sturdier and wider than she remembered and incorporated balustrades with elaborately carved newel posts. The staircase wrapped itself along the panel walls, right up to the fourth storey, where an arched door stood. Her spine tingled. Her father had never let her go beyond level three. A topple over the railing would result in a long fall to your death on the marble mosaic below, but Saige, like any child exploring, had never taken her safety into concern. She had once climbed the stairs all the way to the arched door and was disappointed to find it locked. She'd asked her mother what was beyond the door.

"The staircase leading to the central tower, honey. It's too dangerous to go up there. It hasn't been maintained in years."

After her mother died, Saige's father had become distant. This resulted in a rebellious streak running through his daughter. Saige couldn't remember why she'd done it—possibly to get her father's attention—but she had come to the staircase late at night. She'd ambled loudly up the steps, deliberately stamping her tiny feet. Up and down she went, over and over, making as much noise as was humanly possible. In the end, she had caught something's awareness, but it hadn't been her father's.

No. Don't think about that now. Just find Aunt Violet.

The hallway to the level three bedrooms was just up the next flight.

I can do this. I can do this.

She trod carefully on the first step, then the next. Why did the staircase seem to be growing longer?

It's your head playing tricks.

She was halfway up the flight when she sensed the cold spot around her again. It touched her arms like wispy fingers and made every nerve in her body taut with icy fear. She looked up and gasped. In the centre of the staircase, feet hovering above the floor, was a woman in a long white bridal dress. Her long neck reminded Saige of a swan, only the skin was mangled and saturated with blood. Fat drips ran down her dress and dropped onto the stairs, sinking into each step without leaving a mark. Just like the dream Saige had suffered about her mother, this woman's face was crushed, one side shattered inward like a broken doll, the other sunken but intact, the lips, nose, and eyes bruised black. She danced the waltz with an imaginary partner, her bridal gown spinning around her like a ghostly cloud, her veil snaking out in misty tendrils.

She was exactly how Saige remembered.

Is she...?

Saige recalled what Harriette had conveyed. *"And then there was poor Bridgitt Wolvercraft. She died on her wedding night. Flung herself off the highest tower of this house."*

Apparently, Bridgitt Wolvercraft was sentenced to dance her bridal waltz for all eternity.

A sharp pain clutched Saige's chest. Her lungs burned in spasms.

Okay. Step away. Don't make any sound. You remember what happened last time.

"Saige?"

The voice startled her. She spun around too fast and nearly missed her footing on the step.

Jasper took her arms, steadying her with his firm hands. "Whoa! You okay there? I felt like a jerk before and didn't want you wandering around the house on your own. I know how much you hate it, so I came—"

His eyes found the spectre. Saige bit her lower lip as his fingers gripped her skin in shock. All his facial muscles changed, relaxed one second, panicked and horror-struck the next. He opened his mouth to scream.

Saige clung to his hand. "No! Don't!"

But it was too late.

The wraith's head twisted around. The small bones on display in her torn neck made a horrible sound like a snapped bottle top. Her one eye stood out from the bruised skin on her face. It reminded Saige of a cloudy cataract, or a window frosty and fogged-up. The woman's jaw dropped in a cavernous scream.

Saige smacked her hand on Jasper's shoulder. "Run!"

The creature—Bridgitt—was a hurricane of white mist rolling toward them. The pair slammed their feet on the last of the stairs. They ran, scrambling back in the direction they'd come, their hands still linked. Moonlight must have shone through the trees outside, because flickering shadows danced along the flaking wall colourings, the floor rendered to a morose teal tone. It gave the impression that every closed door was an entry to a mausoleum, that beneath the house's beauty was a skeleton sinking into decay.

Saige led Jasper through various passages and halls. She fancied she could hear doors slamming somewhere in the house behind them, a private composition for just their ears.

Jasper knocked over a chair as he pivoted around a corner, but he didn't stop to put it upright. "What the hell was that, Saige? Was that... was that...?"

"A ghost? Yes, you moron. Now you know why I never wanted to come back to this house."

Saige had no idea why she'd run back into her bedroom. It wasn't exactly safe in there.

Whenever children are afraid, they run into their rooms, don't they?

Jasper shut the door behind him. He darted around Saige's wooden tallboy, about to push it in front of the entry.

She watched him, her eyes still brimming with frightened tears. "What are you doing?"

"What do you think? I'm making sure the ghost can't get in."

"That isn't going to stop a ghost."

He stilled, seeming to realise what she'd said. "Shit! Ghosts are real. Shit! Shit!" His brown eyes found Saige's. "Can ghosts move through walls?"

She dropped onto the end of her bed. The queasy dread in her stomach made her nauseous. "I have no idea."

"Wolvercraft Manor is—" He seemed to struggle to get the last word out. "—haunted?"

"Jasper, calm down. Let me get you a drink of water."

"Water? I'm going to need that with a heavy scotch to get through this."

She ran her fingers through her hair. His panic wasn't helping her think clearly. She sensed colour drain from her cheeks. The ends of her fingertips went tingly.

Oh no.

She knew what this was. She was about to go into a faint.

Breathe, Saige. Breathe.

She focused on her inhales and exhales, her head clearing.

Jasper clicked his fingers in her face. "Hey, Saige. You better not be spacing out on me. We need to be focused right now."

She slapped his hand away. "Can you just give me a moment to think about what I'm going to do?"

And by that I mean how I'm going to stop you from blabbing this to the entire house.

"Going to do what?" He wiped his clammy hands on his pyjamas. "You going to call a ghost exterminator?"

"Don't be ridiculous."

He studied her, his eyebrows raised. "You know, you don't seem nearly as surprised as you should be. How often have you seen…?" He struggled to finish the sentence.

"All the time when I lived here. That one we saw, I call her the screaming bride."

"You gave it a name? It shouldn't exist!"

"Well, it does. You need to calm down. You'll wake the other guests."

"Good. We need to get everyone out of here."

Saige couldn't help it. Her throat cracked in bitter laughter. "Telling people ghosts are real didn't exactly work out so well for me or my mum."

Jasper swore in an undertone. Before Saige realised what was happening, he sat down on the bed and wrapped his arms around her. "I'm so sorry. That's why your family had you institutionalised, right? Because you see… these things."

She shoved him off. She almost wished for the sarcastic, big-headed Jasper back. Anything was preferable to this. He was devastated and traumatised, like an American high school jock who realised he hadn't won prom king.

She tipped her chin up to look at him. "Get a grip, Jasper. It's a ghost. Not the end of the world."

"Are we safe in here?"

"Yes. I think so. Ghosts tend to stay in their zones."

"Zones?"

"It's like a territorial thing, I think. I'm no expert. From all the ghosts I've seen in the manor, they tend to stay in their place."

"So it won't come in here?"

Saige thought about the mysterious window, the way she kept finding it open. "I don't know."

Jasper's brown eyes dilated with fear. "Wait! You said ghosts. Plural. There's more than one?"

"There are a few, actually."

Jasper stood. He paced from one side of the room to the other, his movements frantic. "Okay. Tomorrow we go down to the port, and we get a ferry back to the mainland."

"No can do. The ferries are booked out for the next week. We're stuck on the island."

"Then we get a hotel. We stay somewhere else."

Saige was actually starting to enjoy herself. She reached for a pillow from her headboard and hugged it. All the adrenaline and anxiety must have warped her senses. "Can't. The hotels are booked. Tourists and paparazzi for the wedding, remember?"

Jasper dropped on the chaise lounge. He bent forward, his elbows on his knees and his jaw in his hands. He looked at Saige for a long time. "Then what do we do?"

She smiled, but her lips pinched in the corners. "We do exactly as I have always done. Pretend it never happened."

EIGHT

They both slept in Saige's room that evening—Saige in her bed and Jasper on the chaise lounge. He'd refused to go back to his own room, and eventually Saige had given in. She'd tossed and turned all night. Whenever she stole a glance at Jasper, he was awake and staring at her. As frightened as she was, she was comforted that he was there… and by one thought in particular.

I'm not insane. Neither was my mother. Jasper saw the ghost. These things are not hallucinations. They're real.

Which meant there had to be truth in Harriette's theory.

It wasn't until the first glimpse of daylight peeked under the curtain that Saige finally drifted off to sleep. Hours later, some coherent part of her realised she'd over-slept. She sat upright, feeling smothered by the covers. She checked the clock. 9:20 a.m.

Shit! I have to meet Harriette in forty minutes.

She swung her legs over the side of the bed and went to rouse Jasper. He lay sprawled on the chaise lounge, his cheek pressed into a cushion and his mouth open, his long leg and arm draped over the edge. He looked peaceful, even boyish. Saige had a split second of regret at the thought of what had ended between them.

No. He left me. I will not give in to stupid, reminiscent feelings.

She slapped his cheek. "Jasper, get up."

His eyes popped open in a sleepy daze. "Huh?"

"Get up. I need you out of my room."

"Did you just slap me?"

"I need you out. I have somewhere to be."

Saige ran into the bathroom. She splashed cool water on her face and stared at her reflection in the mirror. Her eyes were bloodshot, and her hair hung in long tangles around her face.

This won't do. I'm sick of always looking like crap.

Saige showered in a hurry, applied minimal make-up, and tossed her hair into a messy, effortless ponytail. Besides last night, it was the first time in a long while that she looked at the mirror and wasn't ashamed by the person on the other side.

Ghosts haunt Wolvercraft Manor, but at least I'm looking better.

She couldn't remember the last time she'd been so fixated on her appearance, but she wanted to wear something nice. Back in her room, she found a pair of skinny jeans in her suitcase, a button-down blue blouse, and a black jacket. Jasper had fallen asleep again, but she didn't fancy getting changed in front of him regardless. She ducked back into the bathroom.

Five minutes later, she was ready. She checked the clock: 9:40 a.m.

Saige took out her phone. Ashvall Island hadn't reached the twenty-first century with Uber, but it did have a small cab service. She organised a ride and focused her attention on Jasper.

He was awake. He sat up, his pillow-styled hair poking out in haphazard angles. His voice was muffled by a yawn. "Are we going to talk about last night?"

"No. You're going to get out of my room."

She forced him onto his feet and pushed him toward the door.

He stretched his arms and rotated them in circles, releasing tension in his shoulders. "You hate this island. Where could you possibly need to be?"

Saige rolled her eyes.

Honestly, a zombie would move faster than him.

She opened the door. "Quit stalling, Jasper. Get out."

He looked at her, at what she was wearing. His face shifted into a frown. "You look nice. Wait, are you meeting someone?"

"Dr Reynolds, if you must know."

"Who's he?"

Saige made her voice sound carelessly polite. "A hunky guy I met last night."

"What?'

She squeezed the bridge of her nose. "Dr Reynolds is a curator and historian. *She* knows about the house's history. I want to talk to her about some of its more *unusual* aspects."

Jasper leaned on the architrave. "Oh."

"Yes, *oh.* Now get out."

In the hallway, the door opposite opened, and a pristine fiftysomething woman in a pink dress suit stepped out. A wolfish smile expanded across the lady's exceptionally pink lips. Saige didn't know who she was, but anyone sleeping in this house had a close connection to either Zoe, Xav, or her father. The last thing Saige needed were reports of a "walk of shame" exiting from her bedroom. The woman's eyes locked on to Jasper's very naked and sculpted chest. It didn't help that Jasper happened to look like a Calvin Klein model. She winked at Saige. "I'm glad to see someone had a good evening."

She sashayed down the hallway before Saige could correct her.

A hint of a smile tugged on Jasper's lips. "It was certainly a wild one."

Saige elbowed him in the stomach.

SAIGE WAITED IN THE DRIVEWAY FOR THE CAB TO arrive. Cold wind blasted her in the face, but the crisp air did a lot to revive her. Grey clouds coasted over the sky, threatening rain. She kept checking the time on her phone in anticipation. She wanted out of here. Wolvercraft Manor seemed to loom over her, the windows its eyes, staring with malevolence. The large front doors had been left open, and Saige could see right through the foyer to the house's magnificent fireplace. Someone had lit it. Flickering light was thrown onto the carved marble reliefs that sat above the mantel—fairies with wings, gargoyles with razor teeth, and witches wearing grave robes. She shivered and looked away.

The fireplace is its heart... the only thing that fuels this abysmal house.

Saige didn't know why she'd thought it, but a part of her knew it was true.

Wolvercraft Manor isn't just a house. It's a living, breathing monster.

Branches clawed at the stone like fingers, and she had the eerie impression that the house was restless behind its opulent façade.

The cab arrived. She jumped in, gave instructions to head for the Ashvall Library, and buckled her seatbelt. The thought of escaping the manor for a while calmed her pumping heart, but before the cab could pull away, someone else climbed in.

Saige squirmed, now cold for an entirely different reason. "Jasper, what are you doing?"

Somehow, since the time she'd kicked him out of her bedroom, he'd managed to dress in black slacks, a red-and-black chequered shirt, and denim jacket. He'd smoothed his hair back, purposely ruffled at the tips, his beard clean and styled. He looked amazing.

Jasper's expression hinted at both amusement and curiosity. "After last night, Saige, I'm fully in."

The cab driver cleared his throat. Saige saw his slightly raised eyebrows in the rear-view mirror.

God knows what he thinks that just meant.

"Fine," Saige snapped to no one in particular. "Just drive, please."

EVEN THROUGH THE CAB, THE WORLD OUTSIDE smelt sharp and earthy. Trees crowded against the road, so thick and cluttered that sunlight failed to reach through the canopies. The darkness between the trees appeared endless. Saige imagined haunted spirits staring back at her. She remembered the stories Xav had told her when they were children. One evening, he and his friend Quinton slipped out of the house and ventured through the Hauteville Woods. They hadn't advanced far when Saige's father and an entire search party of maids and servants had found the pair. But still, Xav couldn't resist telling his little sister the eerie things he saw. A graveyard in the middle of the woods, with crumbling monuments and overgrown vegetation. Rocks and stones had been meticulously placed around the graves. Xav's eyes had been wide and wild while he stage-whispered the story. "Witches' circles," he'd revealed. Saige hadn't been able to sleep for weeks, and her father eventually told her the truth about the cemetery in the woods. "It's where our ancestors are buried. It's nothing to be afraid of, Saige. Many great houses have family cemeteries. Ours is just a little overgrown. As for the stones, well... there are still superstitious people on this island. It's nothing to worry about."

"Saige?"

Jasper's voice pulled her out of her reverie.

"What?"

Concern danced across his face. "I just wanted to know what you were thinking about."

"Nothing." She turned back to the window.

Jasper stretched his long legs. He leaned forward, crossing his arms loosely on the back of the driver's seat. "What's your name, sir?"

"Archer." The cab driver offered a polite wave but didn't glance around.

"Do you know many folktales about the island? Any ghost stories?"

Saige passed Jasper a stern glare, her eyes screaming at him to shut up.

Archer choked on a laugh. "Which one do you want to hear? The island is full of stories about the supernatural. It's great for tourism, of course."

Jasper casually shrugged. "Ever seen a ghost?"

Saige gripped her seat, but what she really wanted to do was reach over and tear his head off.

Archer's hands went stiff on the wheel. "Not me personally, but I have friends who swear they've seen unusual things."

"Like what?"

"Well, one of my mates, he went fishing at Pearl Beach late one night and said he saw a dead woman in white wash up on the shore. She was all mangled and fish-eaten. He was about to call the police, but then her arms and legs twisted, and she started moving. My mate, he said it was like watching a mechanical device click back into place. She crawled into a cave... though crawl isn't the right word to describe it."

Jasper, intrigued, chewed on his thumb. "What do you mean?"

"Well... my mate said she kind of crawled like a spider, legs bent at weird angles. Or maybe it was an alligator. You know how those things move on land and through water. Gives me the heebie-jeebies."

Saige had always feared deep, dark water. She swallowed, trying to clear the image from her mind.

Jasper maintained a curious smile, but his eyes

appeared nervous. "What happened after she disappeared into the cave?"

Archer scratched his unshaven jaw. "He didn't dare go in there, if that's what you're asking. No. He ran back to town and didn't return to the beach. He never fishes there anymore."

"He was that frightened?"

"Wouldn't you be?"

Jasper remained silent.

Saige turned back to the window. They'd left the Hauteville Woods for green pastures and farmlands. They whizzed by houses, which started to fringe closer together until the cab finally pulled into the seafront at St Albert Port. Saige checked her phone: 10:10 a.m.

Great. Harriette must think I'm not coming. She's probably left.

Archer drove the cab through narrow, winding streets. Sometimes the roads rose to high elevation, giving clear views of the rugged coastline, while other times they dropped in such steep declines that Saige was forced to check her seatbelt. The buildings were old but charming. Art galleries, cosy coffee shops, and boutique stores lined the cobbled roads. Each building had high and steeply pitched roofs, decorative façades, flared rafter tails, and stucco finishes. It really was like stepping into a French fairy tale.

Archer dropped them off at the Ashvall Library. Modelled straight off the Opera Garnier, the building had huge Corinthian columns that held a pediment of distinguished figures above the large front doors. Saige guessed they must have been sculptures of scientists, philosophers, and statesmen. The building was finished with an incredible dome capped with a dove. It reminded Saige of the White House and the Parthenon combined, but with a French twist. It wasn't anywhere near as big as Wolvercraft Manor, but it still dwarfed Saige and Jasper as they climbed the stairs toward the threshold.

Jasper grabbed her shoulder. His eyes were wide in elation. "This is just like *Ghostbusters II*, when Sigourney Weaver climbs the stairs to the Manhattan Museum of Art in search of her baby."

Saige broke into disbelieving laughter. Over the past eight hours, Jasper's first—and hopefully only—encounter with a ghost had spun him through the stages of grief. He'd been shocked at first, then in denial. He'd bargained for understanding, then gone through an hour of feeling guilt-ridden and angered before dropping into a storm of depression. By morning, he'd accepted ghosts were real, but now this very strange and unexpected additional stage had occurred.

Is Jasper actually excited to learn about ghosts?

He'd certainly been clingy, like an excitable puppy determined to stick by Saige's side.

They entered the library. Natural light spilled through the windows lining the hall, illuminating the ornate ceiling frescoes and gold spiral pillars. Saige didn't know the exact history, but she was aware that Ashvall Island's original founders had been French. Wanting to compete with the mainland and prove the island's worth, many of Ashvall's buildings had been designed with lavishness. The library was no exception.

Saige scanned the great hall. A feeling like a buzzing of insects soared through her stomach when her eyes rested on Harriette, who was reading in the occult section. The woman waved. Saige held her breath. She'd hoped Harriette would be patient enough to wait, but a small part of her wouldn't have minded if she'd left. Saige wasn't sure which was better: remaining ignorant or learning the truth about Wolvercraft's ghosts.

NINE

They sat in a booth in the main reading room, which was about fifty times the size of Saige's apartment back in London, filled with aisles of books that went on farther than she could see. Libraries were meant to be quiet, but this silence put Saige on edge. All she could hear was Harriette's husky breaths and the dull hum of a florescent lamp that looked out of place among the library's statelier features.

They weren't alone. The occasional sound of turning pages resonated through the library. Saige panicked that they would be overheard. Ghosts was not a subject she wanted anyone, especially a journalist, to hear.

She lowered her voice. "I'm terribly sorry we were late." She shot a dark look at Jasper.

His expression shaped into an affronted frown. "What did I do?"

Harriette didn't seem to share Saige's quiet sentiment, her voice uncomfortably loud and perky. "It's not a problem. It gave me time to collect all the books I required."

Saige didn't doubt her. The books on their table were piled so high she couldn't see to the window. Saige hoped they wouldn't be going through all of them. They'd be in the library till midnight.

Harriette placed a large, overly thick volume in front of Saige. The title read *The History of Wolvercraft Manor.* She flipped to a page she'd bookmarked. "Here. Proof that just about every woman who has married into the Wolvercraft family"—she made quotation marks in the air—"has died an accidental or suicidal death."

Jasper leaned forward and hunched his shoulders, as though coldness had just crept up his spine. "Why did you just do that?"

The curator stared. "Do what?"

"The air quotations?"

It was Saige who answered. "Because Dr Reynolds believes my family is cursed. Any woman who marries into the Wolvercraft family dies."

"Please, call me Harriette." The doctor's eyes sparkled in the subdued light. "And here is your proof." She pointed to the page she'd opened. It was the Wolvercraft family tree, dated back to 1846 when the manor had been officially opened. "It says it right there. Look. Josette Wolvercraft hanged herself in a tree six months after she married Samuel Wolvercraft. Adele Wolvercraft tripped down the stairs and broke her neck. She died instantly. She'd been married nine months. Lucille Wolvercraft married four months before she slit her throat. Bridgitt Wolvercraft... she threw herself off Wolvercraft's highest tower on her wedding night."

Jasper's lip quivered. "We saw her last night. Scary frigging woman. She chased us down the stairs."

Saige threw a sweeping glance around the reading room, afraid someone might have overheard them. "Jasper, keep your voice down."

He waved her off. "No one is listening. Chill." He focused on the historian with an effortless smile. "I was a ghost virgin up until last night." He pointed at the book. "This is definite proof that there is something seriously twisted with that house."

Saige lowered her head and rubbed at her eyes. "It doesn't prove anything other than tragic deaths."

Harriette raised her brows. "You believe in ghosts but not in curses?"

Saige didn't answer. She remembered the dream about her mother. She'd buried Elaine's warning in a deep well in her mind, but now it bubbled to the surface. *"Don't let the wedding go ahead."*

Were the women who married into the Wolvercraft family really cursed to die? Elaine certainly seemed to think so. She wanted Saige to somehow stop her brother's betrothal to Zoe. She and Xav weren't right for each other, but Saige didn't want the relationship ending with Zoe's sudden death. Xav wouldn't cope well as a widower. For reasons Saige would never understand, he adored the elitist, highbrowed supermodel.

Jasper smoothed his hands along the table. "Saige, you're being awfully quiet. I know that's your thinking face."

Harriette had been reading, but her head pricked up like a curious dog. "How do you two know each other, exactly?"

"We were friends in school," Saige blurted before Jasper could answer.

It wasn't exactly a lie.

The curator's lips lifted into a chaffing smile. "Friends who happened to be together in the middle of the night and saw a ghost."

Saige didn't like what she was alluding to. "It's not like that. I was looking for my aunt Violet."

Harriette raised her hands in surrender. "It doesn't matter to me what it is. So long as you and your family are safe in Wolvercraft Manor, that's all that truly counts."

Jasper cleared his throat. "So what causes a family curse in the first place?"

Harriette beamed in delight and wriggled her rather large hips in her chair. "Generational curses are caused by sins. The bible says children are punished for the sins of their fathers. Divorce, incest, adultery, lust."

"Violence, murder. I get it." Jasper stroked his fingers through his short beard. "So someone in Saige's family screwed up big-time."

Harriette winked. "They made a very naughty decision."

She fumbled a pair of plastic gloves over her hands and placed a small briefcase on the table. The briefcase was made of aluminium and looked like something that would transport bacterial diseases. She opened it and took out an old manuscript that Saige couldn't believe she'd managed to get her hands on. Using what appeared to be a pair of oversized tweezers, Harriette turned to a specific page. "This manuscript is a book of fables written by Robert Geoffrey Collinsworth, a British writer who retired to Ashvall in 1837. He began collecting stories about the island."

Jasper leaned forward to examine the handwritten text. "What kind of stories?"

"Folklore. Tales about witches, fairies, ghouls."

Saige bit down hard on her lip. If she allowed herself to go down this rabbit hole, there would be no turning back.

You need answers. You are not insane. Your mother wasn't crazy. We need this.

She felt a pure burst of something that wasn't quite panic but not excitement either.

"Are you listening?" Harriette watched her. She must have caught Saige's unnerved expression.

"Yes. Sorry."

"As I was saying. The curse began essentially at the same time Wolvercraft Manor was completed." Harriette tilted her head to read from the manuscript. "In April 1846, Frederick George Wolvercraft officially opened Wolvercraft Manor to family and friends, hosting a ball for all of Ashvall's wealthier citizens to attend. His lavish life-style, a partiality for gambling, and ongoing construction expenses of the house, which had exceeded the original budget by more than half, brought him to near bank-ruptcy. In June of 1846, Frederick married in a small private ceremony, but his wife tragically died a few days after the wedding. Four months later, he took a second bride. Several years later, his second wife drowned herself in the bathtub."

Jasper laughed, half in surprise. "Only four months? The man worked fast through the ladies."

Saige's face twisted with disbelief. "Out of all of that, that's what you picked up on?"

"Yeah, I mean, that's fast work. The guy must have really hated being alone."

"Or was desperate for money."

"The point is," Harriette interrupted, "Frederick Wolvercraft must have committed a terrible act for the curse to claim both his wives. And now we learn that there are seven victims, not five as I previously believed."

Saige's heart beat faster, but she managed to keep her voice level. "Does the book say anything about what Frederick may have done?"

Harriette leaned back, stiff in the chair. "Not in this manuscript, but in this book—" She pulled out a hardcover from her pile and opened to a page she'd bookmarked. "—it states that Frederick Wolvercraft embraced the idea of spiritualism for guidance."

Jasper dropped his gaze to the book. "Spiritualism?"

"It was a successful religious innovation of the nineteenth century. It united mysticism and science and was on the rise in England."

Saige's eyebrows peaked. "It was all parlour tricks and con artists. Mediums who communicated with the dead?" She threw up her hands. "It was all fake."

There was surprising elasticity in Harriette's smile. "Says the woman who sees ghosts."

Jasper dipped his head. He was trying not to laugh. "She does have a point."

Saige resisted punching him.

"As I was saying," the historian continued, "before Frederick Wolvercraft married his first wife, he engaged Theodosia Sinclair, a highly sought medium, to attend some of his parties and, well... connect with the dead."

Jasper's eyes lit with bad-boy perfection. "Sounds fun."

"The pair were reported to have had a falling-out. Perhaps that is the reason why the family is cursed."

Saige couldn't believe what she was hearing. "You think a medium cursed my family?"

Harriette shrugged. "I think you should be open to the possibility. Ask your aunt Prue about Theodosia Sinclair. A popular belief on the island was that she was a witch. Frederick was reported to have a bad temper. Perhaps he angered her in some way."

Saige's chest constricted so hard it hurt to breathe. "These are just theories and conjecture. I need proof."

Harriette dropped another heavy book in front of her. A dust cloud burst from the pages. "Then start looking for it."

IT WAS MIDAFTERNOON BY THE TIME SAIGE AND Jasper left the library. Harriette remained behind, caught up in her research. Saige had read so many accounts of folklore and tales that her head had grown dizzy. She'd learned nothing new about her ancestor, or Theodosia Sinclair for that matter, and grappled with the disappointment.

Out in the street, the afternoon sun was the brightest it had been in the twenty-four hours she'd been on the island, but grey clouds to the west suggested rain was fast approaching. The sea was choppy and wild, as though a storm might be brewing.

Jasper stretched his arms and yawned. "That is the longest time I've spent in a library."

Saige rolled her eyes. "You don't say."

"I don't know about you, but I'm super hungry. Lunch?"

The thought of spending a second longer in Jasper's presence was nauseating, but the idea of travelling back up to the house, alone in her room with nothing but her thoughts—and ghosts—made her afraid. "Sure."

They found a comfortable-looking pub called The Charming Swan. Inside were red velvet sofas and chairs, a large bar that spanned the entire left side wall, and thick colourful rugs that would be a trip hazard to anyone drunk out of their brains. Saige immediately liked the atmosphere. There were lots of nooks and crannies with private places to sit. They settled at a table by the window, far enough from the bar that they could talk. Jasper ordered a fancy Ashvall beer while Saige settled for tea.

She swallowed the hot, black liquid, formulating something to say. "You don't really think my family was cursed by a spiritualist, do you?"

Jasper sipped his beer. "Once, I would have laughed at the idea. Now, after seeing a ghost, I'm a little more open to the supernatural idea. Theodosia was a witch, right? Makes sense that she'd curse your family if your great-great-great-granddaddy or whatever he was, did something to upset her."

"It must have been something bad to be vengeful on the entire family, even generations later."

"I guess so."

The pair was silent.

Saige fiddled with her hands under the table. Once, she would have loved the thought of confiding in Jasper about the things she saw and heard in the house without him thinking she'd lost her marbles. She'd been too afraid to when they'd been engaged. Now they were estranged, and he was the only one who did believe her. Saige took a moment to appreciate the sad irony.

She leaned forward. "Listen, Jasper. I had a really strange dream about my mother."

"Makes sense. You're on the island where she suicided... or at least made to look like she suicided."

"Right, well...." Saige struggled to find the right words. *Just tell him.*

She inhaled deeply, but the air didn't seem to soothe her spinning mind. "In my dream, my mother told me not to let Xav's wedding go ahead."

Jasper stilled. Tension scrunched his face. "Because of the curse? Zoe is in danger?"

"Yeah, I guess. At the time, I thought my dream was just stress, but now...."

"You have to find a way to end the curse."

Saige stiffened. "What?"

"The alternative is to explain to your brother that he can't marry his fiancée because a curse will kill her. No offence, but with your history, do you really think he or anyone else is going to believe you?"

Saige's shoulders sagged. Jasper was right. Her father would have her shipped off to the nearest mental institution the moment they returned to England.

"Saige." Jasper grabbed her hand, but she pulled away. A flicker of regret danced in his eyes. "I just wanted to say that I'm willing to help. If you'll let me."

The waiter appeared with their meals. They were silent as they ate.

TEN

Saige returned to Wolvercraft Manor with the thought of ghosts jumbled through her mind. Jasper had left to rehearse with the band for the evening's entertainment. She scanned the wedding programme in her hand: *The Roaring Twenties Under the Stars*. She snorted.

Zoe's outdone herself.

She trailed up the stairs and wandered down the various halls that led to her bedroom. Perhaps she'd fire up her laptop and see if she could uncover any information about Theodosia Sinclair. Anything to keep her mind occupied. Otherwise, she'd fret about every bump and groan she heard in the house.

It's just the wood constricting. Old houses do that. But just in case, I'll grab my laptop and head downstairs.

She'd seen people sitting in the drawing room drinking tea. There was safety in numbers.

The floorboard behind her creaked. Saige stilled. It had sounded like the deceptively sly tap of a foot.

A tingly feeling crept up her neck, a sixth sense that

urged her to turn around. Saige slowly moved to face the hallway behind her. It was empty.

"There you are."

She jumped at the voice, her stomach feeling as though it had somersaulted up to her ribs.

Zoe stood behind her, one hand on her hip, the other hand holding a smartphone that had more bling than the crown jewels.

Saige inhaled a steadying breath. Apparently, Zoe's experience with the catwalk had also given her the silent ninja skills to sneak up on others.

Zoe slung her long black hair over her shoulder. Her silver bracelets jingled. "You're late. Where have you been?"

Saige stared. She sensed sweat on her hairline. Cold sweat. "Sorry?"

Zoe's red-painted lips pinched at the corners. "I texted you an hour ago. The dress fitting?"

Her mind whirled. Had she missed something?

Of course you've missed something. Zoe doesn't even like looking at you, let alone talking to you.

Zoe shot her eyes skyward. She looped her arm with Saige's and propelled her down the hallway. "My bridesmaid Luisa is ill with a cold and is lying in bed upstairs. I do not need her ruining my wedding and making all my other bridesmaids sick."

Saige scrambled to check her phone. She had it on silent. There was one text message.

2PM. MY SITTING ROOM. I NEED YOU FOR A DRESS FITTING. DON'T BE LATE!!!

Saige shifted her eyes between their linked arms. She felt like a prisoner being escorted to the gallows. "You need me to sit in for Luisa?"

Zoe's smile was perfectly straight, teeth a flawless white, but her eyes were wolfish. "No. You're now permanent bridesmaid number five."

Before Saige could protest, Zoe pulled back the doors to her private sitting room, which linked with her enormous bed chamber. The bridesmaids were assembled around a dressmaker, who was busy altering each woman's dress and making adjustments to the way the fabric fell around their already picture-perfect bodies. Several stylists sauntered around them, making notes on their clipboards.

Zoe's voice rang smoothly through the room. "Relax, ladies. Here's Luisa's replacement."

Saige didn't appreciate the way everyone's eyes fell on her in... she decided to go with *surprise*.

She unlinked her arm from Zoe's, which she now suspected wasn't an act of endearment but a crafty measure to ensure she couldn't escape. "Can I talk to you privately about this?"

Zoe focused on her phone. "Sure, hon." She shimmied closer, wrapped her arm around Saige, and raised the device above them. "Smile."

Before she was ready, Saige was snapped up in what she hoped wasn't a terrible photo. Zoe examined the image on her phone. "It'll pass."

Saige was convinced that meant "I look great compared to you."

Zoe raised her eyes to the bridesmaids. "What's a good hashtag for a new bridesmaid?"

Various responses were thrown around the room. Saige sat on a chaise lounge, resigned to the fact that she was now a bridesmaid. Her father would be ecstatic. She could imagine his beaming face.

He was probably the one who put Zoe up to it.

The dressmaker, a French woman Saige assumed was a world-renowned fashion designer, handed her Luisa's red-rose sheath gown to change into.

Saige slipped behind a floral-patterned dressing screen. She narrowed her eyes at the dress. A weight of uncertainty pressed down on her. Saige was slim, but she struggled to stuff her midsection and bum into the gown. She seriously fretted she'd rip a seam.

"This isn't going to work," she called through the screen. "It's too small. What a pity, Zo. I can't be your bridesmaid."

Who needs seven bridesmaids, anyway? She'll have to do with six.

Zoe's voice echoed back with excessive authority. "Don't be ridiculous. You're about the same size as Luisa. That's the only reason you got this gig. Fayette, can you attend to her please?"

The dressmaker, unabashed at Saige's half nudity, strode around the divider to assist. In her slim-fitted black dress and fluffy collar, Fayette reminded Saige of an overly pampered poodle. Her broken English came out with an annoyed huff. "You are all sweaty. The dress sticks. You look like red... ah, what are the words?" She rattled off in French. "Ah, bottom look like big, ripe apple. Only lumpy... and saggy."

Saige blew hair off her face to prevent saying something cynical.

And your face looks like an excellent fist target.

Fayette got to work fixing the back of the dress,

pinning extra material around Saige's hips. "We must hide big bottom."

"Gee, thanks."

Finally, the dressmaker was able to zip her into the gown. There was a split that ran up the leg, dangerously close to revealing more than it should. Saige would have to be careful when the wind blew.

She stepped out from behind the divider and caught a glance of herself in the full-length mirror.

I actually don't look half bad.

Who am I kidding? It's the best I've looked in years. With some striking make-up, I might actually be able to pull this off.

She beamed at the other bridesmaids, who assessed her with silent once-overs.

Zoe examined the dress, her perfectly manicured eyebrows curved in a frown. "The hair is wrong."

Saige touched the ends of her hair, which swept past her shoulder in its messy ponytail. "It'll be nice on the day, I promise."

"No. It's the colour. It just doesn't go with the dress."

"I'm not dying my hair, Zoe."

She scrunched her hands into fists and stamped her high heel into the floor. "God, it's so unfair. Luisa had the perfect skin tone and hair colour. She would have completed my wedding photos perfectly. Damn you, Luisa. Getting sick so close to my wedding. I mean, how selfish could she be?"

Her bridesmaids bustled around her, offering her words of sympathy.

Saige stood there, wishing Fayette would come back and get her out of the damn dress.

IT TURNED OUT THE FITTING, GATHERING, GIRLIE get-together—whatever it was—was far from over. Zoe insisted her bridesmaids remain to see her bridal gown. The women appropriately oohed and aahed, clapping their hands in false delight when Zoe stepped out from the dressing screen, her eyes damp with unabashed tears. Saige couldn't help but roll her eyes. The gown was fairy-tale pretty, tight in the bodice but flowing down to the floor in an overly expanded train.

Zoe must think she's royalty. How is she supposed to fit through a door in that thing?

Fayette had really outdone herself. The dress was an artwork of intricate glamour and style, and yet, despite the gown's fluttery chiffon, silk tulle, and beaded lace, Saige got the impression of a marshmallow plopped onto a meringue.

Zoe gave a little squeal of joy as she twirled around. "I'm going for dreamy but feminine. What do you think, girls?"

There were bouts of "You look gorgeous," "It's beautiful," "Xav's not going to know what hit him."

Thankfully, Saige was spared answering when her phone buzzed in her pocket. The screen flashed with a short message from Harriette. The pair had exchanged numbers in the library, but Saige honestly hadn't expected to hear from her so quickly.

I've found something. Talk tonight?

Saige quickly typed back, **Yes**, her insides shrinking into the size of a walnut. If what Harriette suspected was true, Zoe and Xav's wedding was... dangerous. Zoe could be in harm's way.

I have to talk to Zoe.

Saige waited around until the dressmaker and other bridesmaids had left. Zoe now wore a tight pair of jeans and an orange blouse that only she could pull off with her tanned skin and raven-black hair. She had her arms crossed, scrutinising her wedding gown, which had been returned to the mannequin.

Saige meandered closer. An astounded breath escaped her clenched teeth. Now that she was around the partition, she could see what her future sister-in-law evaluated so critically. "You have three dresses?"

Zoe tilted her head to the side to study the array from a different angle. "Yes. My wedding gown for the ceremony, my reception gown, and my after-party dress." She pointed at each one with decisive confidence.

Saige's jaw went slack. Each dress looked skimpier than the last. The after-party dress was practically white lace over a see-through mesh that would barely scrape beneath the buttocks.

Zoe tossed her hair over her shoulder with a trivialising shake of her head. "You don't think it's too much, do you?"

Yes.

Saige slid her hands into her pockets. "No. Of course not. You only get married once, right?"

Though Saige expected Xav would be the first in a long line of men that waited for Zoe down the aisle.

If the curse doesn't claim her first.

A silence hung around them.

Zoe's nose wrinkled. "Do you want something?"

Saige realised she was holding her breath. "I just wanted to know if you're... okay."

"Okay?"

"Yeah, I just...." Saige scrambled for the right words. "I just mean this house is... different. I hope it hasn't frightened you."

God, I am making such a mess of this.

Zoe's eyes went from narrow to slitty. "What are you getting at? Are you having another episode? Xav told me what happened on the yacht. You shouldn't stop taking your medication, Saige. This is my wedding. I don't need you screwing it up."

Screw it up?

Saige's blood boiled like an acidic hot spring.

Fine. I'll just let this curse eat you alive.

But she'd never forgive herself if something happened to Zoe. Stuck up and egotistical as she was, Xav loved her, and Saige didn't want to see her brother suffer. She had to approach this from a different angle.

She remembered her mother's words of caution. *"Don't let the wedding go ahead."*

Could Saige somehow prevent the wedding from happening? Or could she plant doubt in Zoe's head, make her rethink marrying Xav?

No. That will hurt Xav too.

A light-bulb moment struck her mind.

I don't have to stop the wedding. I just have to postpone it.

The women who had died at Wolvercraft Manor had done so because they were on the island. Saige's mother and father had wed in a castle in Scotland and had spent many happy years together. It wasn't until they returned to

Wolvercraft Manor that her mother had supposedly gone crazy and committed suicide. The curse had waited for her, biding its time. Which meant it only affected the women who married into the Wolvercraft family when they arrived on the island. The house welcomed them, luring them in with its romantic, fairy-tale charm, and yet something deep and sinister watched from behind its windows.

Saige nodded vigorously. "Do you really want to get married here? I mean, this place isn't you. Wouldn't you prefer a tropical island? A beach where the sun shines? Not Ashvall? Rain and mist are a real risk to the wedding."

Zoe shot her eyes to the ceiling with impatience. Something that resembled a twisted smile crept over her face. "I cannot believe you are doing this. Are you actually trying to sabotage my wedding?"

Saige tasted panic in her mouth. "No, of course not."

Just trying to postpone it.

"Because it sounds like you are." Zoe adopted a hands-on-hips pose. "I know you don't like me, but I'm marrying your brother and becoming part of this family, so you need to get over it."

Saige managed to hold her voice level—just. "Listen. It's not that... it's just...."

"What? For crying out loud, what is it, you crazy psycho?"

Saige stumbled back. Never, in her entire life, had someone spoken to her like that. The media had been cruel, but at least they'd been sophisticated with their insults. But this? *"Crazy psycho."* That was schoolgirl mean. Saige felt tears threaten to spill in her eyes. She quickly wiped them away. "I'm worried about you. This house... it's not a normal house. Can't you feel it?"

Saige realised as soon as the words were out that it had been the wrong thing to say. Zoe looked at her like she'd sprouted three additional arms and a reptilian head. She lifted a hand to wedge distance between them. "Stay away from me. You're having another one of your... moments. You can stay for the wedding because that's what Xav wants, but after that you get the hell away from both of us. Forget about being a bridesmaid. I'll content myself with only having six."

She turned and dramatically flounced out the door.

Saige watched her shadow disappear. It was the most embarrassed she had ever felt in her life.

Maybe I should let the curse get her.

Saige shook her head, knowing she'd never let that happen.

ELEVEN

SAIGE CRIED HERSELF TO SLEEP THAT AFTERNOON. She would have preferred to never wake again, to be an eternal sleeping beauty who drifted in the dark. But her consciousness pulled itself from its slumber, her lids peeling open. Her bedroom was dark. It was night outside. A single streak of moonlight illuminated the duchess and mirror.

Saige fumbled for her bedside lamp, her hand seeming to stretch into never-ending darkness. She found the switch. The light powered on. Disturbing shadows flickered along the walls. She shivered, aghast by the icy wind that caressed her skin. The window was open.

I definitely closed it.

She climbed off the bed. Even the rug was cold beneath her feet. Chilly air seeped through her socks, numbing her toes.

Something isn't right.

She crept closer to the window. She couldn't see

anything, but she had the distinct impression that something waited outside in the night. Just beyond the curtain. Just beyond Saige's reach.

This is madness. Get out of here.

Get. Out. Of. Here!

The words hung in Saige's mind, but her feet didn't meet the command. Instead of running for the door, her legs wandered closer to the window. She raised her hand. Her fingertips touched the curtain.

Bang! Bang! Bang!

Saige leapt back. Her heart fluctuated in her chest.

Someone was knocking—no, belting against the bedroom door.

"Saige? Are you in there? Are you okay?"

At first she didn't recognise the voice. She'd never heard it spoken with such panic.

Xavier.

"Saige?" His voice was frantic.

Bang, bang, bang.

His fists pounded the door again. The handle rattled. "It's locked," he shouted to someone who must have been in the hallway.

Saige's stomach ached, like there was a little bird inside, fluttering to get out.

No. That's not possible. I didn't lock the door.

"Saige?"

That time it was her father.

She shook her head, driving out the confusion that clouded her mind. She hurried to the door and unlocked it.

"Oh thank God." Her father took her up in his arms. Saige couldn't understand why he was shaking. She peered at her brother. Xav stood in the doorway, his face pale. Sweat soaked his collar.

Her eyes roamed between the pair. "What's wrong?"

Derrick took her shoulders in his hands. "Are you all right?"

"Yes. I was sleeping. For goodness' sake, what's wrong?"

They were acting like she'd been engulfed by a house fire.

Her brother exhaled a disappointed sigh. "We heard about the fitting. Saige, you really frightened Zoe. She doesn't want you anywhere near us. We were afraid that you'd gone and done something...."

He didn't have to finish for her to understand what he meant.

Done something stupid.

Now it was her time to fume, her voice snarky and out of control. "I suppose she made me out as the bad guy while she pretended to be sweet and innocent."

Xav squeezed his eyes shut for half a second. "She was scared."

"She's a good actress."

"She said you told her to end things."

"I told her to postpone the wedding."

"Why the hell would you do that?"

"Because this place isn't safe. I'm trying to save Zoe."

She hadn't meant to yell, but for the briefest moment, it had been satisfying to see Xav wince. Neither her brother nor father had ever truly listened to her, but now she was centre stage and the spotlight was on her, and damn it, they were going to listen.

She'd hoped to sound in control, but her voice teetered

toward hysteria. "It's this place. There's something here. Something evil. Every woman who has married into our family has died. It took Mum."

Her father's stern tone interrupted her. "Saige, that's enough. For heaven's sake. You're frightening your brother."

Disgust transformed Xav's handsome face into something Saige didn't recognise. "You're delusional." His swept his eyes to his father. "I told you bringing her here was a bad idea."

Derrick lowered his head and silently nodded. "Yes. I understand that now." He flinched when he met Saige's glare. "I should never have made you come back to Ashvall. You didn't want to come, and you weren't ready. You need help, Saige. I need to make sure you receive proper care. You're acting... just the way your mother did before she died."

Whatever semblance of control Saige had managed to hold came crashing down. She was a dam that broke, water tearing forward in a wave, washing away everything that was sane. "I'm not crazy. Mum wasn't crazy either."

Hot, angry tears made her vision blurry. Her words had sounded pathetic in her own ears.

Derrick made a sound low in his throat that didn't seem happy. "Let's just get through the next few days. Get through the wedding, and then we'll look at seeing what Dr Grigori can do for you when we return to London. Unfortunately, I can't get her flown into Ashvall."

That's because she has other patients, too, Dad.

Geez, her family really did think the world revolved around them.

Derrick's worry escalated in his voice. "Please stay on your medication."

Saige was trembling with rage. "I never stopped taking it."

Her father had stopped listening, now in full crisis control. His eyes darted between his children. "For now, let's keep this between the three of us and Zoe. Saige, I would like you to dress for dinner and come downstairs, please."

Vehemence rose in her body, exploding into fireworks in her brain.

"Get out," she cried. "Get out."

She realised now why the pair had been so afraid of the door being locked. They feared what she was capable of behind closed doors. That she could hurt herself. Or worse. But Saige wasn't spiralling toward insanity. All she needed was someone to listen. For someone to believe her.

Jasper.

She couldn't believe his name was the first to reach her mind. He'd hurt her. He'd caused her years of suffering. She'd sworn she'd never forgive him, but now she found that he was her only ally.

Derrick leaned back against the duchess, head down, eyes focused on the floor.

Xav shot a nasty glare at his sister. "Stay away from Zoe. And me."

He turned and sped down the hall, his angry footsteps fading away too fast.

Saige sat on the bed silently crying. It hurt knowing that Xav had never actually wanted her at his wedding. That he'd invited her for the sake of their father. Maybe he was more suited to Zoe than Saige realised.

Maybe Xav being cut out of my life isn't such a bad thing. We barely see each other anymore.

But even thinking it caused tears to haze her eyes.

It's going to happen, though. After the wedding. Zoe will make sure of it.

Her father met her stare and smiled, but it was small and strained. "Dinner will be taking place soon. It's going to be quite a show. Please, Saige, I'd like you to join us. I don't want you to remain by yourself."

"Why? Afraid of what I might do?"

"Yes. I am. I'm terrified you'll meet the same end as your mother."

Saige crossed her arms, ready to answer with a very definite *no*, but then she thought of the open window she had never touched, and the door she had never locked. The idea of being alone in this house, the halls dark and empty, her room full of shadows, and that acute, inescapable sense that something was present, watching her, wasn't appealing.

She nodded. She no longer had the strength to fight.

The tension in her father's shoulders lifted. "Thank you, Saige." His eyes moved to her wardrobe. "Good. Fayette brought you a dress. She must have done it in the morning."

Saige turned to the wardrobe. She was positive there'd been nothing hanging in the closet when she'd come barrelling into her room that afternoon and collapsed onto her bed. She hadn't bothered unpacking her suitcase, and just like the window, she was certain the wardrobe doors had been closed. But now they were open. An exquisite black mermaid 1920s flapper dress hung from a hanger. It had a low V-neckline that she didn't think her father would approve of.

Saige had forgotten that tonight's party theme was the Roaring Twenties. Fayette had outdone herself. The dress really did look like something plucked right out of that decade, not something fabricated to look like it had come from that era. She'd have to thank the dressmaker. She'd also have to ask Fayette how she'd managed to sneak the dress into her room. Or maybe Saige really was oblivious to the things happening around her. Maybe the dress had been there all along, and she'd simply never seen it. It wasn't an encouraging thought.

Whether it was the argument or the insurmountable fear that grew inside her, Saige did not want to be alone. At least at a party, she might be able to distract her thoughts.

If I make an effort, Dad and Xav might change their mind. I need to show them that I'm okay.

Saige wanted to feel normal. She was tired of being scared. Tired of being the girl without friends. Tired of the anxiety and depression that clouded her brain. She wanted to be the average twentysomething woman who went out and had fun, not the girl who was haunted.

Another pressing thought flittered into her mind. Harriette's message.

I've found something. Talk tonight?

Saige had to be at the party.

She aimed a determined glance at her father. "Give me fifteen minutes."

Though she knew what she had planned would take her more than half an hour.

DERRICK WOLVERCRAFT HAD SPARED NO EXPENSE. Following her father into the glitzy ballroom, Saige marvelled at the splendour and finery. She felt as though she'd been transported to the age of *The Great Gatsby*. Black and gold balloons floated just beneath the ceiling, accompanied by cascading lights that hung from crystal chandeliers. Excessive volumes of cocktails and canapés were served on gold platters, champagne fountains topped up by waiters. Wherever Saige looked, there were glittering dresses, feather boas, and cabaret wigs. The women were exquisite in their flapper dresses, pearl necklaces, and gold dancing heels. The men were handsome in their tailored pinstriped suits, silk shirts, and black satin bow ties.

And the dancing! Saige never knew people could still dance like that. She identified the Charleston, the Black Bottom, and the Shimmy and wondered if her father had hired professionals to spice up the dance floor. Everyone was wild and carefree. The night was structured on frivolity and looser morals, and Saige loved it. She imagined Wolvercraft Manor really had seen some parties in its time.

A jazz orchestra played all the classic hits. Jasper was among them by the piano, his black tuxedo finished with a gold bow tie and matching handkerchief, his hair slicked straight back with a side part that was glossy in the flashing lights. His fingers ran expertly across the keys. Saige watched him for a moment. He was a talented musician and could play a range of music from various eras, but right now he was in his element. It was like he was meant to have been born in the 1920s.

She recalled a conversation the pair had shared on a date when they'd been in the early stages of their relationship. He'd told her that jazz was the sole reason he'd taken up music in the first place. It was his first love. The other genres had come later. Saige remembered the passion in his eyes when he'd told her.

Her heart dropped. She had missed that look, but most of all, she'd grown—no, taught herself to hate it. Jasper had broken her heart in the cruellest way possible, and she wasn't keen on forgiveness.

She turned away. It was so easy to be sucked in by all the dancing and excitement, but she was here for a reason. Her eyes roamed the guests. She took out her phone and sent a quick text to Harriette.

Are you here? I can't see you?

"Saige, could you come this way please?" Her father clutched her elbow and guided her toward the rest of her family.

Saige's teeth ground together.

Oh God. We're actually doing a receiving line.

The band stopped playing, and the MC on the stage asked everyone to form an orderly line.

Her aunts Violet and Prue started greeting guests, followed by Xav and Zoe. Zoe looked stunning in her blood-red flapper dress, sequinned with black pearls and lace, her dark hair hanging long in loose curls down her side. Her red lips tightened when she saw Saige. Even underneath all that make-up, an angry flush rose in her cheeks. Saige dropped her eyes to the floor. She felt like an intruder in her own family.

So this is why Dad really wanted me at the dinner tonight. To take part in his perfect family image.

Derrick laced his arm with hers and forced her to stand

at his side. He nudged his head close to her ear. "Do this for your brother, please."

A nasty smile tugged on her lips. "Keep up appearances, you mean?"

He flashed her a disapproving glare. "Yes, if that's what you want to call it."

Saige shook hands with guests and spoke polite nothings. She hoped Harriette would appear. Either the historian was running late or she'd boycotted the event.

She said she'd be here.

Saige was desperate to know what she'd discovered.

Damn it, Harriette. Where are you?

"Saige Wolvercraft." The voice was ethereal yet familiar. "It's a pleasure to meet you."

Saige shook the hand of the guest who stood before her. She froze. The woman's fingers were soddened in blood. Saige felt the sickly mess run into her own palm. Nausea made her stomach drop unpleasantly. Even the woman's little finger had been pulverised to a bloody pulp. Saige looked up and screamed. Her mother stared back at her. The left side of Elaine's face appeared as though it had been run over a cheese grater, bone fragments evident in what was left of her flattened cheek. Her lips mashed against her teeth when she smiled.

Elaine's black eyes were dead in their sockets. "Saige, sweetie. She knows."

Saige felt her soul shrivel inside her, forcing her into a catatonic state.

Elaine spoke again, only this time her voice was like the wail of a banshee, hitting Saige with the force of a cyclonic wind. "She. Knows. She. Knows. She. Knows. She. Knows. She. Knows."

Elaine's body shuddered and twitched. Her blood ran down Saige's wrist, creeping over the skin on her arm like running spiders.

"Saige?"

The voice beside her sounded far away.

"Saige?"

Arms shook her.

"Saige? Let go."

Saige jumped, her vision swimming back into focus. Her mother was gone. The woman before her looked frightened, her skin slightly green from fear. Saige had the woman's hand tightly gripped in her own, her fingers pressed so firmly into the lady's skin that Saige was positive she'd leave crescent marks behind.

Saige dropped her hand. "I'm so sorry."

The woman stumbled away, hurtling toward a man who must have been her husband.

What just happened?

Had her mother possessed the guest? Or had Saige imagined the entire episode?

No. That was Mum.

But who was she?

Who was Mum referring to?

Saige didn't think it had anything to do with the woman her mother had possessed. She was just the vessel. A means to transfer a message.

"Saige." Derrick's voice beside her was a confounded reprimand. "What the hell was that? You frightened that woman half to death."

Slowly, shakily, she stared at her father. Her brother and aunts were throwing her sidelong glances as they continued to greet and shake hands with their guests. Saige had no words to explain herself.

I need a frigging drink.

"I'm sorry."

She pushed her way through the crowd toward the bar.

TWELVE

There was no formal dinner organised. Tonight's event was about wolfing down as much finger food as was humanly possible, drinking to excess, partying, gambling, and, above all, embracing frivolity. A section of the ballroom had been set up as a speakeasy—an underground world of poker games, craps tables, and roulette wheels where the drinks kept coming and the dice kept rolling.

Saige took a seat at a round bar table and greedily gulped down her glass of red wine. She didn't have a problem with alcohol, but she sure could have fooled everyone tonight. It was her third glass in an hour. She didn't normally drink, not with all the medication she had to take, but after what had occurred—seeing her mother—Saige needed to dull her senses. Food had become her comfort. She'd collected a plate—her second—of devilled eggs, shrimp tartlets, blue cheese bruschetta, and lamb skewers, and was happily eating away when she felt a tap on her shoulder.

Jasper stared at her overly stuffed plate and smiled. "I'm glad you have an appetite. You need some meat on your bones."

Saige laughed. It was a strange sound.

"You look lovely, by the way."

She didn't know what to say to that. It was the best she'd looked in a long time. The dress fit perfectly, like it was made for her. Her red hair hung in loose curls down her back, the side held with a black brooch.

Something stirred inside her when she met Jasper's eyes. A longing for something she'd once had and lost. She cleared the thought from her mind. "Have you seen Harriette?"

He shook his head.

"She said she would be here tonight. Look."

Saige took out her phone and showed Jasper the message.

"Have you sent her a text?"

"Five times."

"Wow. That's getting stalkerish. Maybe she's just running late."

"It's nine o'clock."

"Some people like to make an entrance."

Saige dropped her fork. Her mother's message echoed through her thoughts.

"She. Knows. She. Knows. She. Knows. She. Knows. She. Knows."

But who was *she*? Who was her mother referring to? Harriette?

A balloon burst somewhere, startling Saige. Her arms broke out into goose bumps.

Jasper gave her a look. "If you're so worried, why don't

you just ask your aunt? Harriette was staying with her, right?"

"Yes, of course." Saige abandoned her plate and half-empty wineglass, about to meander through the crowd, but a tug on her arm pulled her back.

Aunt Violet's overly strong perfume crept up her nose, the woman's breath a bad combination of too much garlic and alcohol. "Saige, my dear. Why aren't you dancing? You must be the only young woman in the room who doesn't have a partner." Her eyes rose appreciatively over Jasper. "The musician will do nicely." She linked Jasper's and Saige's hands together and pushed the pair onto the dance floor. "Come on, you two. Shake your booty. That's what all the young ones are saying these days, isn't it?" She winked at her niece. "You can thank me later."

Saige watched her very drunk aunt disappear through the crowd with wide-eyed confoundment. She started to pull her hand out from Jasper's, but his fingers latched strongly on hers.

A determined expression crossed his face that Saige didn't understand. "Let's take your aunt's advice."

The band's lively jazz melody turned into a slow and soppy tune that made her cringe. Jasper's broad hand against the small of her back expertly guided her through the dance.

She inhaled air too fast and almost choked. "Jasper, we can't dance."

She hated being this close to him. It brought back so many uncomfortable memories. And she really had no time to wander back down memory lane with Jasper. What was he thinking? She had to find Aunt Prue. She had to find Harriette.

He looked at her, a hopeless, desperate silence in his eyes. "Why not?"

"Because I need to find Harriette."

"Maybe she didn't want to come after all. Come on. Let's dance like old friends."

Saige purposefully stood on his foot. "We're not friends. You broke my heart, Jasper." She'd wanted to sound determined and strong, but pain was evident in the way her voice hitched. "When you didn't show up that night... I was so scared. I thought something had happened to you. And then I receive a text at 3:00 a.m. with two words: 'It's over.' The next day, I read online that you'd absconded with some slutty model on a yacht to the Bahamas. So no, I do not want to dance with you. And I am not your friend."

He straightened up, taken aback by the icy tone in her voice.

Something sticky and hot rose in her throat. She hated causing people pain, but God, she was so angry with him. He couldn't just waltz back into her life and expect them to be... what?

What does Jasper want?

There was more she needed to say, more she wanted to shout at him, but someone on the dance floor caught her eye. A lone woman stared intently at her between the dancers. Saige had a sudden impression of herself as a mouse caught in a hawk's predatory gaze. The woman had soft strawberry blonde hair, a smile that stretched too wide for comfort, and eyes painted in thick black makeup.

And she was wearing Saige's dress.

The exact same make.

Saige stared down at the soft material wrapped around

her own body.

Fayette did bring this to my room, right?

One of the LED lights from the stage swept over the woman, and Saige recognised a pale, almost translucent flicker run through her skin. The woman raised a long, slender arm and, with the tips of her fingers, beckoned Saige forward.

Jasper's hand tightened around her lower back. "What is it? What can you see?"

Fear flowed through Saige like electricity. Couples danced ahead, blocking her view. When the dancers were whisked away with the music, the woman was gone.

She shook her head, disbelief fluttering through her. "I'm not sure."

Jasper watched her. He was afraid. She knew by the sheen of sweat along his hairline.

Embarrassed, she pulled away. "I need to find my aunt."

Saige pushed through the crowd, Jasper on her heels.

She found Aunt Prue talking to a bunch of high-society ladies, probably Ashvall's historical society come to sneak a peek at the grandiose event. "Excuse me." She offered a polite smile to the ladies and yanked her aunt away.

"Saige." Aunt Prue trained a startled look on her. "What's gotten into you tonight? That was incredibly rude."

"I'm sorry, but I need to know where Harriette is. She was meant to be here, but I can't find her anywhere."

Aunt Prue's gaze wandered from her niece to Jasper and back again. "I don't understand. What is this about?"

Jasper stepped forward, his voice much calmer than Saige could ever hope to manage. "Harriette had some information to tell us about Ashvall. We were just hoping we could talk to her."

Aunt Prue let out an uneasy laugh. "Heavens. You're both acting like detectives on a murder case and Harriette is your prime suspect." She flicked back an unruly curl with the tip of her feather fan. "Harriette left my house around six and said she'd walk here. It was a lovely evening... at least it had been at the time, so I didn't think anything of it. Are you sure she's not in another part of the house? Zoe and Xav organised parlour games in some of the drawing rooms. I believe there's a murder mystery happening in one of them. Even a seance."

"What?" Saige and Jasper cried in unison.

Before Aunt Prue could respond, the band stopped playing, and the MC stood on the podium. "Hey there, folks. It's great to see so many ladies and gentlemen having a fantastic time tonight. Unfortunately, we're going to have to cut this festivity short."

There was a collection of disappointment from the crowd. Someone booed.

"Now, I don't want to see an end to tonight's celebration either," the MC resumed, "but folks, we have a bad storm on its way. It's out at sea now, but it promises to hit Ashvall in an hour. If anyone needs to travel, you should leave and get back to your accommodation immediately. Those who wish to stay and wait out the storm are welcome to, but please be advised that the storm is expected to last through the night. Met Office has warned that it will be severe."

Startled gasps ensued, followed by a panicked mass exodus for the doors.

"Bloody Ashvall," Saige muttered under her breath.

Jasper watched the fiasco around him. "I'm assuming it's the locals running for their lives. What do they know that I don't?"

"The storms that hit Ashvall are like mini hurricanes."

"Oh good. Nothing better than a dangerous storm to trap you in a haunted house. It's like we're living in a horror movie."

She cast him an unappreciative glance.

Saige remembered hiding down in the basement with her parents and Xav as a little girl. There'd been very little warning that night. The storm had rolled in, taking down trees and smashing all the windows on the house's west side. It had been a costly repair. When they'd ventured outside, all of Ashvall's beaches had been eroded. Ferries had been battered or sunk at their ports. The streets had been cut off by floods. They'd had no power for close to a week. Saige remembered what her father had told her about storms and Ashvall.

"The island is at just the right latitude where cold polar air from the north meets the warmer tropical air from the south. Unfortunately, we're just that little farther west from Guernsey that we're right in the path of storms."

At the time, Saige didn't fully understand what Derrick had meant, but now she did.

Ashvall was screwed.

Aunt Prue closed her eyes tightly. Worry lines formed across her brow. "I should really be getting home. Mr Bubbles gets scared."

Jasper eyed her. "Mr Bubbles?"

"My cat. He doesn't like storms."

"Oh, right."

Saige grabbed her aunt's arm before she could leave.

"What about Harriette?"

"She has to be in the house somewhere, my darling. Don't be so alarmed." Aunt Prue took out her phone, hit a speed dial, and pressed it to her ear. Her expression changed from expectant to disappointment. "She's not answering. The phone rings out."

Saige silently swore. "We need to find her."

Who the hell doesn't have voicemail set up in this day and age?

She typed a quick text into her phone and sent it to Harriette.

Bad storm on its way. Please let me know that you are ok.

The three of them left the ballroom and wandered the first floor of the house in search of the doctor. People mingled everywhere. Hoots of laughter and merriment ricocheted from one room to the next. Saige, Jasper, and Aunt Prue had to force their way through the crowd. It was akin to a high school party where everyone was too inebriated to care much about propriety.

Saige weaved around a couple who were locked in a passionate embrace.

Why do costume parties always drive out people's inhibitions?

The constant flow of chatter and laughter didn't take the edge of eeriness away. These people were not locals but her father's guests. If they'd heard about the impending storm, they didn't seem to care.

And why would you when your bed is upstairs? Party on.

It made Saige feel a little sorry for the locals who were probably hightailing it out of the manor by now, eyes locked in fear on the sky.

Saige studied each of the guests she passed, but there was no sign of the doctor. The three of them swept down halls, through drawing rooms and parlours, past sweeping staircases and a billiards room. Lightning flashed so brightly through the windows that Saige couldn't prevent a startled gasp. The thunder was a menacing boom that roared like a ravenous beast across the sky. When she pressed her hands to the window, she saw towering grey storm clouds veined by white lightning. The flashes were blinding to the point that they painted everything negative in her eyes for a second.

"Stay away from the windows, Saige."

The voice was strict and stern. Derrick Wolvercraft appeared through the crowd. He took his daughter's arm and led her away from the window.

Jasper backed away, too, staying put next to her. "I thought the storm was meant to hit in an hour." He pointed out the window. "*That* definitely makes it look like it's here."

"It is here," Derrick confirmed. "The worst of it is still to come."

Saige's stomach unravelled. "But the locals... outside?"

Exhaustion clouded her father's eyes. "I made sure no one left the house. Saige, Prue, I want you both to go downstairs. I'm encouraging everyone to head to the basement. We can wait the storm out there."

Aunt Prue's bottom lip dropped. "But my house. My cat! I have to get back."

"It's too dangerous. No one leaves Wolvercraft Manor."

Cold fear trickled down the back of Saige's neck. "Dad, have you seen Harriette?"

"Aunt Prue's friend?" He shook his head. The corner of

his lips tightened, the way it always did when Saige recognised he was stressed or afraid. "Have you seen your brother? Zoe?"

"No." Saige could barely get the word out. Her heart squirmed in her chest.

Derrick took her shoulders in his hands, but his gaze wandered to Jasper and Aunt Prue. "Help me warn people. Direct them to the basement. I need to organise the staff and get them to bring flashlights and blankets."

He sped down the hall, walking faster than Saige had ever seen him move before.

Her eyes locked with Jasper's. They didn't need to say words to communicate their thoughts. They pushed through the crowd, warning people of the storm and to get to the basement immediately. Aunt Prue followed them, mumbling about the safety of her cat.

Lightning illuminated the rooms in flashes of white-hot light. Each time the lightning flashed and the thunder roared, comprehension dawned in people's eyes. The party snowballed into full-scale panic, and Saige found herself shoving her elbows out to fight her way through the throng.

She stopped by a drawing room where a murder mystery game was in full swing. On any other occasion, it would have been fun to join in, but the idea that something in the house—something supernatural—really was murdering people made her stomach clench.

"Leave," she cried. "Get down to the basement."

"This storm is severe," Jasper explained behind her.

She didn't wait to see the gamers' reactions. She was already running to the next room when she barrelled into her brother.

Xav's gelled, burnished red hair was in disarray. He looked like he was capable of biting off all his fingernails from worry. "Have you seen Zoe?"

A prickly sensation crawled across Saige's skin. "No. Is she missing?"

"The girls were having a seance. They said Zoe got scared and left the room. Now I can't find her. Not anywhere."

A seance? Really?

She couldn't believe her bad luck tonight.

"Maybe she's already gone down to the basement." Saige knew she didn't sound convincing.

Oh God. First Harriette. Now Zoe.

Her panic subsided only a little when Jasper appeared by her side, then spiked as a thunderclap boomed directly overhead. Aunt Prue staggered away from the window, her lips parted in a perfect circle of shock. The wind outside picked up to a high, breathless whistling, then transformed into something that sounded like a fighter jet had taken off. Rain streamed down in sheets. The windowpanes rattled. Saige couldn't breathe. She was feverish, bursting with adrenaline and anxiety.

A scream tore through the house. It compelled the four of them into the parlour. Saige couldn't believe what she found. This must have been the seance her brother had talked about. The Ouija board on the table looked like a prop from some kind of 1920s horror film. Saige could just make out the letters of the alphabet, the numbers zero to nine, and the words *yes* and *no*. Various graphics meant to depict spirits and demons had been carved into the mahogany board. It was an exquisite piece of art and fine craftsmanship, but it was no simple parlour game.

Around the table sat Zoe's bridesmaids, their faces lit in nervous, giddy anticipation. The table was littered with empty wineglasses that had been discarded for something stronger. Shot glasses had been left around the Ouija board. A vodka bottle had fallen on its side as though someone had intended to play a game of spin the bottle.

If only it had been that innocent.

Saige bit her tongue to refrain from shouting at them all.

All the women had their fingers connected on the planchette, which moved in giant swoops from letter to letter.

Kya squalled, her blonde hair in disarray around her face. "It's saying the same thing over and over again."

"Okay, who's moving it?" another woman cried.

Her accusation met a flurry of headshakes and protests.

It was Aunt Prue who startled everyone in the room. "Where on earth did you find this?"

Kya downed the drink in her shot glass. "It was already here. All set up."

"That's impossible." Aunt Prue was trembling. "This Ouija board belonged to Theodosia Sinclair. It's been missing for decades, presumed stolen."

Kya shot her eyes to the ceiling and looked bored. "Well, I guess the historians got it wrong."

Xav slammed his palm on the wall. "I told you to abandon the game and head for the basement."

Kya raised her hands in surrender. "Okay, okay. Geez, we were just having a bit of fun. I didn't think your soon-to-be-wife would freak out so bad."

Saige's gut reaction was to tear away, to run to the basement where everyone was safe, but instead her voice come out with heightened emotion. "What do you mean, freak out? What did you do?"

Kya's eyes sliced into her. "It was a game. I moved the planchette and spelled out a message. I said the bride had to beware. She was going to die."

Saige felt angry heat climb to her cheeks. "Why would you do that?"

The bridesmaid blinked. "It was a joke. Everyone just needs to calm the hell down."

"Kya!" One of the bridesmaids was crying. "It keeps saying the same thing over and over again." Her eyes were locked on the planchette. "She knows. She knows. She knows."

Fear hit Saige in the chest. It knocked the wind out of her.

Her mother's warning.

It can't be.

Lightning ripped across the sky outside, illuminating a room full of ashen faces. Thunder ruptured, the house seeming to rattle right down to its very foundations. There was a noise in the parlour that Saige struggled to identify at first. It sounded like air deflating from a tyre. Or pressure being squeezed through something impossibly small. For a fleeting moment, she saw spiderwebbing cracks run over the windows, and then the glass burst inward in a cacophonous smash. Shards went flying, splintering through the air, raining down on all of them in a cascading shower.

There was panic. Crying. Screaming.

And then the lights went out.

THIRTEEN

Vertigo spun through Saige's head. At least, she thought it did. She couldn't see anything in the dark. The bridesmaids were hysterical. She suspected more than one of them was sobbing frantically, and, from the loud thump on the floor, one of them had tripped or fallen from her chair. Xav swore. Aunt Prue kept telling everyone to remain calm. Jasper whispered a silent prayer, which struck Saige as odd. He was a devout atheist.

Funny time to find religion.

She gasped as bursts of chain lightning illuminated the parlour like a dysfunctional strobe light. Rain struck her, as powerful as icy bullets. The wind produced a howling effect so intense she felt it reverberate through her skull.

"It's okay. It's okay," a voice called.

Her father appeared with a flashlight. Poor Aunt Violet was behind him, holding a candle that she struggled to keep alight against the wind.

Derrick trained the flashlight across the room. "Everyone, the power has gone out, but we have a backup generator that should go on at any second."

Maybe he'd spoken magic words, because right on cue, the lights switched on. Saige caught a glimpse of startled, frantic faces before another horrendous burst of lightning outside blinded her. The room was thrown into darkness again.

The backup generator. It's failed.

Fear burned through her. She took out her phone and turned the flashlight on. Everyone followed her lead. Sporadic light shone through the suffocating darkness.

A hint of panic crept through her father's voice. "Everyone, follow me. I'm going to lead you down to the basement."

"Dad." Her brother's face appeared in the light's beam. The hard shadows around his eyes made him look almost ghoulish. "Zoe's missing. Dad, I have to find her. She's somewhere in the house... probably terrified."

Somewhere another window smashed. A door slammed upstairs. Wolvercraft Manor's foundations were sturdy, but for a house built of stone, it groaned and rasped like a ship caught out at sea.

Derrick's shoulders visibly tightened. "Xav, you're not searching the house alone. I'll go with you." He handed the flashlight to Aunt Prue. "This storm is getting worse. Lead everyone to the basement. Now!"

No one had to be told twice. Saige's aunt led the terrified bridesmaids down the hall to the stairs, shouting for anyone else who might have somehow failed to flee to follow.

Saige desperately wanted to pursue them, but she felt responsible for Zoe. She couldn't leave her father and brother to search the house by themselves, especially when they had no idea what they were really facing. "I'll help."

Her father's hand clutched her shoulder tight. "Saige, no. It's too dangerous." He turned to Jasper. "Young man, take my daughter down to the basement now."

Saige took a moment to compute that Jasper hadn't left with the others. If anything, he was standing even closer to Saige. "Happy to help, sir. My name is Jasper Young."

Recognition slowly dawned across Derrick's tense face. "You went to school with Xav, right? You're the musician."

"That's me."

"Good man. I wish we were meeting under better circumstances. Please, don't leave Saige's side."

Jasper's hand, warm and firm, clutched her fingers. "I've no intention of doing that, sir."

Saige tore her hand free, ashamed that Jasper's touch caused a spark of fireworks to dance in her belly. "For goodness' sake," she cried at the pair of them. "Let's all stick together."

She couldn't get over Jasper's behaviour.

Sir?

He's acting like he's at a job interview.

"Dad." Xav's voice was filled with impatience. "We should split up. We can search the house much faster."

Derrick shot a resigned look at Saige. "No one is splitting up. If we do this, we do this together. Stay away from the windows, and don't lose sight of each other. Let's go."

The four of them trod carefully down the dark hallway with only the light from their phones for comfort. Trying to navigate their way through the house was arduous. Saige had to press her lips together to prevent a scream when a portrait of a family ancestor was lit up like a grisly spectre. For a split second, she could have sworn the portrait was of a dead person, skin grey and bloated, eyes milky and waxen, staring down at her with a secret behind its smile, but then a staccato effect of lightning lit the hallway, and the image disappeared.

Just my imagination playing tricks.

But she kept her eyes firmly ahead, not willing to glance back.

She kept telling herself there was no reason to be afraid. There was strength in numbers, but she had to convince her mind of that very loudly when they ascended the stairs to the second level. The night air was impossibly cold. Many of the windows had broken. Glass shards crunched under their feet as they wandered down the passages and halls, calling out for Zoe.

"To hell with this," Xav spat. "We're not making progress like this." He ran ahead into the hallway before anyone could stop him. "Zoe! Zoe! Where are you?"

"Xav, come back here," Derrick hissed.

But Xav was like a disobedient dog on a mission. A moment later he was swallowed up by the dark, his voice drowned out by the torrential rain outside.

Derrick swore, the first time in a long time that Saige had heard such resigned anger in her father's voice. "I knew this was a bad idea. That boy is stubborn like his mother." He whipped around to face Saige and Jasper. "Both of you go to the basement. I'll find Xav and bring him back."

A frantic tug pulled inside Saige's chest. "What about Zoe?"

Derrick exhaled an uncomfortable breath. "For all we

know, Zoe could have gone to the basement. It's madness remaining in the house. Go now."

Before she could argue, her father ran into the dark. The faint light from his phone was enveloped by the shadows, as though it had sunk into black water.

This time when Jasper's fingers wrapped around her hand, she didn't pull away. The feeling that they weren't alone returned. She could almost feel that someone, or something, was standing behind her, breathing a fraction too quietly for her to detect. She wasn't sure if she imagined or sensed fingers stretching forward to clasp around her neck. Goose bumps rose across her skin. All the hairs along her arms went erect.

A creak echoed from somewhere deeper in the hall.

A footstep.

Cold sweat trickled down her back. "We need to get to the basement. Now!"

Jasper didn't need to be told twice. His face was blanched white. They careered down the hall, the light from their phones too weak to show anything more than a metre ahead. Saige risked a glance behind her. She gasped. A tumble of limbs in a white dress lurched after them in the dark. Lightning struck outside. It painted the walls and windows too bright, eating up everything in the house and rendering Saige blind. She couldn't be sure if what she'd seen had been real. Her eyes never had enough time to adjust to the disjointed changes, and with the fear eating away at her insides, every fast and sudden movement made her nearly go into a faint.

"Jasper, this isn't the way."

We should have been at the staircase by now.

"Of course it is. This is the way we came in." But he didn't sound so sure.

Saige's tongue had trouble forming the words she wanted to use. "The stairs. They should be here."

All that was evident in the harsh streaks of lightning ahead was the straight, narrow passage. It reminded Saige of a tunnel in a nightmare, one that seemed to grow longer and longer, never showing an end in sight.

Jasper's voice was thick with panic. "That isn't normal. That is most definitely not normal. "

Saige recalled what Harriette had said the first night she'd met her. *"There is something inside Wolvercraft Manor. Something that brings death. Something that doesn't rest."*

She licked her dry lips. All the moisture in her throat had evaporated, leaving an arid sensation in her mouth. She pressed her fingers firmly into Jasper's hand. "Okay. Let's try and think rationally about this. We must have passed the stairs."

But the hallway was equally dark and long behind them. She'd never wandered this part of the house. She was certain of that.

The house. It's playing tricks.

Jasper let go of her hand.

She pivoted around to reach out for him, her phone's light revealing empty space. He was gone.

"Jasper?"

Her heart rate soared.

No. I can't be alone. I just... can't be. He was right here!

"Jasper?"

Her body gave an involuntary shudder. She desperately wanted out of this hallway. She scrambled into an adjoining passage, which led her down another gloomy corridor. Every corner and bend were alien. She'd never seem them before in her life. Saige wanted to look outside the window to get her bearings, but the teeming deluge obstructed her vision.

"Saige!"

Jasper's voice carried down the passage.

"I'm here!" She barely managed to choke out the words. "Jasper! Where are you?"

Silence.

Saige felt her heart being plucked like violin strings. "Jasper!"

She ran in the direction where she'd heard his voice.

"Saige!" Her father's voice travelled down the hallway at her left.

"Dad?"

"Saige, answer me." He sounded frantic.

She sprinted as fast as she could in her heels in the direction of her father.

"Dad?" She couldn't get her voice past a croak.

Why can't I speak any louder? Why is my throat so dry?

This time when her father called back to her, it sounded as though it was coming from upstairs.

There's no way he'd go up to the third level. Not with the storm being this bad.

"Zoe! Saige! Dad!" Xav's voice called from somewhere to her right.

She froze, every part of her suspended as she listened. The sound of feet clattering down stairs reached her ears, drawing closer. She prayed it was her brother. She prayed he'd found the staircase.

I'm here! Xav! I'm here!

She ran. Faster and faster. Every footstep pounded louder and louder despite the soft carpet beneath her. She sped around a corner and nearly faceplanted into a wall. It was a dead end.

What the hell?

The house... it's a maze!

This time when she swivelled around to make her way back, someone waited for her at the end of the hall. The tiniest gasp—the only thing she could manage—worked its way out of her. Lightning rippled through the passage. Saige saw a glimpse of a blood-red flapper dress, black pearls, and long dark hair swept around an ashen face.

Zoe.

She was absorbed by the dark again.

Saige's heart became a ticking bomb.

Her eyes... they looked....

She cringed at the image printed in her mind. The pupils and irises, faded beneath a colourless orb. The skin veined and sunken in shadow.

Thunder cracked. A split second of lightning showed Saige one horrifying revelation. She saw those horrible eyes again and knew she wasn't looking at Zoe.

Yes, it was Zoe's body.

But it wasn't her inside.

Zoe was possessed.

FOURTEEN

SAIGE WAS REMINDED OF THE DAY HER MOTHER died. Elaine's eyes had been the same. An opaque marble, the skin around them darkened by black-purple veins. Whatever had been inside her mother that day now had control of Zoe.

Saige didn't realise she'd scooted back against the wall until she felt the cold pressure of it strike her arm.

God, I'm trapped.

Zoe twitched with an unnatural jerk. The thing inside her raised her slender arm and beckoned Saige to come forward. Saige was struck with déjà vu.

Just like the ghost from the party.

Zoe's lips formed into a malicious smile. She turned and traversed the hallway without taking strides.

"Do you want answers?" The spectre's voice rolled thick and slow through the dark, quiet, yet somehow Saige heard it among the thunder and deluge outside.

Yes.

She wanted to save Zoe. She wanted to spare her

brother heartache. She desperately wanted to know the real reason why her mother died.

Saige forced courage into her heart. She slipped away from the wall, imagining herself as Alice down the rabbit hole. Lightning continued to play havoc with her eyes. She sensed the cold sweat that ran down her back now soak into the half slip beneath her dress.

Zoe disappeared around the corner. The ends of her dress blew after her, reminding Saige of dark, running blood. The spectre didn't move fast, but Saige maintained distance between them as she slipped around the bend and continued her pursuit.

The halls and passages had changed again.

Have the walls sprouted legs and rearranged themselves?

She knew what she was suggesting defied physics, but Saige was starting to realise that little in Wolvercraft Manor could be explained by science.

She followed Zoe to one of the larger, more striking staircases. This one always reminded Saige of the grand staircase from the Opera Garnier, only much narrower and more compact. The white marble staircase was decorated with statue torchères that would have looked more at home in a garden. Tiny cherub faces had been carved into the balustrade, but they were so old and soured by age that their noses had flattened and their smiles now resembled grisly snarls. Saige remembered what her mother had once called them and shivered. *Little demons.*

Zoe drifted up the stairs. The only thing that looked alive about her was the red dress and her long black hair, which moved through the air as though suspended in water. A chill crept across Saige's bones, sinking right into her marrow. Zoe's feet dragged horribly, toes hitting each step and jittering. It was the exact way people's feet twitched when they were hanged.

Oh God! Zoe! What has this thing done to you?

Saige crept up the stairs, trying to pace her breathing, but the tightness in her lungs forced her to gasp for air like she was drowning. Zoe reached the third storey and slid silently down the hall.

I can't let Zoe get hurt, or worse, be killed. It will destroy Xav.

Lightning brightened the windows, thunder following only a few seconds later. It sounded as though the sky and earth had collided. Saige dashed up the last few stairs and hurried into the hallway. She pressed a shaky hand to her chest.

The hallway was empty.

Zoe was gone.

Shit! Shit!

Saige searched her phone for a signal, but the little bars across the top of the screen were empty. She blinked at the useless device in her hand.

A creak made her jump. Saige's ears pricked as she peered into the dark. At the end of the hall, intermittent lightning revealed one of the heavy doors swinging open.

It's just the wind.

But she knew she was lying to herself. Zoe had gone in there.

Saige forced one foot in front of the other, painfully aware of how loud her breathing was. She pressed deeper down the passage. Lightning splashed patchy illuminance across the wall. It wasn't a door that Zoe had entered but a wall panel that had opened, connected on hinges from the inside.

A secret doorway.

Does Dad even know about this? Aunt Prue?

Saige peered inside, but it was too dark to see anything besides grime-caked stone walls. It was a sort of tight passage, barely wide enough for someone to scrape their shoulders through. She moved closer, raising her phone for light. Saige inhaled damp air and mould. She dared to move a little closer.

Someone—or something—latched on to her shoulder.

Saige screamed. Her heart flipped unpleasantly as she twirled around, ready for fight or flight.

"Jesus, Saige! Stop! Stop! It's me! It's me!"

She stumbled backward. The light from her phone bathed Jasper's face.

He stared, open-mouthed. His normally styled hair was a sweat-induced mess around his face. He must have run his fingers through it one too many times. "Where the hell have you been? I've been looking all over the place for you."

His arms encircled her, pulling her in close.

This time, Saige let him. She'd never been happier to see another person in her life. "Don't sneak up on me ever again."

"Okay, I won't, but, Saige, you can't wander off and go on a solo adventure through the house."

"I didn't. Something in this place... it separated us."

Silver radiance shone from his hand. Saige realised that at some point Jasper had gone to the basement and grabbed a flashlight.

He came back for me?

Jasper pressed his lips together. His eyes darted left and

right. "Come on. Let's go. I don't want to spend a moment longer in this part of the house."

"Jasper, we can't!" Saige pointed at the secret trapdoor. "Zoe's down there. I think she's in trouble."

He took one look at the dark entry and shook his head. "Yeah, that's not happening. Saige, I know you're sweet, innocent, annoyingly naïve, but trust me, I've watched enough scary flicks in my life to know rule number one: never go down a creepy passage."

He pulled her away from the door. At the same time, a bloodcurdling scream cut through the eerie stillness inside, rolling up into the house with a chilling echo. Saige clung tighter to Jasper. Then the sound was snuffed out. Like a hand over a mouth. Or a flame gusted by wind.

Or a life meeting a sudden, tragic end.

All comforting thoughts.

Saige grabbed the flashlight out of his hand. She scrambled inside the secret passage.

"Bad idea, Saige."

But he hurried in after her.

It was a tight fit. She manoeuvred her body, sliding carefully along the walls, flinching when stone scoured her exposed skin. The flashlight revealed a few metres ahead, dust mites floating through the dark. Wherever the passage led, the damp stale air smelt like something had died there. Saige coughed. The crushingly cold air made it hard to draw breath.

They clambered into a room filled with malodorous rot. Saige nearly gagged. It was a chamber of some kind. She pointed the flashlight across the walls. Panic skittered in multiple directions through her stomach. Before them stood a line of cells. A wooden gallows occupied the left corner of the room, the noose still intact, as though it waited patiently for its next victim. Rusty electric shock equipment had been left abandoned on a wooden desk, the legs coated in filth. The bars that ran along the cells had tarnished so badly that a coppery stench stained the room.

Her jugular vein pounded. "What is this place?"

She felt Jasper's grip on the back of her dress. She didn't know if he was trying to keep her close or if he was afraid of being left behind. "It's some kind of torture chamber. Look."

He pointed his phone in the direction of the ceiling. Light washed over the stone. Hanging like some kind of twisted consecration cross was a black swastika centred in a white circle and bordered by red. A flag. Still hanging after decades of disuse.

Jasper's brown eyes sought hers. "Ashvall was occupied by the Nazis. Wolvercraft Manor was their headquarters, right?"

Saige swallowed. "Historians always believed the prisons were concealed somewhere beneath the house. Nothing was ever found."

"That's because it's up here, hidden behind Wolvercraft's walls."

She wrapped a hand around her mouth, afraid she'd be sick. How many of Ashvall's citizens had disappeared in this house? How many prisoners and members of the French resistance were secretly shipped from Normandy into Wolvercraft, never to see the light of day again? Where were their bodies? Buried out in the gardens in a mass grave? Entombed in the walls?

Something in one of the cells caught Saige's eye. She tilted forward. The flashlight revealed words scratched into the stone floor.

In life I was afraid. In death I am fearless. They will all pay.

She shivered but shifted closer. She couldn't make out whether the sentences had been scratched into the stone with a rock or... fingernails.

"What is that?" Jasper darted toward something behind the gallows.

Saige hurried after him, afraid to put distance between them. She caught movement too. A horde of cables rasped and groaned against the far wall. They slid down, taut and strained. The high-pitched screech of the cables reminded her of the way pigs squealed when they were stressed or afraid.

It must be carrying something heavy.

Jasper shot her a worried frown. "It's some kind of elevator. It's going down. And by the look of things—" He peered up at the ceiling. There was a square hole where the cables descended. "—it goes up as well. It must travel up and down the house."

Saige bit her lower lip, knowing she must have chewed off most of her red lipstick by now. "A secret elevator... inside the walls?"

Why would Frederick George Wolvercraft, the house's original owner, have a secret elevator built that would ride down into the bowels of the building?

Why is there a frigging torture chamber inside the house?

Jasper flinched. The cables continued to chafe as they descended. "Someone is going down."

Saige aimed the flashlight into the shaft. The light barely surpassed five metres. "It must be Zoe."

Or the thing that has her.

The cables ground to a halt with a deafening shriek. A moment later, they rolled in ascension. The elevator was coming back up.

Something saw the light.

Jasper backed away. "Saige, it's time to leave. I'd very much like for us to go now."

"Agreed."

The tension inside her was engulfing, bordering on smothering. Macabre curiosity and a desire to spare her brother's feelings had brought her down here, but now Saige only sensed evil.

To hell with Zoe. Sorry, Xav.

The cables were climbing faster. The antiquated equipment juddered and grinded up the shaft, moving impossibly fast.

The pair scrambled across the chamber back into the narrow passage.

Saige gasped.

Have the walls moved closer?

The space seemed tighter than she remembered.

"Saige?" Jasper's voice was frantic behind her. "There's something in the chamber."

"I'm hurrying," she cried back.

She could feel it now too. A cold presence that drowned the air with misery and desolation. The frosty sensation drove so deep into her bones that she wondered how she didn't turn into an ice figurine right there. Her breath clouded around her face in white plumes. The flashlight flickered once, twice, and then went out. She reached for Jasper's hand behind her and clung tight, his fingers her only comfort. She never thought of herself as being claustrophobic, but at that moment, she truly feared dying between these walls.

Saige dropped the useless flashlight, feeling the wall to guide her way instead. She'd never been happier to see the erratic flashes of lightning that lit the hallway beyond. She struggled out of the passage and turned to help Jasper. Whatever was behind him was close, but it was too dark to make out its features. All she knew was it was something unearthly and monstrous.

Jasper slammed the trapdoor closed. Together they ran. Down the hallway. Down the stairs. Past empty bedrooms and living chambers. They were nearly upon the staircase that would lead them to the lower floor when Saige spotted something pale and translucent out on the balcony. The woman—the ghost she had seen at the party, the one wearing her dress—stood out in the rain. The glass doors were open, the deluge surging inside, saturating the curtains and carpet. The woman looked completely dry. The torrent showered right through her body, making little razor cuts in her transparent flesh. She smiled at Saige. It wasn't a nice grin.

Jasper's voice faltered beside her. "Saige, it has a knife."

She squeezed her eyes shut, hoping it was an illusion.

But when she opened her eyes, the ghost was still there. Jasper was right. In the spectre's hand was a wicked-looking knife.

The ghost's lips parted. Her voice come out in a piercing cry. "She knows."

Before Saige could register what was happening, the wraith brough the knife to her own throat and slit—

Saige screamed, aghast by the cloud of squirting blood.

She clung to Jasper's lapels and buried her face in his jacket.

Oh my God. She cut her throat. She cut her throat!

Something hot and sticky trickled down her dress. She pulled away from Jasper, the sight of her gown eliciting more screams. Blood ran down her black-and-gold flapper dress, soaking the material.

It's her blood!

I'm wearing her dress!

Saige screeched and flung her arms like she was being attacked by a swarm of hostile

bees. "Get it off me. Get the dress off me."

Jasper's face was tinged green. His fingers ran down the zipper at her back. She scampered out of the dress, not caring that she stood only in a bra and underwear. She cried and ground the heels of her hands into her eyes. Saige was vaguely aware of Jasper holding on to her, trying to soothe her with consoling words, but she was too afraid and nauseated to make much sense out of anything. Her legs collapsed beneath her. Glittering black spots danced across her vision. She was glad when her head hit the floor, drowned in darkness.

FIFTEEN

SAIGE WOKE WITH A HEAD FULL OF NIGHTMARES. All evening she'd had vague notions of drifting in and out of consciousness. She hadn't been sure what was real and what were figments of her imagination, so she'd let the darkness swallow her again, taking her to a sweeter place where there was nothing.

But now she was awake and alert. The memory of last night came crashing down upon her like a wave on the shore. She was in her bed. Someone had dressed her in a nightgown. The window was open once again, the curtains blowing gently in the cool breeze. It wasn't sunny outside, but it wasn't stormy either. Just grey, bleak, and cold.

"Oh heavens, you're awake!"

The voice was animated and shrill.

Saige squirmed.

God, why couldn't you have had mercy on me?

Aunt Violet careered toward her from the corner chair and began fussing with Saige's bedsheets. She pulled them tight around her niece, cocooning Saige inside. "Keep warm, dear. You've had quite the night. It's lucky that young musician was with you. Do you remember what happened?"

Before Saige could answer, her aunt cut her off in a highly theatrical voice. "Well, the doors to the balcony blew open suddenly in that terrible storm, and you were already so frightened and on edge that you fainted. The musician... what's his name? Jack? Jason? Jordan?"

"It's Jasper."

"Oh, yes. Silly of me to forget. Such a handsome man. Jasper brought you here to your room and then came down to the basement to get us, and oh, you were so pale and sweaty. And quite undressed. Your father has questions about that, by the way. I thought you must have been terribly ill with a fever and, in your delirium, stripped off. That happens to people when they get hypothermia, you know. I watched over you for most of the night in the dark, and then the generator came back on, and the storm dissipated. Goodness me! What a night! Half the island doesn't have power. There are trees down cutting off roads. And flooding! The beaches are eroded. And more storms are forecast for this evening, expected to last for several days, in fact. It has the Met Office stumped. Worst storm for Ashvall in thirty years they're predicting. Poor Zoe is beside herself. Her dream of a garden wedding ruined! But between you and me, your father has paid an excessive sum for this event, so the wedding will be going ahead, rain, hail, or shine, though I suspect it will be in the ballroom now, if the windows aren't too damaged, of course. Maybe Zoe could—"

"Zoe's okay?" Saige had struggled to find a pause in her aunt's loud monologue of despair.

Violet had gone red in the face from talking too much. "Yes, dear. She was found passed out in one of the bathrooms upstairs. Drinking to excess, I'm afraid." Her aunt mouthed the next words but failed to keep her voice below a whisper. "Zoe can't remember a thing about last night. Blind drunk. It's disgraceful."

Saige tossed the bedsheets aside and stood on unsteady legs. Her head took a moment to catch up with her. The room spun, but she forced her way to the door and out into the hallway.

"Saige! Take it easy, dear. Where are you going?"

She ignored her aunt. She'd had enough of the eccentric woman to last her a decade. Saige forced strength into her legs and ran down the hallway. A few well-dressed guests on their way to brunch had to flatten themselves against the walls to avoid being hit by her. Saige didn't care that she made a spectacle of herself. She ran up the stairs to the third level and bounded into Zoe's bedroom without knocking. The door swung open so hard it hit the wall with a thud.

Zoe was resting in her bed, her face covered in a green facial mask. She startled awake, and then her eyes turned flat with disappointment. "Great. It's you. What do you want?" Her voice was hollow and lacked its usual cattiness. She flinched at the bleak light that filtered through the curtains. "Jesus. Can you shut that?"

Saige crossed the room and pulled the curtains closed. "How are you feeling?"

She didn't really care. She just wanted to make sure Zoe was... well, Zoe. Not the possessed monster that had taken control of her mind and body.

Zoe glared between slitted eyes. "Are you serious? How does it look like I feel?"

Like you've been intoxicated for the last two days.

Saige studied Zoe for a few moments, taking in the paleness of her long neck and bruise-stippled arms. Scratches ran along her right shoulder. Fingernail scores. "Do you remember anything about last night? Your arms... that all looks painful."

Saige recalled the thin passage to the hidden chamber. The memory of claustrophobia closed in again. The stone walls had been notched and rough. Her own arms were grazed where the skin had abraded with the rock.

Just like Zoe's.

It was the evidence she needed. Whatever *thing* had taken possession of Zoe had come after her and Jasper.

But what is it?

Zoe tossed her a contemptuous look, as though Saige were a silly child asking why the sea was blue. "What are you, a detective?"

Ignoring the jibe, Saige drew closer. The stench of alcohol wafted off Zoe, last night's indulgence not yet lifted. "I'm a concerned sister-in-law."

Zoe rolled her eyes. "Fine. If you must know, I do remember the seance. Kya was a real bitch. She made up a message and told me I was going to die on my wedding night. I mean, seriously? I was upset and wanted to get away from the party. I came upstairs, and then the next thing I know, I'm waking up in a bathroom. Can you get Nurse Tylah? My head hurts like a real—"

"Think," Saige snapped. She didn't know anything about a Nurse Tylah. She was too desperate for information to give a damn about Zoe's comfort. "Did you hear anyone behind you? Did you see anything out of the ordinary?"

Please. Just a clue. Anything.

Anger contorted Zoe's green-smeared features. "For God's sake. I told you what I remember. I passed out." Her lips hardened into a sneer. "Apparently you fainted too. At least I managed to keep my clothes on."

The taunt threw Saige. Anger and humiliation settled inside her. She blurted the first hateful thought that came to mind. "Perhaps you should reflect on Kya's message from the seance. You're a bitch, Zoe. I wouldn't be surprised if someone was coming after you."

A flame of satisfaction lit inside her at the sight of Zoe's appalled face, then dissipated the moment she realised she'd stooped to the hateful model's level. Saige stormed out of the room. Her arms and legs shook, dizziness washing through her in waves.

Maybe I should look for Nurse Tylah for myself.

She stumbled in what she thought was the direction of the bathroom. The walls, floor, ceiling—it all rushed at her.

This house... it's making me go crazy.

Wolvercraft Manor was a beast, the halls and passages its veins, the rooms and parlours its organs.

We are the meal inside.

"Saige."

She turned to find Jasper.

His eyes took her in with quick assessment. "Your aunt told me you were awake. Are you all right?"

Strangely enough, she was. Just having Jasper with her —not being alone—had somehow lessened her anxiety. It was still there but not as prevalent. She could breathe again.

She nodded. "I'm sorry. I just—"

"You don't need to explain. I haven't slept a wink." His lips tightened into a thin line. "What was that thing last night?"

"I don't know." Saige wrapped her arms around herself. "It had possession of Zoe. It was going to take her." The lining of her mouth tasted sticky. She stared at Jasper, unable to keep the emotion from spilling down her cheeks. "I think it took my mother."

"Hey, come here." He gently took her in his arms, holding her tight. She didn't push away. Didn't fight. She was far too exhausted for that. For one contented moment, Saige experienced the illusion of safety sweep through her.

But it only lasted a second.

***

"Do you think we should tell your father about the chamber?" Jasper watched her with curious interest.

They were out in the gardens, underneath the turret-shaped gazebo. When Saige had been a little girl, she'd squealed in happy delight when she'd first seen it, thinking it was a carousel with ponies. She'd cried the entire night when she'd realised her mistake. Back then, the gazebo was a marble structure with grapevine-style designs fashioned in cast iron, but now it was covered in ivy and small white flowers, wet and wilted from the storm but still beautiful.

It was late morning. Rain had settled in, the drizzle

causing clouds of mist to roll across the lawns and curl around Wolvercraft Manor like aimless, wandering souls.

A cold feeling prickled up the back of Saige's neck. She settled on a stone bench, unsure if her legs could support her much longer. "I don't know. I suppose it couldn't hurt. Dad and Aunt Prue would certainly want it investigated."

"Investigated?"

"Yes. People from all over this island disappeared when the Nazis occupied Ashvall. That chamber was probably where their lives ended. Historians will want to see it and research it. Police, too, I would imagine."

Jasper scooted closer. "Okay. So we tell your father? We tell him that last night when we were searching for Zoe, we discovered a hidden door that led to a concealed dungeon. The storm last night... the temperature and pressure changes in the house... they're all reasonable explanations for why that door could have opened."

Saige squeezed her eyes shut until she saw red. "It sounds utterly ridiculous."

"Well, it sounds better than saying, 'Hey, Dad, last night your future daughter-in-law was possessed and chased me out of a concealed torture chamber.' I'm sure that will go down real well."

Saige stared at the ground with reluctance. She knew Jasper was right. She exhaled a long sigh. "We can't say anything. I wouldn't even be able to find that door again. Last night, the house led me down passages I've never seen before."

Jasper dropped onto the bench beside her, his hands held tensely together. He'd always moved with confidence and purpose. It pained Saige to see him this anxious.

No. He hurt me. I don't care how he feels.

But she couldn't help laying her head against his shoulder as Jasper wrapped an arm around her. Human contact, even Jasper's, was better than being alone in this situation.

His breath was warm against her forehead when he spoke. "Then the alternative is to monitor Zoe. We try to keep her as safe as possible until the wedding is over."

"But that's what I'm afraid of." Saige tipped her head to look at him. "All the women who married into the Wolvercraft family died after their weddings. I think the only way to keep Zoe safe is to prevent the wedding from happening."

They were so close together that Saige felt the warmth of body heat in the small space between their mouths. It made her sad to be this close to him. It made her grieve for a time that could never be again. Her heart pounded impossibly fast. Jasper's arms tightened around her. Despite her head shouting at her to move away, she didn't want to.

The wind picked up. Specks of rain drizzled around them, the cold somehow bringing them tighter together. Jasper's dark hair blew off his face. The way he looked at her was so intense. His brown eyes searched hers, seeking the woman behind the fear and madness.

Good luck finding her.

Jasper stroked her cheek with the back of his hand.

"Saige," a voice barked.

They both whirled around.

Xav stood between the gazebo's thick Romanesque columns. His red hair, usually slicked back, was sodden and matted, his coat saturated. He lit a cigarette. The only time Xav smoked was when he was seriously stressed.

Saige thought he'd given up the habit. Her brother inhaled deeply and glared. Not at Saige. At Jasper. His eyes darted between the pair. "What's going on?"

Her already hammering heart edged up another degree. She tore away from Jasper, embarrassingly aware of what this must have looked like to her brother.

Jasper straightened. "We were just talking."

"Talking?" Xav's voice was a sharp, cutting laugh. "What were you talking about?"

"The wedding," Saige blurted before her head could catch up with her.

It's kind of true.

Xav's eyes narrowed. He didn't look like he believed either of them. "If you don't mind, Jasp, I'd like a moment with my sister."

Jasper smiled, but it lacked certainty. He turned to her. "I'll be in the house… if you need me."

She watched him walk out into the rain, the mist wrapping around him until he was entirely lost from view. Saige experienced a deep chill in her bones, like the only light in the dark had gone out.

She mentally slapped herself.

I can't think of Jasper in that way. Not after what he did.

Her brother sat beside her. He studied her, his eyes intent on her face. "What are you doing with Jasper?"

His question was so direct, it caught her off-guard.

Why does he care?

Xav wanted her to stay away from him and Zoe, but now he was stepping in and playing the big brother role again, demanding answers.

Maybe he'd been speaking in the heat of the moment.

Hope flared inside her.

Maybe Xav didn't mean what he said.

She hugged herself, trying to keep warm. "Nothing. Jasper and I were just talking."

"It didn't look like you were *just talking.*" His face transformed into a glare. "Saige, people are saying they've been seeing the two of you together a lot over these last two days."

"What people?"

Xav didn't reply. He tossed his cigarette on the ground and crushed it with his boot.

"When did you pick up that habit again?"

"This morning… when Zoe started behaving strangely." His gaze became intense on hers. "Don't go near Jasper, okay? He's a bad influence, and he'll only lead you to trouble."

So this is the big brother talk.

"I've known Jasper since school," Xav continued. "Girls are a drug for him. A short fix. The guy doesn't like being alone, but he doesn't like commitment either. Keep your distance from him, sis. He's bad news."

Saige felt the blood drain out of her face. "There's nothing going on between us."

If this was the way Xav was behaving now, he could never, ever know the truth about her and Jasper. Xav would probably drown the guy if he knew his school friend was once engaged to his sister.

Good God, this is such a mess.

Xav stared at the house. From this distance, Wolvercraft Manor appeared as though it had been built in the centre of a lake, seen only through a thin sweep of fog that moved in a lazy, hypnotising speed across the water. If the house frightened him, he didn't show it. He lightly punched Saige's arm, the sincere way only big brothers could do. "From the look of things, Jasper has you set in his sights. Don't fall for it. He has a girlfriend."

Her stomach heaved. Those four little words had caused her more pain than she wanted to acknowledge.

He has a girlfriend.

It echoed in her head, taunting and ruthless.

She sucked in a rattling breath she hoped her brother didn't notice. "Xav, I promise. We were just talking."

And I can also promise that I will never be talking to Jasper Young again.

She stood to leave.

"Wait."

Xav fidgeted with his hair. Rainwater trailed down his face. "I came here to tell you some bad news. Aunt Prue sent a message to Dad. That lady you were looking for last night, the one staying with Aunt Prue... the doctor, right?"

"Yes. Harriette Reynolds." A sudden, ebbing fear took hold of Saige.

"She's missing."

SIXTEEN

Saige walked through the fog with slow, stumbling steps. The track through the Hauteville Woods was narrow at the best of times, but with the rain, poor light, and coastal wind gusting through the trees, Saige had to be careful of every step. The tree roots were thick and overgrown. Leaves slipped out beneath her boots, causing her to slide across the mud like an amateur figure skater. She gasped, unsure whether the water running down the back of her neck was sweat or rain.

Damn you, Jasper Young. Damn you!

Her blood frothed like a caffeinated energy drink. She'd purposefully avoided Jasper in the house. He hadn't changed. He was still the immature, womanising player he'd always been. Shame pounded through her, a jackhammer straight to the heart. In the gazebo, Jasper had looked at her like he'd rediscovered his world, like she was a missing piece to a jigsaw. But there were many pieces in a jigsaw, and she was just another unmemorable part.

Women were a conquest to him. She had to remember that.

Saige had seen him waiting by the window in the drawing room, probably scanning the lawns in search of her. Huh! She'd taken an alternate route past the garden and through the old servants' entrance in the back court-yard. She'd grabbed a spare flashlight someone had stored in the kitchen, found a rain jacket—she didn't know whose—and took the back exit out of the house into the Hauteville Woods.

Saige had been proud of her secret breakaway, but now that she was alone in the woods, apprehension did a queasy tap dance in her stomach. The trees loomed over her. Grey clouds coasted over the sun. It was nothing more than a milky coin in the sky, shadows and gloom prevalent throughout the foliage.

Don't be afraid. Focus on what's important here. Harriette is missing.

She knew Harriette would have taken this track through the woods late yesterday afternoon. It was the most direct route from Aunt Prue's house to Wolvercraft Manor. She remembered the chilling message from last night.

"*She. Knows. She. Knows. She. Knows.*"

Saige didn't understand what it meant, but she knew it had something to do with Harriette. The doctor had wanted to talk to her last night. She'd discovered something.

Something that must have put her in harm's way.

Saige had to reach her aunt's house. Aunt Prue would be so distressed.

The police might even be there.

She couldn't let her aunt go through that alone, but just in case something terrible had happened to Harriette last night, Saige took her time through the woods. She searched the ground and surrounding trees with her flashlight, afraid of what she would do if she did find evidence of Harriette's disappearance.

"Saige! Wait! What are you doing out here alone?"

She turned around, aghast.

Light shone through the trees ahead. The figure with the flashlight emerged from the fog.

Shit.

She was grateful that the rain hid the humiliated shade of red in her cheeks.

Jasper had failed to find a raincoat, but at least he was wearing sensible shoes. A pair of white sneakers that probably cost around two thousand pounds. Mud had already stained the laces.

Maybe not so sensible.

He blinked the rain out of his eyes. "What are you doing?"

The flashlight in her face blinded her for a second. She slapped it out of the way. "What do you think I'm doing? I'm searching for Harriette."

He was quiet for a moment, his lower lip slack. "I'm pretty sure that's the police's job."

"Really? Then where are they?"

"It hasn't been twenty-four hours yet."

"Harriette might not have twenty-four hours."

He hung his head. "Saige, please. Come back to the house. Met Office is predicting another storm this afternoon that's going to last well into the evening and possibly for the next few days. This rain bomb has everyone stumped." He reached for her hand. "Let's just go back to the house. We'll tell the police what we know when they come asking."

Saige took a step away. "Oh sure. You want to tell the police that Harriette was taken by a curse."

Jasper laughed, but it lacked humour. "We don't know that's what happened. Come back to the house."

"No."

He dragged his hand down the side of his face. "You know, this is why your family think you're a nutcase. Because you do impulsive, irrational things."

Her lungs knotted, no air going in or out. "You know nothing about me."

You made damn sure of that when you left.

She stormed down the track. She knew she was being unreasonable... but her aunt? Aunt Prue would need comfort. She'd be fretting and scared and alone. And Saige really wanted answers. She'd always wondered how people could throw themselves into dangerous and hopeless situations. Now she knew.

She heard Jasper's heavy footsteps come after her in the rain. The scowl had faded from his face, but he still eyed her shrewdly. "You know what your problem is? You push everyone away. Your dad, your brother, your aunts— they all care about you, but you never give them a chance."

She turned and snapped at him with cold fury. "I never pushed you away."

He took a step back. Regret danced across his face. "What's really going on, Saige? It's more than ghosts and curses, isn't it?"

She didn't want to go there. Not with him. She hadn't told a soul. Not her family, not the doctors or the psychologists. It had been far easier—and smarter—to let them think she was suffering a mental breakdown. But God, she was so tired of holding on to this secret. Dealing with it on her own, growing up with it, had sapped her of energy.

She looked at Jasper, really looked at him, her defences washed away with the rain. He'd seen two ghosts. He was one step closer to her than anyone else had been in her entire life.

Is this something I can tell him?

Her body quaked with nerves, her voice small and afraid. "Ever since my mother's death, I've felt something around me. It's this sense... this presence... watching me, never leaving me alone. And it feels evil. People say we make our own way in life. That we become what we think. But I don't believe that's the case for me. Jasper... I think I'm cursed."

She waited for him to say something, and when he didn't, she looked down at her feet, stiff and lonely in the rain. "Now do you think I'm crazy?"

Of course he does. I think you're frigging crazy.

The hard lines on Jasper's face softened. The saddest expression filled his eyes. "No. I think you're lost and confused and... haunted."

"Then help me find answers."

He didn't say anything.

Saige took the silence for a no, and her tone became more hostile than she intended. "Fine. Go back to the house. I'm going to Aunt Prue's. Don't try to stop me."

She began her descent through the woods. A second later, she heard Jasper's disgruntled sigh before the soles of his trendy sneakers squelched through the mud in pursuit.

TRUE TO JASPER'S WORD, THE RAIN DIDN'T CEASE. IT formed into a torrent, streaming down the trees and turning the mud into a running slush. They plodded heavily along the path, each step slow and cautious, their flashlights doing a poor job of showing them the way.

Great. The weather has done a superb job of hiding evidence.

A part of her wondered if it was the weather to blame or something else? Ashvall was no stranger to storms, but a continuous downpour like this in summer was uncommon.

It's the house. Wolvercraft Manor doesn't want us to leave.

It sounded crazy, but she knew it was true in her heart.

Every last ripple of warmth had vanished from Saige's body. Her teeth chattered, and she worried that if the temperature plummeted farther, she and Jasper could very well be walking through snow. She didn't talk to him at all—didn't even look at him—but when their sleeves brushed, a strange, dicey warmth slipped through her.

Jasper blew warm air onto his fingers and rubbed his hands briskly together. He stilled, his eyes set on something ahead. "What are those?"

Saige turned her flashlight in the direction he pointed. A simple upright slab of stone with a gabled top protruded from the ground. There were other stone markers behind it with rounded and semicircular tops. One had a very distinct cross with a circle.

Saige threw a hesitant glance at Jasper, knowing he

wasn't going to like what she was about to tell him. "They're tombstones."

He stared at her for a moment. "Tombstones? As in… graves?"

"Yes, Jasper. What other kind of tombstones are there?"

A startled look crossed his face. "In the woods?"

Her shoulders slumped. She knew she was going to have to tell him the story. "The graves are centuries old. When they ran out of room in the Ashvall cemetery, people elected to have their loved ones buried in the woods. This is where the Wolvercrafts are. The graves haven't been maintained in decades. It's the reason why Dad never wanted me or Xav to go into the woods. He was afraid it would frighten us."

She stared at the weeping, moss-covered stone sculptures—angels with their eyes closed or sleeping, which she knew was symbolism for a loved one who had passed away. Her mother had told her.

Jasper pointed to something over her shoulder. "And that?"

Saige turned and leapt back. "Jesus!"

A doll hung in a tree, its neck twisted. It was strung up with black nylon rope. The once polished white cheeks were covered in mud. Rusted stains had trickled from the glassy eyes, making it appear as though the doll had been crying. Its smiling face unnerved Saige.

She raised her flashlight. There were more dolls in the trees, some tied to the trunks, others dangling from branches. There were even teddy bears, their fake fur matted. Half of them looked like they'd been pecked at by birds.

Jasper steepled his hand over his mouth, perhaps about to be sick. "What the hell is this?"

Saige's pulse resumed to a normal beat. "It's an island custom. I didn't think people still did this."

"You mean like some sort of creepy voodoo shit?"

"No. The locals are superstitious. They believe the woods are home to witches and fairies. The old stories say fairies would steal children at night and offer them to the witches, so parents started to hang dolls in the trees. The idea being that the fairies would mistake the dolls for children and offer those to the witches instead. By the look of things, it's still a custom people are following."

"That's insane."

"It's tradition. They probably just keep it up for the tourists. People love that kind of theatre. Even when it frightens them."

She dragged her sleeve across her face in a poor attempt to wipe the rain from her eyes. "Come on. Aunt Prue's place isn't far."

They resumed their trek, their path slanting diagonally through the trees. Ten minutes later, they came out to a cottage farmhouse that would have looked more at home in a snowglobe. A pebbled walkway led to a white porch, the house's lower level constructed of stone, the upper storey built with decorative half timbering on the façade. Lattice sash windows and a thatched roof offered a rustic charm.

Saige knocked on the door, surprised when her aunt appeared, hair unbrushed, make-up smudged across her face, her Roaring Twenties attire crinkled from an uncomfortable sleep. The feather on her black headpiece had wilted. Saige thought it was a bad sign that her aunt hadn't bothered to shower or get changed.

Aunt Prue's face clouded with disapproval. "Saige? What are you doing here? You're soaked. Does your father know about this?"

Saige swallowed an angry retort. She really wished people would stop treating her like she was nine years old. "Have you heard anything from Harriette?"

"No. Nothing. I've called the police." Aunt Prue's eyes settled briefly on Jasper. "At least you didn't come alone. Come on. Inside, the pair of you. Out of this rain."

Saige stepped inside, took off her sodden rain jacket, and hung it on the coat stand. She hadn't been to her aunt's house since she was a child. The place seemed to have been stored in a time capsule. Nothing had changed. A nautical theme ran through the entire hallway into the main lounge. Coastal paintings hung on the walls, all of them watercolours Saige was positive would have been purchased from the local art gallery. Dried starfish and little rustic sailboats decorated the mantelpiece. Every bit of furniture was wood, painted in white or ivory. Even the cushions were themed, navy blue with little compass points printed in white.

Aunt Prue directed them to a plush sofa. "Make yourselves comfortable. I'll put on the kettle. Heaven knows I need caffeine."

Jasper dropped unceremoniously onto the couch. He passed an appreciative glance at Saige. "This is nice. I'm digging the beach theme. I'm a little over Wolvercraft's *The Munsters* meets *The Addams Family* vibe, if you know what I mean."

Saige settled in an armchair. She remembered visiting

her aunt as a child, sitting in this chair on long summer nights and reading about the local fairy tales of Ashvall. The recollection of those stories now made her blood solidify in her veins.

Aunt Prue returned with a silver tray, a pot of tea, cups and saucers, and a neat plate of biscuits. Saige found it strange that even with her house guest missing, Aunt Prue still found the energy to play hostess. She smiled, but it was strained. "Tea?"

Saige nodded.

Jasper's eyes lit up. He took a biscuit—something chocolate coated—devoured it in one mouthful, then grabbed two more.

Saige shot him a look.

"What? I'm hungry. I haven't eaten today."

She ignored him and focused on her aunt. Aunt Prue's fingers were trembling. She struggled to pour the tea. The steaming liquid pooled over the cup onto the saucer.

"Let me help." Saige took over. She made three cups of tea and settled back into her chair, then took a sip. It needed milk and sugar. "What did the police say?"

Aunt Prue rubbed a shaky hand across her mouth. "They're on their way. They want to talk to me and look through Harriette's things. They suspect something may have happened to her in the storm last night."

Jasper straightened. "They'll probably put a search party together."

"I honestly don't know. Ashvall's police force is small, and with all this rain, I doubt the Guernsey police force will be able to assist. The island is cut off." Aunt Prue blew into a handkerchief. "They told me to keep ringing Harriette's mobile and see if she answers. It's switched off. I'm keeping my phone on charge just in case she rings, but I have no hope that she will. Oh, Saige. What if something terrible happened? What if Harriette got caught in the storm last night? If she took the path through the woods, she could have slipped and fallen. There have been landslides in the woods before." Her eyes grew wide and alarmed. "You didn't take that track down here, did you? You took the road?"

Saige swallowed. "Of course."

Jasper looked down at his tea and didn't comment.

Aunt Prue gnawed on her lower lip. "Good. That's good." Her eyes travelled around the room, as though she hoped Harriette might pop out from behind a furniture piece. A single tear leaked from her right eye. "Another storm is expected this afternoon."

Saige put her cup and saucer down and moved to sit with her aunt. "Did Harriette say anything to you yesterday that seemed... odd? Something that could explain why she's missing."

Saige watched her aunt closely. She was certain Harriette's disappearance had nothing to do with the weather. It was the curse. Dr Reynolds had learned something she wanted to convey to Saige, but the curse had gotten to her first.

"She. Knows. She. Knows. She. Knows."

The words tormented Saige.

Aunt Prue shook her head. "She was excited to be attending the party. That's all I remember."

"Have you been through her things?" Saige pressed. "Maybe there's something there?"

"Only very briefly. I don't want to intervene with Harriette's things. If something happened... of a crime sort... I don't want to tamper with potential evidence. I'll leave that for the police."

The police. Who are on their way.

Saige knew she was going to have to act quickly if she wanted to find answers.

She stood and wrapped a comforting arm around her aunt's shoulders. "Why don't you shut your eyes and have a rest? Jasper can watch over you and answer the door when the police arrive."

"Yes. That's sounds like a nice idea. Thank you."

Saige grabbed the blanket draped over the back of the sofa and tucked it around her aunt. "I'm just going to duck to the bathroom. Tea and rainwater have made my bladder weak."

She passed a knowing look toward Jasper, hoping he understood the gesture.

Outside in the hall, she ran silently up the stairs. Just as she made it onto the landing, the hall light went out. Saige fiddled with the switch. On and off, on and off, as though flicking it enough times would make it do something different.

Great. Now Aunt Prue's house has lost power.

She imagined the entire island had.

Saige continued down the hall but didn't turn into the bathroom. Instead, she found the guest bedroom and slipped inside.

SEVENTEEN

Her aunt had spared no expense in decorating the guest bedroom to perfection. White and warm sandy neutrals were woven through the bedding and throw pillows. An impressive wicker bed with a beautiful cane headboard had been made into a feature against a teal accent wall, a gorgeous pendant light of seashells sending a kaleidoscope of colour across it. It was like something out of an opulent beach resort, with an untidy, dishevelled, and unorganised holiday maker residing inside. Saige examined the room.

The bedsheets had been thrown back, the pillows on the floor. Library books had been stashed in piles across the white duchess that also doubled as a desk. Chocolate candy wrappers littered a corner of the floor, just a few centimetres from the wicker trash bin. Knowing her aunt, Saige was fairly certain that bin was for decoration purpose only.

Aunt Prue must have had a heart attack when she walked in here.

She stepped over to the desk, recognising some of the books from the previous day's library session—folktales, stories of witches and ghouls, and the early history of Ashvall. Saige went through the books, hoping Harriette might have jotted down notes—anything that may have indicated what she'd learned and been so desperate to convey to Saige. The books were empty. She checked the drawers. There was nothing inside. She ran her hands through Harriette's suitcase, but there were only clothes.

Frustration coursed through Saige to the very tips of her fingers. A loud thunderclap rattled outside, a reminder that there was still very dangerous weather on the way.

A car door slammed. She rushed to the window.

Shit!

A vehicle had pulled up to the curb. Two officers were on their way to the house, a suited detective and an officer in uniform.

I'm running out of time.

She frantically searched through the wardrobe, hoping something may have been left in one of the drawers. They were all empty.

Where's Harriette's computer? Surely she has one.

A heavy knock came on the door downstairs. She heard Jasper's heavy footsteps, on the way to answer.

She checked the bedside table, but there was nothing inside the drawer except a few munched-on chocolate bars. She looked under the bed, not sure what she was hoping to find. About to admit defeat, Saige went back to the desk for one final search. She hadn't noticed it before, but hidden behind several empty styrofoam coffee cups was a small intricate latch. She swept the cups aside and gave the latch a pull. A compartment hidden under the desk's surface opened. Inside was a blue book. She grabbed it and fumbled through the pages.

Voices resonated from below. She froze at the distinct sound of someone coming up the stairs.

Damn it!

Saige rummaged through the notebook, feeling as though her heart ticked in time with a bomb. Handfuls of notes and images spilled from the pages onto the floor. In a panic, she bent down to rake them into a pile.

Icy shock fluttered inside her. Harriette wasn't just fascinated with Saige's family history. She was obsessed with it. There were newspaper clippings, scanned and printed out from archives about accidental deaths that had occurred on the grounds of Wolvercraft Manor. The earliest dated back to 1846. All of them had messy, illegible notes written at the sides. There were pictures of Xav and Zoe cut out from newspapers and magazines. A red circle had been drawn around Zoe's head in all of them.

What the hell is this?

There were photographs of her father at gala events. Photos of Aunt Prue conducting tours in Wolvercraft Manor. Images of Aunt Violet lunching with other socialites. Even pictures of Saige going in and out of her apartment.

I'm going to be sick.

Who is Dr Harriette Reynolds?

A floorboard creaked from the hallway, followed by footsteps.

"It's just down here, right at the end."

That was Aunt Prue.

Saige gathered all the photos together and stuffed them back into the notebook. That was when she saw the black-

and-purple scrap of paper on the floor. It must have fallen out of the book before, and she'd missed it. She picked it up. It was a business card.

GET THE ANSWERS THAT YOU SEEK.
MILDRED TEMPLETON – PSYCHIC MEDIUM AND CLAIRVOYANT.

THERE WAS A DATE AND TIME ON THE BACK OF THE card. Saige's stomach did a backflip. Yesterday at 4:00 p.m.

Harriette met this woman a few hours before she disappeared.

It was vital evidence. Something the police would need.

But I need it more.

She rammed the notebook into her hoodie pocket and fumbled into the bathroom that adjoined Aunt Prue's room, shutting the door gently behind her. To make things more authentic, she flushed the toilet and washed her hands in the basin, then stepped out into the hallway.

"Oh, Saige, there you are." Aunt Prue stood outside the guest bedroom. The police were inside the room, searching Harriette's belongings. "Are you okay, sweetheart? You're pale."

The air in Saige's lungs seemed to vanish. "I'm not entirely well," she lied. "I think maybe I should go back to the house."

Aunt Prue took her hand and gave it a light tap. "I think that's a wise decision. The public coach is taking people to Wolvercraft Manor. One every hour. The final trip is at 2:00 p.m. Make sure you and that young man are on it well before then, please."

Saige frowned. "Taking people to Wolvercraft Manor?"

Her aunt's eyebrows dipped. "Well, yes. Wolvercraft Manor is one of the island's emergency evacuation centres. The other is the town hall. This storm is approaching and is going to be extremely dangerous. Everyone who lives in low-lying areas is encouraged to leave and get to an evacuation centre right away. Your father wants me to leave, too, but I'm not in any danger down here. And I can't leave. Mr Bubbles wouldn't appreciate it."

"Then I guess that settles it. Jasper and I will leave now."

Saige was almost grateful for the news. It meant she had till two o'clock to find this Mildred Templeton.

She ducked past her aunt.

"Oh, Saige. One moment, dear. Please just wait downstairs with that handsome man. The police would like to talk with you first."

Saige's feet suddenly felt rooted to the spot. "Of course."

Shit.

SAIGE SAT ON THE SOFA, BOUNCING HER HEEL IN A nervous tic that she couldn't seem to get rid of. Jasper casually stretched his legs and snacked on another chocolate biscuit. She marvelled at how calm he was. Did he have enough practise with police officers to know how to play it cool? He'd had a bad-boy streak back in school. Regrettably, that was what had first attracted her to him.

She'd read in online magazines that his band members were often in the sights of the police of whatever country they were touring. Something to do with drugs and women. She really hoped that was just the media being... well, the media and sensationalising half-truths.

"Miss Wolvercraft."

Saige jumped.

The short, bald man in the suit appeared, followed by the young, uniformed police officer. Her aunt stood in the doorway behind them, her face lacking colour. The young officer remained standing, his pen poised on a notepad.

The older policeman sat down. His eyes roamed the room, evaluating the family pictures on the mantel, then crossed back to Saige. He seemed to scrutinise her slowly. "I'm Detective Bassi, and this is Officer Hammond. I understand you were meant to meet with Dr Reynolds last evening. She had something important to tell you?"

Saige divided a glance between her aunt and Jasper. It took a moment to find her voice. "Um, yes. That's correct."

"Your aunt tells me that you were extremely worried about Dr Reynolds. Even before the storm occurred."

Saige inhaled a breath. Why did the notebook in her pocket suddenly feel... hot? "I just thought it was unusual that she wasn't there. She didn't seem like the kind of person who would break her word."

"You knew her well?"

"No. Only a few days."

"Was she acting unusual yesterday in the library?"

Detective Bassi's question took a moment to register in her head. "Unusual?"

"Yes. Jittery? Nervous? Anything that seemed odd?"

Saige realised her hands were trembling. She stuffed

them under her thighs. "No. She was telling me about my family history."

It's kind of the truth.

She took them through the events of the day before as best as she could, eliminating the ghosts and supernatural occurrences.

Detective Bassi focused on Jasper. "Do you have anything to add to that, Mr Young?"

Jasper shook his head. "Saige's account sums it up."

There were a few more routine questions, or what Saige supposed were routine questions when someone was missing. It seemed to her that the detective was eliminating possibilities, that he'd already concluded that Harriette's disappearance was due to the severe weather event.

Detective Bassi gave her a stiff smile and stood. "Thank you, Miss Wolvercraft."

"What happens now?" Aunt Prue piped up.

"A recovery mission is being organised as we speak. Ashvall has a small SAR group. It's mostly volunteers, but we'll search the Hauteville Woods until it's no longer safe to do so."

Aunt Prue's lip trembled. "SAR?"

"Search and Rescue, ma'am."

Saige's pulse picked up. She hadn't failed to notice that Detective Bassi had said "recovery mission," not "rescue mission." He really did think Harriette was dead.

Saige knew it was true in her bones. She passed Jasper a tacit let's-get-out-of-here look. She was desperate to have another search through the notebook.

Detective Bassi and Officer Hammond left, far too resigned and slow for Saige's liking.

Aunt Prue paced across the room. "I've decided to pack

a few things and go to the house. I'm bringing Mr Bubbles with me. These storms... he's terrified."

Saige looked at the ginger tabby asleep on the sofa. He hadn't moved once except to glare through slitted eyes at everyone, annoyed by the disturbance.

Terrified indeed.

Aunt Prue aimed a hesitant glance at the clock. "Go back to the house, Saige. Get the next coach."

"Of course." She hung her head, knowing the lie would be evident in her eyes.

She had till 2:00 p.m.

Plenty of time.

SAIGE STEPPED OUT INTO THE RAIN. AUNT PRUE had offered her an umbrella, but honestly, there was no point. The downpour had already doubled in strength and speed. She jogged down the stone path into the street.

Jasper trailed behind her. "Okay, what's going on? Why did you look so guilty back there?"

She raised her eyebrows at him but kept walking. "Listen. I have stuff to do here. Go back to the manor."

God, why did he have to follow her all the time like a lost puppy? This sort of commitment years ago would have made her happiness climb higher than the moon, but now his clingy, dependent attitude was really getting on her nerves.

He has a girlfriend. Keep your distance from him.

Do not let old feelings rise.

Jasper crossed his arms. "You have stuff to do in town? In the pouring rain? Just fancy some shopping, do you?"

His long legs meant he easily kept up to her stride as she hurried along the zebra crossing into town. The street ahead was empty, doors shut and windows boarded up in preparation for the storm. It was strange seeing Ashvall abandoned, like Saige had really stepped into a ghost town. The sign for the White Horse Pub swung in the heavy wind, the galvanised bracket groaning in complaint. The once lively cafés and bakeries seemed lonely without their Parisian-like atmospheres on display. Normally, stagecoaches and horse-drawn carriages passed by every few minutes, offering expensive rides for tourists. Everyone had gone, huddled up in their homes or seeking shelter at Wolvercraft Manor or the town hall. It made Saige afraid that what she was about to do was a bad idea.

She shook the feeling off.

This place is still safer than Wolvercraft Manor.

Jasper watched her with an anxious stare, as though he were afraid her hostile attitude would make her combust into flames. "Come on, Saige. We're partners in crime in this. Let me help."

Partners?

The word infuriated her.

Jasper must have picked up on her aversion, because he stilled. Rain flattened his hair to his forehead, making him appear more boyish and uncertain. "What did your brother say to you back at the gazebo, exactly? You've been acting strange ever since."

That was a conversation she really didn't want to get into. "None of your business."

She ducked beneath the awning of an art gallery and took out Harriette's notebook from her hoodie. "If you insist on helping me, then take a look at what I found.

Harriette has been documenting my family history for years, it would seem." She opened the book. "There are articles in here about my family, dated back from the nineteenth century. Newspaper clippings from the *Ashvall Herald*. And images of Zoe with a red circle around her head."

Saige pointed to the picture.

Jasper's eyebrows shot up. "Did you steal evidence?"

"You're missing the point. Harriette Reynolds knew more than she was letting on. I think she knew exactly what this curse was but needed a final piece of evidence to prove her theory. She was going to tell me last night, but this... the curse got to her first." Her breath came out a little faster. "Jasper, I want you to go back to my aunt's house and make sure she arrives safely at Wolvercraft Manor. She shouldn't be alone."

"If there's anyone who shouldn't be alone, it's you."

Saige shut her eyes. She was too tired to argue. And besides, she really didn't want to be alone in this. It was a pity that it had to be Jasper, but she knew it was safer to have company than to be isolated should something go wrong. And if Saige went ahead with this next step, something could very well go... wrong. "Fine. Just try not to get in the way."

Jasper's cheerful smile returned. "Excellent. Where are we going?"

She shoved the business card against his chest. "To see a clairvoyant."

EIGHTEEN

Saige and Jasper arrived in the heart of town. In the centre of Ashvall's high street stood the island's heraldic white horse, displayed in a magnificent marble centrepiece. Saige shivered. The statue gave her the impression of a tombstone. The beautiful rose and tulip garden surrounding the structure was flattened by the rain, the waterlogged soil sending muddy streaks across the cobbled road. Saige didn't care about stepping in it. Her boots were already filthy—what more could a little dirt do? She snuck a glance at Jasper's feet. His trendy white sneakers were mud-caked and brown, but he didn't seem to care.

He probably has another three pairs waiting for him back at the house.

Jasper studied the business card. A frown creased his handsome face. "Are you sure it's here? This doesn't really look like the place where an establishment like this"—he waved the card—"would be."

Saige examined the tightly crammed bricks-and-mortar

stores, the shop frontages narrow with large windows. The beautiful half-timbered buildings provided the high street with a medieval, fairy-tale charm. Each building had its own distinct flair, but they were harmonised in their variety. Saige had missed it. It was such a contrast to the modern buildings back home, where every new structure was designed to make a statement.

She pointed between two shops. "Right there."

She couldn't blame Jasper for missing it. The door was white and blended in with the white stone of the other shopfronts. Only a small gold-plated number told Saige this was the right address. She hurried forward and knocked.

Jasper wrinkled his nose. "This Mildred Templeton isn't very good with advertising, is she?"

Saige snorted. "I think that's the point."

She had thought Mildred Templeton would be a fraud and believed she'd find a shopfront decked out with ridiculous ornaments of the occult. Now she wasn't so sure.

Jasper jammed his hands in his pockets. "I don't think anyone's home. She's probably gone to the town hall."

Saige lifted the mail slot in the door and peered inside. She could just make out a long, darkened hallway, followed by a small burst of orange colour at the end. "There's a light."

"How can there be a light? The power is out."

"It's a candle."

She drummed her fist on the door again, louder and impatient.

There was the sound of a bolt being drawn back, and then the door flew open. A small, cantankerous woman appeared, her eyes drawn into a suspicious glare. She had a mop of messy grey hair, her face wrinkled and spotted from too much sun.

Not a local to Ashvall, then.

Gold chains glittered from her wrists, and several long, beaded necklaces hung from her neck. Saige couldn't make out exactly what she was wearing. It seemed to be a mishmash of colourful prints and florals, as though she'd collected clothing from various cultures on her travels and sewn them in one chaotic heap.

Saige attempted a small smile. "Mildred Templeton?"

The woman crossed her arms and examined Saige from the top of her drenched head down to her damp boots. She had a thick, Eastern European accent. "I wondered when you'd get here. You better come in."

Saige blinked. "I'm sorry. You were expecting us?"

Mildred inclined her head regally. "I was expecting you, Miss Wolvercraft. I knew you would come. I saw it in a dream. Him...." Her eyes travelled appreciatively over Jasper. "He's a nice surprise. Come on now. Both of you inside." She clapped her hands as though Saige and Jasper were two dogs trained to immediately obey her command.

They stepped into a dark, cluttered hallway and followed Mildred into a dining room. Several cats bounded away, frightened by the new arrivals. Saige counted at least four.

Mildred pulled out a chair for Saige. "Wait here and I'll be back with some tea. You're in luck that I have a gas cooktop and not electric." She disappeared through a beaded curtain.

"We don't need tea," Saige called, but there was no reply.

Jasper rocked back on his heels. "Maybe it's not the kind of tea you drink."

She raised her eyebrows at him. "What other tea is there?"

He elbowed her gently in the side, a smile in his eyes. "Maybe it's tea leaves. Maybe Mildred Templeton is going to read your fortune."

"I don't want my fortune read."

Her past hadn't been great. She was afraid of hearing what her future might be.

I'll end up alone with twelve cats. I'll die, and they'll probably eat me out of sheer starvation.

She shivered at the grim thought. "The entire thing is just a scam made on impressionable people."

Jasper's eyes twinkled. "You see ghosts, but you don't believe someone can read the future?"

Saige shot him a look, sour as poison, and focused instead on the room. She guessed the little house and shop combo must have been a bookstore once, because many of the walls in the room had built-in shelves, now decorated with strange and twisted adornments. She raked her eyes over them. There were carved buffalo skulls, dreamcatchers, rune stones, and crystals. The ceiling had been painted with the constellations of the zodiac. Hanging in a corner was an astrological tapestry with various symbols Saige neither understood nor recognised. The entire place reeked of incense, potpourri, and... something she couldn't place.

"What is that smell?"

Jasper shot her a supercilious look. "Are you really that naïve? It's marijuana, Saige. It seems your clairvoyant is involved in other extracurricular activities."

Mildred sauntered through the beaded curtain with a Moroccan tea set. Her eyes glinted with sly humour. "Are you afraid to sit down? You both look like frightened children on your first day at school."

Saige dropped into a chair. Jasper sat opposite her. The round table was draped in lace cloth, a nine-card tarot spread splayed out in what must have been a previous reading. Saige fidgeted on the fabric of her wet jeans. She didn't know what the images meant, but the cards certainly didn't appear to have foretold a happy future. One revealed a hanged man upside down. Another showed a grim reaper on horseback.

Mildred poured tea for each of them, then settled in her dining chair and smiled blandly at Saige. "I know why you're here. You're looking for the doctor."

Saige swallowed hard. "You know she's missing?"

"I do." Mildred waved to the cards. "That was the reading I gave Dr Reynolds yesterday."

"She came for a reading?"

Mildred sipped her tea. "Not exactly. She came because she had made a discovery. She needed answers, much like you need answers right now."

Saige took out Harriette's notebook and handed it to the medium. "She was studying Wolvercraft Manor." She took out the photos and newspaper clippings and spread them across the table. "Harriette texted me yesterday, said she had something to tell me. Something about the house."

Mildred put her teacup down. "It wasn't about the house, dear. Look at the images. Harriette's interest lay in your family, for that's where the Wolvercraft curse originated."

Saige bit down on her lip. "Do you know something about the curse?"

Mildred leaned forward, her gravelly accent a tad too theatrical for Saige's liking. "I know the Wolvercraft fortune was built on lies and deception." She rubbed her hands across the tablecloth. "Let me tell you about the origins of Wolvercraft Manor. Frederick George Wolvercraft was indeed a very respected and wealthy young man for his time. He loved elegance and extravagance. It's why Wolvercraft Manor resembles a royal palace. He travelled the world looking for just the right furnishings and ornaments. He purchased the surrounding farmland and had it transformed into formal gardens. He often went to London and would bring back a company of young men and women for the season. Parties. Balls. Dinners. All of this came at great expense, but Frederick could never do without. He had to have the finest, most fashionable, and latest things."

Her bright eyes bored into Saige's. "As you can imagine, Frederick's luxuries soon outweighed his means. He ended up bankrupt. To save his house and lavish lifestyle, he endeared himself to Theodosia Sinclair, a woman old enough to be his mother. He had met her on his travels to New York and brought her to the house to conduct seances, communicate with the dead, and to read fortunes at parties, a fad on the rise in the late 1840s. Theodosia was of Romani origin, which may have put a mark on her name, but she was also a wealthy American heiress, and that was enough to make her presence acceptable within Frederick's circle."

Saige slumped back into her chair. She shook her head, her eyes alight with mistrust. "My aunt Prue knows everything there is to know about Wolvercraft's family history. She's never mentioned any of this before."

As soon as the words slipped out, Saige realised it wasn't true. She remembered Aunt Prue's terrified white face the night before when they'd discovered Zoe's bridesmaids around a Ouija board, the game mysteriously set up for them in advance.

"That's impossible. This Ouija board belonged to Theodosia Sinclair. It's been missing for decades, presumed stolen."

Saige shivered in her damp clothes.

Mildred watched her with sharp eyes. Saige couldn't help but feel that the woman's gaze was penetrating right into her soul.

The medium dropped a sugar cube into her tea. "I imagine you have heard of the Roma Witch?"

Memories surfaced in Saige's mind. "Yes. She lived in the Hauteville Woods. She was one of the most powerful witches of the Hauteville Coven. I remember the stories from when I was little." She turned to Jasper to explain. "The dolls we saw in the woods... they're a sort of peace offering to the Roma Witch and her coven."

His head jerked up. "She's the one who stole children?"

Mildred's eyebrows shot up defensively. "She most certainly did not. That is an Ashvall legend entirely made up by the locals who feared Theodosia's powers."

"Powers?" Saige nearly laughed.

Spiritualists are a scam, and you're just an old biddy.

Mildred directed a levelling look her way. "Then what do you call you and me? Are we a scam?"

Saige froze.

That's not possible. Mind-reading... it's not real.

Mildred's lips cracked into a sardonic smile. "Yes, Miss Wolvercraft. You see ghosts. Just like your mother saw them. And your grandmother. And her mother before that. You, unfortunately, refuse to acknowledge your gift."

Saige tried to keep the anger inside her in check but failed. "It's not a gift. It's a nightmare."

"That is your opinion, but I use my talent to help others. To give them hope and courage. I accept spiritualism as a gift. It is my livelihood. I am not a scam. Theodosia Sinclair most certainly was not a scam either."

Saige's skin flushed. Heat filled her cheeks.

Jasper raised a hand. "I thought I should mention that I saw a ghost too. Two, actually. Am I a spiritualist?" His brown eyes stared hopefully at Mildred.

The clairvoyant's tone changed, much sweeter with Jasper. "You've only seen them at the manor?"

He nodded encouragingly.

"Never any before?" she asked with a raised brow.

His shoulders slumped a bit as he shook his head.

"Were you with Miss Wolvercraft when you saw these ghosts?"

"Yes."

"Then no, dear. Chances are her powers impressed upon you. It can happen with powerful spiritualists who remain untrained."

Saige ignored the jibe. She leaned forward, bringing the conversation back on topic. "Did Theodosia marry Frederick Wolvercraft?"

Mildred's eyes turned to the tarot cards on the table. They lingered on the grim reaper. "It was a private ceremony. No one was invited. Frederick kept her around long enough to obtain her money and then dismissed her."

"Dismissed? Do you mean he sent her away?"

Mildred made a noncommittal sound. "No one knows for sure. Theodosia was never seen again. It's assumed that she died. After all, Frederick Wolvercraft did remarry four months later... only for that bride to tragically drown in a bathtub."

Saige sat in silence for a moment. Her mind conjured unimaginable scenarios. "Do you mean to say that's how the curse started?"

Mildred grabbed a shawl that had been draped over her chair and wrapped it around her shoulders. "Theodosia was a talented spiritualist and a powerful witch. She was jilted, her money stolen. If someone did that to you, and you had the means to curse them, would you stand for it? Or would you enact your revenge?"

Jasper's face turned an awful shade of white. He wouldn't look at Saige. She couldn't help but feel a little satisfied. He had done something similar to her, and judging from his expression, he was starting to realise it.

She focused on Mildred. "I wouldn't curse anyone, no matter how badly they hurt me... but I can't speak for others."

Mildred's eyebrows drew together. "I have suspected for a long time that the curse wasn't only directed at Frederick but the entire Wolvercraft family. It flows from generation to generation, taking brides and wives."

"But not all." Saige frowned into the candlelight. "Not all the women who have married into the Wolvercraft family have died. Why do you suppose that is?"

Mildred aimed a sad smile at her. "The curse was made from a broken heart and directed toward those who were in love. Many marriages over the years were made as an alliance… a business arrangement. There was no sentiment involved."

"Which was why the curse never claimed them?"

Mildred nodded. "Dr Reynolds figured that out. She came across an archived newspaper journal that announced Frederick and Theodosia's engagement. Here."

Mildred wandered out of the room and returned with a printout of an old, photographed newspaper. Various parts of the text were circled in red, with the same illegible notes that Saige recognised as Harriette's handwriting. Mildred pointed to a passage and read aloud. "The engagement of Ms T Sinclair to Mr Frederick George Wolvercraft was recently made public. The wedding will take place in a private ceremony in June." She dropped the article on the table and returned to her seat. "Harriette knew enough about Ashvall's history to know who Theodosia was. She just needed me to confirm some of the minor details. That's why she came to visit yesterday afternoon."

Saige sensed Jasper's eyes on her. He looked away the moment she turned to him, his gaze on the medium. "How do you know so much?"

It was a good question. Saige waited for the answer.

An amused glint lit up Mildred's eyes. "Because Theodosia Sinclair was my ancestor. And I have her journal."

NINETEEN

Saige traced her fingers along the journal. "She recorded everything. Every detail of every day."

Theodosia's journal was still in good condition on the outside, but inside the pages had aged, the cursive writing faded to a dull brown. Saige had to bring the candle close to read it. Each entry was a personal and intimate account of Theodosia's thoughts and feelings. There were hopes, dreams, ambitions. Guilt tugged inside Saige. The woman was long dead, but somehow reading her journals still felt intrusive.

Mildred smoothed her mop of curls back. "She was a socialite but also a very private woman."

"There doesn't seem to be any detail about Frederick Wolvercraft. She writes a few times that he's handsome and a suitable match, but that's it."

Saige found that strange.

If you love someone, you'd be bursting with such happiness that surely you'd record it in your journal.

Her eyes inadvertently turned to Jasper. He was

looking at her. The intensity in his stare made her heart fumble.

A slow grin spread over his face. "Maybe Theodosia married for the title. Maybe there was no love involved."

Mildred rubbed a hand across her eyes. "It's possible."

Saige turned another page in the journal. "What's this?"

She lifted a black-and-white photograph that was faded and grainy. Most of the background had been washed out, but the three subjects in the forefront were clear. There was a man on the right who Saige instantly recognised as Frederick Wolvercraft, an older woman in the centre in a stunning dress with lavish furs, and a young girl on the left whose smile was bright, her hair dark, long, and sweeping over her shoulder in thick waves. She couldn't have been any older than seventeen. Saige paused. It had to be a trick of the camera, or simply the aging of the photo, but the girl's eyes were black shadows that seemed to hold in secrets. An intense wave of darkness slid over Saige like a shadow, but it vanished in an instant.

She passed the photo to Mildred. "Who is this girl?"

The clairvoyant put on a pair of winged cat's-eye glasses and examined the picture. Her lips pinched. "That's Theodosia's daughter, Anna Sinclair."

"Theodosia had been married before?"

Mildred nodded. "She was a widow. She had her husband's wealth and an inheritance that made her a target for many a man."

Jasper snorted. "Doesn't sound like you have a very high opinion of men."

Mildred turned on him so fast, Saige wondered how she didn't have a neck ache. "I don't."

His lips tipped into a faint smile, his voice a whisper. "That would explain all the cats."

Saige kicked him under the table. He glared back at her. His hair, which had started to dry, stuck out wildly around his head. Saige hated that he had the messy rock star look down to perfection. Her hair, on the other hand, had turned into a frizzy mess suitable for a bird to nest in.

A quiet shudder passed over Saige that she believed had nothing to do with her wet clothes. She turned back to the other woman. "What happened to Anna?"

Mildred straightened in her chair. One of her cats jumped into her lap and settled into a comfortable ball. She petted it, the dining room filled with appreciative purrs. Mildred looked at Saige with sad, almost kind eyes. "No one knows for certain. After her mother's disappearance, it's said that Anna returned to America, possibly to live with her grandparents."

"Frederick Wolvercraft never helped her?"

"No. I daresay Frederick was the one who instigated her return to America."

Saige slumped back in her chair, disappointed that she had such an arsehole for an ancestor. Her family's legacy, their fortune, was never really theirs. It had been stolen from a widowed woman and the rightful heir. Shame twisted through Saige's veins. "Do you think Frederick... did something to Theodosia?"

Mildred chuckled low under her breath. It wasn't a pleasant laugh. "If you mean murder, then yes, I believe Frederick was most certainly capable of it. Harriette thought so too. That's why we attempted a summoning yesterday afternoon."

Saige nearly fell out of her chair.

Jasper was caught mid-sip and spluttered tea over the table. "I'm sorry, did you say *summoning*?"

"Yes." Mildred stroked her cat absently. "It wasn't successful. We couldn't make a connection with Theodosia. But"—her eyes lingered on Saige—"perhaps Theodosia might be willing to make an appearance if a direct descendent of Frederick's were to, say... be included in the summoning."

Saige opened her mouth, but Jasper interjected before she could get a word out. "Absolutely not. Saige isn't to be involved in any whacky, conjuring, creepy, incantation shit."

Saige returned his gaze with a flat stare. "You speak for me now, do you?"

He flinched.

Mildred's lips tightened. "Very intelligent word choices, Mr Young. I assure you, it's perfectly safe."

His face turned an angry shade of red. "Oh really? It's so safe, in fact, that Harriette can no longer be found."

Mildred ignored him. She turned her beady eyes on Saige, unblinking behind her glasses. "It's up to you, my dear."

Jasper stared at Saige, his eyes pleading silently not to do it.

Saige was divided. She wanted answers, but her stomach tangled in fear every time she thought about a summoning. After all, nothing good ever came out of them in the films she'd seen. Still, she couldn't continue to live like this. Afraid. Alone. Hopeless. Surrounded by a presence she couldn't explain but knew was evil.

She shut her eyes, gathering her thoughts.

If we do this, I might get the answers I need.

I might learn how to break the curse.

I might have a chance for... happiness, whatever that might look like.

She opened her eyes. Her breath was loud and rasped in her ears. "Okay. Let's do it."

MILDRED LIT MORE CANDLES AND TOOK A PEN AND notebook out from a set of drawers. She placed them on the table in front of her.

Saige wondered what the pen and paper could be for.

Mildred smiled kindly. "In case Theodosia wants to communicate."

Jasper shot his eyes skyward. "All ghosts are into writing. Did you know that, Saige?"

Mildred sat down with a heavy grunt. "If you do not wish to participate, young man, you can wait in the parlour."

"The parlour! I'll have the head steward bring me tea in there, shall I?"

"There's no need for sarcasm. If you do not wish to be here, leave."

Jasper's eyes found Saige's, deadly serious. "I'm staying."

The heavy lines in Mildred's face contorted into a grimace. "Fine. But do exactly as I say. Better still, keep your eyes shut for the entire time, please?"

He gave her a sarcastic salute. She glared in return.

Saige watched the pair with nervous interest.

Looks like Jasper's handsome qualities are no longer working in his favour.

She wasn't sure if that was a good thing or not.

Mildred's voice dropped to a whisper. "Join hands, and whatever you do, don't let go. By linking hands we cast a protective circle. If you break the link, you set the spirit free. Theodosia's end was a tragic one. I can't guarantee she won't be... malevolent."

Jasper shot her a contemptuous stare. "How comforting."

Mildred pointed at him. "Not a word. I mean it."

The three of them reached across the table and clasped hands. Saige's fingers trembled in Jasper's. Despite his convictions against a summoning, his skin felt smooth and warm. Her own were clammy and cold, fear and excitement tingling their way to the tips. Mildred's hand was firm by comparison.

She's done this many times. She knows what she's doing.

The thought still didn't give Saige much comfort.

Mildred spoke in a low voice that sounded like a chant. "Theodosia Sinclair, we invoke you to come forward to dwell among us. We seek answers about your tragic demise. We wish to know your story. We do not wish you harm. In exchange, we ask that you do not harm us in return."

Saige's breath was stolen from her lungs. The deathly silence in the room was unnerving. The patter of rain outside grew louder. She wondered if it had started to hail.

A candle flickered. Then another. Saige exchanged an uneasy glance with Jasper. She knew from the way he bristled that he wanted to tug his hands free and leave the room, carrying her away with him. She supposed it said something that he remained.

The temperature plunged. Several of the candles blew right out.

Mildred's jaw tightened. "Theodosia Sinclair, if you are present, make yourself known."

All through the building, the windowpanes rattled. Saige didn't think it had anything to do with the weather outside.

We've made a connection.

She could feel it. A cold prickle on the back of her neck alerted her that there was something else present at the table.

Doors slammed. One of Mildred's cats darted out of the room.

Saige's hands were slippery with sweat. She wondered how Mildred and Jasper had managed not to let go of her fingers.

"Stay calm," Mildred cautioned, then, in a deeper, more histrionic voice, said, "Theodosia Sinclair, show yourself."

A strange, whispered murmur seeped from the walls. A rushing noise that sounded like a waterfall rose into a deafening crescendo. It blocked out every other sound, even the rain.

And then... nothing.

The room went deadly quiet again.

Saige's heart beat impossibly fast. An unpleasant smell had saturated the air, overcoming the incense, potpourri, and marijuana. It clogged her nose and made her eyes water. It smelt of death. It was what she imagined an open grave would smell like.

Mildred had her head down, her shoulders slumped.

Saige feared that something may have happened to her. "Mildred? Mildred, are you okay?"

She cast a frightened glance at Jasper. He stared back with perplexed eyes.

Saige squeezed the medium's hand. "Mildred? Please, can you say somethi—"

Mildred's head sprang up. A horrible gurgling rattle broke from her throat, like she was about to cough up blood. Her voice was not her own but a string of feral, scratchy noises. She turned her head in an unnatural tilt, opaque eyes staring straight into Saige's.

"Saige Wolvercraft." Mildred's tone was a guttural cry. "You must pay for the sins of the father."

A claw of ice fastened around Saige.

Jasper's fingers wound so tightly around hers, she was sure it would cut off her circulation. "Jesus! She's possessed!"

Saige felt Jasper's hand start to slip away. She held on tightly. "You break the circle, you let the ghost out. We have her contained."

"You're an expert now, are you?"

Saige didn't understand how she knew, but she sensed it was right. She stared at Mildred, or the thing that had taken hold of her, ignoring the cold, burning uneasiness inside her. "Theodosia, did Frederick Wolvercraft murder you? Is that why you cursed my family?"

Mildred let out a growl, animalistic and unnatural.

Saige took that as a yes. "What do I have to do to break the curse? What is it that you want?"

Mildred slammed her head back against the chair in a high, cackling laugh. "Pay the sins of the father."

Saige wasn't only scared but frustrated now. "What does that mean?"

Mildred's face pinched into wrinkles. The small woman appeared demonic.

Saige tried another approach. "Where is Harriette? Did you hurt her? Did she find out something you didn't want her to know?"

She seriously worried Harriette had discovered a secret about the family curse. A secret Theodosia had wanted to remain concealed.

What if Theodosia doesn't want the curse broken? What if this is what she's chosen for her afterlife. To watch the Wolvercraft family suffer for all eternity.

Mildred thrashed about in her chair. Her nails dug into Saige's flesh. "Dr Reynolds got too close. Dr Reynolds... is in the ground."

Jasper sat bolt upright. "Are you saying she's dead?"

Saige's mouth tasted sticky. She'd suspected it, but hearing it confirmed sent a spasm of remorse through her gut.

Spittle flew from Mildred's mouth as her lips pulled back in a nasty smile. "No one escapes the curse. She. Knows. She. Knows. She. Knows. She. Knows. She. Knows. She. Knows."

"Who knows?" Saige intervened. "Who is *she*?"

Mildred gasped so loudly that Saige saw all the way to the back of her throat, spotting her black molars. The medium's eyes rolled back in their sockets, and her breathing turned ragged. As though a puppeteer had let go of a marionette, Mildred fell in a boneless heap on the table.

All the colour in Jasper's face had vanished. "Is she dead? Oh geez. What are we going to do with all her cats?"

Saige stared at him, unable to comprehend his asinine comment.

He's in shock. People behave strangely when they're in shock.

She let go of Mildred's hand and reached for the phone in her pocket. "We need to call an ambulance."

She'd dialled two numbers when Mildred sprang up in her chair like a corpse straight out of the ground. The sudden movement elicited screams from Saige and Jasper.

Mildred blinked, startled by the noise. "My goodness. What happened? Did we make a connection?"

Jasper stared at her with his mouth open. "Yeah, you could say that."

Mildred rubbed a hand across her eyes. "You can let go now. The summoning is over."

For a moment, Saige didn't understand, and then she realised her hand was still clasped tight in Jasper's. She pulled away, quick to avert her eyes from his.

Mildred stood up, scrambling to grip the back of her chair. "I apologise. I don't feel so well. Perhaps I should lie down."

Jasper hurried out of his seat and caught the woman before she fell. He carried her through the beaded curtain to the lounge, Saige jostling behind, then set Mildred gently on the couch. She was asleep. Or unconscious. Saige hoped it wasn't the latter.

Jasper tapped his fingers on the table. "I think we should call that ambulance after all."

Her hands shaking, Saige dialled the emergency number.

The ambulance came. The paramedics transported Mildred on a stretcher through the rain, then secured her inside the vehicle, placing an oxygen mask over her face. Saige thought that didn't bode well. She watched from the lounge room window, struggling to swallow the metallic build-up of saliva at the back of her tongue.

Is this my fault?

Jasper was feeding all the cats. "They just keep popping up from everywhere," he cried from the kitchen. "How many cats does this woman own?"

The least they could do was make sure Mildred's animals were tended to. Saige was only partly relieved to learn from one of the paramedics that this wasn't Mildred's first visit to the hospital. They would be able to contact her next of kin, a daughter called Sarah who lived on the other side of the island. That was at least one thing Saige didn't have to worry about. She wouldn't have known where to start otherwise.

She walked around the lower floor, surveying the windows and making sure they were properly shut. Then she checked the bedrooms upstairs. Two cats were sleeping in the main room, curled into two fluffy balls in the middle of a large bed. They didn't even move except to look at her through slitted eyes. Saige checked the window and made sure it was secure. Lightning flashed outside, causing yellow dots to dance across her vision.

"Saige."

She jumped at the voice behind her. She fancied she could even feel cool breath on the back of her neck, but when she twisted around, there was nobody there.

Her heart thumped erratically against her chest.

The voice had been soft. It had sounded like...

Mum.

Something small dropped from the overpacked book-shelf to her right. She crept forward to take a look. It was a plain black book with an embossed sigil on the front. Saige picked it up and flicked through the pages. What appeared to be handwritten spells filled the volume. Saige had read enough about mythology to know this was a grimoire. A spell book.

On the inside cover in the corner was a name.

The Roma Witch.

Saige nearly dropped the book. She couldn't breathe, the air seemingly lodged in her lungs.

Jesus. Did this belong to her? How the hell does Mildred have it?

She went to put it back on the shelf, then second-guessed herself.

What if there are answers inside?

It was far too convenient that it had just fallen from the bookcase.

Okay, Mum. I trust you.

Saige pocketed the book, ignoring the queasy sensation of guilt in her stomach, and made her way downstairs.

"All secure?" Jasper asked when she met him in the hallway.

"All secure."

"Do you think the cats will be all right? You know, with the upcoming storm?"

Saige almost smiled. Almost. "They'll be fine. But I'll try and find a number for Mildred's daughter. She can come and get them."

It took some searching, but finally they came across a small address book in the kitchen and found Sarah's number. Saige hoped the call would go unanswered and she'd be able to leave a voicemail. She was grateful when Jasper followed one of the cats out into the hall to pet it. She didn't want him to hear her balls this up, which she no doubt would do.

How do you tell someone you're partly responsible for putting their mother in hospital?

Sarah picked up on the fourth ring. "Hello?"

Mentally cursing, Saige took a deep breath, introduced herself, and explained the situation.

SAIGE RETURNED TO THE HALL, DEJECTED AND tired. "Sarah is going to the hospital, and then she'll come over here and stay with the cats."

Relief shone on Jasper's face. "Okay. That's good."

"Since when have you liked cats?"

One of the black tabbies was rubbing itself against Jasper's legs and enjoying a nice back scratch from him. "I've always liked cats."

Saige was positive that wasn't always the case. She looked at the time on her phone. "Jasper, it's three minutes to two!"

We're going to miss the last coach!

The pair clambered out of the house into the grey, swampy afternoon. Saige locked the door and dashed into the rain after Jasper. She'd return the key to Sarah or Mildred when she recovered. Or when the storm was over. Whichever came first.

Part of the high street had flooded, the puddles now the size of small, shallow ponds. They took a narrow laneway down to the seafront to the bus stop. The street was empty, but it was madness to even risk standing on the road. The tumultuous sea smashed against the promenade, the waves so powerful that Saige feared they'd rip the balustrade apart. The fiercely briny wind and salt spray stung her eyes.

Jasper's face fell in disappointment. "We definitely missed the coach."

The bus stop looked lonesome and derelict in the rain. The roof seeped, and the wooden bench had a mini waterfall running off it.

There was meant to be a king tide that evening. Saige fretted that the little houses and shopfronts would be inundated by waves. The thought of all that water sent goose bumps up her arms. "Let's head back to the high street. We'll have to stay at the evacuation centre."

Jasper lifted his chin and stared up at the sky as though

the heavens were playing a cosmic joke on him. "Well, at least we'll be away from Wolvercraft Manor."

Saige wrapped her arms around herself. "That's what I'm worried about."

"What do you mean?"

"Zoe. She's fair game to the curse."

"Even if you were at the manor, I really don't think there's anything you could do about it."

Guilt weighed in her heart. Just like with Harriette's notebook, the large pocket in her hoodie seemed to burn where she'd stored her latest finds. "I might have been able to do something with these."

She carefully extracted the spell book and Theodosia's journal.

Jasper blinked in the rain. "Jesus, Saige. How many stolen goods do you have in that hoodie?"

"I think something wanted me to take the grimoire." She swallowed, hoping Jasper wouldn't think it was a far-fetched idea. "I think my mum showed me where it was."

She was almost too afraid to look at his response.

He raked his tousled dark hair out of his eyes. "Well, I'm not against having a ghost on our side for once, but are you sure this is a good idea... messing with something like this?"

"No. Of course not."

They stood there in silence, staring at each other in the rain. Saige's heart pounded. It always did around Jasper, but when he looked at her like that, she couldn't deny the monstrous attraction she still held for him. Her body quaked with nerves at the memory of what nearly occurred between them at the gazebo, and only the recollection of her brother's words snapped her out of the dream and back into reality.

She pulled away as tears she didn't want to deal with built inside her. "Let's head to the town hall. That's about a twenty-minute walk. Maybe half an hour with the rain."

He nodded, disappointment heavy on his face. He strode past her and started the ascent toward the laneway that would take them to the high street. Saige followed. The distance between them hurt.

This is the right thing to do. Jasper doesn't care about anyone but himself. I will not go through that pain again. And he has a girlfriend.

But every step Jasper took away from her felt like the wisp of a lovely dream she could no longer hold on to.

***

THEY WALKED THROUGH THE ONSLAUGHT OF RAIN. Saige had forgotten that the most direct route to the town hall meant going past Ashvall's gated cemetery. She'd always hated being near cemeteries. The sensation that eyes from a place beyond watched her sent her mind into a living nightmare.

If I'm a medium like Mildred said, I suppose that feeling makes sense.

I'm being watched.

By the dead.

She snuck a peek through the high cast-iron fence that had been taken over by crawling ivy. Mist swirled between the grey headstones, which seemed to jut out of the ground like crooked teeth. She wondered if any of her ancestors were buried here or if they were all in the family grave in the Hauteville Woods.

"Saige?"

She jumped.

Jasper was watching her, his face scrunched in concern. "Do you see something in there?"

"No."

She ignored the figures that moved in and out of the twisting fog, refusing to acknowledge her gift.

Seeing the dead. Great.

Her life was already far too complicated as it was.

A car horn tooted. A black cab pulled up to the curb beside them. The window wound down, and a bald man with a tweed golf cap poked his head out. "Are you kids all right? You shouldn't be walking out in this rain. It's too dangerous."

Saige almost laughed. *Kids?* She supposed compared to his age they really were just children. He had to be at least seventy.

Jasper smiled politely. "Archer? That's your name, right?"

Saige drew closer, recognising the cab driver from yesterday.

Archer winked at Jasper. "You have a good memory, kid. You off to the evacuation centre?"

"Could you give us a lift? I can pay you."

Archer waved the suggestion off. "Never mind that. Get inside."

Saige and Jasper settled into the back seat and strapped themselves in.

Archer forced the cab into a small burst of speed, the mad chatter of the windscreen wipers doing a poor job of creating visibility through the rain. "I'm just out here doing a final round in case anyone was stranded. Lots of retirees in Ashvall who need the extra help. It's lucky I found you kids. I was just about to head home. I have my daughter and grandkids there."

Saige pressed back into her seat, wishing to close her eyes and rest, but her moral compass was spinning. She couldn't let this opportunity slip away. "Do you think you could take us to Wolvercraft Manor instead?"

Jasper gripped the seatbelt, his knuckles white. He shook his head at her.

Archer shot a glance at Saige through the rear-view mirror before settling his eyes back on the road ahead. "The lane is windy and narrow to the house, miss. With all this rain, well... it's risky."

"Of course. I understand. It's just...." She heaved a long sigh. "I have a child waiting for me there. She's with family, but I know she'll want me."

Archer's shoulders tensed. "I understand, miss. Children come first. I'll get you to the manor."

He flicked on his indicator and made a slow U-turn down the street.

Saige only felt marginally guilty. She knew the child trick would work, but Jasper's razor-sharp stare cut her deep. She'd never seen him look at her with such... disappointment. Turning away, she focused on the rain outside the window.

How dare he judge me? He's lied enough in his lifetime.

Archer stopped at a set of lights that were out, did a quick look for traffic, and continued down the road. "So how old is your sweet little girl?"

He wasn't staring at Saige in the mirror. He was staring at both of them.

Saige was lost for words for a moment before she finally opened her mouth. "Oh, we're not—"

"She's six," Jasper interrupted. "Loves her mummy and daddy more than anything in the world." He pointed his thumb at Saige. "Can you believe she didn't even tell me about my daughter until recently?"

Saige caught the teasing, acerbic tone in the words.

Archer kept his eyes on the road. She could tell he didn't know what to say to that.

She leaned forward to the cab driver, hoping to change the topic. "Thank you for taking us to the manor."

Archer's good-humoured laugh filled the vehicle. "I can't let a little girl worry over her parents, now can I?"

He gingerly steered the car through another intersection, careful in the rain, which seemed to have doubled in intensity.

Saige stared through the window up to the sky. Cruel flashes of lightning zigzagged through the plum-shaded clouds, the atmosphere charged and tense. She didn't doubt the weather prediction. This storm was going to be bad. She could feel it.

They left St Albert Port, past the pastures and green farmlands, the road narrowing as they climbed to higher elevation. Archer drove about ten miles below the speed limit, which was annoying, but Saige understood the preventive measure. Dense trees packed them in from either side of the road. Saige could see nothing but the vastness of the Hauteville Woods and storm clouds sprouting above the treetops.

Archer had the heater on, but the hairs on Saige's arms

still stood stiff from cold. She blew warm air on her fingers. The tips were wrinkled like a soaked prune. She imagined her toes in her boots hadn't fared much better. She'd left her rain jacket at Aunt Prue's and was grateful she'd decided to wear her waterproof hoodie, but it still didn't stop the cold from sinking into her marrow.

"Not long now, folks." Archer careered the car gently around a bend.

A deafening screech met Saige's ears. She looked up in time to see Archer steer the wheel hard left, the back of the cab fishtailing through the hammering rain, sending them spinning across the road. The wheels locked, the car probably leaving tyre treads scorched in the tarmac. She caught a brief glimpse of Archer's white-knuckled hands gripping the wheel, then Jasper latching on to the granny handle as he slammed into the side of the vehicle. She experienced her own weightlessness, her body lifting from her seat, the belt the only thing keeping her secure.

It all played out in painfully slow seconds before the car swerved to a drastic halt in the middle of the road, the engine rattling. Saige swallowed gulps of air. Her stomach felt like it had flattened to a pancake. She stared through the rain. They were facing the opposite direction, back the way they'd come.

Archer turned to them, his skin ashen and his eyes wide in shock. "Sorry about that. That was messy but necessary. Otherwise, we might have all been drowned." He stole a sad glance at Saige. "I'm sorry, miss, but we're not going to be able to get you to your daughter after all."

Saige opened the door and scrambled out of the car. The road behind them was flooded by a destructive stream of fast-moving water. She knew the road dipped here, but she didn't realise just how low. There was a creek not far. It amazed her that it could have turned into a raging river in so short a time.

Jasper slid out of the car. He stood next to her with a satisfied grin. "Back to the town hall, then? How disappointing for our daughter."

She debated a snide comment, but she was too tired to put any effort into it. "Archer just assumed. I didn't think he'd do that."

His eyes pinned her in place. A muscle in his jaw twitched. "Come on, Saige. Look at the sky. Let's head back. We're putting Archer in danger too."

She swept her gaze to the trees. In the fierce wind, their branches came alive, appearing like fingers beckoning her to come forward. Saige thought about the grimoire in her pocket. Her mother had shown it to her for a reason. There had to be answers inside. Perhaps a way to break the curse. Saving Zoe meant saving her brother pain and heartache. That was worth it.

She exhaled a shuddering breath. "I'm going to the manor. It's only about three miles from here, and I know the way through the woods."

"Are you serious?" Jasper's laugh wasn't quite on pitch. "There's a frigging creek in the woods that's broken its banks."

"There's a footbridge."

"It could be flooded."

"I'm doing this. Get back in the car. Go to the town hall."

Jasper blew out a silent sigh. "You're crazy. You know that?"

He wandered back to the cab while Saige tried to

ignore the empty feeling inside her. She faced the woods, unnerved by the mist that swept through the dark foliage.

I can do this on my own. I have *to do this.*

The engine revved. The sound of the car accelerating downhill grew fainter.

She tried her hardest to keep her emotions inside, but a small tear leaked out. She reluctantly delved into the trees.

"Wait up," a voice called from the road.

She spun around and gave a short, startled laugh.

Jasper walked right past her into the thick fold of the forest, his head held high. "Let's get this over with. I am craving a warm shower, warm pyjamas, and a warm bed. Archer thinks we're mad, by the way." His voice dropped an octave. "He also thinks we're good parents. I'll let your guilt brood over that for a little while, shall I?"

Saige hurried after him. She wanted to frown at Jasper. She wanted to appear annoyed, but deep inside, she was grateful he was with her.

I don't want to be alone. That's all it is. There's nothing more to it.

But she knew it was a lie.

TWENTY-ONE

Saige had always thought the Hauteville Woods were beautiful... because scary could be beautiful, and that was what she found so tragic about it. The woods lured people in with a false sense of harmony, of earthy scents and pure air, while roots and branches waited to snare, hang, and entangle victims like a spider's web. At least, that was the way the woods had always felt to her. She didn't think there was any part of this island she could trust anymore.

Jasper shoved his hands underneath his armpits as he walked beside her, his heavy breath expelling from his mouth in white clouds. Whenever he saw her looking at him, all he seemed to manage was a weak smile. They slogged through the woods in silence, too exhausted, cold, and damp to talk. Fog crept up the tree trunks. Freezing precipitation rained down. Saige feared if the temperature dropped any farther, which she was positive it would by nightfall, they'd be in very real danger of walking in snow.

The manor isn't far. I just need to find the bridge.

She made sure to keep the flooded creek within earshot, but walking beside it was a risk she was unwilling to take. "The bridge can't be far."

Jasper only nodded.

She walked faster, even though her legs felt as stable as cooked spaghetti.

There's a path somewhere that leads to the bridge. It's here somewhere. It has to be.

Panic sweat started to drench her forehead.

It has to be... right?

She wondered if the woods were similar to the manor, stretching its dimensions to keep them trapped inside.

Jasper's arm shot out over her shoulder, pointing through the trees. "It's there."

They tackled their way through the foliage. The violent, dangerous churn of water met them suddenly.

Saige faltered in her step.

No!

The gorge had always held shallow water, the stone footbridge a dreamy picture of a sublime English garden. But now both ends of the bridge were underwater, the arch seeming to point out like a lost island. The flooded creek moved so fast that Saige could no longer differentiate between the water and white foam. It reminded her of a spa bath, if a spa bath could ever go wild.

Jasper's brows pulled together. "Well, that's it. We're stuck."

"We're not stuck." Saige carefully stepped into the mud, spreading her arms to maintain her balance.

"What are you doing?" Jasper's voice sounded strained behind her. "We can't cross."

"What's the alternative? The temperature is dropping,

and the storm is getting worse. Out here, we'll die of exposure. We'll freeze to death."

She didn't wait for him to respond, because she knew there was no alternative.

She stepped onto the bridge, the current stronger than she'd anticipated but not strong enough that it knocked her over. Still, she was happy it wasn't any deeper. The raging surface lapped around her knees, splashing ice-cold water up her legs. Her boots felt heavier, her feet and toes numb as she waded through the water. Relief spurred inside her when she climbed onto the bridge's arch. Jasper shot her a reluctant stare and cautiously stepped into the rising stream.

If I can do it, he can do it. He has much stronger legs than me.

And yet, Jasper seemed to struggle.

Maybe he's... afraid.

She reached out for him. He graciously snapped up her hand, using her weight to pull himself out of the water. His eyes settled on her, almost as stormy as the sky above them. "I will never forgive you for this."

She gave him a droll look. "And there are many things I don't forgive you for."

His lips twitched. "And we're back to that again."

Annoyed by his tone, she strode into the water on the other side of the bridge.

"Careful, Saige. There might be a handrail, but I doubt it will do anything if the rapids catch you."

"Will you shut up? I'm trying to concentrate."

She focused on putting one foot in front of the other, but God, it was getting harder to lift her boots. The force of the water was stronger now.

She reached out for Jasper. "Take my hand. The current is fiercer here. We'll need to hold on to each other."

Their hands touched. Electricity seemed to sear her skin, thawing the cold in her chest.

Jasper waded into the water. This part of the bridge was submerged deeper. The surface of the water now rose to Saige's upper thigh. She suspected it would reach her hips soon, and if that happened, she and Jasper would be in real trouble.

The books.

She could feel Harriette's notebook, Theodosia's journal, and the grimoire pressed against her waist, secure behind her hoodie's waterproof zip. The current tugged at her legs. The stones beneath her feet were slick and mossy from age. One foot in the wrong place, one slip, and it would all be over. The books would be destroyed.

She trod forward, slow and careful.

We're nearly there. Just a few more steps.

The water reached up to her hips.

"Saige!"

The alarm in Jasper's voice made her freeze.

His eyes were wide, his face almost green.

She whirled around and caught what he saw. Panic climbed through every organ in her body. A tree was coming down the flooded creek, branches splayed. The storm, maybe even lightning, had likely caused it to topple. It wasn't a huge tree, but it was large enough that it would do damage when it hit the bridge. Saige had an image of herself and Jasper floating down the creek as bloated bodies, washing out to sea to accompany the little fishes.

She no longer cared about being cautious. Tugging

Jasper's hand, she loped the last few steps across the bridge. Her boots slipped in the bank's dank mud, but she managed to get her grip beneath her again.

Jasper wasn't so lucky. His cry alerted her that he'd fallen. Their locked hands were the only thing that prevented him from being snapped away by the rushing water. It caused Saige to topple. She rolled in the mud, dug her heels in until she found traction, and propelled all her strength into pulling Jasper out.

From the corner of her eye, she saw the dislodged tree approaching fast.

Oh God. No. Please no!

She bit her lip, straining against the pressure in her arms.

Jasper's gaze flicked anxiously to the tree. Emotions she didn't like swept over his face in a heartbeat—fear, regret, acceptance. His face slackened, his body heavier. He was giving up.

Angry tears swam into her eyes. "Don't you dare, Jasper Young."

You started this crazy journey with me when I didn't want you to, and damn it, you are going to finish it.

Maybe it was the fierce glare on her face, or a chemical trigger in his brain causing a last urgent need to survive, but Jasper managed to free his other arm from the water and gripped Saige's hand. He kicked and thrashed against the current while she focused all her energy into pulling him out. Jasper's feet must have found purchase on the bridge again, because like a cork popping out of a champagne bottle, he leapt out of the creek just as the tree swept past him.

Saige's relief was short-lived. She slipped into the mud, Jasper landing right on top of her.

For a moment, all they could do was look at each other. Gratitude and surprise shone in his eyes, and something else. She recognised it. Her insides squeezed.

Desire.

It was evident on his face.

And she was distinctly aware of how evident it was in her own body.

Her brother's warning at the gazebo flared inside her mind, so bright it could have been tattooed on her eyes.

She elbowed Jasper in the stomach. "Get off me."

He groaned. "Ouch. I just had a near-death experience, and that's the first thing you say."

"And you'll have a second near-death experience if you don't move."

He rolled off her, scrambling to get back onto his feet in the sludge. Saige wanted to slap his hand away when he reached down to help her, but she knew she'd never be able to get the strength in her legs to pull herself upright. The mud was like glue. She took his hand, making sure her fingernails bit deep into his skin. He winced, clearly not appreciating the gesture.

They plodded uphill onto less slippery ground, searching for any refuge from the weather. The back of Saige's trousers was covered in mud. Leaves stuck to her hoodie. She doubted anyone would be able to recognise that she was a redhead. The muck gave the impression of black hair dye gone wrong.

Jasper stared at the branches that loomed above him. "Can you explain what happened back there? That was stupid and dangerous... and it nearly got us killed." His voice was cold and lethal.

She raised her eyebrows defiantly. "It was a risk we had to take. We made it. We're close to the manor, so stop complaining and let's keep moving."

He rubbed his hand across his mouth, doing a poor job of concealing an unamused snort. "There's more to it. You're acting like a real bitch."

"And why do you suppose that is? I'm stuck with the person who broke my heart."

She remembered one of the first lessons her mother ever taught her. *"Eventually, the truth will always come out. Sometimes it's just too hard to keep all that emotion contained."*

Elaine Wolvercraft was right.

Saige gulped down lungfuls of air. It was crisp and sharp against her tongue. She told herself that was what made her cry.

Jasper's sharp brown eyes studied her for a few beats. "Saige, I am sorry, truly, about what I did. Trust me when I say that I have lived with guilt every day since I left. But can we just... talk about what's going on here?"

"Going on?"

"Yes, back at the gazebo. There was a moment."

"There was not."

His impatient glare made her squirm inwardly. "Don't pretend it didn't happen. We nearly kissed."

She stared down at her scratched, mud-smeared hands, unable to find her voice.

"Saige, your brother saw us."

"Yes, and Xav warned me about you. A pity that warning came years too late."

Not that she would have listened to her brother's caution when she was in high school... or the second time she and Jasper hooked up.

There will definitely not be a third time.

Jasper's eyes had lost their dark edge. "Come on, Saige. There's still something here... right?"

Does he actually sound hopeful?

She laughed, a pitiful sound to her own ears. "You haven't changed a bit, have you?"

Jasper stepped forward, then thought better of it. "I... I don't understand what you're saying."

"I'm talking about your current girlfriend. When things get too serious for you, you always find a reason to flee commitment. This time you're using me and my brother's wedding as the excuse."

Colour rose in his cheeks. "That is not true. I'm trying to—"

"Jasper, just grow up."

She was tired and overwhelmed. She had a curse to destroy.

Jasper's feelings are not real. He's using you as his excuse to escape his current relationship.

Do not get sucked in.

She continued her trek up the hill.

"Saige, wait. Just be careful. The ground doesn't look stable there!"

A sound she couldn't have possibly imagined in her worst nightmares ripped from beneath her feet. The ground cracked open around her. One second she was standing on leaves and earth, and the next moment she was plunging into darkness, into the unknown. She screamed until the wind was knocked out of her when she hit something solid.

Is that... concrete?

She wasn't sure. She couldn't see anything in the dark. For a frantic moment she was worried she must have hit her head and gone blind.

"Saige! Saige, are you all right? Saige! Can you hear me?"

She blinked against the saturated darkness, her eyes taking a long time to adjust. "Yes, I can hear you. I'm fine."

Apart from shock and a few cuts and bruises, she was okay. She had to be grateful for that.

How far did I fall?

She peered up at the opening. Rain clouds rolled through the trees above.

It's a sinkhole.

She grabbed her small flashlight from her pocket, amazed the battery still had power. Light cut through the dark. Her surroundings morphed into focus.

A tunnel.

Or a catacomb.

A network of exposed roots twisted across the ceiling and down the walls. What she had mistaken for concrete was granite and stone, the texture slimy and smooth from the rain. An earthy, dusty smell filled her nose. It was the scent of rot and abandonment. She remembered the myth about the Nazis. They'd supposedly forced Russian and Polish prisoners of war to build underground tunnels throughout the island.

"Jasper?"

His head appeared just above the aperture. His flashlight beamed down on her.

She climbed onto her feet to get a better look at him. "I think this is one of the Nazis' underground passages."

The tunnel had been hidden away, entirely forgotten, a long-lost secret for decades. Only the storm and rain and her careless footsteps had broken it out of its time capsule.

How is it that Jasper and I found the Nazis' secret torture chamber in the manor, and now we've discovered a tunnel?

Surely that isn't coincidence?

An uneasy sensation rolled through her gut.

She was starting to not believe in coincidences.

"Saige?"

Jasper's voice sounded strange.

She gazed back up.

His flashlight sent patchy rays through the downpour. "I don't think this was built by the Nazis. It's much older than that."

She scrunched her nose. "How do you know?"

"Because I recognise the stone. Saige, this is the same stone from that chamber. I think this tunnel connects with Wolvercraft Manor."

TWENTY-TWO

Saige was too stunned to process Jasper's words at first, but the more she reflected on it, the more she realised he was right. This tunnel led to Wolvercraft Manor.

But which way?

In her mind, she summoned a mental blueprint of the house. This tunnel had to be running parallel to Wolvercraft Manor right now, which meant either direction could have looped around to the house. She shone her flashlight to the left. Ugly streaks of water ran down the walls. Puddles had formed in dips along the ground. She aimed the light in the other direction. It was dank and miserable. A rat scurried along the ground and vanished into the darkness.

"Saige, are you okay?"

The concern in Jasper's voice sent a wave of guilt through her.

She failed to keep her voice calm. "I think we should explore the tunnel. Even if only for a little way."

She waited.

Several beats passed before she heard Jasper's response. "I think that's the stupidest thing you've said all day. I'm going to find a long branch to help pull you out of there."

Annoyance shot up from deep in her core. "We have to know how this tunnel links to the house. In the chamber that night, that... *thing* in the elevator... it was going somewhere before we interrupted it. What if it was coming down here?"

"All the more reason to avoid this place and get the hell away. I'm getting that branch. Don't move a step, Saige. I'm serious. There's a flooded creek not twenty metres away. That means water could be in the tunnel. I don't want you getting washed away."

She couldn't argue with that logic.

That's probably the most intelligent thing he's ever said.

But oh, how she wanted to explore. She hated unsolved puzzles. The haunting of Wolvercraft Manor was a jigsaw that needed piecing together. But she'd seen horror movies and read the books as well, and she knew it was never a good idea to wander into the darkness alone. She stayed put, using her flashlight to discern what was around her.

Come on, Jasper.

If she couldn't explore, then he could at least find that branch quickly and get her out of there.

She rubbed at her arms, trying to secure warmth within her. When she'd been out in the rain, she'd been moving on adrenaline. It had pumped blood hot through her body. But now that she stood waiting, the cold settled in. Her teeth chattered, and she cringed at the soreness that spiked along her shoulders.

She was just about to call out to Jasper again when a noise startled her. A wet pop, like a fish splashing in and out of water. She shone her flashlight in the direction of the noise. The darkness remained empty.

Something tickled up her spine, a sensation that she wasn't alone. She'd always sensed a presence around her, but this was different. This was the same feeling she'd had in the chamber. Evil.

Oh God! It's here!

Her hand began to tremble. The light shakily criss-crossed left and right.

Something was waiting in the dark just beyond. This wasn't a trick of her mind. She could see its faint outline. It appeared human-shaped, but at the same time… monstrous and unearthly, like something that had crawled out of the grave. And the smell. It was a potent, rotting odour, so overwhelming that Saige thought she could even taste it in her mouth.

A taunting cry broke from the darkness. Whatever it was, its voice greeted Saige's ears in a trailing echo. "Wolvercraaaaaaft."

A pale arm shot out of the dark.

Saige screamed.

The thing scuttled toward her. It was above her, beside her, behind her, always moving, always managing to skirt just beyond the flashlight. She heard its wheezy, gasping grunts, felt its sick, cold breath on the back of her neck. And then it had her by her hoodie, slamming her into the wall. Saige's face smashed into the hard stone. She felt blood trickle out of her nostril and squeezed her eyes shut, trying to flush out the fog that clouded her head. But she wasn't fast enough. The thing latched on to her ankle and dragged her across the wet stones. Saige didn't think she'd screamed so loud before in her life. The pain in her ankle was fire. She kicked and thrashed, to no avail. At some point, she'd lost her flashlight. It had rolled on the ground somewhere, causing shadows to dance across the walls. For a moment, she thought she saw a face with pruned, pasty skin, the eyes drained of colour, but it scurried back into the dark before she could be certain. Whatever it was, its fingers bit into her ankle deep enough to draw blood. Saige managed to roll onto her back and lash out with her other boot, surprised when the creature let out a demonic wail. It drew back, but she sensed it was just on the outskirts of her sight, ready to pounce again.

"Jasper! Jasper!" she cried.

Something long and crooked appeared before her. It took her a painful second to realise it was a branch. She grabbed it, forcing herself onto her feet, her ankle making a horrible, cracking sound.

"Pull me up!" she demanded. "Pull me up!"

She saw Jasper above, his lips pressed together as he exerted all his strength in wrenching her out. She was about a metre from the aperture when she realised he wouldn't be able to do it alone for much longer. Saige tugged on some of the exposed roots, grateful they were thick enough not to snap in her hand. She sensed the creature just beneath her, imagined talon-like claws scratching at the soles of her boots. It was shrieking impossible, inhuman screams.

Saige let out a cry of effort and hoisted her upper half through the opening. Jasper grabbed her jeans by the waistband and tugged her out of the sinkhole. He fell back, shock and exhaustion overwhelming his handsome face. She crawled through the mud as far away from the aperture as possible, then burst into tears. The tension inside her didn't subside. If anything, her heart felt like it might explode in her chest.

She looked at her ankle. She expected her flesh to be a bloody, macerated mess, but it was unharmed. The pain had vanished too.

A mind trick. A frigging hallucination!

The knowledge didn't calm her. It just made the creature a hundred times more terrifying than it already had been.

Jasper sat beside her. In her daze, she hadn't even heard him approach. He wrapped his arms around her shoulders. Fear had zapped her energy. Shock had crushed her strength. She broke down in his arms. All the pair could do was hold each other in the rain.

By the time Saige and Jasper reached Wolvercraft Manor, it was nearly dark. The light slipped away in the sky, replaced with churning clouds blacker than Saige had ever seen.

This was it. The storm everyone was worried about had arrived.

It belted its fury on the earth. Wind tore across the lawn, ripping up anything that was loose, and objects that were secure too. Lightning forked in multiple directions, so blinding that Saige couldn't tell where it struck.

But it was the house that frightened her the most. She

thought of it as being alive. A living, breathing creature, the threshold its mouth, welcoming them into its stomach.

Jasper's jaw clenched. "Are you ready for this?"

She gave a tiny nod.

It was a lie. She didn't feel prepared at all.

They walked across the lawn. The precipitation turned icy, enormous snowflakes drifting around them. When Saige looked back at the Hauteville Woods, all she saw was a whiteout of fog. The mist seemed to roll after them, casting an impenetrable wall around the grounds.

A strange feeling fluttered in her stomach.

The house has us now. It won't let go.

They finally reached the snow-covered driveway, Wolvercraft Manor towering before them. Icicles hung from the gables. Water sprouted from the twisted mouths of gargoyles. Wolvercraft Manor might have been Saige's ancestral home, but it was also a mausoleum to her family. There were souls trapped inside. The manor was as much a tomb as it was a house.

Staggering to keep her balance on the snow, she opened the front door and eased her way inside. Jasper trailed after her. When Saige shut the door, it felt final. It felt like the house had already won.

"WHAT ARE YOU DOING HERE?"

Saige was surprised by her father's outburst when she entered the drawing room. Jasper walked in and stood beside her, clutching at his elbows. There was snow in his hair, and the tip of his nose had gone red.

Saige paused, confused. "What do you mean?"

She listened to how quiet the house was. "Where is everyone? Are they all in the basement?"

The house seemed… empty.

But if everyone was in the basement, why was her family alone in the drawing room?

And why were the lights out?

Has the backup generator gone out again?

Derrick Wolvercraft was sitting beside his two sisters. He closed the book he'd been reading and brought his lantern forward, examining Saige's wet clothes and mud-streaked hair. "What the hell happened to you?"

Aunt Prue bit on her fingernail. She stared at Saige with an anxious question in her eyes. Aunt Violet awkwardly sipped from her cup of tea, taking a sudden interest in the carpeted floor.

Saige's brother was also present. Xav was sitting in an armchair, his lips strained, as though he were putting all his mental focus into fighting off a headache. His eyes shot daggers at Jasper.

Someone had started a fire. It was a welcome reprieve from the cold. Saige inched closer to the delicious warmth.

"I don't understand." Her eyes travelled from one person to the other. "What's going on?"

Derrick stood up. "I sent you a text message. I told you to stay away. To seek refuge at the town hall."

Saige checked her phone. She had no signal. "I'm sorry, I didn't get it."

He shook his head with indignation. "How did you get back here?"

She didn't answer.

"Oh, Saige!" Aunt Prue cried. "You didn't walk through the woods, did you?"

"Only a little of the way," she admitted. She left out the part about the flooded road, the creek, and the sinkhole.

Furious colour spread through Derrick's neck. "Saige, I am tired of you taking unnecessary risks. This has got to stop. Do you want to end up like your mother?"

She ignored the hurtful comment. "What's going on? Why aren't you all down in the basement?"

Derrick rubbed a frustrated hand down the side of his face. "I'll show you why, shall I?"

He led Saige out of the drawing room and through the lower level of the house. He opened the door to the basement, took his daughter's hand, and carefully guided her down the stairs. He stopped a few steps short of the ground and raised his lantern. The light wasn't particularly strong, the rays shining across the basement like the distant beams from a lighthouse. "Look."

Saige did. She drew in a sharp breath.

The basement was flooded. A foot of water gently lapped at the walls.

"It's getting deeper," her father confessed. "Xav and I spent all morning trying to figure out where the water was coming in, but we couldn't find anything. People couldn't stay here, so I had the coaches return everyone to town."

Saige's thoughts darted frantically. "So... everyone's at the town hall?"

"Yes."

"We're alone?"

"Yes."

She tasted an ironic laugh in the back of her throat. She and Jasper had fought so hard to return to the manor, to try and protect people from the curse, only for everyone to have left.

Derrick's eyes flicked over her face. She knew he wasn't really angry with her. He was just worried and afraid. He swallowed hard. "The power's out. The generator is down. But we have food. The taps are still supplying us with water."

"Why didn't you all go to the town hall? Why did you stay behind?"

She was actually grateful they had remained. She didn't like the idea of her and Jasper arriving to an empty house.

Worry lines creased around her father's eyes. "Zoe and the bridesmaids are ill. Dr Ahmadi was one of the wedding guests and kindly offered to stay to monitor them. He doesn't know what's wrong with them. He's never seen anything like it."

Fear fluttered through Saige's veins.

It's the curse.

"They're too weak to be moved. Xav refused to leave Zoe. I refused to leave him. My sisters refused to leave without the pair of us. So we're all here. Alone." He smiled nervously. "Come on. Let's get out of this cold basement."

Her father might have been putting on a brave front, but upstairs in the hallway, where the lantern was stronger, she saw his face go slack with defeat.

"Dad?"

"We'll be all right, Saige. I've had the windows in the second-level bedrooms secured. We'll all sleep in those rooms tonight. Now go have a shower and wash all the muck off you while we still have hot water."

He walked away with uneasy steps.

Saige stood transfixed, her thoughts frantic.

Great.

We're trapped in a haunted house.

The roads are flooded.
We have no phone signal.
We have no power.
And there's a storm battering down.
Yeah, Dad. We're going to be perfectly all right.

TWENTY-THREE

Saige shut her eyes and let the hot shower soak her body. She knew she should spend no longer than five minutes under the water. Without power or the luxury of a backup generator, the hot water wouldn't last long, and there were others in the house who wouldn't appreciate a cold shower. She washed her hair quickly, did her best to towel-dry it, and changed into a fresh set of jeans.

Maybe it was because the electricity was out, but back in her room, Saige distinctly felt that the temperature had dropped. Someone had boarded the window with temporary storm shutters. Even with a candle going, her room seemed abysmally dark. There was no risk of the window opening mysteriously, but Saige still didn't want to sleep in the room. At least not alone.

Out in the hallway, she found her brother leaning against the opposite door, massaging his temple.

"Do you have a headache?"

Xav jumped. The contours of his face tightened from exhaustion. "I took painkillers. They haven't kicked in yet." He pointed into the bedroom. "Dr Ahmadi is with Zoe right now. I can't go to bed until I know she's... comfortable."

"You make it sound like she's dying."

Saige immediately regretted what she said. For all she knew, Zoe and her bridesmaids really could be dying.

Xav tossed her an unappreciative stare.

"I'm sorry. That was insensitive of me." Saige traced her finger along a loose thread in her sleeve. "Maybe Dr Ahmadi will have good news. It can't be anything more than the common flu, surely?"

She hoped it was nothing more than the common flu, but when Dr Ahmadi returned, she knew it was much worse than either she or Xav was expecting.

The doctor didn't shut the door all the way, maybe to keep an ear out should his patient call back for him. The lantern he carried revealed all the hard lines in his face. His expression was flustered, as though he had a mathematical equation he had no idea how to solve. He dropped his voice to a whisper. "I have never seen anything quite like it. She's complaining of a headache and abdominal pain. There's much vomiting. She has a fever but says she's experiencing chills. Her glands are swollen. Even drinking water is difficult. The other young ladies have similar symptoms."

Xav's chest rose and fell with sharp, urgent breaths. "Is there anything you can give her."

Vertigo gripped Saige. This entire experience... well, it felt like she'd been transported to the manor's earlier years, where doctors paid house visits with tonics. Dark, difficult days where leeches were used to alleviate illness.

How many people have died in this house?

Dr Ahmadi's posture went stiff. "Apart from cold and flu tablets, which she's already taken six of today, there really isn't much that can be done other than rest, I'm afraid."

Saige saw how irritable her brother was becoming, his knuckles white where his fingers balled into fists. Cigarette smoke wafted off him. She wondered just how many of the supposed stress relievers he'd indulged in.

She stepped forward and intervened before he said something he'd regret. "What do you think it is?"

Dr Ahmadi snuck an awkward peek through the gap in the door, as though he was afraid his patient might hear him. He turned his attention back to Saige. "To me, well... it looks like scarlet fever, but of course, without a proper medical examination, I can't be certain."

Xav's jaw dropped. "Scarlet fever? Does that still exist?"

The doctor nodded. "It is incredibly rare."

Xav squeezed the bridge of his nose.

Saige realised she was shivering, and not entirely from the cold.

The curse... it wants to kill Zoe.

It will *kill Zoe if I don't do something.*

She doubted medical treatment would help. This illness sprang from supernatural means, which meant it would require a supernatural cure.

There has to be something in that grimoire. My mother wouldn't have shown it to me otherwise.

Her voice sounded thick and anguished when she spoke. "Is there anything we can do?"

The doctor silently nodded. "Keep your distance. Anything the young ladies have touched will be contaminated. Scarlet fever is very contagious. They will have to remain isolated. There really is nothing we can do but ensure they keep their fluids up and rest. When the storm finishes, we'll be able to get them the treatment they require."

Whatever small restraint Xav had held on to burst. "But the storm is expected to last for days."

Saige took his elbow, forcing him to take a step back. "I think Dr Ahmadi is right. Zoe needs rest, and so do you."

Her brother flinched. He opened his mouth, maybe to yell at her, but then his shoulders shook. He gave a relenting sigh. She couldn't remember the last time she'd seen Xav cry.

No. She could.

Mum's funeral.

Xav ground the heels of his palms into his bloodshot eyes. A single tear streaked down his cheek.

"Come on," Saige pressed. "There's a gas cooktop in the kitchen downstairs. I'll make you a cup of tea."

"There is? Which kitchen?"

"The original, down in the old servants' halls."

She fancied a cup of tea herself. And food. She'd need all her strength to attempt what she had planned later that night.

SAIGE DIDN'T KNOW HOW THE ORIGINAL household staff survived the cold in the servants' quarters. She knew this part of the house had been preserved for the tourist groups. Except for a new stove and cooktop for hygiene reasons, the downstairs hadn't seen much modernisation in the last hundred years.

Venturing past the sleeping quarters, scullery, pantry, and various larders, Saige and her brother entered the kitchen. It was an oblong room, dominated by a large kitchen bench where the household cook had once tended to the meals. Xav sat on a stool and hunched over the table, looking increasingly like a drunk brooding at a bar. Saige set to work with the tea. She boiled a pot of water on the gas cooktop and searched through the two commercial storage fridges that had been brought in for the wedding.

Probably not enough room for them in the upstairs kitchen.

Without power, she wondered how long the food would last. She found a loaf of bread, cheese, avocado, ham, and tomato and made two sandwiches.

They ate in silence. Xav picked at his food. Saige devoured hers and wouldn't have minded eating whatever her brother left. Apart from tea at both Aunt Prue's and Mildred's, she hadn't had anything all day. A headache had formed at the tip of her skull, but the food and tea helped. She already felt stronger. But her brother? Sadness seeped off him. His head drooped down, like he might have fallen asleep.

A worried stirring churned in Saige's stomach. "I'm sorry about the wedding."

He looked up. His voice took on an edge she'd never heard before. "Why? Evidently it wasn't meant to be."

"Maybe it's for the best. You can marry soon enough, just not here at the manor."

And far away from Ashvall, where the curse can't find you.

Xav smiled, but there was no warmth in it. "Yeah. If there even is a wedding."

"What do you mean?"

He tossed his head back and threw an aggravated sigh to the ceiling. "Zoe never wanted to get married at the manor. She blames me for all of this."

"She didn't?"

"No, of course not. You have met my fiancée, right?"

"Fair point."

"She wanted to get married in the Bahamas or someplace like that."

"So why did you come here?"

The temperature in Xav's cheeks rose. "Because that's what Dad wanted."

Saige's skin tingled ominously. "Dad?"

"Yeah. He wrote a letter to us. Told us it was our responsibility to honour the Wolvercraft name... to marry at our ancestral home or some crap like that."

"A letter? But why didn't he just call you?"

"I don't frigging know, Saige. The man is obsessed with family image."

She couldn't deny that part about him. The Wolvercraft legacy was everything to their dad. Sometimes she thought he didn't belong in this era and would have been better suited to living a century ago.

She bit her lip, pondering why their father always intervened. "I'm sorry, Xav. Let's not worry about the wedding, okay? Let's focus on surviving this storm and getting Zoe better. I, for one, would rather enjoy a trip to the Bahamas... but this time," she added with a bitter tone, "please don't invite Jasper Young to perform at the reception."

Xav jerked his head up. "I didn't invite Jasper."

"Then make sure your fiancée doesn't invite him."

"No, Saige… I meant neither Zoe nor I invited Jasper to the wedding. I hadn't spoken to him in years, and, honestly, I was surprised when he contacted me and asked to perform."

Saige was silent for a moment.

That did not add up with what Jasper had told her.

Why would Jasper lie to me?

Xav snorted, a low sound of amusement. "Probably used the wedding as an excuse to get away from his current girlfriend. You have been keeping away from him, haven't you?"

Saige swallowed her tea. It burned her mouth. "Of course."

"It's just… when you returned to the manor this evening, you looked like you'd spent the entire day rolling with him in the mud."

"Don't be crude."

"Well?"

She set her mug down. "We shared a cab back to the manor. The road was flooded. We had to hike the rest of the way."

Xav had his eyebrow raised. "If you say so."

They ate in silence.

Xav downed his tea and took a flask out of his coat. "Want some?"

Saige nodded.

Somehow, drinking seemed like the only way she'd survive the night.

After Saige made sure her brother finished his sandwich, crusts and all, she helped him back upstairs to his room and waited beside him until he fell asleep. His freckles were more pronounced in the lantern light, his pale skin soft beneath the tangerine glow of the flames.

I'm so sorry, Xav. You came here to get married, and now it looks like your bride might die.

She cringed, aghast by her own macabre thought.

No. I will do everything in my power to make sure that doesn't happen. The curse will not claim Zoe.

Saige tiptoed out of the room, shut the door gently behind her, and moved silently down the hall. Except for the resonant tick of a grandfather clock and the storm outside, everything was quiet. She imagined things moving in the shadows, imagined faces in the flashes of lightning, but blamed it on tricks played by the weather. The window at the end of the hall hadn't been boarded up. Maybe there hadn't been time.

Large, swirling flakes of snow drilled into the glass like flying bullets. She hurried to her bedroom, not wanting to remain in the hallway a second longer. Her hand paused just above the door handle as a frigid draft crept over her skin.

She turned around.

Zoe's bedroom door was open.

Did Dr Ahmadi forget to shut it?

She doubted it. He'd made it plainly abundant that no one besides himself was to enter Zoe's room.

But then... why is the door open?

Saige stepped forward.

Maybe Zoe, in a delirious state, could have felt feverish and overly warm. She may have wanted fresh air.

Saige stood in the doorway and examined the room. A pungent, sickly odour permeated everything. Apart from a small candle burning fiercely on a side table, the room was shrouded in shadow. It was a deep black... almost an unearthly darkness.

A small voice at the back of Saige's mind protested that this wasn't a good idea, but as if driven by a trance, she stepped inside.

Zoe was asleep on the bed, the blanket pulled back, her white nightdress soaked from sweat. Her face appeared as bleached as driftwood. Raised blotches ran down the entire length of her neck, chest, and arms, scratched red-raw. To Saige's horror, they were oozing. Zoe's long hair was splayed across her pillow. It no longer looked sleek and stylish but damp and knotted.

My God! Zoe.

You look like a plague victim.

For one terrifying moment, Saige thought Zoe might actually be dead, but then she saw the model's chest rise shallowly. Soft, wheezing spurts broke through her lips. Saige wondered whether there was too much fluid in Zoe's chest.

Perhaps I should get Dr Ahmadi.

She was about to leave when a bright flash of lightning lit the room. Zoe's wedding gown came into view. For the briefest second, Saige could have sworn a pale figure was inside it, arms long and loose by the bodice, but then another streak of lightning must have branched over the house, and the image disappeared.

Saige's heart resumed a normal beat.

Jesus, I really am jumping at everything now.

The dress was certainly an over-the-top garment and

something she'd never wear, but seeing it reminded her of an opportunity ripped away. She had searched for a wedding dress during her engagement, something simple and elegant. She'd been certain she'd found the right gown, but then Jasper's true colours had shown, and all her dreams had shattered.

Saige didn't want to be in this room anymore. The wedding dress was a reminder of a happy time that had crumbled into misery. She turned around, ready to run out the door, but slammed straight into a body.

She let out a stifled cry. Her foot slid out beneath her.

Arms gripped her. In the lightning, Jasper's face merged into focus. His expression shifted from pity, to disbelief, to shock. "Saige, what are you doing in here?"

She slapped his hands off her. "I could ask you the same thing."

"I saw you enter and thought, 'Jeez, that can't be good.' Do you want to get sick?"

"No, of course not. And I won't get sick. What Zoe has... it's the curse."

"Are you sure about that?"

"Yes."

Jasper fixed a steel-like gaze on the immobile woman. "I think you might be right. That there is something straight out of *The Exorcist*."

Saige punched his shoulder. "Quiet. She's waking up."

Zoe had started to stir. She mumbled something incoherent, words that didn't sound English. No, not a mumble. A chant! The more Saige listened, the more her heart throbbed. Fear prickled through every fibre of her body.

Zoe's voice was scratchy and hoarse. She arched her

back suddenly, legs ramrod straight, arms flapping about like fish out of the sea. Her head twisted at an uncomfortable angle. When she opened her eyes, there was nothing remotely human about them. They were black and ringed in red.

Saige inadvertently gripped Jasper's hand. "Out! Out now!"

She didn't have to tell him twice.

They ran into the hall, Zoe's demonic hymn resonating behind them.

TWENTY-FOUR

Jasper paced in the downstairs drawing room. It made Saige dizzy to watch him.

She shook her head, trying to remain composed and not appear frazzled. "Jasper, can you please sit down? I can't think with you prancing around like that."

His face went blank for a moment, as though he'd forgotten she was in the room. "Yes, sorry."

He sat beside her. Both of them listened to the wild thrashing of the storm outside. Each blaze of lightning, each clap of thunder sounded like it came from directly inside the house.

Saige's stomach rolled. She imagined herself on a luxurious cruise ship out at sea, waves pummelling down, determined to split the vessel in half. They might as well have been on a ship in the middle of nowhere for all it mattered. Wolvercraft Manor was just as isolated surrounded in its banks of fog and thick-forested terrain.

Jasper pressed his hands together, maybe to stop them from trembling. "How does someone recover from something like that? Did you see her body? The way it just... bent?"

Saige nodded. She really didn't want to remember the disturbing movement.

"What if we can't help her?" Jasper whispered.

"We can." Saige took out the grimoire from the pocket in her knee-length cardigan. She'd decided to carry it with her everywhere. "This has to have an answer in it. My mother gave it to me for a reason."

"That's if your mother is on our side."

Saige gazed at him for a long time, trying to figure out his meaning.

Jasper rubbed at his eyes. "All I'm saying is that for the most part, nothing has worked in our favour. We go one step forward and five steps backward."

Saige slid off the couch and sat cross-legged on the carpet. She rested the grimoire on the coffee table and flicked through the pages.

"Saige. Listen, I didn't mean to offend you. It's just that—"

"Go to sleep, Jasper. You look exhausted. I'm going to stay up a bit and read this."

He did look tired. There were bags under his eyes. He rotated his arms in wide circles, probably to release tension.

Fat chance of that happening. This entire house is filled with tension.

He yawned loudly. "I can't possibly sleep. Not when you're still awake. Not after everything that's happened."

But five minutes later, he was sprawled on the couch, lightly snoring.

Saige was tired, too, but she forced herself to stay awake.

I should have drunk coffee instead of tea.

She continued to scan the grimoire's contents, marvelling at the incredible detail and intricate drawings on each page. Not all of them were exactly what she'd describe as pleasant images. There were skulls and demonic faces, half-moons and full moons, and symbols she neither understood nor had seen before. She found a section that focused on spells and rituals to remove unwanted ghosts and settled in.

STEP 1 - CLEANSE THE SPACE BY BURNING SAGE OR smudging. Throw salt in the entrances and corners.

Step 2 – Speak to the ghost. Announce your presence. Convince the entity that you mean no harm.

Step 3 – Perform a banishing spell.

THAT WAS THE GENERAL GIST OF IT.

Are you serious? That's all there is?

Her family really would think she'd gone insane if they caught her hurling salt around the manor. She doubted something that simple would actually work, anyway.

Frustrated, she tossed the grimoire onto the floor, thinking the most suitable place for it would be a fire. An old photograph tumbled out, and her eye landed on a figure she recognised.

Saige picked it up. It was once a black-and-white photo, now aged and yellowing. Theodosia Sinclair and her daughter, Anna, stood proudly before a ring of vertical standing slabs, topped by connecting horizontal stones.

Table des Pions! The fairy ring!

Saige remembered the place as a little girl. Her mother had taken her to visit the attraction, along with all the tourists, to show Saige a part of Ashvall's history. All Saige had wanted to see were fairies. She'd been disappointed when none had arrived. Not even a glimpse.

"What are you looking at?"

Saige jumped at the voice.

Jasper stretched his arms. His shirt lifted, revealing a hard, flat stomach.

She looked away. "Will you please stop doing that?"

"Doing what?"

"Scaring me. You have the worst timing."

"Well, actually... when you think about it, I have very good timing. I've saved you enough times."

She glared at him.

Jasper raised his hands in a placating gesture. "Point taken."

He bent down and sat on the carpet beside her. "What is that? Are they who I think they are?"

She passed him the photo. "Yes. Looks like Theodosia and Anna were having a mother-daughter day."

"And what is that behind them?"

"Table des Pions, otherwise called the fairy ring."

"A fairy ring? Seriously?"

"Don't be so cynical. It's part of Ashvall's history. People believed it was where fairies, witches, and elves gathered. It's said that many weddings took place there, and that people's love imbued the fairy magic. Supposedly, if a loved one is lost, their partner can lay their body in the circle for an entire night. If the fairies deem the couple's love to be true, the deceased's soul will be returned."

He snorted. "That's the worst fairy tale I have ever heard."

"It's meant to be romantic."

"You sure it's not a burial mound? A place where people were sacrificed by Ashvall's earliest inhabitants?"

Saige lifted her nose at him. "You've seen too many horror films, you know that?"

"And look how well I've survived." He waved his arms, indicating the house. "The films have trained me well."

She ignored him.

An idea crept into her mind.

Mildred had an image of Theodosia when she conducted the seance.

If I'm a medium, could I perhaps…?

No. It's too silly. A far-fetched idea.

Jasper was watching her, his eyes alert with suspicion. "You have that look on your face."

"What look?"

"The one that says you're about to do something that will get us both into trouble."

She glanced away, sheepish. "I think we should hold a seance. I think we should try and communicate with Theodosia Sinclair."

Jasper stared at the floor. "I knew I should have stayed asleep."

SAIGE REFUSED TO ALLOW JASPER TO CHANGE HER mind. If she listened to his warnings, his hesitation, she'd lose her nerve.

She shot him a stern glare. "We have to at least try."

Knowing our luck, nothing will happen. Theodosia might not make contact.

She found a spot on the other side of the coffee table and sat down.

Jasper gave her a last pleading look and then, seeming to realise there was no changing her mind, grudgingly took up her hands when she offered them to him across the table. "I thought you needed at least three people to do a seance? Something about creating a safe circle."

"Where'd you hear that?"

"I think I saw it in a movie."

She scoffed. "Because movies are so accurate."

"Saige, I'm serious." He took a sweeping glance around the room, as though he expected something to jump out from the shadows. "Mildred was a professional medium. Look what happened to her. I can't get an ambulance for you if something goes wrong."

His dark eyes flashed with worry. Despite her head telling her she was still angry with him, she had the growing urge to comfort Jasper. His fingers trembled, much like her own. Just the touch of his skin on hers sent a fluttering sensation through her stomach.

He's afraid. It's not fair that I'm doing this to him.

She pulled her hands away. "I can do this on my own. You don't have to be involved."

To her surprise, he reached out and wrapped his fingers through hers again. There was a strange look in his eyes she suspected was mounting anxiety and, just maybe, fear that the seance might actually work. "We try it once. If it doesn't happen the first time, that's it. Got it? No more attempts."

She nodded. "I promise."

He swallowed hard and shook out his shoulders. "If I ever write a memoir, at least this will make an interesting chapter."

He shut his eyes.

Saige closed hers too. She breathed in deeply, trying to remember what Mildred had spoken when she'd conducted the seance. "Theodosia Sinclair, we invoke you to come forward to dwell among us. We seek answers about your tragic demise. We wish to know your story. We do not wish you harm. In exchange, we ask that you do not harm us in return."

Jasper snorted. "Because that's likely."

Saige wished she could kick him under the table, but she sat cross-legged and had to resort to a forceful squeeze of his hands. "Shut up. We need to be serious."

Her entire body tensed with anticipation. "Theodosia Sinclair, we invoke you to come forward to dwell among us. We seek answers about your tragic dem—"

One of the candles hissed and went out.

Saige couldn't help it. She opened her eyes.

One after another, all the candles flickered and dimmed, the flames dissolving into smoke. Shadows crept forward. There was something unusual about the way the darkness rose to the ceiling. Heavy gusts tore at the house outside, whispers layered on each other in the storm. Or was that a trick of the wind?

Saige's phone buzzed in her pocket.

Her heart thudded into her ribs.

But I have no reception.

She let go of Jasper's hand and plunged her fingers into her pocket. She shook so badly she could barely decipher the message on the screen.

STOP! DO NOT DO THIS!

Saige blinked at the words.

This time, her heart threatened to rupture in her chest.

Dr Harriette Reynolds had sent the text.

No. That's not possible. Harriette is dead.

The message faded, replaced with another.

RUN! GO TO YOUR ROOM AND LOCK THE DOOR!

The phone buzzed again.

SHE. KNOWS. SHE. KNOWS. SHE. KNOWS. SHE. KNOWS. SHE. KNOWS.

More messages came through, the same words repeated over and over again until Saige thought her eyes might burst from the sight of them.

Jasper's sudden gasp alerted her that something was wrong. His eyes were trained on the window. "Saige... I think she's here."

A silhouette appeared through the mist outside. Woman-shaped, hunched, and reeking of death, the creature didn't seem to have the full use of its legs. Its feet dragged horribly on the stone beneath the window, its gasps loud and grisly enough to be heard over the wind. There was a *clack-dah-clack-clack-clack* sound. Saige fancied it was the creature's bones clicking into place, as though the thing really had just climbed out of a grave.

Its face appeared in the window. Saige recognised the strong draw and black widow's peak from the photograph.

It's Theodosia!

Her eyes were reduced to black stains, her skin shrivelled and torn in places where insects had feasted on her.

Chills broke out over Saige's body. She was on her own feet now, her legs threatening to buckle as dizziness washed over her.

I really have summoned Theodosia from her burial place.

Theodosia's crooked fingers scraped against the window. Her nails left scores in the glass. She didn't say anything, but the way she kept peering behind her, terror alight in her dark eyes, told Saige there was something worse just beyond.

What is she afraid of?

Saige's adrenaline spiked. "How do I help you? What can I do to break the curse?"

Theodosia kept peering over her shoulder. She frantically scratched at the window. When that didn't work, she began pounding her fists against the glass. Spiderwebbing cracks appeared across the surface.

"What do you want?" Saige persevered.

Theodosia turned and looked at her, pure hatred in her eyes. Stubbed teeth sank into her lower lip before she screamed, her voice piercing, "Pay the sins of the father."

The window exploded. Glass fragments burst through the air, momentarily beautiful as they reflected shadow and light, and then, like projectiles, dived toward Saige and Jasper.

Saige felt something strong tug her. Jasper pulled her from the room, the strength in his arm forcing her to run. "Come on. Move!"

She heard a frightening crash of glass behind her and had no objection to fleeing for her life.

They scrambled up the flight of stairs to the second level, speeding through the maze of passages. Saige's legs ached and her lungs burned, but she didn't inhale an easy breath until they were in her room and the door was locked securely behind them.

She checked her phone. No new messages.

She wiped tears out of her eyes.

I think I just made everything worse.

TWENTY-FIVE

Saige's entire body had gone rigid. She sat on the edge of her bed, her eyes tracing the patterns in the carpet. Icy tension crept up her arms.

Did I just free Theodosia's spirt?

Is she more powerful?

The window is broken. Now she's… in the house.

It took her a moment to realise that Jasper had bent down in front of her, her fingers snugly gripped in his. His face was frightfully ashen against his dark curls. A sheen of sweat licked his hairline.

She showed him the texts from Harriette.

The reckless half of her brain laughed. "I screwed up, didn't I?"

Jasper dropped his head. His voice was so soft, it was almost a whisper. "Saige, have you considered that maybe there is no way to end this curse? Sometimes, things are beyond our control, and we have to learn to live with that. What's happening in this house… it's beyond our understanding."

She flinched. "Pay the sins of the father. That's what I have to do."

"And we don't even know what that means."

Disappointment flooded her. She waited for the ache in her chest to abate. "So we just give up? What about Zoe? We let the curse take her?"

"She's not married to Xav. If Dr Ahmadi can keep her comfortable, maybe she'll recover, and we can all leave this place together when the storm ends."

She tipped her chin up to look at him. Really look at him. "You don't believe that."

"I believe in doing what's best for everyone. Too many people have been hurt. Harriette is dead. Mildred is in hospital. We've intervened too many times. Theodosia is probably coming for us next."

Saige looked at the door. She imagined the handle slowly twisting around, a shadow looming through the crack beneath the entry.

Theodosia could be just beyond the door.

She shivered and looked away.

Jasper tilted his head to study her. "So we're in agreement. We stay out of it. No more looking for trouble? No more ghost encounters?"

She pulled her hands free from his and wiped away the tear that streaked down her cheek. "I bet you really regret asking my brother if you could sing at his wedding, don't you?"

He stilled.

Saige knew this wasn't the appropriate time, but with Jasper locked in her room and too afraid to leave, this might have been the only opportunity for answers. She failed at keeping her voice calm. "Xav told me the truth.

Why did you really come to the island, Jasper? It wasn't to sing."

He drew away. His stride was fast as he crossed to the other side of the room. He leaned a shoulder on the wall and faced her but didn't say anything.

Saige's pulse beat into a crescendo in her temples. "Are you running away again? Because if you are, you need to do the right thing by your girlfriend and end things properly."

A small smile latched on to his mouth. "So Xav told you that, too, did he?"

"Will you do the right thing... for once?"

"I already have."

"You did?"

"Don't look so surprised. I am capable of learning from my mistakes."

"Right... well, good. Well... I mean not good for her, obviously."

She might have a broken heart now, but at least she'll never be left wondering why.

The muscles in Jasper's neck tightened. "If anything, I think she was relieved. We weren't a good match."

"Just like you and I weren't."

Saige immediately regretted saying it. She sensed Jasper's mood darken a shade.

He set his eyes straight ahead, staring at the small clock on the duchess. "We weren't?"

"Of course we weren't. You left, remember?"

Without even giving me the courtesy of explaining why.

Maybe it was the heightened fear, the stress of the last several days, or years of built-up resentment, but Saige really wanted an answer. Now.

Don't do it. It won't make a difference anymore.

She bit her lip, determined to keep the question inside, but the urge to know was too powerful. "Why did you end things between us?"

The air in the room felt thick and suffocating. Awkward tension sizzled between them. Saige wondered if it outweighed even the intensity of the storm outside.

Jasper's sigh was a tense, tired sound. "I rushed into things with you. I'm sorry if it causes you pain to hear it, but that's the truth. I wasn't ready to get married... and instead of finding the courage to tell you, I chose to be a coward." He raked his fingers down his face. "I should never have asked you to marry me. I'm sorry."

She'd wanted answers, but not pain and humiliation all over again. She wished she could drown all her feelings when it came to Jasper. She despised herself for still loving him, for still hoping there might have been a chance. But most of all, she hated the absolute lonely emptiness that haunted her day and night.

And the presence.

She loathed that icy feeling that something was near, always enjoying her misery. Never letting her escape from it.

Saige dug her nails into her palms. She wanted to hide her face in a pillow, cocoon herself in bedsheets, and never see the world again.

Her life with Jasper had been a fairy tale, only she didn't get the happily ever after.

Damn you, Disney. You have a lot to answer for.

Something inside her gave an unpleasant twitch when she realised Jasper was staring.

The tightness in his face softened. "Saige, I came to the island for—"

Boom! Boom! Boom!

The pounding on the door startled them both. Saige leapt up from the bed. From the corner of her eye, she saw Jasper stiffen.

The door handle moved, making a whiny, creaky noise.

I did lock it, didn't I?

The handle turned the opposite direction, then back again, rattling faster and louder. Someone was determined to get inside.

Boom! Boom! Boom!

The pounding echoed across Saige's bedroom.

It sounded like someone stood on the other side of the door with a baseball bat.

Jasper gave Saige an anxious glance, his eyes communicating one thought.

Theodosia.

Saige couldn't think. Couldn't move.

She's here to end us.

Another pounding.

"Saige," a voice called. "Are you in there?"

The tension inside her crumbled apart. "Dad?"

"Yes. Why do you have the door locked?"

Jasper legged it to the bathroom with the speed of an athlete.

Saige rolled her eyes.

It's like high school all over again.

She slid the latch and opened the door. Derrick Wolvercraft stood in the hallway with a candle, the flame casting harsh shadows across the hard lines in his face. He looked like he'd aged five years in the last several days.

He stepped inside, his eyes keenly sweeping around the room. "Who were you talking to?"

"Myself. It's a bad habit."

His lips set in a grim line. "Your mother used to talk to herself too."

"Talking to yourself is completely normal. Therapeutic, even."

Please stop trying to pinpoint everything on my fragile mental state.

Derrick stopped examining her room and faced her. "Private counselling sessions or not, don't lock your door. What if there was a house fire and we couldn't get you out?"

"I'm sure the rain would put out a fire."

He grunted, seeming not to appreciate his daughter's snide comment. "You know what I mean."

"Yes, okay. I get it. I won't lock the door."

She crossed her fingers behind her back.

Derrick breathed in deeply, his nostrils flaring. "Miraculously, somehow Zoe has managed to get out of bed and is wandering the house. She's in some sort of delirious, sleepwalking state. Dr Ahmadi is stumped by her behaviour. Xav and I are searching for her now. I just wanted you to know in case she comes knocking on your door."

A tide of fear crushed over Saige. "I should help."

"No. It's far too dangerous. One of the windows downstairs has smashed in this storm. Stay in your room. Better still, I think I'll go get Aunt Prue to stay with you."

He started to walk away, but Saige stopped him. "Don't disturb Aunt Prue. It's late, and she's had an awful day. I'll be fine."

She tried her best to look... normal, like a sane person.

If that even exists.

Her father's shoulders drooped. "Fine, Saige. I'm not going to argue with you. Just keep your door unlocked."

She waited until he disappeared down the hall before she firmly shut the door and locked it.

Jasper poked his head out of the bathroom. "Is it safe?"

Saige's hand remained on the handle, knuckles bulged white from tension. "Did you hear what my dad said? Zoe is wandering around the house again."

"She's possessed. It's not Zoe."

"I know that. It's Theodosia."

It's my fault.

Jasper sat down, the lines on his forehead creased in a frown. "All the more reason we need to remain here. Harriette's spooky text message didn't warn us to stay here for no reason." His eyes flashed with exhaustion. "I'm tired. I'm sleeping on this very uncomfortable excuse for a sofa lounge."

"It's a chaise lounge. It's designed for sitting."

"That explains why it's so uncomfortable."

She watched him settle onto the furniture piece. He wrapped the blanket from the previous night around his body. "Night, Saige. Get some sleep."

Get some sleep. Sure. There's a possessed lunatic running around the house.

Saige crawled into bed and closed her eyes. Exhaustion clouded her mind, her head heavy and spinning. "Jasper?"

"What?"

"Wouldn't you prefer to sleep in your own bed?"

The room was silent.

Jasper's voice sounded strained. "I'm not leaving you, Saige. Not this time. Not ever."

Her thoughts slid deeper into her sleepy subconscious. She couldn't be certain if Jasper spoke the words or if she imagined them.

SAIGE STOOD IN THE HALL JUST BEYOND THE DOORS that opened to the ballroom. She was jittery. Anticipation boiled inside her. She dared a glimpse in the mirror, amazed how her pale skin now looked creamy and flawless, her make-up natural and to perfection. She swept her hands down the waist of her dress, smoothing out any imaginary creases. Her wedding gown was a simple white satin garment with ivory lace and pearl beading. It was comfortable and fit snugly. Happiness flowed through every vein in Saige's body.

Definitely the right choice.

The only thing that was wrong were the tight nerves in her stomach.

It's excitement, Saige. Nervous excitement.

But there was something else not right.

She examined the hallway. Colours didn't seem quite natural, like she was viewing everything through an artist's impression. There was something else, too, but she couldn't put her finger on it.

One of her bridesmaids handed Saige a bouquet, a beautiful display of white roses and peonies. Saige raised the flowers to her nose to inhale their scent. She smelt nothing.

That's strange.

She shook her head.

Excitement, Saige. It's excitement playing with your senses.

Someone tapped her on the shoulder.

She turned around to find her bridesmaid beaming at her. "Are you ready? There's no turning back now."

Saige smiled, but the corners of her lips dropped. She didn't recognise the woman.

I must know her somehow. She's my maid of honour.

But Saige couldn't be certain that was the case.

How do I know her again?

She watched the woman join the other bridesmaids in the wedding procession. The trains of their crimson dresses trailed behind them like a blood-red river as they walked down the aisle.

"Saige?"

Her father appeared. Tears welled in Derrick's eyes. "You look beautiful, my darling."

"Thank you."

There was more she wanted to say, but she couldn't find the words.

He offered her his arm. "Are you ready?"

"Yes. More than ever."

Saige and her father stepped through the grand doors into the manor's impressive ballroom. Bowers of ivy, white flowers, and candles decorated the aisle runner. The guests were seated on either side, watching the bride with cheerful expressions. She saw her brother and Zoe wave at her. Zoe blew her a kiss, which Saige pretended to catch. Aunt Prue had delighted tears running down her cheeks. Aunt Violet was sobbing. She blew loudly into a handkerchief.

Saige swept her eyes over the guests again. She didn't recognise any of them.

Why are they smiling like that?

Their expressions were stiff and unnatural, and something about their faces almost appeared... waxy.

Saige blinked.

Just nerves.

She was too contented to give it much more thought.

It's my wedding day.

Walking down the aisle stretched into one long happy blur, but as the seconds ticked by, Saige had trouble holding her smile together.

This is taking a long time.

She looked ahead.

The aisle didn't end. It went on and on.

Her joyful mood evaporated. "Dad?"

She tugged on her father's arm, but when she looked up, it wasn't his eyes she was greeted with.

It was her mother's.

Elaine Wolvercraft's pale lips pulled too far back, revealing all the crushed bones in her jaw. She set her cold, dead hand on Saige's cheek. "My sweet baby girl. All grown up."

Panic swelled inside Saige. It started in her stomach, traversing all the way into her throat. She couldn't breathe. The air shook out from her lungs, but oxygen refused to come back in. She pulled her arm away and stumbled backward.

Her mother's smile faded. "What's wrong, sweetie? Don't you want to get married?"

This isn't real. This isn't real!

She glanced at the wedding guests. All their heads

lolled at the same time, as though attached to their shoulders by broken necks.

Oh my God! They're dead!

"Saige, my darling?" Her mother offered her arm again. "Don't be afraid."

Saige bolted down the aisle back the way she came. But this end of the aisle didn't finish either. It stretched ahead, never ending. From the corner of her eye, she saw the flowers and bowers of ivory bleed, their petals wilting. Blood flowed in rivers between the chairs, the white runner beneath Saige's feet soaked red.

Her mother's voice called to her. "My darling, you're going the wrong way."

Saige couldn't outrun the lingering chill that crept over her body. Her beautiful dress, which had moulded perfectly to her body before, was now tight and constrictive. It was suffocating her. Saige had an image of herself squeezed into an airtight bag.

The gown... it's possessed!

It's going to kill me.

She tripped on the long skirt and tumbled forward.

Saige screamed.

There was no floor to catch her.

She plunged into darkness. Wind lashed at her face, tearing her hair out of its beautiful braid.

Something latched on to her arm, spinning her upright. The force jolted her out of the nightmare.

Saige woke up. Freezing-cold rain pelted her body, the icy water streaming down her back and shoulders. Lightning ripped through the sky, illuminating the manor's limestone façade. It was met with an earth-shattering thunderclap that made her cry out again.

I'm outside?

Outside the manor!

Her teeth sank into her tongue as the hand that latched around her arm heaved, trying to pull her up. A twist of shock zapped through Saige at the realisation that there was nothing beneath her. Her feet kicked wildly through air. She looked down and wished she hadn't. The ground was a long way below, the fog rising like an ethereal sea to drown her.

She peered up. The person holding her ducked his head. She got a good look at him for the first time. "Jasper?"

His lips pressed tight together as he strained to pull her up.

She saw beyond him, recognising the steeply pitched roof that pierced the sky like a needle.

Oh my God! I'm hanging off the tower!

TWENTY-SIX

Saige was screaming. Screaming loud enough for all of Ashvall to hear her. "Jasper, please! Don't let go, please!"

The veins in his hands bulged from the tension. The rain sliding down his fingers didn't help. His teeth clenched as he groaned from the exertion. "Yeah, the not-letting-go part is obvious to me, Saige." He was in a precarious position himself, straddling the balustrade so he could lean over and hold on to her arm. "Give me your other hand."

She lifted her arm. Their fingers just missed. Saige felt the friction release between them. She started to fall. Gravity pulled her down.

With insane speed, Jasper leaned forward and caught her wrist, nearly toppling over in the process.

Saige heard a frantic voice. Her brother appeared by Jasper's side, his pyjamas already soaked through by the rain. True panic flashed through his eyes when he saw her.

She swung her arm up, happiness flooding her when her hand connected with her brother's.

I might be okay.

Jasper and Xav managed to haul her up and over the balustrade. She stood on shaky legs, grateful to be standing. The upper level of the tower had been built as an observation deck with three-hundred-and sixty-degree views of the landscape. Its use was never intended for storms or wild weather, which meant the tile floors were slippery. Rain lashed from every direction. Against the veiny streaks of lightning, the masterfully sculpted gargoyles were sleek and grotesque.

Saige's eyes connected with Jasper's. Relief shone on his face, but something else appeared when he examined her for injuries. He was... stunned. And not in a good way.

Xav's hooded eyes evaluated her with fury. "What are you wearing?"

She looked down. Shocking familiarity enveloped her.

Zoe's wedding dress.

But... how?

How am I wearing this?

The dress was ripped and waterlogged, the white chiffon stained. Something dark ran down the front of the gown. It took a moment for Saige to realise it was blood.

I'm not hurt.

At least... I don't feel hurt.

But that wasn't the problem.

There was a pattern to the blood.

Saige realised with horror that it spelled words.

YOU'RE NEXT.

"Saige?"

She looked up to see her father. His eyes creased,

resentment flaring across his face. Aunt Prue and Aunt Violet appeared behind him. Unable to pull their gazes away from their niece, their lips parted in surprise.

Aunt Prue raised a hand to her mouth. "Oh, Saige, my dear. What have you done?"

Saige watched all their expressions shift from shock to anger, finally settling on fear.

They... they think I did this on purpose.

They think I ripped apart Zoe's wedding dress, graffitied it, and wore it as I jumped off the tower.

She stared at them all, grappling to find an appropriate response. A way to explain that this wasn't her doing, but that would just make her sound crazier.

Her father stabbed a finger in her direction. His voice choked as furious tears spilled from his eyes. "That's it, Saige. This is enough. I can't let this keep happening anymore. You need help." He turned to Aunt Prue. "Go get Dr Ahmadi and instruct him to bring the sedatives."

"Sedatives?" Saige hoped she'd heard wrong.

Her father wouldn't look at her. "Yes. I had some brought to the house, just in case one of your episodes made an appearance."

Saige gasped feebly. "But I didn't do this."

Aunt Violet hurried forward and wrapped Saige in her arms. "We know, sweetie. It's the illness. That's why we're going to get you help. You do need help. You know that... don't you?"

Saige tugged free more violently than she intended. It knocked her aunt right over.

"Saige, that is enough." Derrick's voice boomed through the tower. "Xav, help me get your sister downstairs and back to her room."

The panic inside Saige reached its crescendo. She wondered if this was what an animal felt like when predators were herding it. "I can walk downstairs myself."

But her father and brother refused to listen. They took her by her arms and dragged her down the tower.

Saige peered over her shoulder. Jasper trailed behind, his face a mask of distress. An understanding that hadn't been there before rose in his expression, and Saige knew he was thinking the same thing.

Theodosia did this.

Fear crept up from her belly into her chest.

Theodosia possessed me. She made me dream. She made me sleepwalk. She made me jump off the tower.

She was numb to everything now but shock, unable to do anything except be led through the house to her room. Her father and brother bundled her brusquely onto the bed. She was aware of Dr Ahmadi by her side, aware of the syringe, aware of the needle that pierced her skin, but she was too weak to do anything about it. The floor seemed to roll out beneath her bed, the walls shifting. Voices became slow and distant, the conversation muffled. Dizziness closed in. Her eyes wanted rest.

Where is Jasper?

She fought very hard to lift her head, but she couldn't see him.

He's not here.

It was her last conscious thought.

SAIGE HAD ALWAYS LOVED WOLVERCRAFT'S beautiful rose garden, so it made sense that she'd dream about it. The sun was out, the wind warm and soft against her skin. Her red hair looked more strawberry than auburn in this light, the way she'd always wanted it to appear. Her pale skin lacked the freckles she despised. She wondered if her eyes were blue like her mother's or if they'd remained hazel-green.

She inhaled the roses' fragrant perfume. Birds chirped. Wind rustled in the leaves. The gentle tinkling of running water could be heard somewhere in the woods. She wandered among the beautiful red and white flowers. The petals were lush and full. Pearl-shaped water droplets glistened on their vivid leaves.

It must have rained recently.

The grass was wet between her toes. The damp blades tickled her soles.

"Saige? Saige, darling? Where are you?"

Elaine's voice floated through the garden, faint and waiflike, as though the wind was whispering it.

Saige stopped moving.

No. She can't be here.

The sun dipped behind a cloud, the warm air now saturated by cold. Saige rubbed at her bare arms. The sky overhead churned, thick with roiling clouds. The first drop of rain splashed like ice on her forehead. Then another on her arm. She gasped, staring above. Violent, grey storm clouds glowered down, the rain breaking from it in a torrent.

The rosebushes no longer resembled a fairy garden. In seconds, they'd grown to an astronomical size, blocking out whatever light still existed. Saige had an impression of herself as a mouse trapped in a maze. Vines and brambles slithered out of the ground like serpentine monsters, climbing higher in a grotesque braid. They surrounded her. Walled her in.

"No, please! No!"

Thorns cut her skin. Branches scratched her arms. The grass beneath her feet no longer felt like grass. It was supple and wet. Horror seized Saige when she realised she was sinking in mud. Quick mud. It swallowed her ankles, latched on to her calves, spilled over her knees.

It's going to pull me under.

She tried to hold on to a vine, but it twisted up her arm instead.

"Saige."

For a moment, the shock of not being alone overshadowed her fear, and then it came tearing back. Panic suffocated her.

Dead brides surrounded Saige. Their pupils grew darker, bleeding through the whites, dripping past their cheeks until all that was left was a horrible black stain. Her mother was there, smiling. At least the good half smiled. What was left on the other side was pummelled meat with sticky, gelatinous blood. The stench of it made Saige's stomach heave.

She recognised the other brides. The hanged woman from the woods, her neck long and bent from where the noose had broken it. The lady with the slit throat. Blood still spilled over her beautiful black-and-gold flapper dress. The dancing bride in the tower. And there were others. Women with horrible things that had been done to them. One had a hole in her head, probably from a gunshot. A woman clawed at Saige's arm, her nails sinking into her flesh. Saige screamed. The wraith's discoloured fingers were pruned, the skin grooved and soggy.

She must have drowned.

The women were everywhere. They rose in the mud, looming over Saige, pushing her down. The sludge was to her chest now. She knew kicking and thrashing would only serve to sink her faster, but her fear took over and she did it anyway. The filth and muck climbed to her neck.

Saige had never been religious, but she managed to scramble enough energy to say a final prayer.

Please, let it be fast. Don't let my death be prolonged.

The idea of drowning always freaked her out. The thought of being compacted in mud for all eternity terrified her.

Fingers curled beneath Saige's chin, forcing her head up.

Her eyes bulged.

Theodosia.

She'd never noticed before, but Theodosia's green dress was marred with blood. It pooled from a gash in her throat, soaking the gown.

Her throat... it was cut!

Theodosia knelt down, smiling with quiet menace. "Pay the sins of the father, Saige. A life for a life."

She transferred her hand to the top of Saige's head and pushed down.

Saige shrieked hysterically. She scrambled to stay upright, but her feet felt like they'd been strapped with concrete blocks.

The mud scaled up her face, forcing itself into her eyes.

Her nose.

Her mouth.

TWENTY-SEVEN

Saige gasped, jerking upright. Her sheets were tangled around her, her pillow hanging at an odd angle half off the bed. Sweat licked her hairline and made her underarms itch. Someone had changed her into a night-dress. It clung to her. She inhaled the cold air, grateful her throat wasn't packed with mud.

Just a dream.

No. A nightmare.

Or had it been something else?

Was that ... a warning? A... message?

Theodosia's words returned with a swift chill up her spine. *"Pay the sins of the father, Saige. A life for a life."*

But what does that mean?

She dropped back in the bed, wishing she could close her eyes and fall asleep to merciful darkness. No dreams. No nightmares. No thoughts. Just pure, raw subconscious.

"Good morning, Saige."

She flicked her eyes open. With the window boarded up and the door closed, very little light had managed to leak into the room. Saige was surprised to find it was morning. She rose to sit and leaned against the headboard. Her eyes strained to see in the dark. Someone was sitting in a rocking chair beside her bed. A single candle on the side table provided just enough light for her to trace their outline.

She squinted. "Aunt Prue?"

In the candle's subdued glow, Aunt Prue's hair looked the colour of caramel. The heavy lines on her face were weighed down by concern. "Did you rest well?"

Saige swallowed. "Sort of."

Her aunt didn't speak for a long time. "We're all worried about you. What you did last night.... Saige, please... what's happening to you?"

I'm being haunted. That's what's happening to me!

But Saige knew she could never say those words. Everyone would think it was just another cry for help, another twisted episode.

She raked her fingers through her hair, hating that she was lying through her teeth. "I don't know what that was. Honestly, I think I must have been sleepwalking. It wasn't intentional."

"Intentional? Saige, you could have died."

"Yes, I am painfully aware of that."

Aunt Prue clasped her hands together in her lap. "When the storm is over and it's safe to leave the island, your father is going to have you hospitalised."

Saige didn't say anything. She'd expected it.

A spark of emotion flicked over Aunt Prue's face. "Until then, you will be watched twenty-four hours. Dr Ahmadi will be able to provide something to help you sleep."

"I don't want to sleep."

"Are you hungry?"

Saige shook her head.

"I've brought magazines and a few books up from the library. Would you like to read any of them?"

Saige flicked her eyes grumpily at her aunt. "Are you saying I'm not allowed to leave this room?"

"Dr Ahmadi doesn't think it would be wise for you to wander the house."

"So I'm a prisoner?"

"No. We're doing this for your own good."

Saige laughed, hostile and angry. "You're keeping me here against my will. That's called imprisoning someone."

Her aunt huffed. "Oh, Saige, for heaven's sake. Stop acting like a belligerent schoolchild. Honestly, I don't understand you sometimes. You have everything anyone could possibly want. A family who cares for you. Wealth you can command at a click of your fingers. You could have the life of a socialite if you wanted it. You could work with your brother and father for once and help with the family business, but instead you... you sit around, glum and mopey."

Saige swept her eyebrows up, surprised by the blatant remark. "I do not sit around all sullen and negative. I have a job. I give my money to charity because I prefer to earn my living. And Dad and Xav don't want me involved in the business. They're ashamed of me. They're ashamed of how I'm just like Mum."

The look Aunt Prue directed at her held the tiniest hint of disgust. "Is that what you think? Oh, Saige. You are in worse shape than I thought. I honestly have no idea how my brother handles you sometimes."

Saige's fury escalated. "Then I guess it's a good thing you ended up a miserable old spinster, isn't it? No husband. No kids. Nothing to worry about."

She immediately regretted it the moment the words slipped out.

Her aunt froze in the rocking chair. She looked at the floor, not saying anything, but Saige could see the hurt that had settled on her face.

Jesus, it's like I've just killed Bambi.

She wanted to apologise, but the door popped open.

"Yoo-hooooooo. Is my little niece awake?" Aunt Violet appeared with a tray of tea and boiled eggs. Her vibrant pink flower dress made her look like a housewife straight out of the 1950s. The print reminded Saige of the roses from the dream. She didn't think she'd ever be able to look at flowers again.

Aunt Prue stood up, refusing to even look at Saige. "I'll take my leave."

She moved briskly to the door and shut it behind her with a louder-than-necessary slam.

Aunt Violet's gaze travelled to Saige, confusion in her wide eyes. "Did I interrupt something?"

Saige scrunched up into a ball and dropped her head onto her knees. "Just the nastiest, most undeserved insult in the entire world."

Aunt Violet laughed. "You forget that she's my sister. Whatever you said couldn't have been as bad as some of the nasty things we've called each other in the past." She placed the tray on the bedside table and poured the tea. "No toast, I'm afraid. I could only make what could be cooked or boiled on the gas cooktop."

Saige wasn't hungry, but now wasn't the time to insult

another aunt. She took the tray and used the teaspoon to crack the egg.

Aunt Violet settled into the rocking chair. "What did you say?"

Saige sipped her tea. At that moment, she wouldn't have minded being prodded at with another sedative. Anything to stop her from feeling the guilt and hurt inside. She told her aunt what had occurred.

Aunt Violet lost her good-humoured smile. "Oh, well, that is… difficult."

"I didn't mean what I said. It was in the heat of the moment."

"I know it was, but… oh, Saige. Aunt Prue wasn't always alone. She was engaged once. Back when she was very young."

Saige moved too fast and had to grip the tray before it slipped off her lap. "Wait. What are you saying? Aunt Prue was going to marry?"

Aunt Violet rose from the rocking chair and settled on the bed. She smoothed out some of the creases in the quilt. "Prue was eighteen. I was only twelve at the time and didn't really understand, but I remember our father being furious."

"Because she was so young?"

"No, many girls married young back then. Your grandfather didn't approve of the match."

"Why not?"

"His name was Samuel Wiles. He was a fisherman. Not exactly what your grandfather classed as a suitable addition to the Wolvercraft family. Samuel wasn't a wealthy man."

"So Grandfather separated them?"

"I believe that was his intention, but he didn't have to in the end. A violent storm, much like the one we're experiencing now, hit the island. The fishing trawler Samuel was working on capsized. I still remember the funeral. Twelve fishermen dead. It rocked the entire island. Everyone was so sad for the families who had lost a loved one, but the most distraught person was Prue. I think that's why she refuses to leave the island."

Saige had been feeling bad before, but now it was combined with guilt and shame. "I never knew. Why wouldn't Dad have told me?"

Aunt Violet's eyes darted uncomfortably back to the quilt. "I guess... after what happened with your mother... maybe Derrick thought it was best not to upset you with Prue's tragedy. Our family has had a history of being unlucky in love."

Saige stilled. A horrible new thought struck her.

What if the storm that killed Samuel was no natural weather event? What if it was the curse? Harriette said the curse targeted women who married into the Wolvercraft family, but what if...?

She grappled to put the two loose ends together.

"Aunt Violet?" Saige tried to keep her voice level. "Would you very much mind getting me some more tea?"

I really need you to leave the room.

Her aunt dabbed at her eyes with a handkerchief. "Of course, dear. It's good to see you have an appetite." She took the tray and scuttled into the hallway. To Saige's dismay, Aunt Violet shut the door. A second later, she heard the unmistakable turning of a key.

What the fu...? She's locked me in?

She thought about the way her father had reproached her for the very same thing.

Frigging hypocrite.

At least she was alone. For now.

She wrestled out of her blankets and swung out of the bed. Tiptoeing her way across the room to the duchess, she opened the bottom drawer, pulled out the extra blanket, and found Theodosia's journal in the same place she'd hidden it the night before. Despite her waterproof hoodie, the book was damp from Saige's travels through the woods, but she was grateful it wasn't damaged.

She hurried back into bed and brought the candle close.

Jasper's warning floated into her mind. *"Too many people have been hurt. Harriette is dead. Mildred is in hospital. We've intervened too many times. Theodosia is probably coming for us next."*

Saige never promised Jasper that she'd stop searching for answers. She didn't owe him a promise.

I can't let anyone else suffer an unhappy ending.

She stared at the shadows stretched across her room, taking a moment to convince herself this was the right thing to do.

I need answers.

Saige opened the journal, wondering what madness she was about to delve into.

MAY 31, 1846

. . .

Frederick's letters claimed that Ashvall is beautiful. I suppose it is, if wild and rugged can be described as beautiful. Anna loves it. As long as she is happy, I can endure cold weather and constant gloom. I do not think the sun has shone once since our arrival. Anna walks along the beach every day, even in the rain. Sometimes she will take her shoes off and jump the waves, or talk to the seagulls. I am sure her governess hates me for allowing it. Miss Preston does not like to get wet.

Wolvercraft Manor is an exceptionally grand house. I did not quite believe the rumours back in New York, but Frederick really has spared no expense. Tonight is the Summer Ball to mark the change of the seasons. Anna is excited. Frederick organised a gown to be tailored for her, and she is impatient to wear it. I wish she would not be so boisterous in the house. She is still so young and ignorant of the world, and so foolishly headstrong that I fail to see how she will mature in the coming weeks. I must train her to behave, or otherwise I risk Frederick sending her away.

I wonder how many people are coming to the party tonight just to leer at me. To see what a spirit-medium is and to laugh and poke fun. I have seen it before. The non-believers are harsh. Some people will, of course, want me to conduct a seance, and I will be happy to oblige. I must learn to acquaint myself with Frederick's guests and to be patient and calm. For Anna's sake. Wolvercraft Manor is home now. Everything is dependent on this. Frederick has told me that tonight he will announce the engagement.

SAIGE SET THE MAGAZINE DOWN THAT SHE'D hidden the journal inside. Aunt Violet's loud snores messed with her concentration. Saige's father had been serious when he'd said she was not to be left alone. Aunt Violet had returned with more tea, had settled into the rocking chair with a magazine, and had dozed off to sleep in less than five minutes. Her mouth now hung open, her head lolled to the side. With her violent red hair, she resembled a clown head at a fair, only broken, flaccid, and plump.

Saige crept out of bed and went to check the door. It was locked.

Great.

Her legs complained beneath her. Her entire body shook.

Probably the result of being sedated.

She snuck around her aunt and checked her phone on the mantelpiece, hoping that maybe... just maybe....

It was dead.

Damn it.

Saige settled back in her bed, grinding the heels of her palms into her eyes. Theodosia's book rested beside her, still open. There really had been nothing in there to suggest that Theodosia was a vindictive, manipulative bitch hellbent on destroying happiness and people's lives. The journal was exactly that—a journal detailing her life, hopes, and dreams.

What happened to you, Theodosia?

A chill crept over her when she remembered the woman's cold, dead words in the dream. *"Pay the sins of the father, Saige. A life for a life."*

Just imagining the feel of Theodosia's hands pushing

her down into the mud sent icy spasms along her body. She didn't want to live through that horror again.

The sins of the father.

She assumed that meant Frederick Wolvercraft.

Frederick did something to Theodosia and her daughter. I'm going to find out what it was.

Saige took up the book again.

TWENTY-EIGHT

June 1, 1846

There was a woman at the party last night. She had hair the colour of fire and skin so fair it seemed as luminous as the moon. I did not like the way she watched my Anna. Perhaps it is mother's intuition, or my ability to see beyond what the normal eye can accept, but I sense evil in this woman. Many people here in Ashvall believe evil witches live among us. I think they may be right.

This woman did not seem shocked by Frederick's announcement of the engagement, but she did not look pleased by it either. Many times throughout the evening I saw her approach Frederick. I did not like the way she spoke to him with such familiarity, or the way she touched his arm with a firmness that was almost possessive. At any time I happened the chance to glance upon them, they stood so close that not even the smallest margin of air could breathe past.

I asked around. Her name is Margaret Thronesby. She has lived on the island for two years with her aunt. An orphan with no prospects. Perhaps that is why she looks so unfavourably at Anna and me. Perhaps she has her eyes set on Frederick.

JUNE 12, 1846

MARGARET THRONESBY AND HER AUNT, A MRS RIXON, have dined with us eight times in the last two weeks. I am told by the housekeeper that the pair are frequent guests at the manor. The evidence is there. I am convinced Miss Thronesby is no mere acquaintance to Frederick. She is familiar with Wolvercraft Manor. She touches everything as though it already belongs to her. She watches me and my Anna with an intensity that is, dare I say it, as cruel and forbidding as a demon. I do not like the way her lips move when she speaks. Her voice is sweet and kind, but there is something heartless hidden beneath.

I know what Margaret Thronesby intends. She hopes to marry Frederick. It is laughable. Preposterous. I tell myself she is a lovesick girl who has set her sights too high, but deep inside I do not think she is a girl. Maybe not even a woman. She is something else. There is a savagery inside her that only I am able to see.

SAIGE FROWNED, UNSURE WHAT TO MAKE OF THE journal entries. She had been reading Theodosia's journal on and off all day, only stopping to drink tea and eat when food was brought to her. Aunt Violet had been replaced by her father, then Dr Ahmadi, and now Xav. Her brother sat in the rocking chair, pretending to read. Saige knew by the way his hands were so highly strung, the veins protruding out of the white skin, that he was too tense to lose himself in a book.

She looked at the small wall clock: 8:00 p.m. The day had disappeared too fast. It seemed to have just melted away. She focused back on the journal.

Theodosia doesn't come across as mad in any of these entries. She was certainly suspicious about Margaret Thronesby. I wonder if Aunt Prue has ever heard of her.

Saige read through more of the entries. The storm outside continued to rage. The thunder was the worst. Saige remembered her father sitting her down to tell her what thunder was when she was seven years old. *"It can't hurt you, sweetie. It's God moving his furniture upstairs. He has a very loud way of doing it."*

Saige looked up at the ceiling, listening to the angry forces in the sky.

If God's moving his furniture, he must be relocating a piano.

Her brother stood up and stretched. "I'm going to make a sandwich. You want one?"

"Ham, cheese, and tomato, please."

Xav left. He locked the door behind him, the click of the key reminding her that she was a prisoner in her own room.

She wasn't really hungry. All she wanted was twenty minutes or so to herself. She checked her phone. Still dead.

Did you really expect any different?

Harriette isn't going to contact you again when you're locked in a room and useless.

She focused on the journal once more.

JUNE 19, 1846

WE ARE LEAVING. THE ENGAGEMENT IS OFF. I HAVE instructed Anna to pack and to be ready at 11:00 p.m. I have secured us passage to Guernsey on a small fishing drifter and paid the captain to remain quiet. We cannot stay at Wolvercraft Manor. Frederick is not faithful. I saw him kissing Margaret Thronesby in the library. They thought they were alone. They thought they were discreet. I heard her whisper to him, and it did not sound like any known language on this earth. It was a spell. I am positive she is a witch.

I hid and listened to their plan for a long time. She has bewitched Frederick. She has convinced him to marry for my fortune and, when he possesses it, to remove me and my Anna. Then Frederick will marry Margaret.

I have learned a great many sad truths today. Frederick is bankrupt. He gambles often and loses frequently. He drinks to excess and treats his staff with appalling indifference. The house, its loveliness and extravagance, is a ploy to hide his ugliness. He can no longer afford the house or his indulgent lifestyle. That is why he needs me. My money.

Anna and I are in danger. I fear that if we remain another day longer in this house, we will be killed.

.   .   .

Saige sat ramrod straight. A ripple of fear spread through her.

What did he do to you, Theodosia?

To Anna?

She turned the page, surprised to find no words on the next sheet.

Saige stared at the empty page for a long time.

Did Frederick kill them?

Do we have a murderer in our family?

She instinctively felt that the answer was yes.

Saige stepped out of bed, dizzy from the truth. She went to the bathroom to wash her face and calm her shock. She stared at herself in the mirror. Her hair was long and unbrushed, almost a golden red in the candlelight. Dark smudges ringed her eyes. She looked too thin in her white nightdress. It ballooned around her.

I've lost weight. I look dead. I look like a... ghost.

I wonder if this is what Theodosia and Anna felt like when they learned the truth.

She reeled around when someone tapped on the bedroom door.

She darted back into her room. "Xav?"

No answer.

Xav has a key. He wouldn't need to knock.

Blood rose in her neck.

What if it's Theodosia? What if she knows I've discovered her secret?

Candlelight sent flickering shadows across the door.

Tap. Tap. Tap.

Her stomach heaved when a shadow fell beneath the door's diminutive gap.

Tap. Tap. Tap.

"Saige, are you there?" The whisper was tight and hoarse.

Saige inhaled a relieved breath. She ran to the door. "Jasper?"

"Yes. I've been waiting hours for your brother to leave."

"He'll be back. You shouldn't be out in the hall alone. Not when Theodosia...."

Could sneak up and kill you.

The terrifying thought made her entire body ache. "Jasper, go back to your room. Lock the door."

He laughed, but the tone held a hint of tension. "Saige, I...."

She waited.

Has something else happened?

For a moment, she wondered if he had left. She pressed her hand to the door. "Jasper?"

"I want to talk."

Despair and longing seeped from his voice. She wondered if there was sorrow in his gaze too. No matter how much she told herself she despised Jasper, hated him for what he'd done to her, her heart disagreed. It was a battle she'd been fighting for years, burning her from the inside out. She was too tired to contest it.

His voice was uneven. "I'm sorry... for what I did. I've missed you. I didn't come to the island for Xav's wedding. I think you've already figured that out. I came back for you."

She couldn't speak. She hugged her elbows, wishing she could extract all the heartache from her body as she silently dropped to the floor and cried. It had crossed her mind that Jasper had come to the island for her. She'd told herself it wasn't true, but her feelings had betrayed her better judgement and had made her hope.

Why did he have to confess this now?

"Saige? When all of this is over... can we try *us* again?"

A sob caught in her throat. She sat against the wall, afraid she'd unravel and break down completely. "You've seen what's happened in this house. You've seen how... my family look at me. I'll be hospitalised."

"That won't happen."

"It will."

"Then I'll tell your father the truth. About everything."

Saige couldn't help a short, unamused laugh. "If you do that, you'll be locked away in a

mental asylum too."

"I don't mean the ghosts." The insistence in his voice frightened her. "I mean us. I'll

tell him about our previous engagement."

She felt her desperation reignite. "That will just make him hate you."

"I'm willing to risk that. I love you, Saige. If I have to wait, then that's what I'll do."

Saige couldn't speak. Her emotions became a disjointed mess. Love. Elation. Terror. Regret. It all flowed out of her, cinching into a knot that tightened her airways and left her puzzled and unsure. Against her better judgement, against her self-respect, she'd fantasised hearing Jasper say those words for years, and now that he finally had, it was impossible for them to be together. If she told him she loved him, too, the curse would claim him.

Her eyes were damp and swollen. Afraid she'd lose her resolve if she didn't act quickly, she wiped the tears from her face. "Jasper, please make me a promise."

"Anything."

"When this storm is over, leave the island the first

chance you have. This curse... I don't think it applies only to women who marry into the Wolvercraft family."

"What do you mean?"

"I've been reading Theodosia's journal. I think the curse applies to any member of the

Wolvercraft family. If we love someone, that person dies. Married or not. Aunt Prue lost her fiancé. Jasper, you need to stay away from me."

He was quiet for a moment. "So you do love me?"

Her spine stiffened. She had two choices.

Confess everything?

Or force him away?

The curse will claim him. I can't let that happen.

There is no happy ending for us.

"Saige?"

She was unable to control the quiver in her lower lip. "Please stay away. Don't come near me."

"I told you I can wait. When all of this is over and we're far from this house, we can be together."

It took a moment for his words to settle in.

Is it possible? Could we do that?

She shook her head. She let go of the fantasy, watching it slip away like a balloon blown in a heavy gust.

Theodosia won't let that happen.

And I will not be the reason Jasper dies.

She focused on keeping her voice level, but her heart broke inside. "I don't love you. Please just go away."

He was quiet for a moment. "Is that what you really want?"

He sounded like he didn't believe her.

She bit down on her lip. The sharp, fiery pain of the lie threatened to rip her in two.

"Yes. You hurt me. I don't forgive you. I'll never forgive. Now leave."

It was the silence on the other side of the door that hurt her the most. She'd been convincing. He'd left.

Goodbye, Jasper.

She tried to make sense of what just happened, of hopes and dreams shattered and gone forever. Her breathing was shallow and choppy. She ran to the bathroom and knelt over the toilet, unable to stop the retching. The poisonous heartache had made her insides sicken. Her skin was lathered in cold sweat, and the more she cried, the more the tiled floor seemed to rush at her.

I'm dizzy. I just need to lie down.

At the basin, she pressed a wet cloth to her face, then drank some of the cold water from the faucet, hoping to expel the foul taste in her mouth. In the mirror, her red eyes stared back at her. She looked miserable. Her shoulders sagged, her skin so pale she couldn't help but wonder if her family would think she was chronically ill.

Why do I never get a happy ending?

Saige couldn't take it anymore. She ran back into her room, jumped into bed, and threw the covers over herself. She had wrapped her body in a dark cocoon where there was nothing but reflection and agony.

To hell if Xav returns to find me like this. He already thinks I'm nuts.

She wished for sleep to take her pain away, to numb her. But it took a long time for the dark waters of her unconscious to drown her mind, and by the time it did, a patch in Saige's pillow was soaked through by tears.

TWENTY-NINE

SAIGE HAD BEEN DREAMING AGAIN. DREAMING OF
something wicked that climbed up Wolvercraft's limestone
wall as she slept. Its hooked, crooked fingers dug into the
mortar, head darting from side to side as it searched for a
point of entry. It came to the bedroom window. Saige saw
it through the glass. A veil concealed its face—something
that had been lacy and pearl-white but was now torn,
blackened, and stained. Dark hair fell in a tangled mess
past it shoulders. A foamy scum grew in those strands. It
resembled an algae Saige was positive only grew on a
water's surface.

The creature lifted a long finger to the glass and, with a
single tap, pushed the window open. Fear seeped into the
very marrow in Saige's bones. She couldn't move. Her body
felt bound to the bed, her legs and arms too heavy to
budge. All she could manage was a slight raise of her head.
She watched the twisted form tumble in an ungainly heap
on the floor. It crawled, startingly crablike, soaking the

carpet with its waterlogged body. The entire room filled with an odour that was septic and fishy. Saige held her breath, too afraid that the slightest inhale would draw its attention.

My God! Is that... a wedding dress?

The creature wore a long white skirt that Saige recognised as part of a bridal gown, only it was ripped and discoloured, soaked by rain and dirtied by mud. Oily stains oozed from small bite-size chunks missing in the creature's dress and torso.

It's partly decomposing. I'm looking at a corpse!

The carcass reached for the door handle.

Saige gasped.

And immediately wished she hadn't.

The creature turned around.

Saige was startled awake. She jerked upright, her body free from the dream that had weighed her down like stone.

Just a nightmare.

The annoying, tense feeling continued to linger in her muscles, the air a wave of ice across her skin.

Cold air?

The candle was out, but light managed to stream into her bedroom. Her eyes adjusted, and she nearly cried out with fright. Her window was open. The wooden shutter that boarded it was missing. Weak light from a growing moon shone into the room, shadows suddenly vanishing and reappearing in the insane flashes of lightning. Snow and icy sleet blew into the room, sending shivers across Saige's skin.

She pulled her blanket over her.

That was when she saw the door.

It was open.

It's not possible.

It was a dream!

But she knew she was lying to herself.

She climbed out of bed and tiptoed to the door. The hallway outside was shrouded in shadow. Saige wondered if the darkness hid eyes that stared back at her.

A chill danced across her bare feet.

The carpet, it's... sodden?

She recalled the way the creature had sidled across her room, dripping water and mud.

It wasn't a dream!

Oh God! Where is Xav?

The rocking chair was empty.

He'd gone to make a sandwich. Perhaps he never came back.

She checked the clock. That was two hours ago.

Agitated questions popped in her mind.

Xav wouldn't do that. He'd be right back here.

She wondered if he'd ignored Dr Ahmadi's order and was with Zoe.

She looked across the hall to the model's bedroom. The door was open.

Something sickly curdled in her stomach. Before she could talk herself out of it, she darted across the hallway.

It was hard to tell what was in Zoe's bedroom at first. There was no light, and the window was boarded up. A burst of sporadic lightning illuminated the duchess. For a split second, Saige saw a flashlight. She raced toward it, fumbling with her sweaty fingers to switch it on. The beam of light shone into the darkness. Zoe's bedroom was empty. The sheets had been pulled back on the bed, smeared with a dark stain that looked like coffee. Saige drew closer.

Not coffee. Blood.

She stepped back. The flashlight emitted a shaky ray across the room. She didn't want to be here. She sensed... evil.

Saige hurried back into the hallway.

Where is Zoe? Where is Xav?

Something was very, very wrong. The best thing she could do now was alert her father.

She turned, the expanse of hall before her seeming endless. A small, weak cry sprang from her throat. Every door in the hallway was open.

Dad!

Aunt Prue!

Aunt Violet!

She prayed they were asleep in their beds, unaware of the danger that had infiltrated the house, because Saige was sure of it now. That *thing* that had climbed its way through her bedroom window was Theodosia. It was her corpse reanimated.

Saige stumbled forward, tripping on her long night-dress. Her head whirled as she nearly went into a faint. She checked each room, shining the flashlight inside. Despair clutched her heart when she discovered every bed was empty.

What has Theodosia done with them all?

Where are they?

She drew in several sharp breaths. There was one room she hadn't checked.

Jasper!

She bolted back the way she'd came, nearly barrelling into the architrave as she sped into his room.

Jasper was absent.

She knows.

Turning Jasper away last night didn't work. It didn't save him from the curse.

Horror scraped against her bones.

Theodosia knows I love him.

She hurried back into her room and quickly dressed in a pair of jeans, a T-shirt, and a jumper. She strapped on her boots, wishing for a stroke of impossible luck to guide her. She'd search the entire house. Theodosia couldn't have taken her family far. They had to be in the manor somewhere. She grabbed her flashlight, forcing herself to swallow her fear, and stepped into the hall.

Wolvercraft Manor was abysmally dark. She wandered the halls of the second floor, searching every empty room and bathroom. Saige tried to move fast but also keep her footsteps soft and agile, alert for anything that might jump out at her.

After about twenty minutes of frantic searching, she came to the inevitable conclusion that her family wasn't on the second floor.

Check the ground floor.

She silently crept down the staircase, portraits of her ancestors seeming to watch her, their expressions stiff and apathetic. She stopped by the space of the missing portrait, recalling Aunt Prue's explanation. *"That is a mystery of the*

Wolvercraft Household. I suppose at some stage the portrait was damaged and taken down for repairing. Perhaps it was lost."

Saige now understood why the vacant space unsettled her.

Is this where Theodosia's portrait had been?

Could Frederick no longer stand to look at her, to see her eyes follow him every time he passed this way?

Because he... murdered her?

Saige was positive of it.

She continued down the flight of stairs into the foyer. The ground floor was as empty and unoccupied as the second floor. She searched the parlour, the drawing rooms, the large dining hall, and the ballroom, every vacant space staring back at her with silent mockery. Saige wondered how many people had died in the house, if the shells of them were still here, watching her.

Has my family gone to join them?

She wiped a tear from her eye. She couldn't afford to think like that.

Be strong. You'll have to travel deeper.

She found the staircase that led to the old servants' quarters. The kitchen, scullery, and pastry room were smoky and stuffy from two centuries of use. She cried when she saw four pieces of bread on the bench. Butter, ham, tomato, and cheese sat untouched beside them.

Xav.

Did he even see what came for him? Or did he simply... vanish?

She almost hoped it was the latter. At least that would have spared him any terror.

Saige turned away, refusing to let the sight shake her. She checked the servants'

quarters, found them all empty, and reluctantly went back upstairs.

They're not on the ground floor or the second floor, which means I'll have to check the upper levels.

Or...?

Saige remembered the basement.

No. They couldn't be down there. That place was filling with water.

But she couldn't risk not checking.

She hurried down the hall that led to the basement. The door was open, the stairs leading to a darkness that not even the flashlight could breach. The light seemed to just bleed into the inky black.

I can do this. I can do this.

She stepped gingerly down the stairs, cold moisture hitting her face. The damp, musty scent of mildew assaulted her nose. She really hoped only fungi bred in the dank base-ment. Running water met her ears. Saige was reminded of the flooded creek that had nearly claimed Jasper's life, and of the tunnel that had nearly claimed hers. It was entirely possible that water ran thick and fast beneath the house.

She descended several more steps and stopped. A sense of danger settled over her skin. The hazy beam from her flashlight revealed the lower steps were flooded.

The water has risen. It's much deeper than it was.

She imagined bloated bodies beneath the water, waiting to pull her down.

Your family is not here. Get out of this place. Get out!

She didn't feel alone. There was something in the basement. Something Saige sensed breathed the same air as her but wasn't alive.

She turned away, and that was when her flashlight shone on something that paralysed her. Someone stood in the water.

She leaned over the rail, sending the light forward. Her lungs expanded, threatening to burst into a scream when she recognised the familiar shape—her father, pale and soaked, his eyes wide and unblinking. His hands were linked to two others. Saige traced the flashlight over them. Aunt Prue's ashen body appeared. Her right hand was linked to Xav's, which in turn was linked to Zoe's. Dr Ahmadi stood beside the model, his hand united with Aunt Violet's. Saige trained her flashlight on the next unfortunate victim. Zoe's bridesmaids appeared in the traces of light, circling back to Derrick. They were all holding hands, standing in a circle with their backs facing each other. Saige couldn't quite believe what she was seeing. Their eyes were black and unblinking, their hair and clothes soaked against their sallow skin.

They've been... spelled.

They were alive. She saw the shallow rise and fall of their chests.

Do they know I'm here? Can they sense anything?

Or are they just marionettes, plucked on strings to do Theodosia's bidding?

The sight of them linked together like some sort of human Stonehenge was too much for her to bear. Saige bent over and vomited. She was afraid and irresolute about what to do. She couldn't think. And she had to think. Her family's survival depended on it.

If Theodosia hasn't killed them, then that means they're

not part of her true intention. She's brought them down here to keep them out of the way.

The realisation made something deep inside her churn.

Jasper!

Where is he?

His absence woke Saige from her stupor. She fought her way out of the dark basement, mindful of the slick steps that caused a trip hazard with every tread. Anger had overcome her fear, and she no longer cared about being cautious. She dashed through the halls into the foyer, back up the stairs, past the second level to the upper landing.

Eerie light flashed through the third level, the lightning outside more powerful and dangerous. A rumble that sounded capable of splitting the very foundations of the house tore through the sky, making each of the walls groan and shake. Every door Saige came across was open.

This is a mind game. Theodosia is deliberately making my search difficult.

Saige didn't know whether she should call out for Jasper. Drawing attention to herself was unwise.

I am the mouse, and Theodosia is the cat. And a cat always knows when a mouse is present. It just bides its time before it pounces.

There was no sense in keeping quiet.

"Jasper!"

Her shout rolled down the hall, swallowed by the dark. She kept calling out to him, racing down every passage, checking every room that she passed. She didn't know what she would do if something happened to him. It was ironic. So many years of hating Jasper, of pushing away the memory of him and despising every article written about his music, and now she would do anything to have him by her side.

Wild with impatience, she sped down the last of the halls.

She froze, her mind settling on one disturbing thought.

The hidden chamber!

Saige barrelled forward, hoping she wasn't too late.

THIRTY

Saige didn't want to go down there. The passage to the hidden chamber was dark, like a rabbit hole that descended to nowhere but madness, or a gateway to the fiery depths of hell. Her flashlight did a poor job of revealing anything. The walls were uneven and damp, slick with mould and something that resembled black tar. It dripped in horrible fat drops. Saige stepped away, certain she was looking at blood.

Is the house... bleeding?

Again, she sensed the manor was alive. The chamber was its beating heart, the halls and passages its veins. Every room was a network, a part of something that was alert and aware. She had an image of herself as a piece of meat, slowly devoured by the house over time. Were she and her family really just... a food source?

My God, Theodosia. What has your curse done to this place?

Saige focused on the passage again. The walls seemed

to close in before her, the light intermittent. She realised her hand was trembling.

Stay calm.

She willed her heart to stop its palpitations.

I can do this. I have to do this.

She stepped into the passage, her shoulders snagging the tight walls. Warm liquid pressed against her arms. Saige was reminded of the blood and had to press her lips together to keep from gagging. Her panic escalated. She desperately needed to throw up. Cobwebs clung to her face and hair. She sensed tiny legs scrambling all over her scalp.

Turn back. Turn back!

Her flashlight went out.

A spike of chills ricocheted through her bones. She clambered backward, but the hall wasn't there. Had she somehow lost her sense of direction? Was she, in fact, going deeper into the passage?

Panic consumed her.

Get out! Get out!

But she couldn't tell which direction was which. She couldn't see where she was going. Saige put one foot in front of the other, sliding forward. Her legs felt as stable as water, the floor seeming to shift under her boots. She clung to the walls, her fingers scraping through blood and bone.

The house... it really is flesh.

She could feel hot chunks of meat between her fingers.

Saige couldn't help it. She screamed. Her cries echoed off the walls, rebounding back into her head. She saw nothing but twisted shadows. She was in an abyss. A black hole. A deep, empty pit where the walls were too hard to climb.

Terror choked her heart. She couldn't breathe. Saige welcomed the dizziness that pulled her down. Anything to get her away from the impenetrable dark.

Her knees buckled.

Yes, sweet mercy. Take me away.

Hands latched on to her waist, stopping her from hitting the hard floor.

Saige blinked against the sudden light.

Recognition slammed into her hard.

She was in the hallway.

But... how is this possible?

I was in the passage that led to the torture chamber.

Her skin was dampened by sweat. Cool air soaked through her clothes. There wasn't a trace of blood on her hands. She gazed back at the passage. It was empty. The walls were simple, jagged, uneven stone. No blood. No oozing flesh. The passage seemed to watch her with mock calmness.

"Saige! Saige can you hear me?"

Someone tapped her cheek. No. They were slapping her.

"Wake up! Saige, wake up!"

She tilted forward, fighting to gain strength back in her body. The person holding her helped her to her feet. They never let go, their hands like gauntlets around her arms. Clarity spun into focus when she looked at his face. Hot tears tumbled down her cheeks, the panic inside her deflating. She made a whimpering sound of relief and sagged into Jasper's embrace.

"Holy shit, Saige." He drew in a rocky breath. "You were in some sort of trance. Your eyes had rolled back. I thought you were about to have a fit."

Saige's heart couldn't carry a steady rhythm. "It was Theodosia. Some kind of mind trick. She made me think I was in there."

She pointed to the passage. She refused to look at it again. If she did, the horror would come tearing its way back to her.

Jasper stroked her arms, either for comfort or to keep her warm. "Why were you even up here?"

"I thought you were in the chamber."

He laughed. "Saige, that is literally the last place I would hide."

"I thought... I thought Theodosia had taken you," she admitted with a sob.

Jasper's face turned the colour of cornstarch. "Why would she come after me?"

Saige didn't say anything. She couldn't admit it. Not to Jasper. Not to herself.

Theodosia already knows anyway. It's why she was messing with your head.

But Saige knew saying those three little words out loud would put Jasper in more danger.

She tried to pull free, but he held her tighter. "Saige, why would Theodosia come after me?"

Her silence was speaking more than her words ever could. She wanted to stay in his embrace, ignore the feeling of terror she sensed coming for them from every direction, but in the end she turned away, every step painful.

I will not put Jasper in any more danger than I already have.

But he had other ideas. He reached for her hand and

reeled her back in, tightening his arms protectively around her, the space between them closing in.

Saige stood there, scarcely breathing, second-guessing herself and all her decisions. Her heart accelerated, beating wildly.

All her inner turmoil scattered away as Jasper's lips grazed hers, soft and unsure at first, then hungry and powerful. Saige lost herself in the sheer sensation of their mouths pressed together. The ground spun beneath her in the best way. She forgot about the danger. Forgot about the fear. All that mattered was her and Jasper. She deepened the kiss, pulling him closer and absorbing the heat from his body. She could feel his mouth smiling against hers. Memories of a happier time returned to her mind, filling her with hope and desire and love. She realised this was where she'd wanted to be for a long time. This was where Jasper had wanted her to be.

A rumble of thunder reeled above the house. The walls shuddered. Lightning burned through all the windows. Saige was jerked to the present. She broke the kiss, startled by the strange atmosphere that amassed in the house. Jasper's fingers wrapped around her own. His eyes darted frantically from wall to wall, as though he expected something to jump out at them at any moment.

Saige opened her mouth to speak but was cut off by a terrible scream. It pierced through the entire manor, full of pain, anguish, and sorrow. It came from above. But there was something else too. Something Saige wished she didn't recognise.

Rage.

"Jasper." She shook so badly she couldn't make her

voice clear. "I think that was the lady in the attic. I think that was... Theodosia."

She'd never actually seen the ghost she'd dubbed "the lady in the attic," but that scream was definitely Theodosia's. They were one and the same.

All the doors in the hallway slammed shut with impossible speed. She felt Jasper jump beside her, her own heart thrashing against her ribs. Doors banged closed downstairs, followed by upstairs.

Saige passed a stricken look at Jasper. She stared at their interlocked hands.

What have I done?

She'd angered Theodosia.

Saige reluctantly let go of Jasper's hand, but he refused to let her step away.

Tormented defiance lit in his eyes. "It's too late, Saige. We've nowhere to run. I love you. And you love me. She knows. The only thing we can do now is face her together."

Saige knew it was the truth. There was no way they could flee the house and escape through the woods. The storm would kill them. The flooded roads would kill them.

The house could very well kill us too.

She nodded, unable to control the quiver in her lower lip.

It wasn't just Jasper in danger. It was her family too.

She had to confront Theodosia. She had to try and end this.

Pay the sins of the father. A life for a life.

She really hoped she could achieve whatever that meant.

Saige was stuck in a daze, one triggered by fear. She

sensed her feet moving beneath her, one step in front of the other, farther and farther down the hall, Jasper right at her side.

His mouth quirked into a brief smile. He squeezed her hand. "We can do this."

That was another thing about Jasper that Saige had forgotten. How his optimism had the ability to take away all her common sense, because for the briefest moment, she did think everything would be all right.

But she also knew they faced an obstacle neither of them understood. Saige compared herself and Jasper to a dream.

And at some point, all happy dreams had to end.

THIRTY-ONE

The screams never ceased. They weren't just sobs but wails, guttural and howling, full of torment and regret.

Saige and Jasper reached the top of the stairs and took a left into the hall that led to the attic door. They followed the sounds of the weeping. It was a deep song of grief and mourning.

Saige's fear ascended to an all-time high as she turned the handle, the door creaking on its hinges as it opened. It reminded her of screeching pipes. The staircase ahead was wooden and narrow, the steps lined with a thick coat of dust. They climbed, their feet sending clouds of grime into the air. Saige fought a sneeze. Her footfalls were quiet. Jasper's were heavier. Some of the stairs groaned under his weight. Saige shot him a look, which he returned with a shrug.

She was terrified, but she was also torn. Listening to those gutted cries broke her heart. No one deserved to be tormented like that.

What did Frederick do to you?

The staircase became tighter the farther they ascended. At the landing, Saige gripped the dangling pull cord, which appeared to have never been replaced, the rope dry and wiry to touch. She gave Jasper a hesitant look, a last chance to turn back.

He silently nodded, but his face was damp with perspiration.

Saige counted down from three in her head and tugged the cord. Her chest felt like it could very well explode. She didn't pull away when Jasper took her hand. She climbed the first step, then the next, her head screaming at her to turn around and flee. Wetting her lips, finding her courage, she crossed the threshold. At first, all she saw was darkness, her eyes struggling to see into the attic.

Jasper's voice was a whisper beside her. "Why are attics always so creepy?"

She couldn't have agreed more.

The attic is the brain of the house, filled with memories, past passions, and dreams.

And secrets.

A raw, aching scream tore through the darkness.

Jasper and Saige shone their flashlights in the direction of the sound. Objects draped in white sheets appeared intermittently in the scattered light. Together, they stepped blindly into the musty attic. Saige cast her flashlight up toward the sloping roof. Cobwebs drooped from every beam. In the distorted light, they appeared deceptively like lace catching the slivers of early sunrise. Rain dripped from damp patches in the ceiling. A drop fell onto Saige's forehead. It was unnaturally cold.

This is no normal rain.

She'd always suspected the storm outside had nothing to do with the weather but rather the supernatural. Now she was certain of it.

A wail rose from somewhere to their left.

Jasper flinched and nearly barrelled right into Saige. He grabbed her arm, his fingers biting deep through the fabric of her jacket. She was sure he'd leave crescent bruises on her skin.

She shook her head, urging him to not make a sound.

He nodded. His eyes were bugging out of his head.

They followed the haunting cries. A sweep of their flashlights cast a muted haze across overstuffed, fraying furniture. The attic was a disorganised maze. Volumes of books had been stacked upon each other. A broken piano was covered in layers of cobwebs. Saige and Jasper started when they came across a dressmaker's dummy, the face white and waxy, the eyes discoloured.

"Jesus. That isn't creepy, is it?" Jasper's voice was tense in Saige's ear.

They passed dozens of old trunks piled on top of each other. Saige cast her light down onto the floor. Some of the boards were rotten, and those that appeared sturdy creaked beneath her boots when she stood on them. Every step she and Jasper made was met with a groan. Saige cringed, terrified that Theodosia would suddenly be upon them, a screaming banshee hellbent on tearing their bodies apart.

She's somewhere in here.

Theodosia's mournful cries drifted across every surface, making it difficult to know which direction they came from. Saige knew she was being watched. It was an intense feeling of awareness from somewhere behind her... then in front of her. It was moving every second. Circling. Eyes that bored into her soul, sending horrible tingling sensations all over her skin.

Jasper moved toward an object covered in a white sheet. It looked tall and sturdy enough to be human.

"Jasper, what are you doing?" Her voice came out in a frantic hiss.

She didn't like this sudden burst of confidence he'd gained.

He tore the sheet down. A floor-length mirror met them in a cloud of disturbed dust mites, little specks dancing through the flashlights' beams. Saige swatted the haze away. She caught a glimpse of her distorted reflection in the mirror. For a second, she could have sworn she saw a pale face by her shoulder, staring at her with lifeless eyes, but it had disappeared too fast for her to be certain.

Saige clung to the front of Jasper's jacket and forced him away from the mirror. "Why did you do that?"

She whipped her head around in a panic, afraid something monstrous would creep up on them.

Jasper's eyebrows shot up. "They do it in the movies. I thought maybe it might have been Theodosia and we had the upper hand... for once."

"We never have the upper hand. Please, just don't do anything else, okay?"

"Okay. Promise."

She wondered if he had his fingers crossed behind his back.

Another tormented scream filled the attic. This time it sounded like the cries of a drowning woman.

Saige spun on instinct. Her scalp tightened as dread coursed through every vein and artery in her body. She gripped Jasper's hand, afraid he'd attempt another act of bravado.

"This way," she insisted, hating that she couldn't keep her voice steady.

But Jasper didn't move. He pointed to Saige's left, his face so pale even his sun-kissed freckles had faded to a blanched white.

Saige slowly turned around. Her heart buckled, caving down to her stomach.

Crouched on the floor in the northwest corner of the attic, a woman rocked back and forth. The movement reminded Saige of a pendulum swinging chaotically out of control. She recognised the translucent, sallow skin of the wraith.

Theodosia.

The spectre was crying heart-rending sobs. Tears slipped down her discoloured cheeks, her hair a black mess of twisted curls. Every so often, her fingers hooked into the strands, tearing them out from her scalp and discarding them on the floor.

Saige found it difficult to breathe, her throat clogged with panic. Her feet seemed to take a life of their own, pacing toward the spectre without any direction from her brain. She was terrified, but she also had the strongest urge to help.

She was about five feet away from the ghost when she paused. Blood soaked thick and fast through Theodosia's emerald gown. It spilled over the floorboards, sinking like droplets of oil through the gaps.

Theodosia reached for something ahead. Saige cast her flashlight toward it. It was a portrait, something aged and covered in a thick coating of grime. She recognised the bronzed vintage-carved frame. It was the same as the portraits downstairs in the foyer.

The missing portrait.

Saige leaned forward, perplexed by the image. It was of a handsome couple in wedding attire. Saige knew the unsmiling man. Frederick George Wolvercraft. The writing in the corner, the artist's stamp, confirmed it. It also confirmed something that sent icy fear fluttering through her chest. The bride in the portrait was young, much younger than even Frederick, her smile full of hope and happiness. Saige recognised her face. Her cheeks drained of blood as realisation struck home.

Anna.

Only that wasn't her name in the stamp.

Tianna Wolvercraft.

Saige leapt back. All her discoveries over the last couple days rushed at her, her thoughts frantic. She mentally brought up Theodosia's journal entries in her head. Not once had Theodosia written "my engagement." She'd referred to it as "the engagement."

Saige's shock spiralled toward despair.

Theodosia had never been writing about herself. She'd been writing about her daughter, Anna. Whose real name was Tianna.

Saige remembered the news article she'd read in Mildred's dining room. *"The engagement of Ms T Sinclair to Mr Frederick George Wolvercraft was recently made public. The wedding will take place in a private ceremony in June."*

Saige wanted to slam the heel of her palm into her head. How could she have gotten it so wrong?

"Sssaaaiiiggggeeee."

She leapt at the sound of Theodosia's voice. Blood seeped out from the corners of the ghost's lips. She opened her mouth, her words barely discernible. "She... kno... she... knowwws."

Saige felt sick. "What?"

Theodosia squeezed her eyes shut. Frightening determination settled into the rotting features of her face. Then she screamed, her voice causing Saige's eardrums to throb. "She knows. She's here!"

Theodosia snapped her head toward Jasper, pointing a crooked finger at him.

A blast of wind lifted him off his feet, slamming him against a wall. He dropped onto the floor, paralysed with shock.

Saige cried out and ran to him, horrified when an invisible force dragged him across the floor, thrashing him about like a human piñata. The closer she got to him, the farther he was hauled away. She didn't care that she collided with discarded furniture or knocked-over boxes. Papers and old bundles of newspaper were strewn in front of her, creating obstacles in her path.

She came to the end of the attic and froze. Jasper was in the air, his head down and arms outstretched, as though he'd been crucified on an invisible cross.

"Jasper. Oh God, Jasper!" She searched for something to help get him down.

"Saige."

She swivelled on the balls of her feet, surprised by the voice. Alarm crossed her face, shock settling into despair. "Anna!"

And that was when I struck her hard across the head.

She toppled back, her body rigid on the floor. Her

glassy eyes stared at me for a second longer, her mind desperate to remain conscious. Dull acceptance glinted on her sweaty face. "H-How?"

I didn't answer.

Then her eyes shut, her consciousness swallowed by the dark.

Saige has always known she was haunted by a presence.

And she's right.

She just didn't know it was me.

I've followed her since she was a little girl, the shadow that was always behind her. I watched her grow up into the young, nervous woman she was, witnessing every fumble she made in life. She was as useless and pathetic as the rest of the Wolvercraft clan, but there was something about her that reminded me of myself. A naïve girl, too scared to venture out of her comfort zone, too ignorant to know that people in this world were self-centred and cruel.

Saige is a loner because I made her so. I gave her night-mares in the evenings, messed with her emotions during the day, and destroyed her ambitions. It wasn't difficult. My winning card was dividing her and Jasper. My curse couldn't claim the young musician, not when he wasn't in Ashvall, but I could still break the pair apart. He was easy to influence. I planted whispers in his head while he slept, encouraging him to marry Saige. He'd been a puppet on my strings when he proposed. And just as easily, I convinced him to break it off, leaving her desperate, afraid, and alone. She was wrapped in nothing but misery and self-loathing. I wanted her to experience the joy of love, like I had, and then be crushed by disappointment. I couldn't let her find happiness, not when I was trapped in this house, on this island, with her as my only escape. The daughter of the Wolvercraft bloodline doesn't deserve love, not when mine had been my killer. Love was my curse, and I'll be damned if I don't see it destroy the Wolvercraft family.

Saige and I are, in a way, sharing a soul. Perhaps it was the deaths of our mothers that so strongly linked us—that same unbearable, gut-wrenching pain that surrounds Saige's ongoing life and my short one. When I learned that Xavier Wolvercraft was to be married, my connection with Saige was easy to manipulate. I possessed her in her sleep. It wasn't hard to write to her brother and confess my deepest, cherished desires that he and his fiancée wed at Wolvercraft Manor. Saige wasn't even aware that she wrote the letter or posted it. I signed it "Dad," knowing Xavier would never disobey his father.

Derrick Wolvercraft.

Even the name makes my stomach curdle. He is in every way like my Frederick. Arrogant. Selfish. Obsessed with self-image and his own entitled worth.

Yes, I watched them all arrive at Wolvercraft Manor. Every one of them pawns falling into my trap, each piece moved across the chessboard of my own making.

Dr Harriette Reynolds was not part of the plan. Her research led her to connect the curse to me, its instigator.

Interfering, prying, meddlesome woman. I couldn't let her tell Saige and ruin everything I had worked so hard to achieve. I stalked Dr Reynolds though the Hauteville Woods on the evening of the party. It was a foolish choice to travel on her own. I felt the fear hang in her chest when she realised she wasn't alone. Her panic was heavy and debilitating, her movements sloppy through the trees. My echoing, beating footsteps pulsed in her ears as I gained closer. At the last second, at the moment she realised I was behind her, she turned around, her eyes filled with dawning horror. I bared my teeth in a dark, bitter smile and snapped her thick neck. She fell in a limp mess. Her body I gave to the earth, a deep hole where no one would find her.

You will understand why I did it. The descendants of Frederick are a disease on this earth. I hate them with a passion that stirs my blood and makes the darkest part of my heart bleed. Frederick George Wolvercraft took everything. My mother. My fortune. My life.

My soul.

And as long as I walk the halls of Wolvercraft Manor, I have vowed his descendants will pay the price.

And they have.

They always will.

Generation after generation.

I will be there for every death.

Now it's time you learn my story.

Tianna Sinclair

THIRTY-THREE

Ashvall Island was drearily grey. It wasn't at all like the hot summers of New York City I'd grown up with. Even the cold in Ashvall lacked atmosphere. Back at home, winters were magical. The icy spells during Christmas cast a winter wonderland across the entire city. It had taken my breath away. I missed home so much. I wanted to explore the glamourous boutiques and rustic markets one more time. I longed to walk the city's leafy boulevards lined with resplendent architecture, but this was my home now. Ashvall Island.

The sea was rough, the *Adventure* slicing through the water between other smaller steamships as it navigated its way to an empty port at the dock. I couldn't help but be a little disappointed at my first sight of the island. The wind off the sea was chilly, the mist and spray too thick to see much beyond the rugged coastline. I could vaguely discern a small township, lights twinkling ahead in the distance, before it, too, was consumed by fog.

That must be St Albert Port.

Frederick had told me about the quaint little town. He said I would love it. I hoped he was right.

"Come along, Anna. Don't dawdle." My mother linked her arm with mine, weaving us through the disembarking crowd. She was an extraordinarily handsome woman. Confident and poised, she was the envy of many a high-society lady. I'd inherited her long, dark hair and lustrous curls, but that was all. While my mother stood tall, her tanned skin and vibrant beauty catching the eye of sailors left and right, I stood next to her with my shoulders hunched, my eyes downcast to the wooden boards beneath my feet. My mother always did tell me I was too shy for my own good. She was right. Without her help, I'd never have accomplished such a fortuitous match. I often had to pinch myself just to make sure it was real.

We followed the passengers across the gangplank to the wharf. Tugs ploughed their way through the dark water, carrying baggage and all sort of boxes heaped with cargo. As soon as I took my first step onto the island, the dull-coloured sky opened its floodgates. Rain drummed down on us, my mother's straw bonnet losing its shape, the brim catching water like a cistern.

Her voice was sharp in my ear. "Hurry. I do not want you catching a cold. Not after everything I have been through to secure this match. Mr Wolvercraft wishes to marry quickly. I cannot have you ill in bed the first week we arrive."

"But why must we marry so quickly?" I stumbled past some damp-looking sailors, all of them shouting in French. My engagement to the love of my life had been long. Three months, to be precise. I desperately wanted to be by Frederick's side, to be wed, but what were a few more weeks' wait in the grand scheme of things? We had our entire lives together waiting for us.

My mother lifted her nose ever so slightly to show me she wasn't impressed. "My dear, matches are not made out of love. They are a business arrangement, and as your mother, it is my responsibility to ensure you are well provided for. You have looks, you are sweet and well mannered, and you possess an impressive dowry, but there are other young ladies out there who have Mr Wolvercraft in their sights. Women with inheritances and dowries too. A man's affection can easily be led astray when it comes to money."

"But Frederick told me he loved me back in New York. He wouldn't do such a thing."

"Matches made out of love have been ruined before. And do not call Mr Wolvercraft by his Christian name until you are married. Understood?"

"But he told me to."

"I do not care what he said. You are not married yet. And until you are, you will be proper and respectful."

I nodded silently. I was exhausted and overwhelmed. My wet shoes caused my feet to go numb, my gloves doing a poor job of retaining any warmth in my hands. The transatlantic passage from New York to Southammon, and then to Ashvall Island, had taken over nineteen days. Mother said I should have been grateful it wasn't on a sailing ship. Now, I wanted to do nothing else but curl up in a ball and go to sleep in a warm bed, to have pleasant dreams about Frederick and the excitement of our upcoming nuptials.

My mother practically dragged me to the end of the

wharf, where we were met by a footman in front of a gleaming black carriage wet with rain.

Disappointment washed over me.

Frederick isn't here to meet us.

Mother discussed something I couldn't hear with the footman. We were both helped into the carriage. It wasn't warm inside like I'd hoped, but at least it was dry. The seats were comfortable, richly decorated with plush red velvet and gold-tasselled curtains. I couldn't help but smile.

That would have been Frederick's choice, of course. He does love beautiful things.

I wondered if that was why he loved me. If I grew old and ended up half as beautiful as my mother, then I had nothing to fear. I'd heard the affection between a married couple dwindled over time, but I knew in my heart that would never be me and my Frederick. We'd be inseparable. We'd be in love.

The massive diamond on my finger glistened, reminding me of the future ahead.

I am the luckiest woman alive.

So why, when the carriage lurched forward through the rain, did a strange wave of dread tackle my stomach?

***

FREDERICK WASN'T LYING WHEN HE SAID HIS HOUSE was a feast for the eyes. It was magnificent. A beautiful Renaissance-inspired manor, every room decorated with scenes from folklore and poetry. I loved exploring the walled courtyards and expansive gardens. I was accustomed to lavish things—my mother's profession afforded us small luxuries—but this was an extravagance of a different sort. Even the red carpet beneath my feet, with its intricate gold patterns, was softer than any Aubusson rug.

My mother and I had been at Wolvercraft Manor for over a week. There had been no talk of my marriage to Frederick. No date had been set. Except for the evenings at dinner, or the occasional chaperoned walk around the gardens, I hadn't even seen him. Mother told me he was a gentleman and would often be detained by business. An absent husband was something I'd need to learn to contend with. But it was difficult. As much as I loved the house, I didn't want to be stuck in it alone, with only my handmaid and mother for company. The housekeeper and butler were civil when spoken to, but there was something about them that was difficult to define. They watched me often. I didn't like what I saw in their eyes. It wasn't mistrust. No. It was—with a heavy heart, I realised— dislike. I asked my mother about it.

"Forget them, my darling," she told me on the night of the Summer Ball. "They are beneath you and jealous. Once you are married to Mr Wolvercraft, they will look at you as the lady of the house. You wait and see. Tonight, Mr Wolvercraft will be announcing your engagement to the entire room. Focus on that." She waved her feather fan, though it was far from humid in the massive ballroom.

I danced many sets that evening, but none with Frederick. Was that not strange? After announcing our engagement, he never once asked me to dance. I was disappointed, but rather than letting my feelings show, I kept to my mother's side, meeting guests and thanking them for their kind words and congratulations. New acquaintances taught me the origin of the Summer Ball. It was one of the most celebrated traditions on the island. Witches used to reside in the Hauteville Woods and would bless the land in a dance. My mother scoffed, but I was willing to believe it. Mother was a spiritualist, after all. If she could communicate with the dead, why couldn't witches exist? I was intrigued by the stories of the Roma Witch, the leader of the Hauteville Coven. I'd get Frederick to tell me all about Ashvall's legends when we were married.

The ballroom was a masterpiece of summer cheer. I loved dancing, the sets moving in time, skirts becoming colourful, swirling rows, the music haunting but melodious. It was exactly like the beauty of the Venetian balls I'd read about, the entire party carrying an air of mystery and intrigue. Frederick certainly knew how to entertain, but how much must this all have cost him? I wondered if he would share that information with me.

Later that evening, news of my mother's talents had travelled across the room. Encouraged by curious participants and onlookers, she conducted a seance in the parlour. It was the first time I could breathe all night. I loved my mother dearly, but it was exhausting to constantly live up to her expectations.

I watched the dancing, but I wasn't alone for long. A young lady in a superb red gown with strawberry-coloured hair approached, her smile genuine and lovely. My goodness, she was beautiful. And confident for a woman of her standing. She introduced herself as Margaret Thronesby. We talked till the early hours of the morning. We really did have much in common. She lived with her aunt, Mrs Rixon, and had been on the island for two years. She was only a little older than me. Finally, I had found someone I could talk to. A companion of sorts. We decided to promenade the next day in St Albert Port. It was my first adventure into the town, and I very much looked forward to taking a stroll on the beach and watching the seagulls fly. Miss Thronesby promised me we would do just that.

I settled into life at Wolvercraft Manor. The weeks seemed to drift away. They were going too fast yet, at the same time, so slow. I spent most of my time with Miss Thronesby. She was a gem and a perfect lady. I supposed she had not received any matches because she had no fortune. That saddened me. She was such a beautiful, tolerant, caring creature. She deserved every happiness.

In confidence, she told me not to worry about Frederick's lack of affection.

"He is not indifferent, Miss Sinclair. A man has a great many things to settle before he weds. Wait and see. All will be set right once you are married."

Despite Margaret's comforting words, I was seriously worried that Frederick had changed his mind. Mother grew agitated too. On my return from St Albert Port one day to dress for dinner, I found her waiting in my room. A beautifully wrapped parcel with red ribbon sat on my bed.

Mother's nose crinkled, as though she'd smelt something bad. "You've been walking on the beach again, haven't you?"

"Of course. It's been a pleasant afternoon."

For the first time since I'd left the *Adventure*, sunlight

had sparingly glimpsed its way through the dull-coloured clouds.

Mother snorted with contempt. "Look at the state of your shoes. Sand everywhere. Get them off this instant."

I did as she demanded, shielding my eyes from her, fearful they'd start to tear. I hated disappointing my mother.

She sashayed over to the window, closed it with a jarring thud, and drew the curtains. "I do not understand why you insist on keeping this window open. You will catch a cold."

"It helps me to sleep."

It stops the bad dreams and night sweats.

Something I had never told my mother about. Something my lady's maid had been good enough to hide.

"Come here." There was a nervous slip in my mother's voice.

I was both shocked and pleasantly surprised when she pulled me into a comforting hug.

She brushed an unruly curl behind my ear. "I am sorry, my sweet girl. I am only very... worried."

"About what?"

I didn't like the creases that suddenly formed across her forehead. They made her look years older.

"Anna, my darling. Please stay away from Miss Thronesby."

I pulled away, shaken by her tone. "I don't understand. Miss Thronesby is my friend. She has been a great comfort these last several weeks. I've taken guidance from her and value her friendship."

"You sew and buy ribbons together. That does not

make you friends. Miss Thronesby is not to be trusted. She watches Frederick. She watches you."

A cold ripple of alarm swept through me. "What are you saying?"

Mother brushed her thumb across my cheek. "Mr Wolvercraft has set a date for the wedding. It will be a private affair. In three days, you will be married."

Private affair?

That was very unlike Frederick. He never passed a moment to flaunt his worth.

Mother raised her chin. "I believe Miss Thronesby hopes to make a match with Mr Wolvercraft. She will do what she can to break your engagement. Stay away from her, Anna. That woman is a malicious vixen."

I couldn't help but laugh. What my mother suggested was absurd.

"Anna." The icy glint in her eyes silenced me. She moved to the bed and unwrapped the parcel. I held my breath. It was an exquisite white gown. My cheeks flushed with warmth as happiness exploded inside me. It was a wedding gown, one of the most beautiful dresses I'd ever seen. Silk brocade and tulle trimmings. Pearl beading and ivory lace. A long, two-tier bridal veil fit for a queen.

Mother looked down at the dress appreciatively. "Mr Wolvercraft has organised your wedding portrait to be painted tomorrow. After that, he will be attending to business in London. He will be back for the wedding."

My smile dropped. "But isn't it bad luck for the groom to see the dress before the wedding?"

My mother tsked at me. "Silly superstitions. Anna, in three days' time, all of this will be yours." She waved her hands around the room to emphasise her point. "Three days. Stay in the house. Do not accept any visits from Miss Thronesby. Do I make myself clear?"

"Mother, you're frightening me. I can't believe Miss Thronesby would do such a thing. And I don't believe Fred... Mr Wolvercraft would be capable of backing out of an engagement. It would not be right."

She held me in her gaze with pity. "My dearest girl. You are so naïve and ignorant of everything evil in this world."

"Then tell me. What gives you cause to distrust Miss Thronesby?"

And Frederick?

Evil?

My mother turned away. She raised a gloved hand to her head, as though she had a migraine. "Be ready at nine o'clock tomorrow morning. I will make sure your lady's maid is here at seven thirty. We must have you looking your best for the portrait. I will see you at dinner."

She swept out of the room with that air of indifference she was so good at presenting.

I tried not to let the confrontation hurt me, but my face crumpled in humiliation.

What is she so afraid of?

And why won't she tell me?

THIRTY-FOUR

I didn't sleep well. Bad dreams haunted me. Ever since my wedding portrait had been painted and hung above the mezzanine, my head had been assaulted by a persistent headache that had lasted two days and two nights. But it was on the eve of my wedding when the real nightmare began. I sensed someone was in my room. I was still half asleep, barely conscious. A nagging sensation in my chest told me to open my eyes. Why couldn't I? My lids refused to flutter apart. My legs were stiff, my arms incapacitated. Was someone holding me down? Yes, someone was. Their hand was pressing against my mouth, pinching my nose, stopping the air flowing in and out.

Kick. Wriggle. Do something. Fight them off!

But I couldn't. My body wouldn't meet the demands my brain screamed for them to do.

Cold sweat latched on to my body. It saturated my nightdress and soaked into the sheets.

Please, someone help me!

Help me!

"Anna, wake up. Anna! Anna!"

Hands slapped my cheeks, rousing me into the waking world. I gasped, my jaw stiff, my lips heavy where fingers had smothered them.

My mother bent over me, her face paler than I'd ever seen. "Anna, sweetheart, get dressed this instant."

"What?" I blinked through the darkness, surprised when she pulled me out of bed.

My mother held a candle. Its flame was small and insubstantial compared to the overwhelming shadows that had settled around us. "Get dressed and meet me in the foyer. Do not make a sound. Do you understand?"

I struggled to make sense of what she was asking. "Yes, but... Mother, why? What time is it?"

"It is late. Wear something warm."

"Mother, you're frightening me?"

"Just do as I say. Immediately, Anna."

My mother hurried out of the room, slipping away into the shadows of the hall.

I stood beside my bed, unsure what to do. My mother had been acting so strange lately. She'd been stressed by my upcoming nuptials, but I'd never realised just how far it had gone.

Is she hysterical?

Is she paranoid?

All the evidence pointed to yes.

But I was a dutiful daughter. Whatever my mother was going through, I'd be there for her.

I hurried to my wardrobe and found my favourite winter dress and coat. Would I need a hat? Surely we weren't going outside. And what about my hair? I needed Sophia, my lady's maid, to attend to it. It wouldn't be proper to go downstairs without being dressed. My mother knew that.

Perhaps I should ring the bell. Call for help. Frederick will understand. My mother is ill.

My body was both hot and cold. Perspiration dripped from my hairline. I had to open a window. I needed cool air. The room was so dark and stuffy.

I'd just undone the latch, relishing in the feel of brisk wind against my skin, when Sophia appeared.

She bent in a small curtsy in the doorway. "Miss Sinclair. I'm here to dress you."

"Did my mother send you?"

Sophia's delicate face crinkled into a frown. "No, miss. Mr Wolvercraft did. He arrived late this evening and waits downstairs with your mother. You're to be married tonight."

"Tonight?"

This was all happening too fast. Not to mention how very strange it was.

Sophia gave me a small smile. "Mr Wolvercraft must leave again in the morning. He wishes to wed immediately. He'll be away for some time."

It struck a nerve with me that even the household staff knew more about my fiancé than I did.

I moved toward the wardrobe and took out my wedding dress, admiring the way the white fabric glimmered against Sophia's candle. "Mr Wolvercraft spent a small fortune on this gown. While we may not be getting married the way I imagined, it would be a waste not to wear the dress."

"Yes, indeed it would be, miss."

"Help me get dressed, please. And even if our time is

short, please see if you can do something worthy of a bride for my hair."

"Of course, Miss Sinclair."

I glanced at myself in the mirror, my nightdress stained with yellow splotches where I'd sweated.

I will look beautiful for my husband. I will look dignified for my mother.

SOPHIA DID A SPLENDID JOB. SHE HAD MANAGED perfection in twenty minutes. I never thought of myself as being vain, but in that moment, looking at my reflection in the mirror, I couldn't help but see a princess out of a fairy book, about to marry her prince. The dress fit me in all the right places, snug and tight near the bodice and loose and flowing at the waist.

Sophia gently placed the veil over my head. She beamed at me. "You're exquisite, Miss Sinclair. I hope that wasn't too bold to say."

"Of course not." I squeezed her hand. "You have done an amazing job as always. You truly are a lady's maid to be trusted. I hope I never lose you."

Sophia's warm smile waned. She curtsied. "Mr Wolvercraft asked me to accompany you to the chapel."

"Chapel? I didn't know there was one in the house."

Sophia only nodded.

I stole one more glance at myself in the mirror. It wasn't the wedding day I'd hoped for, but I had no reason to complain. I was about to marry the man I loved. United forever. My smile proved I was the happiest woman in the world. "We best not keep Mr Wolvercraft waiting any longer."

Or my mother.

MOONLIGHT SPILLED OFF THE POLISHED SURFACE OF the floor. Sophia led me down various hallways I hadn't known existed. The corridors felt like a maze. I'd forgotten just how huge Wolvercraft Manor truly was. That evening, the interior really did look like the inside of a cathedral, or a resplendent castle somewhere in France, but there was something off about the beautifully carved cherubs that stood as features at every corner. Their faces weren't quite as angelic but rather appeared strained and cruel in the dim light. It must have been a trick of the dark. I shivered, ill at ease.

"This way, Miss Sinclair. The chapel is just down here." Sophia entered a long passage with identical doors and hurried at a brisk pace.

I struggled to keep up in my long dress. "Sophia, please slow down."

She didn't.

"Sophia, are you sure this is the way?"

It seemed incredible that a chapel would be located at the end of a very dark and lonely passage. And then it struck me. Sophia had said Mr Wolvercraft was in the foyer. *"He arrived late this evening and waits downstairs with your mother."*

I stopped, suddenly afraid of the tiny, delicate creature before me. "Sophia?"

She tugged hard on a candelabra fastened to the wall.

A loud grating tore through the passage. A doorway opened up from the panelling.

I stepped back.

A secret doorway.

I was so startled my entire body shook. "Sophia, what is going on?"

She stared back at me with sad eyes. "I'm sorry, miss, but they made me do it."

Her eyes flicked behind me.

I pivoted around, barely having time to recognise the butler and footman ascend upon me. They clamped their hands around my upper arms, hard enough to hurt. I wasn't afraid anymore. I was furious.

"What are you doing?" My voice was shrill. Surely someone must have heard me. "Let me go this instant."

But there was no stopping the men. They dragged me toward the hidden doorway. It was my nightmare all over again. I wrenched backward, kicked and thrashed, screamed until my own eardrums felt like they'd shattered.

"Silence her. Now!" Sophia's voice was a harsh demand.

I glared at her with a look of utter, hurtful betrayal. Was she jealous of me? Did she want Mr Wolvercraft for herself? She had to know that a man of his position would never marry a servant girl.

I screamed again, only this time my ribs were met with a devastating punch that knocked the wind from my chest. My feet stumbled, my legs failing to hold me up. The footman covered my mouth with a cloth, something wet with a horrible stench. The world turned much darker. The floor tilted beneath me.

They've poisoned me! They've poisoned me!

Someone lifted me off the floor. I couldn't tell if it was the butler or the footman. Every sensation in my body had gone numb. Even my neck no longer felt secure. My head lolled to the side. I had a fleeting image of passing the hidden door, of hard stone walls and flickering candlelight, before everything went dark.

THIRTY-FIVE

I WOKE TO DARKNESS, MORE PROFOUND THAN anything I had ever known. Not a trace of light leaked through the suffocating black that greeted me from every angle. It was amazing that in the face of blindness, every other sensation grew stronger. I sensed a flagstone floor beneath me. It was damp from cold, the chill bleeding through my clothes into every fibre of my body. The air that hit my nose was dry and musty, tainted with the stench of death and rot.

Death and rot!

My heart raged into an erratic pounding.

The butler and footman. Sophia's betrayal!

Where am I? What is this place?

I scrambled onto my hands and knees. A wave of pain crept over my skull, an intense throbbing that latched on to the back of my head. Something sour rose from my stomach. I toppled over and was sick, the fatty, acrid scent of bile everywhere.

My beautiful dress.

"Anna!"

I froze, momentarily shocked.

That voice

For a split second, I actually believed everything would be all right.

"Anna. Are you there? Is that you?"

"Mother?" Tears bled from my eyes. I wasn't sure if they were from relief or despair that we were both trapped in here. "Mother, where are we? What is this place?"

"I do not know, my darling." There was panic in her voice, but also a strange tone of acceptance. "I think it is a cell. There is a wall between us."

I scrambled toward her voice, not caring that my wedding gown tore on the stone floor beneath me. I hit my palms against the wall. It was solid rock. Unbreakable. I traced my fingers along the stones, hoping to find a handle or a door.

Don't be ridiculous, Anna. Cells are designed to keep their prisoner contained. There is no door.

I slumped to the ground, emotion pulling me under.

"Anna." There was a sob in my mother's voice. "My lovely girl, we have been fooled."

"What's happening?" I swallowed a shallow breath. I couldn't get enough air in my lungs. The mindless terror had me clutched in its inescapable claws.

How had this happened? Where was Frederick? I was meant to be marrying him. To be a wife. Not a prisoner in a cell.

"Anna, I did try to get us out of here. Please forgive me. This is all my fault."

"I don't understand."

My ears were ringing. The pain in my head threatened to toss me back into unconsciousness.

Maybe that isn't such a bad thing.

"I have been so foolish," my mother confessed. "Anna, Margaret Thronesby is the Roma Witch. This is her doing."

"The *what*? Mother, please, you're not making any sense."

A gasp split the still air. My mother sounded like she was choking on her tears. "This has all been a ploy. Margaret and Frederick... they planned this."

"Indeed we did." The cold voice ripped through the darkness.

A sudden bloom of light ignited the dark, bringing my surroundings into relief. Margaret stood by the rusty cell bars, her right hand clutching a burning torch. There was nothing sweet or gentle in her expression. This was not the Margaret I had grown to be friends with. The woman before me was someone else.

Mother is right. Margaret is... a witch.

The Roma Witch.

Her delicately curved lips, which I had always envied, were now tipped in a sinful smile, her blue eyes burning like ice, her red hair an orange glow of fire. She was an angel of hell. A demon waiting for me at the gates.

I stared, horrified and still.

Margaret stepped forward, her cruel eyes never leaving mine. "Dear, poor, gullible Anna. You really should have listened to your mother and left Wolvercraft Manor when you had the chance."

I felt something heavy press against my chest. Fear. It was paralysing me. "I thought you were my friend."

Callous laughter erupted from her. "I was never your

friend, Anna. Stupid girl. Do you really think Frederick could love something as small, weak, and pathetic as you? He is mine. We planned this together. Designed Wolvercraft Manor together." Her smile dropped. "We were meant to be married and live happily together in our new home... but money became an obstacle."

"You mean your lack of it," my mother spat from her cell. "Anna, that is why we were dragged into this. Our fortune. That is what they want. They have planned this for months. Frederick found us in New York with the intention of bringing us to Ashvall Island. He is bankrupt, Anna. He needs our money."

It burned me to hear those words.

The fortune I'm set to inherit when my mother passes. That's all Frederick ever wanted.

Tears flowed angrily down my cheeks, fuelling my hatred.

Up until that moment, I'd hoped this was an awful ruse planned by Margaret. I'd hoped Frederick was ignorant of it, that he'd find me in this cell and save me and my mother. But that was a fantasy. His love had been an illusion. A trick. A deceitful, painful lie. He was the instigator of this cruel plan. Him and his witch.

I stared at Margaret, wishing I could walk through the cell bars and strangle her. "Why us? Why send Frederick all the way to New York to swindle us?"

There were eligible ladies in England, even France, with exorbitant fortunes.

My vision wasn't at full capacity, but I detected the smallest hint of cruel delight on Margaret's face. "This isn't just about money, sweet Anna. Sacrificing another witch during the full moon means a lifetime of wealth for my entire family for generations to come." She patted her stomach softly. "And I really need to assure that my family are taken care of."

I swallowed, wishing for the first time that my eyes hadn't adjusted to the poor light. Margaret's small baby bump was on full display. She must have been at least three months along. She'd hidden it so well with full skirts and corsets that no one had noticed.

I wanted to smack my head, or smash it against the stone wall.

I have been so blind.

I gasped in great sucking drafts. "I'm not a witch. Margaret, please. Let my mother and me go. This is madness."

Her eyes gleamed like razors. "Not a witch? That's where you're wrong. Your mother is a medium. She's the link to the dead. Powers like that do not come to any mere human. She's a witch. And that makes *you* a witch, sweet Anna."

"Stop calling me that." My voice had risen to a shout.

Shout. That's what I need to do.

"Help me, please," I screamed so loud I was surprised my lungs didn't burst. "Please. Someone. I'm in here. Please, help!"

Margaret heaved a bored sigh. "No one can hear you, Anna. Frederick and I made sure of that when we had this little chamber built into the house. Now, let's not waste any more time, shall we?" She fastened her torch in a bracket on the wall, took out a parchment from her dress pocket, and through the bars flattened it against a small wooden step stool. A fountain pen and inkwell were already on the stool, prepared earlier. "Come here, Anna. You will sign this."

I stretched forward to see what it was, then scurried back the moment I realised. "No. Never."

A marriage certificate.

"Do not sign it," my mother cried from her cell. "It is infused with magic. Once you sign, her spell is complete."

Margaret slapped her hands on her hips. Something hot and angry flickered beneath her gaze. "This grows tiresome." She waved her hand. The click of a lock resonated through the chamber, a cell door rasping open with screaming hinges.

Margaret disappeared into the cell. A moment later, she returned with her hand secured on the back of my mother's head. The Roma Witch held a knife to Mother's throat.

I struggled forward, my last grip on composure gone. The dress ripped beneath me, the fabric no longer soft and delicate to the touch but a hindrance to all my movements. My voice broke in a desperate cry. "No, please. Let her go, please."

The blade was so sharp that already a trickle of blood seeped from my mother's neck. It was a weapon unlike anything I had seen before. On any other occasion, I would have thought the green-jewelled hilt was beautiful, but all I could see now was a cold blade of steel that would rip the life from my mother.

Margaret's eyes narrowed, the skin around them hardened by lines like cracks in paint. "Then sign the certificate."

"Do not sign," my mother snapped. She whimpered when the blade pressed more firmly into her skin.

It agonised me to see her like that. A beautiful woman, reduced to a captive at the whims of a crazy witch. And I was partly to blame. My ignorance had led us down this path. Mother had told me to dress quickly and meet her in the foyer. We could have escaped Wolvercraft Manor together, but instead I believed Sophia's lie. I'd allowed myself to be deceived because of some stupid fantasy.

It's all my fault.

Margaret tugged on my mother's hair with impatience. Mother gasped from the pain, her long swanlike neck exposed to the blade.

I didn't doubt Margaret's motivation or her wickedness.

I grabbed the fountain pen with shaky fingers, and signed my name next to Frederick's.

Margaret's lips stretched into a cunning smile. Her voice was etched with sarcasm. "Thank you, Mrs Wolvercraft. A pity that you are now an orphan."

Margaret dragged the blade across Mother's throat.

I screamed, louder than I knew I was capable of. Loud enough to break glass. Loud enough to make dogs bark in St Albert Port. But it was useless. No one could hear me.

Surprise filled my mother's eyes, followed by shock and agony. The colour in her face drained to white.

Margaret dropped her. She stepped away as my mother's body sagged to the floor, her blood a thick, dark stream down the front of her gown. It pooled on the stones, flowing through the grating in a river of red.

Margaret wiped the blade clean on my mother's dress. Then she turned her beady eyes, which had thinned into black slits, on me. "Oh, Anna." She shook her head with pity. "How gullible you truly are. Your mother had to die. You couldn't inherit her fortune if she lived."

She swept down and retrieved the marriage certificate. "Now that you are Mrs Wolvercraft, your money belongs to Frederick. Everyone will be so saddened for Frederick when his young bride succumbs to illness, but they'll rejoice when he finds new love and remarries. This was how it was always going to be, Anna."

Frustrated and terrified all in that moment, I scrambled backward, unable to tear my eyes from my mother's lifeless body, unable to look at the woman who I thought was my friend.

Margaret watched me with curious interest. "Three days until the full moon, little Anna. It will all be over then. You will be reunited with your mother."

She's going to kill me!

She took up the torch, giving me a final once-over. "That dress was supposed to be mine. A pity you had to ruin it."

Her smile was like a grinning skull's. "Pleasant dreams, sweet Anna."

She slipped away into the dark, the light bleeding out.

I WAS BROKEN. TORN.

I didn't know how many hours had passed. Time was unmeasurable in the dark. Tears streamed from my eyes, so unstoppable that I imagined there was enough to fill Niagara Falls. I shouted for help, beat my fists against the walls, tried to break the lock on my cell door, but nothing worked. I was trapped in this eternal darkness.

My mother's body had never been carried out. She must have been cold by now. I didn't want to think of her that way, but the alternative was to imagine her alive and happy, her arms wrapped around me in a way only a mother's love could protect you from the world. That just made me cry harder. I would never experience that again. I was alone. I would die in this place.

I drifted in and out of sleep, sometimes not knowing if I had actually woken or if everything was a nightmare. At one point, a horrible smell roused me awake. I gagged, choking on the odour that permeated the cell. There was no mistaking that scent. Death. It was everywhere. My mother's body had started to decompose.

I crawled into the farthest corner away from where she fell.

I'm so sorry. I'm so sorry.

My ignorance, my naivety, had been our downfall.

It had killed my mother.

It would kill me too.

IT HAD TO BE AT LEAST TWO DAYS SINCE MY MOTHER died. I was deliriously hungry. I begged for death to find me quickly, to take me away and unite me with my mother. Every time I was close to losing consciousness, my groaning stomach dragged me back to the waking world. I couldn't concentrate. Irritable, angry thoughts racked my mind. Sometimes I thought there were others in the cell with me. Voices spoke, but I didn't have the energy to talk back. I wondered if it was death, if the Grim Reaper had arrived to take me away, but in the end there was always that empty darkness. There was no escaping the eternal black.

I realised this had been Margaret's intention. To starve me.

Please, hurry it along.

It would have been far more merciful if Margaret had plunged that dagger into my heart. But that would have been too quick. Prolonging my pain was her way of rewarding her macabre appetite. I imagined her sitting in the drawing room, drinking tea, wondering if it was time to check on me and see if I'd finally succumbed to death.

When I next woke, a sliver of silvery light had penetrated the darkness. It had to be moonlight. It must have slipped between the stones in the wall. It was weak but still strong enough for me to see a small, sharp rock in my cell.

I crawled toward it, my legs trembling beneath me. I struggled to grab the rock at first. My mind just couldn't seem to instruct my fingers to grip it. Or maybe my hand wasn't listening. Finally, I clasped it.

I didn't know what made me write it. Most likely delirium, but once I started, I couldn't stop. I scratched the words into the stone floor, over and over again. The one time I would be heard. A final message. A reminder that I had been here and wouldn't be forgotten.

IN LIFE I WAS AFRAID. IN DEATH I AM FEARLESS. They will all pay.

THEY WILL PAY?

How will they pay, Anna?

How can you be fearless in death?

I was too tired to answer the question.

I WOKE GRIEVING FOR THE THINGS THAT WOULD never be. I would never see my mother again. I would never fall in love. I would never marry and have children. Frederick and Margaret had stolen my future, cut my life short. They would have everything that should have been mine.

Rage filled every vein in my body. It was the only emotion I could accomplish. I was too drained to cry, too exhausted to scream. All I had left was my anger.

I hate them.

I hate the baby that grows inside the witch.

I hate Wolvercraft Manor, a house paid for with stolen money, deception, and lies.

I hate the Wolvercraft family.

But most of all, I hated myself.

Too naïve. Too gullible. Too sweet and innocent to see what was really happening.

The end was drawing close. My organs felt like they'd shrivelled up inside me. My muscles were numb. My head pounded from pain.

Margaret has won.

I prayed and prayed to God to avenge me. To curse the Wolvercraft family and their legacy. Love had been my downfall. Now I wanted love to be a curse for the entire Wolvercraft bloodline.

Please, please, please. If you have any justice, send them the angel of darkness. Destroy them like they have destroyed me.

I closed my eyes, waiting for the sweet mercy of death to take me.

I will never forget.

And I will never forgive.

THIRTY-SIX

I STOOD OVER MY BODY, UNABLE TO MOURN THE loss through my rage.

The butler stared at my mother's body for a long time. Her veins were a dark purple against her grey skin, her eyes locked in a final display of horrified surprise. Her beautiful dress that she'd loved so much was no longer green but now a dry sheet of blood. The stone around her was caked in it. Would someone even clean it, or would my mother's essence remain etched to the stone, a permanent reminder of the horror that befell her there?

Margaret held a cloth to her nose, offended by the smell that came off our bodies. The Roma Witch hadn't checked on me in several days. In the torchlight, I dared not look at what I had become.

In the end, there had been no angel to greet me. No long tunnel to go down. No pearly white gates. I was trapped in this cell, still alone, with only my dead body and my mother's for company. I had hoped my mother would be here. Perhaps God was kinder to her and had taken her soul to heaven.

Why am I still here?

"We need to remove them." Margaret's voice was an emotionless command. "We'll go through the tunnel."

The butler, a beefy sort of man who liked his food and alcohol, sweated profusely. "The tunnel, Miss Thronesby?" Sweat perspired from his bald head, running down the back of his neck. The air around him smelt of body odour.

Margaret grinned. It wasn't a pleasant smile. "Follow me, gentlemen."

The butler bent down and scraped my mother off the floor. Her legs and arms were limp and floppy, making her a cumbersome heap in his hold. Her head lolled back on his shoulder, exposing the long slit across her throat. It was crusted over with dried blood and something that resembled yellow mucus.

It pained me to see my mother reduced to that. It had always been her wish to be buried in the family plot in New York City, not in a shallow grave where no one could mourn for her.

The footman slipped into the cell. He carried my body out, my dress and veil catching on the stone. I watched them take my body away. The footman hauled me over his shoulder like a sack of wheat, my long dress and veil adding an extra burden to my weight. He cursed at the unfairness of it all. Some of the white pearls caught the light from the torch, sending brief glitters across the dress, a reminder of the beauty it had once been. I had been dead several hours, my body cold and inflexible to the touch. The young footman struggled with my dead weight, my long hair hanging over his arm.

Will they bury my mother and me together?

That seemed far too kind a mercy for the likes of Margaret Thronesby.

The Roma Witch clicked her fingers at the men. "Don't dawdle."

She directed them to a device I had never seen before. It was tall and slim with intricate wrought-iron scrollwork. It reminded me of a birdcage but had the confinement of a coffin.

The footman stared with an open mouth, his youthful face sallow in the torchlight. "What is that?"

Margaret pressed her lips together with impatience. "It's called an elevator. A rarity for now, but soon every great house and building will have one. Now get inside. We will have to travel one at a time."

The footman blinked. "But what about the bodies, miss?"

Margaret's gaze slid over the pair. Her green eyes narrowed. "The elevator is spacious enough to carry two. I had it purposely designed that way. Now get inside."

She grabbed the footman by the shoulder and shoved him in the cage, my body stiff beside his. He barely had time to comprehend what was happening when the door was latched shut and some sort of chain on a pulley system groaned above. With a jolt, we descended into darkness. It must have been a narrow shaft of sorts, because every so often, the caged ironwork scraped against the walls. I felt the tension in the footman's body, sensed the blood pounding through his veins, the driving rhythm of his heart. He was afraid.

The chains above rasped, each jolt causing his breathing to intensify. I didn't feel sorry for him. He was an accomplice to hiding a murder. I wanted terror to bore into his soul. I wanted horror to squeeze him until he begged for it to end. I wanted to drive my cold dead hands inside him and tear his limbs apart. He clutched at his necktie, trying to loosen the knot. He was lucky I did not tighten it.

Can I even do that?

Fiery illumination pierced the darkness above. Margaret was peering down, the flames from her torch blazing across the compacted walls. It allowed me to see the beads of sweat that ran down the footman's face in rivulets.

The farther we descended, the colder the air became.

The elevator jerked suddenly. He unhooked the latch and scrambled out, nearly dropping my body in the process.

"Miss Thronesby," he cried out. "I can't see anything down here."

His voice travelled up the shaft, an echo that became thin and muted.

The elevator rattled. He watched with wide eyes as it ascended, leaving him in this alien world with only my corpse for comfort.

"Miss!" His voice trembled up to the dark. "Miss, please!"

The waiting seemed endless.

When the elevator arrived again, Margaret stepped out and glared at him with an annihilating look, teeth bared. The flames from her torch shone against her milky skin. Her beauty was no longer soft and angelic. Down here, in the underworld where she belonged, she was hardened by cruelty. She approached the footman with a panther-like grace. "Keep your voice down."

When the butler arrived, my mother's body like a wilted flower in his arms, Margaret stepped forward. Her torch revealed a long tunnel that stretched farther than the light could penetrate. Rats scurried in and out of the shadows. The scratching of their tiny claws sounded much louder in the dark.

"Follow me." Margaret's voice was a ruthless command. She marched ahead, not caring that the footman whimpered and the butler sniffled.

The deeper we ventured into the tunnel, the more its structure changed. The walls were no longer smooth but jagged, and the texture beneath my feet turned into something that had a weak, resistant force. I drew closer to Margaret. The red glow from her torch revealed sand and tiny seashells, which she crushed with her heavy boots. The briny scent of ocean air saturated my nose, and my ears filled with the sudden crash of foamy waves.

A sea cave.

Margaret led the company up a set of stairs chiselled into the stone. The passage was narrow and winding. It seemed endless as it drifted up, step after step. It was definitely not constructed for stealthy escapes.

It was built to hide secrets.

We came to an opening in the rock, the starless sky above us. The moon cast a deceptively tranquil illuminance across the ragged sea cliffs. Even the waves looked silver, their crests sparkling as they broke on the shore, tugging shells and seaweed back in the undertow. It was a beautiful night. Not the night for dumping corpses.

Cool air swept across my skin. The harsh tangle of

weeds wrapped around my dress. *Can I even call it skin? Or a dress?*

I was here, and yet... I wasn't.

Am I a ghost?

Mother had communicated with countless spirits during her seances. Was it possible that they had all ended up like this? Wandering aimlessly. Something that existed but was never seen in the physical world.

I really hoped there was more to it than that. I wanted there to be a reason.

Margaret marshalled the group along a path surrounded by rocky outcroppings. We arrived at a deep gorge with a steep cliff wall, the water below black and fierce. Waves beat the rocks, the roar so powerful it overpowered Margaret's voice.

She shouted to be heard. "Throw them in. The mother first."

The butler approached the edge of the cliff face with reluctance. The heel of his shoe scraped against loose pebbles. The small stones plummeted over the edge. They took a long time to land in the water below.

The butler visibly shivered. "Miss Thronesby, is this a good idea? The sea could very well bring them back to shore. Wouldn't a grave be more suitable?"

The footman directed an uncertain glance between his mistress and his boss.

Margaret approached the edge with confident strides. She looked down at the rocky void, her torch casting a ghostly glow around her. In comparison, the steep rock wall and black water below appeared to end in pervasive darkness.

The corners of her lips twitched. She seemed to watch

the water with silent fascination. "You do not need to fear the current. Witches have used this gorge for centuries to rid themselves of bodies. The tide will take them out." She nodded at the butler. "Now do as you are told."

He dropped my mother by the edge of the cliff and effortlessly kicked her body into the gorge. There was no splash. We were far too high to hear it if there was. I couldn't look. The fear in my mind already played the scene for me. My mother, tossed and tumbled like a piece of seaweed, sinking into the deep for the little fishes to eat.

"Now the girl," Margaret demanded.

The butler stepped forward, aggravation in his eyes. His voice was gruff and uneven. "Just one moment. What about our payment?"

Margaret laughed, a sweet yet conniving sound. "I cannot believe you are asking for money now. The job is only half done."

"My part is complete in this. Now, I want the money you owe me."

Margaret didn't say anything. She smiled at the footman, who'd gone so white in the face he looked ready to be sick. "Put her down there." She pointed to the edge of the cliff. "I will pay you both for your hard work. And, of course, for your nondisclosure."

The footman approached the edge of the cliff. He looked at my face, which was grey and bloated, my lips colourless, my eyelids closed and pale. I thought maybe he was about to offer me a silent apology, to seek forgiveness, but instead he dropped me on the ground. He swivelled around, his eyes alight for the first time all evening when he saw the sum of money Margaret took out from her dress pocket.

She was still smiling. "Your reward."

There was nothing overly mean in her voice, but I felt the evil radiate off her in waves. The way she drifted forward reminded me of a stalking lion. Before either man could accept the money, she shoved both of them, using her full strength to drive them over the edge. Their screams were barely audible in the wind.

Margaret's face remained impassive as she stepped through the reeds and focused on my body. "Goodbye, sweet Anna."

She kicked me over the edge. Gravity caught my body, the wind dragging me down, my long hair splayed around my face. My wedding gown almost looked silver in the moonlight, my veil a ribbon of white, like a shooting star beelining from the heavens for earth.

My body sliced through the cold water. For a moment, I seemed suspended in time, frozen in that single moment, but then the waves washed over me, shutting out the moonlight, shutting out the rocks and the surface.

My body sank, lower and lower.

Into the deep.

Into the dark.

Into the unknown.

THIRTY-SEVEN

I THOUGHT THAT WOULD BE THE END. I THOUGHT... no, I'd hoped to wake up and be reunited with my mother.

But the Roma Witch's curse had only begun.

When I opened my eyes, I was propelled by a magnetic force. A sense to move toward something I didn't understand.

Time could not be measured down here in my watery grave. It could have been days, weeks, months, years. The marine life had made a biological system out of my body. I was a skeleton with half-eaten flesh, small crabs crawling in and out of what was left of my skin.

There it was. That pull again. That drive to move. To do something.

Move. Move. Move.

The stiffness in my legs dissipated. The reeds that held me captive scattered, the current driving me forward. Strength returned to my arms. The numbness that had plagued me for so long had dissolved in a heartbeat. And yet my heart remained an un-beating drum in my chest.

Move. Move. Move.

The sensation marshalled me out from my watery tomb.

I crawled through the coral, across the flat abyssal plains, over the rocks and gigantic sand beds. Eventually the waves latched on to me. They tossed me in a multitude of directions, a helpless spinning I couldn't fight. I washed up onto the beach, a corpse battered by the sea, pollution tossed away and disregarded by the ocean. And yet I still had that urge to move.

No air filled my lungs. I was animated by something else. Something extraordinary and powerful. My fingers bit into the sand like the taloned claws of a monster. I inched my way up the beach, that drive urging me forward.

Move. Move. Move.

My body had no control. My legs clicked back into place, my sockets popping, limbs reunited. My long bridal gown, wet, dripping, and mouldy, flowed around my body. I must have resembled a dead queen from the sea, or a goddess returning with a vengeance. Was I even walking? Or was it that strange force that impelled me up the sand, through the hazy fog that settled over Ashvall's cemetery, and into the Hauteville Woods?

Moonlight guided my way. I made no sound, the ground undisturbed. No leaves crunched beneath my feet. Fog blanketed the foliage, slipping in and around the trees like lost, wandering souls. An owl hooted on a branch. Its big eyes stared at me with surprise, and then, seeming to think better of it, it flew away into the black night. The chill of the evening didn't affect my mangled body. I had the power of a storm inside me, building silently and fast. Who would be the victim of my wrath?

The trees ahead thinned, giving me a glimpse of my destination.

Wolvercraft Manor.

Why on earth did that force bring me here? Hadn't I been punished enough?

The manor loomed large against the dark sky, a white-stone monstrosity surrounded by a sea of endless fog. White was meant to symbolise innocence. Purity. But what lived behind that façade was nothing but evil. Except for the occasional flickering light, all the windows were dark.

My feet dragged horribly against the wet grass, the force thrusting me closer. When I'd first arrived at Wolvercraft Manor, everything about the house had been new, fresh, and exciting. Now, water stains had accumulated over some of the bricks. The flying buttresses and balustrades were stained with mildew. Even one of the gargoyle figures had its face flattened down by age, the fangs in its gaping jaws broken.

How long had I been in the sea?

I crossed the smooth stretch of grass, but the mystery strength that propelled me onward led me past the entry and around to the side of the house. My bedroom window, high above on the second floor, stared down at me like a dead eye.

My entry.

The thought was alien in my head. Not my own.

Automatically, my hands latched on to the brickwork, pulling me up. I climbed, my fingernails sinking into the mortar. It sounded like the scraping of dead tree branches. At the window, the glass reflected empty space, my face nonexistent. I pushed it, expecting it to remain closed, but it swung gently forward. My body toppled inside, sagging on the carpet.

Move. Move. Move.

The foreign thought in my head compelled me out of the room. The passages and halls were vast and dark. The interior hadn't changed since I'd last wandered the halls. Marble-tiled floors, high arched ceilings, cathedral-like windows built to impress. Memories of a happier, innocent time filled me, driving something hot and angry through my mind.

This is my house.

They stole my fortune, my inheritance, my life, to pay for Wolvercraft Manor.

It's mine.

Mine.

The strange presence inside my body drove me forward. I climbed the heavily varnished staircase that led to the third floor and found the main bedroom where I knew the master and lady of the manor slept.

The bedchamber was large and richly furnished, all decorated with golds and reds that matched the mahogany furniture. Fire crackled in the hearth, its golden glow spreading across the four-poster bed. The bed was empty, but there in the corner of the room, soaking and relaxed in a tin bathtub, was Margaret. I drew closer. Her red hair was wet and neatly washed. A small, satisfied smile stretched across her face as she lathered herself in the soapy water. I wondered how many servants it had taken to carry the heated water from the kitchens, how many maids it took to pour the steaming water over their flawless mistress.

Margaret settled back in the tub and closed her eyes.

I studied her. Rage filled my essence. This woman had taken everything from me. And just like that, I knew what the mystery *force* wanted me to do. Destroy her. Throw her life into the eternal dark. She couldn't see me. She didn't know I was there. It would be easy.

I crept closer, reaching out, the tips of my fingers so close to her face. The hot, vapoury steam of the water touched my skin. It flowed right through me, and yet my hands seemed solid enough to perform my task. I latched on to her head, my fingers twisting into her wet hair, and plunged her into the water. I'd always hated the idea of drowning kittens simply to remove an inconvenience, but now I found it to be a practical solution. Margaret hadn't even had the time to scream. She kicked and thrashed in the water. Her long legs lifted up to the surface, the bubbles around her like a piranha feeding frenzy. She was much stronger than I'd anticipated, and I had to press more strength into my arms to keep her under. That didn't matter. It had taken me three days to die. I wanted her to feel every panicked second it took for her to reach the end.

She went limp, her eyes open and glassy when her body rose, her mouth open in a permanent circle of surprise.

Just like my mother had died.

I wished that Margaret remained there forever in that tub, stuck in the water to slowly decompose, but a maid would find her soon. She would be given the proper burial, the proper rites read, but this witch would not be going to heaven.

Goodbye, sweet Margaret.

My task over, I must admit I was rather lost. I paced the length of the halls, gazing into the pitch-black shadows of the house, wondering if I was just as terrifying as the darkness. Somewhere, a grandfather clock ticked, booming the early morning hour. I wandered past a door, nothing out of the ordinary, but a nagging sensation compelled me to go inside.

It was a child's bedroom. A boy slept in a bed far too big for his small size. He had to be at least five. I sat down next to him, staring at his white skin which was spotted with small freckles. His strawberry blonde hair shone in the moonlight that trailed through his bedroom window.

I knelt down, listening to the tiny sounds of his breathing.

Margaret's child.

Frederick's son.

The heir to Wolvercraft Manor.

I didn't know what his name was. I didn't care. I reached forward to gently cover his nose and mouth. That same maddening rage took hold again, my blood fizzing inside me, fuelling my resentment. I wanted to do it. I wanted to rip the life away from this small child, the spawn of evil.

But I couldn't.

Not yet.

Not until he was grown up. Not until he felt love, and love was returned.

I'd wait. I'd wait till he was married. Wait till he was happy. Wait till he had his own child. Then I'd return to tear his family apart.

Love was a curse. Loneliness was a curse.

This boy would grow up to realise both.

I SPENT MY TIME TRAPPED BETWEEN MY WATERY tomb and Wolvercraft Manor. Sometimes I'd wake, sentenced to wander the great halls alone, shadows skittering over the walls as the evenings closed over the sun, bathing the manor in darkness. Other times I was a prisoner in the sea, caught in the long strands of coral, with no company but the fishes. It was a lonely, painful existence. Many times I wished it to end. Nonexistence would be better than this miserable presence, but the Roma Witch's curse hung tight, refusing to release me from this nightmare.

I remembered dying. I remembered praying to God to avenge me. To make the Wolvercraft family suffer. Perhaps it was not God who answered but the devil. Maybe this was not the work of Margaret's spell but a curse I had settled on myself, for when that urge to return to Wolvercraft Manor came, it did so with murderous intent. I drowned Margaret, but that wasn't enough. Over the years, I'd slit women's throats, hanged them from trees, driven them to suicide through possessions. It wasn't just women, though. I took men's lives too. Anyone who loved a Wolvercraft, and whose love was returned, was greeted with death.

I had said the Wolvercraft family would pay.

And I'd meant it.

Generation after generation.

Through the decades.

Until that moment I saw Elaine Wolvercraft.

She was a beautiful woman. Intelligent, confident, strong. Married to one of the most influential media tycoons in the world. She reminded me of my own mother, and her daughter, little Saige Wolvercraft, reminded me of myself. I watched the pair from a distance when they played in the rose gardens. I watched Saige sleep at night, knowing that soon she would lose her mother to my curse. It never pained me to think about Elaine's fate, but this little girl, who was so much like me, would suffer just as I had. The sentiment never lasted long. The person I had been when I was alive had died, leaving a monster in her place. A monster that cared for nothing but revenge.

Over the years, more of the Wolvercraft family had left the island, broadening their horizons overseas, learning their education at different universities or colleges, earning money from respectable jobs. Little Saige Wolvercraft had all of that in front of her. She would inherit everything that should have been mine.

Will she even come back to the island?

She'd fall in love when she was older. My curse would never reach her if she didn't return to the manor.

That morning in the rose garden, I set out on my plan. I floated into Elaine's body, taking full possession of her mind. The poor woman didn't know what was happening. Saige knew immediately something was wrong, but she was too young to understand. I dropped the doll, some hideous smiling thing, its face smashing the moment it hit a rock, and wove through the hedges to the woods. Saige hurried behind me. She kept calling out, "Mummy," which only served to infuriate me. Her fingers clutched at mine, but before I could clasp on to her tiny hand, she pulled away. She must have sensed the cold, dead presence in her mother's skin.

Good.

The sun had dipped behind the treetops, shrouding the woods in heavy shadow. Decayed leaves crumbled under my feet. Branches scratched at my arms, the wild call of animals echoing in the distance. Even the wind sounded like a ghostly whisper, urging me to take Elaine's life.

I sensed Saige behind me. If I closed my eyes and forced out every other sound from my mind, I fancied I could hear the erratic pulse of her heart, the panic fluttering through her veins.

Yes!

We came out onto the Cliffs of Eden. The wind blew strong in Elaine's hair, flowing around her face, causing a hindrance to my own vision. Storm clouds dotted the horizon ahead, the rain whipping into eddies around me. I stepped out to the edge. The sea was a vicious swirl of waves below. They battered against the line of the cliffs, smashing onto the rocks with terrifying force.

"Mum? Please, what are you doing?"

I smiled. Saige's frightened voice was a precious melody to my soul.

I turned around to face her.

She gasped and stepped back.

It hadn't been my intention for Saige to see her mother like this, eyes colourless, skin pale as death, lips tinged blue, but I enjoyed the horror that took over the little girl's face.

Mother and daughter, parted for ever.

It was the cruellest punishment.

And the most satisfying.

I flung myself off the cliff, my soul extracted from Elaine's body as she dropped through the open air, gravity spinning her in spirals. The waves reached up like an open mouth to swallow her. She slammed onto the dark rocks below, her legs twisted at odd angles. Water washed over her marred body. For a moment, I was afraid the waves would rip her off the rocks into the sea. I didn't want that. Derrick Wolvercraft had to find his dead wife. Her death had to destroy him and his family.

I had watched all this from the cliff. A cry broke through the tense air behind me. I turned, alarmed to discover Saige screaming... at me. Frightened tears ran down her cheeks. She shook her head in disbelief. She knew I had killed her mother—she'd witnessed it. Horror had paralysed her small body, her breathing rapid and uneven.

She can see me?

Margaret's magic may have skipped generations, but I sensed it in Saige now like a beacon lit at night. Elaine, too, had descended from a family of witches. The two magical bloodlines flowing through Saige's veins made her a powerful medium. A powerful witch.

I had spent nearly two centuries alone, either rotting in the sea or walking the halls of Wolvercraft Manor. I could not face another two. My mother had told me about life-long possessions. Ghosts who lingered in a medium's body. Most mediums were strong and powerful enough to block the spirit, but this little girl had no clue about her talent or her heritage. She would be easy to possess.

Why did I have to remain in this miserable existence when there was an escape right here?

I descended upon Saige. My veil swirled around us, securing us in our own little world on the cliff. She was so terrified, so disoriented, she couldn't move. I touched her cheek, felt how alive her skin was, and desperately wished for my own life in return.

Yes. I would escape Wolvercraft Manor. I'd escape the island.

If only for a little while.

Because I knew one day, Saige would have to return.

My curse would claim her loved one.

It had to.

I shut my eyes, feeling my essence break into a thick, rolling fog, and sank into Saige's flesh.

We were one. Two souls sharing the same body.

And I would never let her go.

Not until the time was right.

THIRTY-EIGHT

Saige

Sleep paralysis had been a long torment of mine, but I'd never experienced it quite like this. I knew I was lying numb on the cold, dusty floor in the attic. The blow to my head had been like a red-hot poker straight through my temple. Each stab of pain made my entire skull feel like it was being ripped open. I had vague impressions of moving in and out of consciousness, some- times aware of what was happening around me but power- less to do anything about it. Other times, I was trapped in Anna's twisted memory, her tragic demise playing out for me like scenes in a horror film.

Anna.

The girl who'd had dreams and ambition.

Anna.

The girl who'd been brutally murdered.

Anna!

The girl who'd turned into a monster.

I'd always known there was a presence that lingered around me. What I hadn't understood was that Anna had not only haunted me but possessed me. The pained, lonely sensations that plagued me night and day hadn't always been mine. They'd been Anna's, her emotions, her desire for revenge, polluting my mind and soul.

I did, truly, feel sorry for Anna. Her life had been taken from her, but she'd taken mine too. She'd brought terror and sorrow to generations of my family. The Wolvercrafts may have descended from a murderer, but we weren't the Roma Witch. Xavier and Zoe were not Frederick and Margaret.

Jasper and I are not Frederick and Margaret.

My heart shattered.

God, Anna has Jasper!

I strained, demanding all my muscles to wake, but my body refused to move. It was ironic. Now that my thoughts were my own for the first time, I was helpless to do anything about them. I loved Jasper so much it hurt. The world had been wonderful and exciting with him, and we'd already been parted once by Anna.

I will not let that happen again.

I will not let her... kill him.

Move. Move.

My heart was beating. Blood pounded through my veins, but my body remained paralysed.

Move. Move. Move!

The spell broke. Sensation rushed back into my arms

and legs. I jerked up, gasping for breath, and gingerly got to my feet. Nausea swept through my stomach, the pain in my head causing black dots to span across my sight, but I wouldn't give up. Not now. Not ever. I'd been on the sidelines of my own life for far too long. It was time for me to take control.

And that started with confronting my fear.

I picked up Jasper's discarded flashlight, flicked it on, and followed the sounds of Theodosia's cries, which sharply rose in volume. She was still kneeling in front of Anna's wedding portrait. Her translucent hands stroked her daughter's painted face. I wondered if she was trying to remember Anna as the person she once was. Was Theodosia mourning a daughter she'd lost? A daughter who'd turned into a twisted version of herself?

The stiffness in my muscles made me feel like a tense coil of rusty wire, but I moved toward Theodosia. The boards creaked under my weight. She turned her head, her death wound still evident on her long neck. The slit still bled, the blood saturating her elegant green gown.

My mouth curled into a pathetic smile. Anything to show her I was on her side. "Please. How do I end this curse? How do I stop Anna?"

How do I save Jasper?

Theodosia bared her teeth and let out a demonic wail that caused my insides to loop themselves into knots. She pointed to something against the far wall. I strained to see in the darkness. Besides cobwebs that hung like the loose, broken threads of a ghost ship, all I saw were shadows. Then lightning spilled through cracks in the roof, revealing what I'd missed. A room in the southeast corner of the attic. Its open door faced me, inviting me into the dark.

Don't be afraid. You can do this.

But just to be sure, I checked with Theodosia. "In there?"

She nodded.

I walked toward the doorway. Slivers of lightning leaked through the boarded-up windows inside, the cobwebs dancing in the cold air. If anything waited in the darkness beyond, say a massive spider waiting to gobble me whole, I was fair game.

It's for Jasper. The answer is in this room.

I parted the cobwebs as though they were draperies and stepped into the dark. My flashlight shakily criss-crossed left and right, revealing scattered objects that would have looked more at home in Mildred's house. Grimoires, crumpled and covered in grime, lined the bookcases. Some of the shelves had collapsed, books and paper scattered across the floor. My eyes swept over crystals of all shapes and colours, skulls that didn't look like they'd been made out of face moulds, and drawings of constellations. And candles. So many black and purple candles.

I drew closer. The candles surrounded a large black pot. Images of witches around a boiling cauldron leapt to mind. Not the childhood fantasy type but the murderous, heinous men and women who cast curses and hexes.

Margaret was the Roma Witch. Did all of this belong to her?

I jumped, sensing something behind me. Fear pushed out through my chest.

Theodosia was standing in the doorway. She flickered

in and out like a static image on a screen. Her eyes bored into mine, her voice an eerie rasp. "In there."

I aimed my flashlight in the direction she pointed. An antique wooden chest, something I imagined pirate treasure would be hidden in, was concealed behind one of the crooked bookcases. I moved toward it, running my fingers over the intricate domed lid. A name had been inscribed on a plate just above the lock.

Margaret Wolvercraft.

This belonged to her.

Nervous with either adrenaline or terror, I opened the chest. The most exquisite dresses, silks, ribbons, and priceless jewellery were inside. Frederick really had lavished his second bride with the most expensive and finest gifts.

But how do these help me?

Theodosia's voice rolled through the dark. "Dig deeper."

I lifted the beautiful dresses and jewellery out of the chest, almost feeling guilty when I dropped them onto the filthy floorboards. One object remained inside—a black velvet bag. I pulled the drawstring. Inside was a blade with green gems along the silver hilt. Inscriptions of runes and other symbols I didn't understand ran down the length of the knife.

Margaret's blade. Some kind of witch's tool.

Recognition started to solidify within me. "This is what Margaret used to kill you."

Theodosia's voice sounded like the thunder outside. "The gorge. That is where Anna has taken him. You do not have long."

She turned around, floating eerily back to the wedding portrait, her feet hovering a few inches off the floor.

I looked at the blade in my hand. It wasn't heavy, but it was alien to me. I knew what Theodosia wanted me to do. She'd given me the answer days ago, I just hadn't understood. Now I did. My mind felt like it was being sucked down into something the size of a pinhole as acceptance closed in.

I would do this for Jasper.

For my family.

Maybe even for Anna too.

I TORE OUT OF THE ATTIC. MY LEGS STRUGGLED with the instructions from my brain, or maybe it was my mounting anxiety taking control again, because my feet were as loose and slippery as butter. I took the staircase that twisted down to the fourth floor, feeling as though every part of me might rupture.

Please. Please. Please.

Don't let me be too late.

I'd never been a firm believer in religion, but right then, I was willing to pray to any of them that would listen.

Jasper.

What horror must he be going through?

More windows had shattered on the third floor, the carpets littered with shards of coloured glass, the curtains and drapes blowing like flags in a heavy gale. Doors slammed. The chandelier lights along the ceiling juddered, as though Wolvercraft Manor was positioned on a fault line.

My ears strained to hear anything above the violent

storm, so it was a surprise when I tore around the corner into the next hallway to see a figure hobbling toward me. My shock was eclipsed by immediate terror. It was the woman from the woods, the one who hung from the tree, only now she was very much animated and... active. She shuffled toward me. Her neck was snapped, the veins black where the pressure of the noose had suffocated the life out of her. Her eyes bulged from their sockets.

I darted back the way I'd come.

Someone else waited at the end of the hall. The woman in the bridal dress, the one Anna had thrown off the clock tower. She lurched toward me, wobbling like she was inebriated, only her eyes were locked on me with a clarity that was frightening. Her veil was torn, bits of it arranged in grotesque threads through her hair.

I dashed into the hall on my right and kept running, my mind frantic to bring up a mental blueprint of the house.

I have to get to the chamber.

There was no way I'd get to the gorge without going underground. The storm and flood made sure of that. I had to use the tunnel.

At the end of this hall, turn right, then left. There's another staircase.

Soft shuffling resonated behind me. I stole a glance over my shoulder. The dead brides were coming after me. They hobbled down the hall in fast pursuit, arms outstretched. More joined them. Men and women—all victims of Anna's horrible vengeance. Some of them were missing limbs or faces, and some had the implements of their deaths still embedded in their bodies.

Anna is trying to stop me.

She'd summoned her dead captives, controlling them like marionettes.

I reached the end of the hall, twisted round into the passage on my right, and scrambled into a separate corridor. I kept going, turn after turn, long passage after passage, but there was never any sight of the staircase.

No. Not again.

Anna was playing mind games. I was a mouse caught in her maze.

I whipped my head around to see how far back the corpses were. The floor suddenly went out beneath me, swallowing me into the yawning deep. I screamed, my lungs wedged between my ribs. The sensation of falling, of being tossed down something with a straight blunt edge, over and over again, knocked the wind out of me. I rolled onto soft carpet, blinking to get my surroundings in focus. My flashlight lay a metre ahead. Silver light streaked onto a staircase.

The frigging staircase.

In my haste, I'd fallen down it.

Anna's puppets descended the stairs in creepy unison, eyes not blinking, faces pallid from putrefaction. The smell of them brought something toxic up from my stomach.

I scrambled onto my feet, grabbed the flashlight, and darted into the corridor opposite. I kept running, past doors, past windows, never looking back. I didn't want to know if the corpses were close. I just focused on getting the hell out of there.

Sweat beaded on my skin, my scalp itchy from it.

Where is the chamber?

"Saige."

I nearly screamed at the sound of the voice.

My mother stood at the end of the hallway, flickering in and out like a static image on a screen. She stood by the secret door that led into the chamber. It was open.

Her smile faded. "Hurry, sweetheart. Jasper's time is running out."

THIRTY-NINE

I TRIED TO KEEP MY BREATHING SHALLOW SO I wouldn't panic, but the terror inside me climbed. The walls of the secret passage were so close, it was a miracle even a ghost could have slipped between them. Water trickled from the ceiling, the once-jagged edges now slick with whatever fungus had grown over the last two centuries. They dripped over my hair and down my face, sending icy shivers all through my body.

A breeze blew from the black depths ahead. I reached out, intending to guide myself with the wall, but my fingers met cold air. A small cry escaped from deep within me. I'd made it to the chamber. Somehow, the large expanse around me now seemed worse. Anything could latch on to me from any direction.

I directed my flashlight around the dank, miserable prison. It hadn't changed since the last time I'd been in here with Jasper. The dark stain on the stone floor, which I was now painfully aware was remnants of Theodosia's blood, looked deceptively like rust. I stepped over it and headed for the birdcage elevator in the far corner. It meant passing the cell where Anna was imprisoned. The words she'd carved in the floor stood out like a warning sign on a road. *"In life I was afraid. In death I am fearless. They will all pay."*

My heart thundered. Blood rushed to my head. It was a reminder of the formidable force Anna had become.

I reached the elevator and scrambled inside. It shuddered hard when I yanked the lever, the unstable floor beneath me seeming to lurch. My compact space descended, slow yet at the same time too fast.

How many levels of the house have I passed? How far underground is the tunnel?

A jolt startled me. The cables above groaned in complaint, making me think that at any second they would snap apart.

It can't be much longer.

Fast-moving water reached my ears. I'd barely had time to comprehend it when a cold, black wave spilled through the wrought-iron scrollwork from every side. The water swept up to my knees, then to my thighs, splashing up to my waist. I screamed.

The heavy shudder through my feet announced I'd reached the tunnel floor. I clambered out of the elevator, wading into the flooded channel.

If there was one thing I hated more than cold, dark places, it was cold, dark, wet places. I kept imagining bodies floating up around me like bobbing apples, skin grey, teeth mouldy but sharp.

I swallowed damp air.

This is the only way out.

This is the only way to save Jasper.

I knew the direction from the memory Anna had shown me. I hurried through the muddy floodwater, slipping twice. My heart pounded so loudly it drowned out all sound. The beam from my flashlight crisscrossed left and right, revealing all the rats that swam on the water's surface, their little feet scampering up the walls. A smell akin to raw sewage made my stomach heave.

Maybe it's a good thing I can't see what's floating around me.

I followed turn after turn, my flashlight barely cutting through the darkness ahead.

Anna manipulated the space in Wolvercraft Manor. Is it possible she's doing the same thing here?

Is she making the tunnel longer?

The horrifying thought was thrust aside at the appearance of a heavy, dark lump ahead. Rats scurried over it, nibbling at something that was definitely fleshy and human. I leapt back, shallow gasps not properly filling my lungs. The eyes were wild and ringed in white, the hair ripped from the scalp, leaving bloody patches in its place. Teeth exposed. Lips pecked at. The tongue was the worst. It was purple and swollen, the saliva inky and blotted around it. Or maybe that was congealed blood. And the neck... had been snapped, the head supported at an angle on the shoulder.

Harriette!

Anna, what did you do to her?

The sight was too horrible. My legs waded backward through the water without any instruction from my brain. I had to get away from Harriette's body. I couldn't look at the gruesome, mangled thing she had become.

What if Anna did that to Jasper?

But more selfishly, I was afraid that if I remained a moment longer with Harriette's body, I, too, would become a corpse left to rot in this miserable place.

I continued as fast as possible down the tunnel, tears burning my eyes from the guilt that rushed at me.

If I survive this, I will inform the police that Harriette is down here. Aunt Prue and I will give her a proper burial.

The darkness changed ahead. Grey light spilled from the ceiling, bleeding into the dark water below. It reminded me of moonlight descending through a natural oculus in a sea cave. Familiarity clouded my head. Rain fell from a large expanse, creating a waterfall that would have been pleasant if it wasn't so damn cold.

I've been here before.

This is where the ground collapsed beneath me in the Hauteville Woods.

A mental projection of the island popped into my mind. I had about a half mile to go before I reached the cliffs.

Jasper, I'm on my way.

I splashed through the flooded tunnel, following the turns and folds. Water rose ever so slowly to my chest and then dropped back down to my waist as I travelled the various dips and ascents. Everything was drab and dark and wet. My feet felt slimy in my thick boots. The thought of trench foot started to worry me just as much as the shadows.

The faintest scent of an ocean breeze wafted around me.

The stairs can't be far.

I pressed my hand against the wall, relieved to feel

pointy, serrated rock, some of the edges smoothed by erosion.

Like rocks near the sea.

My hope ignited, I directed my flashlight with more enthusiasm, scanning the rock walls for an opening, a hewn step—anything that would get me out of the forsaken tunnel.

A loud pop startled me. It had sounded like a bubble bursting.

I stood frozen.

There was another.

Pop. Pop. Pop. Pop.

I shone the light back the way I'd come. The water rippled. A little moan escaped my lips. A head emerged, followed by another, then another. Three, then four. Five. Six. They rose, all of them wet and slimy, as if they'd been decomposing in a bottomless swamp for decades. They dragged themselves through the dark water, malicious contempt in their eyes. I didn't know how Anna had managed to get her dead puppets to follow me down here —to be honest, I didn't want to know—but their sudden shrieks and lunatic giggles iced me to the core.

I turned and ran.

The creatures loped after me, hungry to rip their teeth into my body, to tear me apart, to drown me.

What does Anna have intended for me?

Or could she sense that I was getting closer? Was this simply a method to try and prevent me from reaching Jasper?

The thought spurred me on, but every step I took seemed to be slow and heavy, as though I were crawling through a nightmare. I tried frantically to recall where the stairs had been in Anna's memory. A lot had changed in two centuries. I trained the flashlight across the walls, looking through every dark hole and crevice.

What if the stairs no longer exist? What if they collapsed at some point?

A wheezy screech right at my ear snapped my attention away. I ducked as the corpse with the bent neck lunged for me. Her swollen fingers scraped the air in another attempt to seize me, her mouth open in a scream, revealing rotten teeth and a mouth soured by decay. All of them crept forward, reminding me of hunting lions, slow at first but moving in for the kill. Death, it seemed, had made them faster.

I twisted and pulled away as they lunged forward in a hideous cacophony of screams, terrified by their wicked grins and relentless eyes. My foot slipped out beneath me, and I tumbled back into a large fissure, hitting stone. There was something strange about its shape. It wasn't natural but cut straight. Not perfect, but—

As though cut with chisels and axes!

I looked up to see hewn stairs, aged from weather. Finally, something had worked in my favour.

I climbed onto my feet, barely missing the dead hands that attempted to grab my shoulders, and barrelled up the steps. They were tight, the rough walls pulling against my jacket. Sand and algae made it difficult, creating a trip hazard with each step, the soles of my boots sometimes failing to find traction. Anna's dead marionettes trailed behind me, their grisly screams an unfriendly reminder that they were gaining.

I gasped, half in surprise, half in relief when the first

drops of rain fell across my face. I reached the final step and came out to the cliffs that overlooked the ocean. Wind pummelled me, throwing my wet hair into disarray. Thunder, which had sounded subdued in the tunnel, split the air with resounding impact. Lightning streaked the sky in a multitude of purple and white flashes, like a strobe light on acid.

But it was the ocean that frightened me the most, because only fifty metres away was the gorge, and standing right on the edge was Jasper.

Anna's and Theodosia's bodies were thrown into the sea in that very spot. Is this some kind of poetic justice in Anna's mind?

I hurried along the dirt path surrounded by rocky outcroppings. Overgrown reeds twisted around my legs, the rain and wind threatening to bowl me over like a pin.

Lightning flashed once more, making it bright as day for a split second. In that tense moment, I saw Anna's profile against the dark backdrop, her wedding dress blowing around her, as though she were made of mist and cloud. She was standing behind Jasper. I feared that at any given second she would push him over the edge and watch him sink into the watery abyss below.

My sides ached from exertion. Every muscle in my body complained, yet I kept running. "Anna!"

I reached the gorge. My voice had been no match against the wind, but she heard me.

She turned slowly. Her pale skin was streaked with dark, purple veins, her eyes oily and slitted. Her long hair moved through the wind as though suspended in water. She was beautiful and terrifying at the same time. A goddess put on this earth to enact her revenge.

"Please," I gasped. "Don't do this to Jasper. He doesn't deserve it. We are not Frederick and Margaret."

It was the wrong thing to say.

Jasper raised his foot, about to step off the cliff.

Oh God! She has him under her spell!

"Please," I begged. My jugular pounded overtime.

There was no reasoning with Anna. She hated every Wolvercraft. I saw it in the way she looked at me. Those deep, dark eyes, which had been kind and full of hope when she was alive, struck me with intense loathing. She was cursed into despising the Wolvercraft family, but also herself. Why else would she have possessed me? She'd been a monster in a painful existence. A long, lonely continuation that would never cease, her resentment for my family the only thing fuelling her. What happened to her hadn't been fair. What happened to all her victims hadn't been right.

There was only one way to stop Anna.

Something transformed in the air behind her. Another ghostly manifestation appeared, soft and translucent at first but slowly becoming more corporeal. I recognised the smiling face, no longer flattened by the sea rocks she had plunged onto but round and perfect.

Mum.

Her lips pulled into another gentle smile. She nodded, affirming my thoughts. It was the final piece of conviction I needed.

"Pay the sins of the father, Saige. A life for a life."

I took Margaret's green-hilted knife out of my pocket.

Anna's face contorted into animalistic fury. She moved toward me, a predator about to play with its meal before devouring it.

"Anna." My voice cracked as a fresh wave of tears spilled from my eyes. "Frederick deceived you. Margaret left you to die. The Wolvercrafts took your life and cursed your soul. Now a Wolvercraft is giving you a chance to be free." I raised the knife. "A life for a life."

I brought the blade down. The dagger pierced my skin, breaking through my stomach, sending excruciating agony through my body. The pain was hot and cold all at once, as though I were burning alive in the middle of an Arctic night.

Anna stared. She wasn't surprised or shocked. Relief slowly crossed her face, her eyes now more brown than dark. The wedding dress she wore was no longer wet or polluted by dirt and sea slime but had transformed into something white and magnificent. She was pure again. She was Anna Sinclair. The dark goddess, the cursed bride, was gone.

Another figure coalesced beside her. Theodosia. No longer wearing her death wounds, Theodosia was a tall, proud, and regal woman in a majestic green gown. She took Anna's hand, sealing a kiss on her daughter's forehead. They wrapped their arms around each other. A glow enveloped them, brighter than sunlight, something that belonged here but was also unnatural to the earth. An essence, an aura from beyond. It grew so bright that I could barely look at it. I squeezed my eyes shut. When I opened them, Anna and Theodosia were gone.

They've moved on. Anna is finally free.

My relief lasted about half a second. I collapsed on the ground, clutching at the useless piece of steel impaled in my stomach. The grassy earth beneath me, though soaked through with mud, was soft and a nice reprieve from the torture that racked my body. I rolled onto my back and lay there, looking up at the dark, churning storm clouds, wondering if an angel would come from the heavens and lift my soul free. That would have been nice.

"Saige!"

Jasper appeared, his forehead threaded with worry lines. He examined my body, cursing. My blood had leaked all over the ground, staining his jeans.

He's okay. He's safe. Anna no longer has control of him.

"I saved... you," I choked out, surprised by how difficult it was to speak. "I... saved... Anna."

"Don't talk, Saige. Keep your strength."

He burst into a slew of panicked rumbling. There was no service on the island. He couldn't call for help.

I reached for his hand, clasping my fingers tight around his. "It's... okay."

I wish I had the chance to say goodbye to Xav and to Aunt Prue. Even Dad and Aunt Violet. But I knew it was a sweet mercy that I was even able to look Jasper in the eyes one last time. At least I could say goodbye to him.

I gave his hand a final squeeze. I couldn't tell if he was crying or if it was rain running down his cheeks. I told myself it was the former.

If Anna and Theodosia were finally reunited, then surely one day I will be reunited with my family too.

Mum.

I'm going to see her soon.

The thought raised a smile to my lips.

The pain disappeared, my body numb, all sensation of life gone.

I closed my eyes, letting the cool black waters of death wash over me.

FORTY

Light burnt my eyes, blinding and painful at first, then soft and gentle. The air was crisp with the scent of earthen forest and briny sea air. Seagulls squawked. Yeasty waves smashed soothingly on a beach in the distance.

This must be heaven.

But when my eyes peeled open, I realised I was far from the paradise my mind imagined. Sunlight streamed down from the blue sky, barely a cloud to be seen. Large stone slabs loomed over me, wrapped in a tangled mess of ivy. For a moment, I wondered whether I was in a grave-yard and these were the crooked tombs, defaced and toppled by age.

The grass beneath me was damp, soaked through by rain. If it hadn't been for the warm, intoxicating sun, I'd surely be a human popsicle by now.

Where am I?

I sat up. I remembered the knife piercing my belly, but there was no pain. Blood had dried into my clothes, but when I lifted my shirt, all I saw was a two-inch white scar, already healed.

How is this possible?

"Saige?"

I turned in surprise, not willing myself to hope, but my eyes didn't deceive me.

"Jasper."

He was sitting beside me, his clothes drenched, the back of his jeans dampened by mud. His hair was mussed and long around his face, no longer in a cool rock star vibe but tangled and matted by the elements. The strained anxiety that had racked his face for days softened, and any trace of fear vanished from his eyes. He leaned forward and caught me in an embrace. "Thank God, it worked."

He kissed me on the top of my head. The contact radiated warmth through me.

"Worked?" I pulled back to look at him, then took a closer inspection of my surroundings. The stones stood in a ring, topped by connecting horizontal slabs. "Table des Pions! The fairy ring!"

I looked at Jasper for confirmation, but I knew that was where we were. We'd been here all night. Me as a corpse, and Jasper sleeping right beside me.

He slept in the storm. In the rain. I'm surprised he doesn't have hypothermia. Or even a cold.

Jasper glanced down at the grass. A sheepish smile tipped the corner of his lips. "I do listen to what you say, you know. When you died last night, I was scared and angry that I'd lost you. That you'd... sacrificed yourself. And then I remembered the story you told me about the fairy ring. The place where fairies and witches gathered for weddings, and... well, I'm sure there were other titillating activities occurring, too, but the point is, you said if someone lost a loved one, they could bring their partner's body to the circle."

Elation filled me. "And if the fairies deem the couple's love to be true, the deceased's soul will be returned."

For the first time in a long time, it was happy tears that stung my eyes.

He snorted. "Still the worst fairy tale I've ever heard, but I thought if ghosts were real, then it was worth seeing if the power in these stones was real too." He tucked a lock of hair behind my ear. "And I'm grateful it was."

I nodded wordlessly and snuggled closer to him.

Jasper pressed his lips against mine, the kiss long and slow and perfect.

He whispered into my ear, "Let's not break up again?"

I smiled. "Agreed."

EPILOGUE

THREE YEARS LATER

THE SUNSHINE IS GLORIOUS THIS SUMMER. I unpacked the picnic basket and set the rug on the freshly mowed grass a little while ago. It was difficult bending over. Being six months pregnant with my daughter has made some movements impossible, especially when it comes to Connor. He's eighteen months and, now that he's learned to run, is like Speedy Gonzales around the house. Aunt Prue chased after him through the rose garden while I was setting up. She brought him back a few minutes ago, a smiling little boy with dark hair like his father's and two cute dimples. He was giggling but behaved and made a beeline for the cupcakes when he saw them.

It's our first picnic of the summer, a tradition my family started now that Jasper and I reside in Wolvercraft Manor. Dad took two weeks off from work to join us, mainly to see his grandson, who he spoils like there's no other kid in the world. Aunt Prue and Aunt Violet moved in with us and now live in their own private chamber in the house. I'm eternally grateful that they do. Jasper often goes on tour for months at a time, and Connor can be a handful when his dad is absent.

My little boy sits calmly now in Jasper's lap, eating his cupcake and making a terrible mess on his clothes. I wonder what he'll be like when his sister is born and he's no longer the centre of attention all the time.

Aunt Prue sits beside me and makes the tea. Dad and Aunt Violet pull faces at Connor. My little boy bursts into laughter. Anything brings him into hysterics. Even Xav and Aimee, decked out on the sunchairs, are smiling at how silly their nephew is acting.

Xav broke things off with Zoe not long after they left Wolvercraft Manor. He'd known in his heart that she didn't love him. After all, Anna hadn't killed her for a reason. Zoe's possession had been about frightening me, nothing more. It had been hard for Xav at first, but then he'd met Aimee. The pair had married in the gardens at Wolvercraft Manor, just a small family event, at the end of last year.

After I'd set Anna free on that fateful day, Jasper and I had returned to the manor to find everything completely... normal. Well, as normal as things could have been. My family, Zoe, and the bridesmaids had been sitting in the drawing room, drinking tea and coffee. My family had no recollection of that night in the basement, or how they'd kept me a prisoner in my room, and Zoe and her brides-maids had returned to full health. For them, they'd simply woken in the morning to discover the storm had passed and the power was back on.

Jasper and I had lied, making up a story about getting up early and going on a long walk to inspect the damage on the island. We'd found the tunnel and made the unfortunate discovery of poor Harriette inside. The police had investigated. Harriette, it seemed, had slipped and fallen in the Hauteville Woods, the rain eventually washing her body into the underground passage. It pained me that no one would ever know the truth. Harriette didn't deserve the horror that had befallen her. And neither had Anna.

Jasper and I waited a year before we got married, but it came with its obstacles. I could never leave Ashvall for long. The magic that had returned my life had also bound me to the island and to Wolvercraft Manor. We'd discovered that when we went back to London. After three weeks, I'd fallen violently ill. Not even the doctors could understand my symptoms, especially when all my results proved I was perfectly healthy. During that confusing time, I was certain of one thing: I had to get back to the island, to the house... to my home.

Wolvercraft Manor is a part of me now. I live and breathe it. I run historic tours of the house, and yes, I do host ghost tours and parties. Halloween Night at Wolvercraft Manor is a spectacular event for the entire island. I've become an advocate for the National Heritage Trust of Ashvall and even do freelance writing on the side for magazines and papers.

I look at my wonderful husband and amazing son and feel... grateful. My eyes travel to my beautiful house, charming and gothic, the white stone bathed in sunlight, the windows staring down at me like inquisitive eyes. I know every room, every furniture piece, every ornament to heart, but there's one additional piece I had made—a portrait of Anna and Theodosia. The true owners of Wolvercraft Manor now stand proudly above the mezzanine, looking down upon anyone who enters their house.

I'd wanted their portrait put there as a reminder. For a house isn't just bricks and mortar, or a place to call home. It isn't just a dwelling where we dream and spend our family time. It's a space where we conceal agendas. Where we hide and bury lies.

Because in the end, all houses have secrets.

ABOUT THE AUTHOR

From a young age, Cas E Crowe knew she wanted to be a writer. As a child, she spent her lunchtimes at school creating weird and haunting stories for her classmates to listen to. An admirer of all things spooky and quirky, her grandfather recognised her unusual hobby as a gift and built her a haunted doll's house to stage her stories.

Cas studied a creative arts degree majoring in design and a minor in creative writing, followed by a graduate certificate in animation at the Queensland University of Technology in Brisbane, Australia. She has worked as a shop assistant, a graphic designer, an office manager, and now pursues her dream of writing.

Cas loves to read and write fantasy, horror, and paranormal stories and is passionate about supporting other authors. She loves to write while listening to film soundtracks. Amongst Cas's likes are travel, drawing, writing, reading, gardening, painting, and whatever else she can fit in a day. She resides in Brisbane, Australia.

Don't miss out on new releases, exclusive giveaways, and much more!
Join my newsletter: casecrowe.com/contact/
I'd love to hear from you directly too. Please feel free to email me at cas@casecrowe.com or check out my website www.casecrowe.com for updates.

facebook.com/casecroweauthor
twitter.com/CroweCas
instagram.com/casecroweauthor
goodreads.com/casecrowe
bookbub.com/authors/cas-e-crowe

ACKNOWLEDGMENTS

Writing a story is the easy part, but it takes an entire team of people to publish a novel. A big thank you to the Brisbane NightWriters—Gillian, Stuart, Tom, Stacey, and Shannon—for listening to chapters of the story and providing feedback and advice. Thank you to the Brisbane Young Adult Writers Group (BYAWG) for offering so much support and advice with everything to do with writing and marketing.

An enormous thanks to the beta reading team at Tangled Tree Publishing—Kim Deister, Rebecca Allman, Paula White, Andrea Robinson, and Donna Pemberton—who found all the little inconsistencies and plot holes and offered kind words of encouragement throughout the manuscript.

The cover design for this novel is beautiful, and thanks is owed to Claire at BookSmith Designs for creating such an eye-catching book cover.

Thank you to Becky Johnson and the Tangled Tree Publishing team for taking a chance on this newly emerging author and for supporting me on the writing journey for *Wolvercraft Manor*. And finally, a big thank-you to my editor, Kristin Scearce, who has edited all of my novels and always takes the time and patience to improve my stories. She has taught me so much about writing and editing, and for that I am eternally grateful.

ABOUT THE PUBLISHER

Tangled Tree Publishing loves all things tangled and aims to bring darker, twisted, and more mind-boggling books to its readers. Publishing adult and new adult fiction, TTPubs are all about diverse reads in mystery, suspense, thrillers, and crime.

For more details, head to www.TANGLEDTREEPUBLISHING.COM

facebook.com/tangledtreepublishing

twitter.com/ttpubs

tiktok.com/@hottreepublishing

www.ingramcontent.com/pod-product-compliance
Lightning Source LLC
Chambersburg PA
CBHW030143200726
48285CB00004BC/1330